SLAY THE DAWN

SUPERNATURAL LEGACY 3

EVERLY FROST

Frost, Everly
Slay the Dawn

Cover design by Claire Holt with Luminescence Covers
www.luminescencecovers.com

For information on reproducing sections of this book or sales of this book,
go to
www.EverlyFrost.com
everlyfrost@gmail.com

DISCOVER THE EVER REALMS

Seven series. One world.

Suggested Reading Order:

Bright Wicked
Storm Princess
Assassin's Magic
Soul Bitten Shifter
Supernatural Legacy
Dark Magic Shifters
Kingdom of Betrayal

Free your fire.

CHAPTER ONE

I stifle the scream rising to my throat.

Callan is dead.

A burning pain I can't control rushes through my chest.

I can hardly think. Hardly process that the dragon standing opposite me, whose burning grip brands my arm and anchors me to the spot, is no longer the man I love.

He is Atrox Imperator, Callan's dragon. A dragon who wants to destroy the world and has the power to do it.

This monstrous beast was responsible for starting the war between angels and dragon shifters. He was complicit in the death of the last Avenging Angel. He is a murderer, a thief, and now he has broken my world.

He has killed the man who mattered most to me.

Oh. My heart.

The scream I'm trying to control pushes at my chest, driven by sharp pain. *How can my heart feel this much agony and continue to beat?*

In the last day, I've lost so much. It's as if, with every new piece of information I gained about myself, I paid a price. I found out that my mother is a warrior angel named Melisma— and then she slipped through my fingers. I found out that

Solomon Grudge was my half-brother, and it was his act of taking me into the moonlight when I was a baby that triggered what remained of a fire dragon inside me. What he did fundamentally altered my basic nature. He told me the truth before he died in my arms. A senseless death that hurt my heart.

And now, I've discovered that the volatile dragon that Callan has carried within himself—the dragon that would force him into a fiery shift if any supernatural touched him, the dragon that forced him to live his life separate and alone—is none other than the deadliest, most hated dragon of all.

And now that dragon is in control.

We stand on a gleaming, white marble floor inside a prison that's located within the veil between Earth and the heavenly realm. I was brought here by the Roden-Darr, an elite group of angels who were meant to serve me but were instead sent to capture me.

This prison doesn't have bars. It's made up of endless night that stretches in every direction. There is no visible escape. No doors or walls that can be broken through. I have no idea what other magical enchantments could shroud this place and make it impossible to leave.

One thing I learned quickly is that sound creates light here. It's a phenomenon that means darkness is creeping back now that the clash of battle is fading. Only the space immediately in front of me is still bright, but the light is fading fast.

Shadows grow across Atrox's face. Heat waves shimmer around him, creating iridescent ripples in the gloom. He smells like ash, and the scent is so savage that it burns my throat when I inhale.

In his partially shifted form, his eyes are pure gold, and his skin is overlaid with golden scales. He stands at nearly seven feet tall—as tall as Callan—and he has the same slight hint of a cleft in his strong jaw. His shoulders are broad, and his biceps are sculpted.

Sweat glistens on his naked chest, mingling with the drying

blood of his healed wounds. He inflicted those wounds on Callan to break Callan's mind and take control of his body. He had clawed and bitten and nearly torn Callan apart. Callan's blood still pools on the floor not more than ten paces away, a glistening sheen in the dark.

In the background, Atrox's brother, Audax, is a mere outline in the gloom but is no less intimidating. His eyes are juniper-green but appear silvery in the dark. He stands as tall as Atrox, his shoulders as broad, and his body from his feet to his neck gleams because of the golden armor he's wearing. The armor belongs to Atrox. It was all part of the two brothers' ruse to trick the angels into imprisoning Audax instead of Atrox.

Atrox's lips stretch into a cold smile that's at odds with the heat growing around his body. He holds the dual-horned golden helmet that goes with his armor.

Every muscle in my body is tense as I prepare to fight my way free of his hold.

"Asper Ashen-Varr." He speaks slowly, his golden eyes reflective and shiny as he pulls me closer to him. "You know who I am, but you've yet to formally meet my brother, Dominus Audax, whom you will address as 'Master Dominus.' Likewise, you will address me as 'Master Atrox.'"

In the background, Dominus Audax watches me with anticipation, as if he can't wait for me to show a hint of submission.

Before I can utter a retort, Atrox closes in, an increasingly dark shadow towering over me. "Think wisely before you respond, Asper. Callan Steele gave you choices, but I will not. You think you can fight us or maybe run from us, but you will only die trying. The sooner you accept your place beside us, the less painful your path will be."

My breathing is ragged. My face and body ache from the bruises I already suffered last night. I don't have my golden feathers to fill the gaps in my broken left wing, so I can't fly. My glaive is gone. The only dragon's gold I still wear is my armband and the bracelets Callan gave me.

The ruby-heart charm on one of the bracelets was my beacon to Callan, a device that allowed him to find me when I needed his help. It's cold against my skin now. The connection between Callan and me is lost.

This fucking monster took away the only goodness in my life.

"You say I don't have choices," I reply, my voice seething with rage. "You believe I'm not strong enough to fight you. But you're wrong. I do have a choice." The corners of my mouth draw down as I snarl. "I *choose* to die trying."

Atrox's eyebrows rise, as if I've surprised him a little.

I give a scream of fury, letting out my pain in a torrent of sound, as my fist flies out.

My shout drives back the darkness, wiping away the shadows from Atrox's face. My knuckles glance across his cheekbone, busting through his iridescent dragon scales and cracking them. I succeed in drawing blood, but his scales are so hard that I feel the bones in my hand shift and pain rockets up my arm all the way to my right shoulder.

Atrox retaliates swiftly and with full force.

Wrenching me toward him and nearly dislocating my arm, he swings the golden helmet that he holds in his left hand at the side of my head. His hard grip means I have nowhere to go and the metal cracks across the side of my face before I can evade it.

The force of the strike drives me to my left, and his unyielding hold on me risks breaking my arm. Both of my wings shoot out and the tip of my left wing bone rams against the floor to counteract his attack.

Despite my blurred vision, as I jolt to the left, I manage to grab the arm with which Atrox holds me. My instinct is to strike my armband down against his forearm to try to make him let go of me, but that will only wrench my already injured left shoulder further.

My fingers close around his muscled forearm, gripping him as tightly as he's gripping me. Using the momentum of my near-fall to the left, I allow my weight to drop to that side so that I can kick up my right leg, bent at the knee, and shove it into his stomach. His scales protect his chest from my attack, but I manage to unbalance him enough that he finally lets go of my arm.

His torso becomes a springboard, which I kick off so that I can leap away from him. I don't lift off the ground high enough to risk tottering or beat my wings in any way that means the gap in my left wing unbalances me.

My landing on the floor is so light that I barely create any sound and the entire space around me is now filled with shadows.

I hold my wings back and off the ground as I crouch in the darkness, rapidly assessing my surroundings.

A throne sits behind me. It's as black as this prison and fashioned out of the bones of an enormous creature's ribcage. Dominus was imprisoned on it, bound to the throne with unbreakable chains. When I freed him, I was trying to save Callan's life, but I was already too late.

Off to my right, Dominus's hammer is vaguely visible where it rests on the other side of the throne. The hammer's shaft is made of black bone similar to the bones that form the throne and its head is a thick block of gold inscribed with runes. Dominus left the hammer there after he used it to wake Callan.

It must be made from dragon's gold because I can sense its bloody history—all the lives it has taken and the deaths it has coldly caused—but its nature is somehow heavy within my senses, as if it's weighed down. I certainly can't call it to me across the air like I could call my golden feathers to my wing. Even if I could run to it, my single attempt to use it against Dominus was easily foiled, so I have no guarantees I can use it against Atrox.

Blood drips down my face, the muscles in my left arm are strained, and my shoulder throbs.

Atrox barely gives me a second's reprieve.

He drops the helmet to the floor with a clang, and then he's a silent blur, his footfalls so quiet that he creates only the faintest glow as he plows toward me.

My focus is momentarily diverted to his helmet. Unlike the golden hammer, it isn't weighted down and the dragon's gold from which it's made sings to me.

A sweet melody of savage death.

I refocus on the danger right in front of me.

I manage to dart out of the way fast enough that Atrox's fist smashes into one of the enormous bones behind me, instead of my head. The *crack* of the impact lights up the space around us like fireworks, but the bone doesn't splinter.

Ducking just in time, I avoid the next fist Atrox aims at me, the swing of his arm so unrestrained that the rush of wind creates sparks of light that flash across his enormous biceps.

He drives me around the back of the throne, and it takes all of my concentration to avoid his fists in the flickering light. His attacks are swift and agile—far more fluid than I was expecting —but his fighting style reminds me of Callan's from that time he and I sparred with wooden fighting sticks in his gym.

It's a painful memory now.

I've had enough of evasion. It's time to attack.

Retracting my wings, I leap upward and grab hold of one of the higher rib bones that forms the back of the throne so that I can swing from it.

I time my kick to perfection.

As Atrox steps forward, swinging his fist once more, my right boot collides with his jaw. The impact knocks him back so fast that he stumbles. It takes him a second to recover, and I use that moment to maximum effect, throwing myself forward, letting go of the bone as I hook my right leg around his neck and drop my weight to the left. We're going to crash to the floor and it's a dangerous move that could go either way—he could just as easily fall on me and crush me—but he was already headed backward, so he goes down first.

There's no way I can break his neck. His scales are too hard. But I don't waste a second as we drop to the marbled floor, my right fist hammering his cheekbone three times in quick succession. Right where I cracked his scales before. It opens up his cheek and temple, making the flesh of his face vulnerable.

At the same time, I fix firmly in my mind the image of his helmet. Specifically, the horn that sits on the right side atop it.

He lands heavily, his blood splattering the marble, while light splashes out around us, but my focus has become narrow. My concentration complete.

I may only have this one chance.

As I hit the floor on top of his chest, my left hand on his shoulder, my right having just delivered the third blow, I scream a mental command at his helmet. *Come to me!*

There's a glint of gold in the distance as the helmet rends, one of the horns rips off the top, and the horn shoots into my hand. The moment my palm closes around it, its nature explodes through my senses, an instant influx of hatred and rage. This gold wants death, and it doesn't care whose life it takes. Even its own master's.

I drive the tip toward Atrox's exposed temple.

But he isn't lying idle beneath me. His big fist closes around my wrist and it's like hitting a wall.

He stops the horn's descent just as it breaks his skin.

The horn's tip rests against his temple, pricking his skin and drawing droplets of blood that trickle toward his hairline.

I grit my teeth as his grip threatens to break the bones in my wrist and hand. The more tightly he holds me, the harder I push.

Two forces pushing relentlessly against each other.

His other hand whips around my neck and I gasp for breath, but I'm not deterred. He needs both of his hands to break my neck, but I only need one to impale him.

"Brother!" Dominus's shout creates light across the distance and his running footfalls pound in my hearing.

Atrox's response is sharp. "Stay where you are!"

Dominus's footfalls stop, and I judge he's still ten paces away from us.

Atrox doesn't take his golden eyes off me.

My muscles strain, blood drips from my face to his, and sweat beads across my forehead. "You won't be fine soon."

Only days ago, I found out why the angels consider me to be corrupted. As an Avenging Angel, I'm expected to remain pure above all others. I should not have blood on my hands. Apparently, it's my desire to kill the wicked that makes me corrupted.

The Avenging Angel whom Atrox encountered in his past lifetime—the one named Eva Ashen-Varr—never took a life. She imprisoned the creatures she fought. She never killed them.

My hand is going numb, but I'm locked in this position and with every passing second, the horn's tip moves just a little farther inward.

"You forget that I'm not an ordinary Avenging Angel," I say to Atrox, my voice low and strained, but I'm determined. "I *can* and I *will* kill you."

"Which is exactly why I want you at my side," he replies through gritted teeth.

Impossibly, despite the effort it's taking him to restrain my hand, his grip around my neck softens. His thumb grazes the edge of my jaw, a soft exploration. "You're tainted, Asper. A wild thing. You've tasted true power—the power to take life—and embraced its consequences. And yet you haven't come anywhere near to tapping into your full potential. Imagine what you could do if you weren't weighed down with guilt or self-loathing."

Callan tried to convince me that I wasn't really corrupted—that it was my choices that define me. Not my impulses. Not my birthright. Not even my fucking scars. There was a part of me that desperately wanted to believe him, but there was also a deeply ingrained part of me that had experienced true heartlessness. That cold moment when I would choose to take life and I would feel nothing doing it.

The leader of the Roden-Darr, an angel named Isaac, who was betrayed by the others, said I had the capacity to hunt the dark ones without risk of my emotions getting in the way.

But... which side does killing Atrox fall on? Am I taking out a monstrous beast or killing the only part of Callan that remains in this world?

Atrox's left hand softens even more, his fingertips stroking down my neck to my shoulder. It's a far more relaxed exploration than I was expecting, given the way the muscles of his other arm are bunched as he continues to keep the horn at bay.

"I know how your mind works, Asper," he says. "I know what you need."

"You have no fucking idea what I need," I say, drawing out my response as I struggle to force the horn to move.

"Don't I?" he asks, trailing his forefinger across the top of my shoulder.

I'm wearing the garment that Callan gave me. Long, black pants, while the top is a fitted bodice with straps that extend up to a halter neck. The straps leave triangular sections of my pale skin exposed between the top of the bodice and my neck.

Atrox traces the shape of the straps as his fingertips dance across the top of my breasts. "I know everything that Callan knew. I know what makes your breath hitch." His voice lowers. "I know what makes you ache and what makes you scream."

I can't bat him away with my left hand without losing my leverage on the other side of his head, so I'm forced to tolerate his touch.

"I threw off my shackles," he continues. "When I was wronged, I let go of all misconceptions of right and wrong, and I took revenge against those who persecuted me. You can, too."

"By that reasoning, nothing should stop me from killing you," I say.

I'm acutely aware of the helmet lying on its side in the

9

distance. There's another horn on its top and the gold calls to me. I calculate how fast I could snatch it out of the air with my left hand and drive it into his throat. Even if I weren't fast enough—or strong enough to break through his scales, since they aren't already cracked—it could distract him sufficiently for me to kill him with the first horn.

As the darkness closes in around us again and finally obscures his features, I pretend that he doesn't have Callan's body and that he isn't wearing Callan's face. I tell myself I'm not about to destroy what remains of the man I love.

I could never hurt Callan—never *kill* Callan.

But *Atrox. Oh.* I want nothing more than to fucking destroy him and remove the taste of murder flooding my mouth. The overwhelming tang of copper and the scent of ash that continues to fill my chest with every breath I take.

His golden eyes glint up at me. Unnatural and reflective. Light glimmers around his mouth as he speaks. "You won't kill me," he says, sounding far too certain.

"Why not?" I ask as I prepare to call the other horn to me.

"Because there's a part of you that still believes Callan is alive. If you destroy me, then you destroy any hope of his revival."

My breath catches. Atrox's declaration cuts to the heart of my fears. Callan was everything good in my life, a goodness that was so precious to me, I should have known it would be torn away.

A creature like me doesn't deserve goodness.

I was never fucking worthy of the hope or kindness that Callan showed me. A hunter like me deserves only the rage and retribution that's coming my way.

And yet...

How can I kill my own hope?

I can't stop the moan of pain leaving my lips as the pain becomes too much.

Is this how a heart breaks?

The hurt in my chest is too great for me to constrain, an agony that burrows inward.

Little fractures that shatter so completely.

The shards left behind are turning their sharp points toward my mind and soul, cutting through me as they bury themselves deep. They tear at my rage first because that's where I've always found my strength. Then they slice through my need for vengeance, shredding my instincts into smaller and smaller pieces until it's difficult to think. To reason.

My shoulders hunch and my breathing becomes ragged while my hands start to shake.

"You won't kill me," Atrox repeats. "To strike me down is to destroy yourself."

My moment of vulnerability is my undoing.

He moves so fast that I barely anticipate his attack.

His left hand closes around one of the straps he was playing with and he yanks my head down to his, headbutting me.

Smack!

Pain explodes through my face.

I struggle to maintain hold of the horn, making a final attempt to drive it into his flesh, but he wrenches my arm away from his face, dragging the horn from my grasp. It clatters away from us across the floor, while he shoves my shoulder with his other hand and rolls us over just as fast.

Before I can take a breath or clear my vision from the head-butt, I'm pinned beneath him, his body weighing me down. He doesn't even have to plant a knee on my stomach or chest; he's bulky enough that his sheer weight overwhelms my smaller, lighter frame.

His right hand rests beneath my head like a spiteful cushion. His left is planted on my chest right across my sternum. There was a time when I yearned for Callan to touch me without exploding into flames. Now, the hands that used to be his make me shudder.

Atrox smiles down at me as blood drips from his temple to

his jaw and the scales I broke on his face begin to heal. "This may conflict with your nature as a hunter, but surely, you must realize that you are—now and always—my prey."

I'm suddenly, horrifyingly, aware that he *let me* hold the horn to his head for as long as I did. He could have headbutted me at any time. He wanted to speak to me, so he did.

Fuck!

I underestimated him and I can't do it again.

I try to clear my head, try to focus on his features through the pain still ricocheting around my skull and down my spine.

Shimmers of heat build around his form as he speaks clearly enough to beat back the darkness around us. "I will give you a single choice, Asper. Right here and now. But it's the only choice I will ever give you, so consider your decision wisely."

I can't look away as his eyes shift, his irises returning to the juniper-green that reminds me of a field of burned grass. The color of Callan's anger.

"You can choose to join me willingly or unwillingly," he says.

That's the choice?

My eyes widen a little that he isn't asking me to choose between living and dying, but to decide if I'm *willing* to stand at his side. He assumes that he can make me join him no matter what. *Arrogant, fucking...*

My mental cursing stops when he continues.

"If you follow me, I will help you get revenge for what you've suffered at the hands of the angels."

It's not a deal I expected him to make, and he seems to know it. He pauses, as if he wants his promise to sink in.

"They caged you," he snarls. "Scarred you. Sent you out to kill dragons and then called you a monster because of the deaths you caused. The Celestial Ascendant, the Serene Commander, and every other angel deserve all the fucking pain I can cause them for their sins against you. Give yourself to me, do everything I ask of you, and I will give you all that you desire and deserve."

I stare up at him, my lips parted in surprise.

It's a seductive promise. A promise that, to some extent, doesn't clash with my own goals. But revenge was never something I sought. I only ever wanted my freedom.

I wanted Callan.

"What if I refuse?" I ask.

The scales across his jaw shimmer as his muscles clench. His voice hardens. "Then I will do worse to you than they ever did, and you'll still be mine."

CHAPTER TWO

My lips press slowly together, and a deep anger builds inside me. Despite the pain in my chest, my shattered heart, and all I've lost tonight, it seems that there's still rage inside me. Strip away everything else, and beneath it, I will always have that.

I push upward against Atrox's palm, and he not only lets me rise a little, but one of his big hands cradles my head, bringing me nearer to him. He watches me with a crease in his forehead and a curious light in his eyes, as if he can't anticipate my decision.

I stop when my lips are only inches away from his. This close to him, my head swims with the scent of ash and blood. Where Callan once calmed me, Atrox agitates every nerve in my body.

"Fuck your promises," I whisper. "You have nothing to offer me. You already took away the only thing I ever wanted."

Callan. He was my path to my own heart. The one who gave me the tools to connect with my emotions and understand that I'm capable of so much more than hatred.

Atrox's features harden, but he persists, as if he wants to give me another chance. "You underestimate the pain I can cause you, Asper Ashen-Varr."

He said he knows everything that Callan knew, but it seems Atrox doesn't yet comprehend one of the most fundamental aspects of my personality.

My safety isn't important.

Callan knew that about me. He lived with that truth every night I went out to track the Sentinels, and he didn't know if I would come back alive. Achieving my purpose has always been more important to me than my wellbeing.

From this moment on, my only goal is to end Atrox once and for all.

No matter what it costs me.

My teeth snap together before I say, "You can't hurt me more than you already have."

"Don't fucking count on that." Atrox's hand closes around the back of my head, his fingers tangle in my hair, and he wrenches me upward.

Pain explodes through my scalp, but I don't focus on the discomfort, only on his cruel eyes.

He *wants* me to scream. He wants me to regret my choice. But I fucking won't.

My wings shoot out beneath my back, pushing me upward at the same rate he's pulling me, which eases the tension across my scalp. At the same time, I grab his wrist with both hands so that when he drags me fully upright, practically dangling me opposite him, I'm holding myself up. He doesn't rip my hair out and the pain stops.

My biceps strain a little, but my frame is light, and it doesn't take as much effort to keep myself in the air as it might have if my body were heavier.

His gaze flashes up and down the length of me as if he's cataloging all of my potential pain points—including my wings.

I fully retract them and prepare to kick my foot into his face. I picture myself smacking him right where I cracked his scales.

Before I can move, he says, "Perhaps I should rephrase. You underestimate the pain I can cause the dragons you care about."

I freeze, my muscles tense, on the verge of lashing out, but I restrain myself as he continues.

"You care about Sophia," he says. "And Beatrix and Felix. Even Callan's sister, Zahra. And especially Callan's niece, Emika." He pauses, as if he wants to make sure I'm listening. "They will all believe that I'm Callan. Imagine the damage I could cause by pretending to be him."

My blood runs cold. Sophia, Beatrix, and Felix are all dragons in the Dread clan. They're all loyal to Callan, and I formed bonds with them. Friendships I never expected to have. Each of them defended me at different times from different threats. I could never cause them harm or allow harm to come to them.

As for Zahra, Callan's sister, she and I had finally come to an understanding before the Roden-Darr captured me. She agreed to accept my help, even if she doesn't fully trust me. I won't allow harm to come to her, and I would die before I allow Atrox to hurt her five-year-old daughter, Emika.

"Imagine how easily I could crush Emika's tiny body," Atrox says, lifting his free hand and curling his fingers in the air as if he holds her already.

It's a very real threat. Unless the Dread are warned, they would believe that Atrox is Callan. Atrox is currently partially shifted, his skin covered in golden scales, his height and body mass increased, but all he has to do is shift fully back into his human form, and the differences in appearance between him and Callan will be barely discernible.

The only real visible difference would be Atrox's juniper-green eyes. But Callan's eyes turned that color when he was angry, so it wouldn't immediately give Atrox away.

I now face a choice that goes against my basic nature. I could lie to Atrox and tell him that I will follow him willingly. But it would be a lie, and the taste of sour lemons—the mark of a liar—combines with the ashy flavor already coating my tongue.

Or I can continue to fight him, and trust that I can protect those I care about.

But... can I?

I couldn't protect Callan. I thought I could, and I fucking failed. *How can I be sure I'll be able to protect anyone else I care about?*

To my right, Atrox's brother skirts around the puddle of blood on the floor to retrieve his hammer. He nonchalantly hefts the weapon over his shoulder as he approaches us.

"Enough, brother," Dominus says. "Let me cave in her skull and we can be done with her."

Atrox flashes his brother an unexpectedly furious glance. "I'll be done with her when I *say* I'm done with her."

Dominus appears unperturbed by Atrox's anger. He shrugs. "Very well. That is your choice."

Atrox's eyes are like cold gems as he returns his attention to me. "I'll ask you one last time, Asper. Will you choose to stand at my side, to accept what I'm offering you, or will your future be filled with pain?"

My breathing is so rapid now that I may as well have sprinted a mile. Blood and sweat drip down my face. Big, fat drops. One of them splashes to the floor, creating a miniature explosion of crimson light.

That tiny visual disturbance is like a trigger.

A scream tears out of me. A fucking useless, furious scream that carries enough force that the space around us lights up like daytime. Everything becomes bright: the throne, Atrox, Dominus, and the emptiness that stretches as far as I can see. An emptiness that is outside and *within* me and it's tearing me apart from the inside.

My heart refuses to break quietly.

I thrash against Atrox's hold, digging my fingernails as hard as I can against his scales as I use his arm as leverage to kick my right foot into his face. My boot connects and the *thump* adds to the volume of my scream, turning the air so white that it's nearly blinding.

I struggle to see Atrox opposite me, but I hear his grunt of pain and, the moment I sense the loosening of his hand around my head, I ram my armband against his forearm so hard that the *crack* his scales make is audible despite my continuing scream.

He lurches away from me, but I drop to the ground and leap through the white air after him. I knock into his big chest, my fists flying. Uncontrolled. Unable to stop.

A final, desperate attack, even though I know I have no way to escape him. I need to prove to him that I'm a threat. A danger. And that subduing me will not be easy. I may not be strong enough to finish him—I know that now—but I sure as fuck want to cause him even a little of the pain he's promised to cause me.

I crack the scales across his chest, his shoulder, and once again, his left cheekbone before he can react. Somewhere in the back of my mind, I'm coldly aware that the wound I've reopened on his face—the spot where I pressed the tip of the horn—isn't healing as quickly this time. I've struck at that spot over and over and my attacks seem to be having a more lasting impact now.

I'm also aware of the shimmer in the air between us. The heat waves rising off his body. His heated exhalations that warn me his fire is only heartbeats away.

Before I can pound him again, the golden hammer glints at the edge of my vision. Dominus strides to our sides, his outline appearing through the white air, swinging the hammer directly at my head.

I barely have time to twist before the weapon hits me.

I avoid the worst of the blow, but the edge of the hammer's head clips my forehead. Pain explodes through my head, but it's not the physical force that has the most impact.

A surge of energy shoots through me from the contact point

all the way down my spine and it's like a burning cord that immobilizes my neck and back and locks up my limbs.

Oh, fuck...

I lose control of my evasive move, my body lifting off the floor before I land heavily and roll stiffly. Even when I stop rolling, finding myself on my back, the force of the hit was so great that I continue to slide across the marble. My left arm is outstretched and I can't seem to pull it in. My right arm is wedged against my side while my left leg is bent at the knee. None of my limbs are responding to my commands.

The white air swims above me when I finally come to a stop, lying on my back and staring up at the nothingness above me.

It's difficult to focus. The pain across the right side of my face is intense, and I'm worried that the hammer might have damaged my right eye because my vision is swaying and shimmering. The surge of energy that flowed through me at the hammer's impact continues to burn slowly, a hot sensation down my spin.

A *thud* right beside my head makes my whole body jolt, but I can't do more than swivel my gaze to find Dominus has dropped the hammer's head on the floor in line with my left shoulder.

He crouches beside me, his left hand resting on the hammer's hilt. "This weapon is infused with light magic," he says. "What you're experiencing now is an overwhelming surge of magic that your body is trying to process. It's only because my brother wants you alive that I won't finish you off now. He gave you the chance to willingly become our ally, but you have chosen the path of pain."

Several strands of my hair have fallen across my face, sticking to my cheek in the still-flowing blood. Dominus pushes them off my face before he gestures at our surroundings. "Do you know why this prison is made of darkness, Asper Ashen-Varr?"

I'm not confident that I'll be able to speak, but I manage to find my voice. "I'm sure you're about to tell me."

He snorts at my bravado, but shadows lurk behind his eyes as he leans a little closer. "Because nothing creates light in this prison like screams of pain."

A chill passes down my spine that's at odds with the burning sensation. I must have stopped crying when the hammer hit me, and the shadows are once again growing at the edges of the bright space around us, drawing relentlessly inward.

Dominus runs his fingertips down the side of my face to my chin. "Flap your wings as hard as you can, little bird. Beat yourself bloody against the bars of this cage if you will."

He smiles as his brother appears behind him. "You won't escape us."

CHAPTER THREE

*D*ominus rises to his feet, looming over me. Where before he considered me with disdain—the look an apex predator gives easy prey—there's now a hint of anticipation in his voice as he speaks to his brother. "I see now why you don't want to kill her. She's nothing like the Avenging Angel I fought."

"A lesser creature would have died from the hit of your hammer." Atrox presses his hand to the wound across his temple, checking the blood on his fingertips. The crack I made in his scales is only now healing. I definitely hurt him. Which means I could do it again.

He doesn't seem concerned. He dismisses the blood on his hands. "She's a wild thing." A smile plays around his mouth. "But Callan tamed her. I will, too."

I exhale quietly. Callan didn't 'tame' me. He took the time to understand me, to comprehend my nature and how my past experiences influenced my decisions, and then he gave me the freedom to choose my path.

He trusted me when no other dragon would have.

"Callan may have conquered the angel, but you are now

contending with her dragon," Dominus replies. "Your ability to control Asper will be determined by who her fire dragon is."

Over the course of my stay with Callan, I learned more about the nature of the dragon shifters' dragons. Sophia didn't have a dragon until last week. She had spent her whole life practically human—unable to manifest wings and scales like other dragons could, and without the physical strength of most dragon shifters. Then, when she was faced with the danger of my fire, her dragon surfaced for the first time. She briefly heard her dragon's voice and, before it faded, it told Sophia that its name is Bella Vorago. Later, we discovered that Bella Vorago was a water dragon who once lived in the time when dragons freely roamed the Earth. Bella Vorago was killed by angels when she was somehow led astray by none other than Atrox.

Now, Bella Vorago lives again within Sophia, giving Sophia power over water, the same way that Atrox lived within Callan and allowed him to breathe fire—even if nobody knew that was who Callan's dragon was.

Similarly, Solomon Grudge's dragon was the forest dragon named Magnus Grim. Magnus spoke to me during my fight with Solomon and it became apparent that Solomon had found a way to live symbiotically with Magnus, the two working together and making each other stronger. Solomon could do things that other dragon shifters can't—like shifting different parts of his body at will and not casting a dragon shadow when he was exposed to moonlight. When Magnus Grim spoke to me, he had the power to compel me—and even Callan at the time—to stop fighting Solomon.

Atrox rubs his jaw as he peers down at me. "The question is whether or not we deliberately draw out her dragon or try to keep it subdued."

"Better to know who her dragon is and ascertain whether or not it's our enemy than have it rise up when we don't expect it," Dominus says.

Atrox grunts his agreement. "If her dragon is one of our enemies, we can crush it before it gains any further strength."

I'm not sure how they plan to draw out my dragon, let alone how they could crush it without killing me. Of course, the possibility that they might kill me might not worry them.

Atrox crouches to me and the gleam in his eyes makes my blood run even colder. "There's also the possibility that Asper's dragon might be an ally. In which case, she may be forced to comply with its wishes once we draw it out."

He runs his fingertips up the side of my face, skirting around the bruise that must be forming on my cheek where Dominus hit me and stopping at my hairline where the hammer clipped me.

Dominus crouches, too, and now he tips his head, his dark hair swishing across his cheek as he contemplates me with what appears to be curiosity. "Why isn't she healing?"

"She can't," Atrox says. "She doesn't know why—and Callan didn't, either—but I have a theory that it's connected with her dragon. The only times she has healed herself quickly were when she connected with her most basic dragon traits."

"Which ones?"

"Fire and gold." Atrox's fingertips lower to my neck, stroking down the side of it. "When she breathes fire, she can heal any wounds that might be on her neck—which is where the fire scorches. Also, some old scars on her back disappeared after dragon's gold lashed her. That second instance is more curious, but I believe the gold was in the process of transformation and she was harnessing her dragon's power to control it at the time."

They both stare down at me with identical juniper-green eyes, their ashy scents nearly indistinguishable.

"Then we should proceed even more carefully in drawing out her dragon," Dominus says. "No matter who it is, once we uncover it, she's likely to heal more quickly. Her wing might even repair itself. It will be harder to subdue her."

Atrox grins. "I welcome the challenge."

The fact that they're speaking so openly in front of me about strengths I may, or may not, attain tells me they're confident they will be able to restrain me no matter what. As for my ability to heal myself...

I've only known for a short time that I have a dragon. Solomon Grudge revealed that fact to me before he died. When I woke up in this prison, I had no idea how much time had passed. It could have been a day. Or less. Or more. And it was only moments after I woke that Dominus revealed to me his theory that my dragon is a fire dragon. I haven't had enough time to process how I feel about any of it. But if drawing out my dragon means my wing might heal, then I'm anxious to make it happen. Of course, I'm ignoring the fact that the process might destroy me, or that my dragon might be my enemy.

Atrox breaks his scrutiny of me. "We need a place to work and figure out our next move. We can't hurry out into the world without a plan. The world has changed a lot since you were last in it, brother."

Dominus nods. "I expected as much. What happened to you after I was captured?"

Atrox's gaze flashes to me. His voice lowers and he speaks more carefully, as if he's now guarding what he says. "I kept searching for what was stolen from us, just as I promised. My only hope was to find the Book of Light Magic, since it would point the way, but it took me many years to find it. The book was being guarded by the forest fae and, in turn, Magnus Grim was protecting the fae. He would not let me pass." Atrox's lips press with apparent frustration. "He claimed he was doing me a favor. He said the book had become volatile and was too dangerous for anyone to read. He said it would kill me."

Atrox gives an unhappy growl. "I tried to get past him, but I underestimated his strength. We fought, and we both suffered mortal wounds."

"You killed each other?" Dominus asks.

Atrox nods. "The forest fae carried Magnus Grim back into the woods to die—"

"And left you to rot, no doubt," Dominus says.

"No," Atrox says quietly, making his brother's eyebrows rise. "They gave me a mercy I wasn't expecting. They carried me all the way to Viviana's grave so that I could take my last breaths where she was buried."

The angry crease in Dominus's forehead smooths out, his shoulders slump, and his lips lose their cruel twist. At the mention of Viviana—whoever she was—he is suddenly quiet, his gaze downcast.

Finally, he asks, quietly, "What of your sword?"

Atrox shakes his head. "I don't know what became of it. It may have been buried with me or stolen. I doubt I will ever find it after so many years."

Atrox stares into the distance. "You took my place in this prison because I was sure that if I had more time, I could take back what was ours and avenge Viviana. Instead, my life ended."

Heat grows around his body again and the scent of ash deepens. "I failed you, and I failed her. I won't forsake you again."

Dominus reaches out to place his hand on his brother's shoulder. "*We* won't fail again."

Atrox exhales heavily before he considers our surroundings. "The question is: How the fuck do we get out of this prison?"

"Now that my chains are broken, the Roden-Darr will let us out," Dominus replies. "The breaking of the chains will have triggered alarms within this place, but I asked them to hold off until I gave them the signal that I had Asper under control. From what I glimpsed of the veil before the previous Roden-Darr imprisoned me in this place, there is much more to this place than what we see here. A hidden palace lies beyond this prison. We can remain there while we regain our strength."

Atrox rolls his shoulders and stretches his neck. "I need to rediscover my ability to fully shift into my dragon form and to recover complete control of my flames."

"As do I," Dominus replies. "The chains constrained my power and it's been millennia since I fully shifted. Whatever we need, the Roden-Darr will provide."

"But they think you're me." Atrox growls. "Will they follow us once they discover you lied to them?"

A sly smile appears on Dominus's face. "Brother, don't doubt me. These angels were created to be followers. They are as easily persuaded and controlled as sheep. Without their Avenging Angel, they are thirsty for purpose and direction."

He holds up the hammer as if it were proof. "They gave me back my hammer and your armor when they brought you to me yesterday. They killed their own kind for me. They have blood on their hands and nowhere else to turn. I assure you they will gladly obey us."

He rises to his feet and steps away from me. "If you will permit me to use your armor one last time, brother? I need to continue our ruse just a little longer."

At Atrox's nod, Dominus holds out his free hand in the direction of Atrox's helmet and its broken horn. The two pieces lie on the floor several paces away, but they both fly to Dominus's hand, the gold seeming to obey his unspoken command. The horn fits itself neatly back onto the helmet, appearing to seal again. Even though the golden armor belongs to Atrox, I suppose that after so many years with Dominus, it has formed an affinity with him.

Dominus places the helmet on his head, dressed once again as he was when I first saw him and mistook him for Atrox.

At the moment he pulls on the helmet, the armor he's wearing ripples. Despite Dominus's control over them, it's as if the plates are aware that their true owner stands nearby, and they wish to fly to Atrox.

Feeling is returning to my left side and my fingers twitch, but I force myself to lie still. There's no point using more of my energy fighting the dragons now—not until an escape from this prison presents itself.

Atrox remains towering beside me, his back now partially turned to me.

His brother strides across the darkness to the throne on which he was chained and lifts the hammer high above his head. He aims it at the back of the chair, where black bones rise upward.

With a grunt, he swings the hammer sideways, smashing it into the black bones. Instead of breaking, light bursts through the bones with a *clang* that vibrates through me.

Light ripples across the air high above us like a hundred shooting stars. They streak away to my left, all of them angling toward the same spot in the far distance.

That spot suddenly floods with light and it's as if a hatch opened in the darkness. A wide column of light beams down from high above and a cascade of white-winged male angels descends through it, their wings curved to slow their path before they alight on the ground.

They stride toward us, approaching from the side, which allows me to see them clearly even while I remain lying down. They're all dressed in simple clothing: white sweatpants, a white T-shirt, and ivory boots. Their pristine clothing makes them practically glow in the dark, while the gold watches they wear around their wrists glint. From experience, I know that their gold watches transform into poleaxes that they're trained to use to full effect.

The angel striding ahead of them is named Zadkiel. He is tall, like his brethren, with black hair and flawless skin. If I couldn't sense his true nature, I might consider him to be beautiful, but the taste that fills my mouth makes me gag.

All of these men carry the stench of traitors. It's a strong tang of copper, underlaid with the heavy scent of violets and the gritty texture of mud, as if my mouth is filled with rotting flowers and old copper coins.

There used to be twenty Roden-Darr, but now there are only ten. Zadkiel was second-in-command, and his leader was a white-haired angel named Isaac. Zadkiel and the other nine who now stand before me murdered Isaac and their fellow Roden-Darr right after I was captured. They couldn't allow Isaac to stop them from bringing me and Callan to Dominus.

Dominus takes a few steps forward as the angels approach, positioning himself in front of Atrox and me while the Roden-Darr line up and take a knee.

Zadkiel is the only one who keeps his head raised. "Atrox Imperator," he says, greeting Dominus. "We rejoice to see that you have been freed."

"Thank you, my brothers," Dominus says.

Zadkiel's focus flickers to Atrox, and his forehead creases a little. As Atrox said, these angels don't know who is who. When they brought Callan here, he was unconscious, and they must be wary to see the dragon they think is Callan Steele standing freely at their master's back.

"Forgive me, Master Atrox, but why is Callan Steele still alive?"

"Zadkiel, you must listen to me carefully," Dominus says, demanding the attention of Zadkiel and the other Roden-Darr alike. "You have lived too long in the shadow of the veil. You were left without a leader, abandoned by the Celestial Ascendant, and told that you had no purpose. Your strength was denied, and your true potential was ignored.

"You chose to follow me when I was branded a monster. You risked the hatred of your people merely by standing at my side. You have given me your faith and belief and I promised to reward you. Did I not?"

Zadkiel and the others nod, their eyes now raised to Dominus.

Murderous fucking sheep.

Dominus sweeps his arms wide. "Now is your time, my brothers. You *will* be given purpose, and you will find glory, but you must take another leap of faith."

Dominus pauses. His gaze runs over them and his voice

lowers. "My name is Dominus Audax," he says, watching the Roden-Darr carefully.

I can't help but notice the way Dominus reaches for his hammer and his grip tightens on its hilt, as if he's preparing to kill them if they rebel.

"Dominus... Audax...?" Zadkiel falters. "But..."

Dominus raises his voice. "Your predecessors lied to you." He growls. "I am not Atrox Imperator, as you were led to believe."

There's a flurry of murmurs among the Roden-Darr, and all the while, Dominus's hand tightens on his hammer.

Still watching the angels, Dominus gestures with his free hand to his brother. "I have liberated Atrox Imperator from the shifter who caged him. This dragon is no longer Callan Steele. He is no longer your enemy. He is my brother, and your new master, Atrox Imperator."

There's silence among the angels as their focus comes to rest on Atrox.

Now that Atrox's attention is drawn nearly completely to the Roden-Darr, I test my ability to rise to my knees. I make it only halfway up before my head swims and I'm forced to plant my palms on the floor, crouching on all fours as I wait for my vision to clear. I haven't yet ascertained the full extent of my head wound, and there's a part of me that doesn't want to know. I want to believe that the only consequences are blurred vision and a pounding headache, and that no structural damage has been caused.

I tell myself to get the fuck up, even if I can only make it up to my knees, and even if my arms hang at my sides.

Zadkiel has quickly gathered himself after Dominus's revelations and responds as a true zealot would. He stands and turns to his comrades. "We have gladly served Dominus Audax. He gave us purpose when we had none. We pledged our faith to Atrox Imperator and now he has been delivered to us. Who are we to question what form he comes in?"

Zadkiel casts a challenging stare at the other angels, but

none of them speaks up against him. "In fact, we should rejoice. Not only have we freed the dragon who gave our lives meaning these past years, but we have contributed to the liberation of his brother." His voice lowers. "What other purpose can be more righteous than this?"

Once again, he casts a challenging look at the other angels where they remain on one knee, but it's a slower contemplation this time. "Do any among you doubt this? If so, speak now."

Not a single Roden-Darr voices an objection.

"Then we are agreed," Zadkiel says. "We will be the army standing at the backs of Dominus Audax and Atrox Imperator. We will serve them faithfully and give our lives to their cause. Fate willing, we will live to see the day when their fire cleanses the world of all evil."

Dominus finally releases the handle of his weapon and closes the gap between himself and Zadkiel, standing eye to eye with the angel. As powerful as the Roden-Darr are, Zadkiel's presence seems to pale in comparison to Dominus's.

"My brother and I are tired and in need of rest," Dominus says to Zadkiel. "I trust you have prepared lodgings for me within this veil."

"We have," Zadkiel replies. "Although we were not aware that multiple lodgings would be required. I will send some of my men ahead to prepare another room."

His focus finally lands on me, and his disdain for me is clear in his voice. "What do you wish us to do with Asper Ashen-Varr? Will she require a cage?"

Atrox speaks up for the first time since the Roden-Darr arrived. "She will." He grabs my arm, yanking me up at his side. "She belongs with the mindless beasts."

Zadkiel's eyes light up. "We have the perfect place."

CHAPTER FOUR

Zadkiel bows once again to Dominus and Atrox. "Please follow us."

At his words, the other Roden-Darr rise to their feet. In near unison, they reach for their watches, flick them upward, and then neatly catch them before the watches transform into poleaxes.

Together, the angels strike the ends of their weapons onto the floor. The light they create with the sound spreads across the room, brightening the space around me from the floor beneath my feet all the way up Atrox's towering form. Without the shadows, it's easier to see just how tightly he's gripping my arm, his fingers pressing into my bicep.

He peers down at me with angry eyes, and his voice carries an undeniable threat. "You will walk beside me at all times. If you fail to obey me or you stray from my side, I will leave you in this dark place to scream until you have no breath left."

A retort rests on the tip of my tongue, but I swallow it.

He yanks me hard against his side, a demonstration of how quickly he can subdue me if he wants to. "Test me, and I will give my brother permission to kill you."

I rapidly consider my options and my chances of fighting to free myself from this situation. But the fact is, I can't do anything to help myself if I don't get out of here first. If survival means standing obediently at Atrox's side for now, then I'll do it.

For a time.

Not forever.

Besides, he's planning on putting me with beasts, and as far as I'm concerned, animals will be a step up from having to spend further time in his presence.

As I make that decision, the memory of Callan's voice pricks my heart like a needle.

Sometimes the hardest thing is to do nothing.

Damn… it's fucking hard.

Just as I once promised Callan that I would give him time to show me who his people are, I will now give myself time to learn about my environment and my enemies so that when I strike, I can strike hard.

While his brother and the angels wait, Atrox watches me closely, as if he expects me to immediately retaliate against his command.

The longer he waits, the more apparent it becomes that he expects a verbal agreement from me.

I'm not meek. I've never been submissive. But I give Atrox my response without even a hint of sour lemon on my tongue. "I won't test you."

The moment I finish speaking, he grabs my chin, tipping my face up to his as he scrutinizes me. I suppose he's looking for a lie. Whatever he sees in my eyes, it seems to please him.

"Good," is all he says before he returns his attention to Zadkiel.

The Roden-Darr are poised to proceed, and the dark-haired angel gestures us forward.

Atrox doesn't let go of my arm as we follow the angels to the column of light in the distance. I'm still sluggish from the blow to my head, but Atrox propels me along at his side until we reach the light.

"All you need to do is step inside the light," Zadkiel explains as several of the angels precede us. "It will transport you upward."

Atrox steps into the ring of light without hesitation while Dominus is a step behind us.

The light enfolds us, filling my vision so completely that it feels like the briefest sensation of rushing air, and then our environment changes.

The air is now as pure as a crisp, winter's day. It's such a startling contrast to the darkness we left behind that it over-comes the burning scent of Atrox's nearness.

My eyes had adjusted to the prison's darkness and my surroundings are now so bright that it takes me a few seconds to focus.

While my eyesight catches up, my other senses fill the gaps. My hearing tells me that we've entered another large space, given that the footfalls of the angels surrounding us echo outward and don't bounce back.

The crispness of the air reminds me of an icy lake—not that I think there's any water nearby—but it's an absence of scents that tells me the entire space is devoid of life, other than the angels and dragons nearby.

I don't detect any new threats.

I'm gratified that it also takes Atrox a moment to adjust—or so it seems, since he stops where he stands, instead of immedi-ately dragging me after Zadkiel.

The angel's silhouette is barely discernable against the white background. "We're currently situated at the deepest level of the veil and can only ascend from here."

His footfalls stop, and so does the procession of the other angels around us, as they wait for the two dragon brothers to resume walking.

When they do, it's at a slower pace.

My eyesight finally adjusts, and I make out another seemingly endless space, also lined with a white marble floor.

I'm dismayed to realize that there are no obvious exits from this place—no apparent means of leaving, although the outline of a single structure becomes visible in the near distance and my hopes rise again.

As we approach, the structure's shape becomes more distinct and I eye it with curiosity.

It's a spiral staircase.

Each step is wide and deep and hangs in space without any railings or any other structure to support it.

The whole staircase extends up into the air for what looks like about fifty feet, curving gently, until it abruptly stops. The uppermost step appears to sit in space high above us, leading nowhere.

I was unconscious when the Roden-Darr brought me to the veil, so I'm seeing all of this for the first time, and the staircase's design puzzles me.

"We call this 'the central stairway,'" Zadkiel says. "You must take these steps if you wish to go anywhere within our territory."

Dominus peers upward. "Can we fly up?"

Zadkiel shakes his head. "You must take each step to your destination. In the veil, the path is as important as the destination. Unless you proceed by the steps, the doors won't open to you."

"Doors?" Dominus asks.

"They open to every part of our territory within the veil," Zadkiel replies. "They will appear as you ascend the staircase. Your lodgings are behind the doors that will appear at the top. They are the most opulent quarters. The door to the angel's cage is located on the second step. The lower the step, the darker the cell. Do you wish to proceed to her cage first?"

"Take us to our quarters first," Atrox says with a sharp glance in my direction. "I want her to see what she could have had."

I remain in step with Atrox as he moves toward the stairway. The less I tug against his hold, the less his iron grip around my bicep hurts.

Dominus falls in behind me, a guard at my back, and I suspect they still don't believe that I won't cause trouble along the way.

The stairs appear wide enough that Zadkiel will be able to walk beside Atrox, and each individual step looks deep enough that it will take us several paces before we reach the next step up.

"The bottom step merely begins the journey," Zadkiel says. "The doors will begin to manifest from the second step."

As Atrox ascends onto the bottom step with me, Zadkiel gives a warning. "You must remain on the stairway once you begin to ascend. If you step off the stairway into the air around it, you will plunge into the uncontrolled part of the veil. There, you will find yourself in the dark space between Earth and the heavenly realm. It is a space from which you may never escape."

It sounds like a bad way to try to leave. I'm hoping Zadkiel will let slip how to exit the veil, but, as if Dominus reads my mind, he speaks up from behind me.

"When we are alone, you will tell us how to leave the veil," Dominus says to Zadkiel. "But none of you will mention the way out in front of the Avenging Angel."

Zadkiel inclines his head. "Of course."

Just as Zadkiel said, nothing happens on the bottom step, but the moment his foot touches the next step up, doors appear at each side of it. The bottom of each door sits against the surface of the step, but otherwise, the doors stand upright in the air. No other structure becomes visible around them, not even a doorframe.

"Each of these doors leads to another part of our territory," Zadkiel explains. "These lower levels contain the prisons while the upper levels give access to our living quarters, as well as a library, training rooms, and a food hall."

"How many other prisoners are being kept here?" Dominus asks, remaining behind me.

"All of the creatures that the former Avenging Angel captured," Zadkiel replies. "That is, those that are still alive. It has been a long time since she was killed. You are one of the few who survived this long."

"Dragons live long lives," Dominus mutters. "Unless they are hunted and killed."

Zadkiel pauses on the next step. His forehead creases and a new tension settles around his mouth. "We can tell you about each of the other prisoners when you're ready. If you have any allies among them, we would not object to releasing them."

Beside me, Atrox gives a non-committal grunt but says, "I doubt there would be any here who were allied to us in our time."

Dominus mirrors that sentiment. "Our goal is not to create chaos."

I don't imagine it would be a smart move on the brothers' part to release any prisoner who's their enemy. They will have enough enemies as it is.

Since Atrox wanted to see his quarters first, Zadkiel continues up the stairway. When we reach the higher levels, he points out the doors that lead to the library, the training rooms, and the food hall. He also points out the Roden-Darr's sleeping quarters, which sit behind a door on the third-to-last step.

When Atrox and Zadkiel reach the uppermost step, a golden door appears on the right, and a silver door materializes on the left.

Zadkiel gestures to the golden door. "These quarters once belonged to the first of the Roden-Darr, a pious angel named Isaac," he says. "His lodgings are now yours, Dominus Audax. I hope you will find them to your liking."

I quietly bristle at Zadkiel's description of Isaac. In my interactions with him, I didn't find him sanctimonious. He was determined and dedicated, and he believed in my ability to hunt down and capture those who prey on the vulnerable and innocent. His anger toward me was fueled by his bitterness and grief that I was born with the ability to take life. It meant he was left without a leader—a leader he had trained his whole life to serve.

Dominus veers out from behind me to take the step up and push open the gold door. Beyond it lies an opulent room with threads of silver and gold interlinked across ivory walls. I catch sight of plush furniture before Dominus turns back, his tall frame blocking my view.

He wears a smile. "It is acceptable."

Zadkiel then gestures to the silver door. "These quarters were designated to the Avenging Angel." His focus flickers to me before returning to Atrox. "Until today, it has been many years since anyone entered this room." He shuffles a little. "In fact, none but the first of the Roden-Darr is permitted to enter. As such, I have never seen inside this room. If there is anything lacking about its appearance or amenity, please tell us and we will fix it."

The rule about not entering must be so well ingrained that Zadkiel doesn't even reach for the silver door's handle. He steps back so that Atrox can reach for it.

The door swings open to reveal a short corridor. The corridor's lighting is soft and silvery, and its walls appear to be made from white stone with decorative arches along the top. A glimpse of the ceiling from where I'm standing reveals that it's painted with vines that twine around large, silver roses.

At the end of the corridor is what looks like a waterfall of silver petals that fall from the ceiling to the floor and disappear into the ground. The cascade is so thick that it's impossible to see what lies beyond it.

It seems that the Avenging Angel's privacy was absolute.

Atrox is stiff beside me. If he wanted me to see what I'm missing out on, then I guess he's disappointed.

"You should take me to my cage now," I whisper.

Atrox's lips twist as he wrenches me around and plows down the steps, dragging me with him. It's only because my reflexes are quick that I keep my feet.

He stops on the step near the bottom that will lead to my new prison, taking angry breaths and staring from the black door on our left to the dark-blue door on our right. "Which one?" he demands to know.

Zadkiel hurries to open the black door before he stands aside so we can see what lies within this part of the veil.

A long, dark corridor stretches out in front of me.

On either side of it are cages—the traditional kind, with metal bars and large, metal locks on the hinged doors. The cages nearest to the door appear smaller, but the ones farther along are larger, judging by the distance between the doors.

Each cell is completely dark except for a column of light that beams down from the ceiling and lights up a circular patch in the center.

The sound of metal scraping across rock reaches me from the distance, but when I focus in that direction, all I see is a chain disappearing out of the circle of light.

I can't make out the occupants of the cages since they must be keeping to the dark corners, but, hell, I can sense them and the explosion of wrath that washes over me is like a wall of flames, burning hot and unstoppable.

I can't stop the gasp that leaves my lips.

My hands are suddenly shaking and there's no way that I can hide my response from Atrox.

He yanks me closer, pulling on my arm, and I'm forced to stand on my tiptoes so he doesn't dislocate my shoulder.

"It's just like walking into a den of Scorn dragons, isn't it, Asper?" he whispers, reminding me of the moment I stepped into Sienna Scorn's dining hall. The fog of guilt hanging over the dragons in her clan hit me with full force.

Once more, I'm about to be surrounded by monsters who

have killed, hurt, maimed, and abused others for their own cruel purposes.

All I want is to end them.

The difference this time is that I'm about to be housed with them.

CHAPTER FIVE

"Which cage?" Atrox asks Zadkiel.

"The last cell on the right," Zadkiel replies. "I'll bring the key."

Atrox drags me into the darkness along the corridor. The cold air hits me immediately and I wish it would wash away the overwhelming reaction I'm having.

As if he senses I might snap, Atrox hurries me along. The deeper we go, the darker the corridor becomes until it's nearly pitch black at the end. The sense of misery around me also increases, mingling with the sharpness of malice pouring toward me.

The occupants of the other cages remain incredibly still and none of them move into the column of light within their cage, but I feel their eyes on me with every quick step I'm forced to take. By the time I reach my cell, it feels like I'm crunching glass between my teeth and swallowing blood.

I try to cling to the memory of the night of the dinner with the Scorn, and the way Beatrix calmly leaned in and told me...

There's nothing like looking into the face of a true monster to put your own sins into context.

I focus on the memory of her voice and the sense of calm

Callan gave me then, and it takes the edge off the influx of guilt around me. Just enough to control my impulses until we reach my cell.

Atrox stops in front of what is undoubtedly the largest cage, but I can't tell if I'll be alone in it because it's impossible to distinguish one malicious creature from the myriad of others hiding in the dark corners around me.

The clatter of the keys as Zadkiel hurries to reach us is the final straw.

I strike out with my palm straight into Atrox's nose, satisfied to hear his bone snap when his scales don't manifest fast enough to protect him.

His roar is muffled, but the wound heals far too fast for my liking and when I try to dart past him, he snatches me off my feet and up into his arms. Dominus is close behind him, but there isn't enough room in the corridor to swing his hammer without risking hitting his brother instead—especially with how wildly I'm attacking Atrox. I'm kicking with my feet. Ramming my elbows into his neck and chest.

"Get the fucking door open!" Atrox roars, holding on to me as I fight him.

I'm too busy trying to free myself to see who opens the cage —the flurry of white wings means it could be Zadkiel or one of the other angels. All I'm aware of is my rage and the force with which Atrox hurls me inside the cell.

My fingernails catch his arm and scrape all the way to his wrist as he shoves me. I don't draw blood—my nails glance off his scales—but the unexpected smell of burning skin fills the air and the heat in my hand is intense as I fly backward.

The cage is so large that I don't hit the back wall, even though I land on my knees and slide through the center spotlight. I finally come to a stop on the other side of the light.

My breathing is ragged, and my chest is heaving.

Atrox turns the key in the lock before I can get back to my feet.

I look up through the matted strands of my hair, snarling at him like the now-caged animal that I am.

The cell is wide enough that there's room for Zadkiel and the other nine Roden-Darr to gather outside it alongside the bars, their outlines glowing in the dark. In contrast, Atrox and Dominus both shimmer with amber flames.

It's the way the angels shift their focus from me to the corners of the cage, and the anticipation in their faces, that makes me most wary.

What the hell is in this cage with me?

Even though the breath is still seething in and out of my mouth, I rise as quietly as I can to my feet, not making any sudden moves as I remain at the edge of the column of light.

One of the straps that adorned my top is now torn through and flops across my chest. I tear it free and wrap it around the palm of my right hand to protect my already-bleeding knuckles. The material is just long enough to tie the ends together.

Then I force myself to close my eyes. I don't dare immerse myself in my senses, since there's too much negative input around me. Instead, I attempt only to focus on what I can hear...

The faint brushing of the angels' palms against the cage bars as they lean forward.

Atrox's angry breathing.

I sink a little within my mind, seeking the sound of heart-beats, which I count carefully. There are the hearts of Atrox, Dominus, and the angels beating opposite me. But it's the ones closer to me that matter.

Finally, I identify the heartbeat of a creature behind me and to my right. And another to my left, also behind me. A third is near the front left corner of the cage. And finally, the quietest heartbeat is near the front right-hand side of the cage. That one is unexpectedly close to where Atrox stands outside the cell, as if the creature isn't afraid of him.

My own heartbeat quickens with the realization that there

are *four* creatures in here with me—one in each corner—but it's the quietest creature I'll need to worry about the most. That one's calm heartbeat indicates that it doesn't fear me—or anyone else for that matter—while the other three creatures are agitated, their heartbeats drumming in my senses.

Outside the cage, Atrox checks his arm and his face for blood before he narrows his eyes at the cage. "What's in there with her?"

"Mindless beasts, just as you requested, Master Atrox." Zadkiel gives Atrox a bloodthirsty smile before he turns back to the cage, the light of anticipation growing in his eyes.

Atrox doesn't look quite as happy. He told his brother that he wanted to keep me alive, but he probably should have mentioned that to Zadkiel. He asked for me to be caged with mindless beasts. He didn't specify that they shouldn't be able to kill me.

He grips one of the bars with his big hand, his focus drawn to the corner closest to him—the one where the quietest creature lurks. Maybe his senses are also alerting him that that beast is the most dangerous.

Just as he takes a breath and appears about to speak, a soft snarl sounds within the cage. It comes from the back corner on my left—diagonally opposite the quietest creature.

The hairs on my arms stand on end and a shiver runs down my spine. I've never heard a sound quite like it. It's not a wolf or a bear or any creature I'm familiar with.

I have no idea how old these beasts are or what era they come from, given the passage of time since the last Ashen-Varr died.

They could be anything.

A second later, another snarl sounds from the front corner, also on my left. This beast's voice is deeper, and it's accompanied by a soft scraping sound—possibly claws on stone because there's a flash of silver that seems intended to draw my attention.

I don't fall for it.

I'm sure that the growls from the beasts on my left are intended to be diversions. These creatures are bound to work together to push me toward the right-hand side of the cage into the path of the quiet beast.

I don't have another second to think.

The ones on the left race toward me, their footsteps quick and light. Multiple silver points flash in the darkness. Teeth. Claws. I don't have time to figure out which before they're upon me.

At the same time, the quiet footfalls of the most dangerous beast speed toward me from my right. That beast will take me down the moment I jump away from my first two attackers and into its path.

I react purely on instinct, leaping into the air and to my right —just as the quiet beast wants—but I tuck my arms close and throw myself into a spin, gaining speed. At the last moment as I fly through the air, I drop my hands, plant them firmly on the creature's back, and use its hindquarters as a springboard into the darkness.

With an unearthly scream of rage, it spins, its reflexes astoundingly fast. Long, curved, silver teeth and steel-like claws flash in the dark as it twists and takes a swipe at me.

It's only because I haven't stopped moving that the beast doesn't cut my head from my shoulders.

I still don't have a good sense of what these creatures are, and I don't have time to figure it out because my evasive move has taken me right into the path of the final animal—the one that was in the back corner to my right, its heartbeat the most rapid of all.

Twitchy mad fucker.

It leaps at me through the dark, its silver claws flashing from both left and right too fast for me to follow. The air shifts across my left shoulder as I throw myself back to the right, desperately trying to evade its attack.

Pain rips through my senses.

I'm aware of another set of silver claws cutting across the fleshy part of my upper arm, and then I hit the ground, my body sliding into the center spotlight, leaving a trail of blood in my wake.

A scream rises to my throat at the sheer fucking pain ricocheting through my arm and the threat of the powerful bodies converging on me.

All four leap into the light, silver eyes and teeth and claws emerging from the darkness.

They're big cats, the size of panthers, their fur ochre-black.

Right at the last moment before they would reach me, another sound reaches me.

It's the soft scrape of metal on stone.

Chains!

With a scream, each beast is halted midair. Black metal collars wrench at their necks and their bodies twist as the chains that bind them are pulled taut, forcing them back to the ground, where they writhe and struggle to reach me.

Each one lands at equidistance from one another around the spotlight—although I've ended up closest to the quiet one.

The four beasts gnash their teeth and swipe at me, reaching forward as far as they can with their forelegs. Their claws are like silver steel, and their teeth are long and curved, sharp enough to disembowel me or tear out my jugular with a single swipe.

I flinch left and right away from each one, adjusting my position as I seek the only safe spot—right in the very center of the spotlight—where the panthers can't reach me.

Their silver eyes flash at me from the darkness at the edge of the circle, their presence immense in my senses. They're each like a void, sucking at the light that floods the floor around my feet.

Their snarls become more frustrated when they fail to reach me.

Now that I can see the beasts, I'm startled to realize that I recognize them. There were drawings of them in the Book of Angelic Monsters, which chronicled the work of the previous Avenging Angel, Eva Ashen-Varr. She imprisoned these beasts not long before she died.

My heart is hammering in my chest as I check the wound across my left shoulder.

I quickly look away. Squeeze my eyes shut. Then unravel my loose bodice strap from around my knuckles and tie it around my left arm instead, gritting my teeth and groaning with pain as I tighten it.

I sink to my knees, trying to calm my breathing and attempting to ignore the shifting air as the panthers strain at their chains and take repeated swipes at me.

I tell myself over and over until my heart stops hammering that if I stay exactly where I am, they can't reach me.

That is, assuming they don't break their chains.

Atrox's voice breaks through the mire within my mind, asking the question I might not want answered.

His voice is low and angry. "Will the chains hold?"

It's only then that I pay attention once more to the angels and dragons. Blinking away the tears of pain from my eyes, I focus on the monsters outside the cage.

The angels have backed away from the bars and only Atrox and Dominus remain directly in front of me. Atrox is pacing, while Dominus has repositioned himself off to my right and is watching his brother closely.

"The chains are unbreakable, master." Zadkiel speaks up but doesn't move toward Atrox. The dark-haired angel looks a little less triumphant than he did before, and I'm not sure what I missed while I was evading the panthers.

Zadkiel gestures toward the end of the corridor. "There's a lever that will open the clasps that keep the chains pinned to the floor. But the lever was melted into place when the panthers were first brought here so that nobody can accidentally release the beasts."

Atrox gives a grunt, but the heat continues to swirl around him, a sign of his continuing rage.

His brother peers through the bars at the beasts.

"Fucking shadow panthers." The heat shimmering around Dominus's face reveals the unhappy press of his lips. I'm surprised to see him appear so unsettled. When he continues, it becomes apparent that his concern isn't on my behalf. "It's been a long time since we've seen these creatures."

Zadkiel and the other angels appear startled. "You know them?"

"We encountered this pack once in our time," Dominus says. "There were only ever these four. We'd never seen beasts like them before and we didn't encounter them again. They are creatures of the purest form of dark magic. That is to say, they are formed from pure malice."

Zadkiel's eyes are wide. "The ancient Roden-Darr never discovered where they came from or which dark witch or warlock conjured them."

"Not a witch or warlock," Atrox snaps, exchanging a look with his brother. "These four appeared right after the bright elves disappeared from the face of the Earth. There were many theories at the time. One was that gargoyles slaughtered the bright elves and used the darkest magic to conjure these creatures as a warning to anyone wanting to avenge the elves' deaths."

Dominus is nodding. "Another theory was that *dark* elves did the slaughtering—although they denied it. And yet another rumor was that the bright elves left by choice—although fuck knows where they went. But no matter the theory, the four shadow panthers were seen as a warning that, because the bright elves took their light with them, one day, dark magic will overcome the Earth."

The angels murmur among themselves and many shake their heads in disagreement.

"Light magic will always prevail," Zadkiel says.

"Will it?" Atrox asks, a sharp question as he looks Zadkiel up and down, as if he doesn't think much of Zadkiel's power.

I discovered from fighting the Roden-Darr that none of them are as powerful as their former leader, Isaac. It was only because of Isaac's light that the others could subdue me to bring me to the veil.

Zadkiel stands firm in the face of Atrox's anger. "The light of your flames has the power to destroy all darkness."

Some of Atrox's anger vanishes as he appraises Zadkiel. "An angel who knows where power truly lies." He growls before turning away from the Roden-Darr once more.

I guess Zadkiel and the other Roden-Darr have well and truly bought into the belief that they're on the right side of history right now.

Dominus gains Atrox's attention. "What do you want to do with Asper now, brother?"

"As I said before, I want her kept alive," Atrox says, his eyes narrowing at his brother. "But I want her weakened so she won't be able to fight us when we come back for her."

Dominus scowls when Atrox says he wants me kept alive, but he quickly wipes his expression clean. He has now asked multiple times for permission to kill me and each time Atrox has said *no*.

Zadkiel speaks up from behind them and I guess he's smart enough to sense the sudden friction between the brothers because he's more hesitant than before. "If your orders are to keep her alive, then we can ensure that she will live. The prisoners are fed and given water at regular intervals, so you can be assured she won't starve or die of thirst."

"Then she can stay where she is," Atrox says firmly, without taking his eyes off his brother. "We'll come back for her when we're ready to discover her dragon. She'll be too frail by then to cause any trouble."

He pauses to give a pointed stare at Zadkiel. "You may leave us now."

Zadkiel bows deeply before he and the other Roden-Darr proceed toward the exit.

Once the door closes behind them, Atrox speaks in a low voice. "The stench of treachery is strong around those angels. If they betrayed their leader before, they could do it again."

"They're a means to an end," Dominus promises. "If they stray from the path we set for them, we will kill them."

"Good," Atrox replies.

Without a backward glance at me, Atrox strides away from my cage.

Dominus lingers a little longer, looking down at me through the bars. He doesn't say anything, but his silence is more unsettling than any verbal threat he could make.

He turns away and within moments, I'm alone in the overly bright spotlight, surrounded by beasts that want to tear me apart.

CHAPTER SIX

I hunch over my knees, close my eyes, and try to block
out the snarling animals, the rush of air as they
continue to swipe their paws at me, and the warm blood
seeping from beneath the makeshift bandage I wrapped around
my upper arm.

I try to focus on my golden bracelets as well as the subtly
vengeful nature of my armband.

The armband is defensive armor, so I guess that's why Atrox
hasn't bothered to take it off me.

As for the bracelets, they were never weapons. The one on
my left wrist is a solid band inlaid with three little sapphires. It
saved my wing from being cleaved off during my fight with the
Serene Commander. The other one is an interlinked chain. The
heart-shaped charm on it is cold and dull, and I'm not sure if
Atrox would be able to tap into its magic to track my location,
but it certainly doesn't hurt him to leave the bracelets on me.

All the gold does is remind me of what I've lost.

I stay curled up like that for a long time before the panthers
grow tired of trying to reach me and slink back into their dark
corners. Every few minutes, they growl, as if to remind me of

their presence and the threat they pose if I dare move from the safe spot I found for myself.

An hour passes. Maybe more.

As each long minute ticks by, my most basic needs become a problem. I'm dehydrated. Hungry. I've lost more blood than I care to think about. I need to sleep, but nodding off or passing out will leave me dangerously vulnerable.

My head sinks lower until I'm curled over my knees and the mental screams I hurl at myself to stay awake become softer and weaker. Unimportant compared with the numbness overtaking my body. I'm overcome with the overwhelming need to just... go to... sleep...

I jolt.

My eyes fly open.

A soft, snuffling sound close to my right draws my focus.

The quiet panther rests at the edge of the light, silently observing me, its silver eyes glowing in the dark. When it blinks, its eyes disappear from view completely. Just like its claws when they're retracted and its teeth when it isn't snarling. Unless it chooses to reveal itself, it blends completely into the dark.

It sniffs at the drying blood on the stone floor before it hisses at me. Its teeth are like daggers in the dark. Then it slinks back to its corner.

Satisfied that it still can't reach me, I lower my head to my knees once more, determined to conserve my energy as much as I can.

Once again, I lose track of time.

At some point, the Roden-Darr bring food and water to the cages, a process that they undertake with surprising careless-ness, wheeling a trolley with squeaky wheels down the corridor as they go.

I count only three other cages to which they deliver food, which reinforces the fact that there are few prisoners still alive now. Each cage has a different-shaped opening in the bars for this task—some with a small hatch high up, others with a narrow hatch down low. They throw the food into the dark corners, and I don't see any sign of the inhabitants to know what or who they are.

When the two angels reach my cage, they unlock a hatch in the cage door that opens at their eye-height. They take turns throwing large chunks of raw meat into each corner of the cage before one of them pitches me a hard loaf of bread and a leather pouch that sounds like it's filled with water.

The loaf of bread nearly rolls past me, but I catch it just in time. The leather pouch lands in the danger zone just outside the spotlight. I stare at it, as if glaring could bring the pouch closer to me.

The angels lock the hatch again and take a moment to smirk at me through the bars.

"Eat quickly," one of them says. "The rain will arrive soon."

Their mention of rain doesn't make sense, but I file it away as another thing to be wary of.

While the angels disappear back along the corridor with their squeaky cart, I listen carefully to the panthers snuffling and eating. I take the chance to slip forward and snatch the water pouch, jolting back in time to avoid the deadly swipe the quiet panther aims at me.

It slinks back into the darkness, a piece of its food gripped between its teeth.

That fucker really wants my blood.

Checking that I'm carefully back in my safe spot, I pace myself as I consume the bread and water, determined not to eat or drink so fast that I bring any of it up again.

I've only made it through half of the bread when the darkness filling most of the cell begins to swirl, wisps of gray appearing as if storm clouds are forming above us.

Seconds later, I gasp when needle-sharp rain beats down on me, a torrent so fast and thick that I'm driven to the floor. It's difficult to lift my head or see through the downpour, but it seems that rain is filling every cage, not just mine.

It lasts a solid ten minutes and when it finally eases, I'm left hunched, shivering, and clutching the soggy remains of my bread.

The water that was pooling around me quickly drains away, and I listen carefully to discern that it runs toward the back of the cage and then through what sounds like an open grate.

Moments later, I also hear the sound of the panthers lapping at water, and I judge that there must be troughs in the floor near the sides of the cage, which the rain has now filled.

I shiver in the cold and check the wound on my upper arm, finding it washed clean. So is the previously bloody floor.

Hours pass after that. Long hours. Maybe half a day.

And then the cycle repeats.

Another two angels—different ones this time—come in to feed us, dragging their squeaky trolley along the corridor and throwing food into the cells. I receive another loaf of bread and another leather pouch of water.

Soon after the angels leave, the rain pelts down again, and I soon recognize it as a mechanism to fill the troughs with water, as well as a means of cleaning each cell. After all, the panthers aren't toilet trained.

But the rain poses a continual danger to me because it leaves me chilled and, combined with my continued blood loss, I'm dangerously unable to regulate my temperature. My teeth begin to chatter and the energy it's taking to keep myself warm is draining the small reserves I have.

When I turn my senses inward, my heartbeat is thready and my body is slow to respond to my commands.

The brothers might have thought to leave me in here for days to weaken me, but I don't think I'll last that long.

Some fucking Avenging Angel I am that blood loss can defeat me so completely.

Finally, I have no choice but to sink into a meditative state, which allows me to conserve my energy and maintain a regular temperature, but also requires me to let down the mental guards that are keeping the malice of my fellow prisoners at bay.

I'm too tired to scream as the vile taste of copper fills my mouth, and the darkness around me becomes darker and heavier.

Thankfully, the deeper I immerse myself, the farther away the violence feels, and I can finally gain some relief from the heavy wash of rage.

Until another emotion replaces it, overwhelming me with an intensity that I'm not prepared for.

Grief.

It's a hot burn within me, even more powerful than anger, welling up from the deepest parts of my heart.

I lost Solomon, the half-brother who could have raised me and changed the course of my life. I lost Isaac, the first of the Roden-Darr who was born to serve me and didn't deserve to die.

And Callan.

Those gentle parts of my soul that I was once convinced I could cut out of myself... Well... They are not so gentle after all. They are as sharp as daggers. Blades burning so intensely as they cut through me that I'm gasping for breath within my mind, struggling to endure this pain that is far worse than any physical agony I've ever felt.

Worse than the Serene Commander's lash.

Worse than the crunch of a Dread dragon's fists against my ribs.

Worse than a golden noose around my neck.

Callan convinced me that I was worthy of love, and I believed him. I returned that love to him, and I loved *all* of him. His calm. His reason. The way he would consider his next move, even though he was the strongest in the room and could have forced everyone to obey him. The way he chose kindness when he could have used brute strength. I even loved his volatile dragon and the flames that could destroy me. Not because of their power, but because they were part of him.

I had love... I *knew* love... and I lost it.

And now... I would give anything to get it back.

The deeper I sink into my mind, the stronger my memories become until Callan could be curled up beside me, his wing resting across my back and his lips brushing my forehead.

His question is a whisper that echoes around and around within my mind.

Do you know why I call you 'Not-Lana'?

The memory of his voice and the warm light in his eyes draws me deeper until we could be floating in a dark ocean together, suspended in the calm, surrounded by pain that only his wing is keeping at bay.

You're complicated. You're important. You matter. Your life is yours to weave.

I want you by my side.

Will you come with me, Not-Lana?

Some of my pain eases. Only the smallest amount, but it's enough to make it bearable as I remain in Callan's arms within my mind, floating in the dark.

I can still sense my surroundings—the cage and the panthers—but only vaguely. The passage of time becomes unimportant, and so is the presence of angels when they next bring food. The slap of another water pouch hitting the ground is like a pebble hitting the water's surface far above me. The object that tumbles past me must be another loaf of bread. Then there's more rain, but I'm already immersed, so it doesn't matter to me.

There I remain, curled up and no longer shivering.

At some point, after what might be days, I'm aware of sharp whispers and a sense of anxiety flowing from the two angels who hover for longer than usual outside my cage.

The bread will have washed away, so they won't know that I haven't eaten it, and I'm not sure where the water pouches have ended up—maybe they're stuck against the front of the cage—but my persistent stillness could be worrying the angels.

I don't give them another thought when they hurry away.

That is, until a different presence breaks my trance.

The scent of ash wafts across me, burning embers floating through the ocean around me and making me feel like my chest is filling with dust and death.

"Little bird." Dominus's growl reaches me through the mire inside my mind, gripping me like a hook and dragging me upward against my will.

I fight it with all my might, screaming within my mind as Callan's wing slips from my back and he tumbles away from me through the dark.

No! Come back!

"Trapped in a cage," Dominus continues, the barbs in his voice feeling like nails grabbing every inch of skin across my body and yanking me back to myself. "Your heart will be ripe for carving now."

I return to myself with a groan. My body is stiff and it's nearly impossible to raise my head to see him. I'm not too concerned about that yet, since I sense Dominus has remained outside the cell. I suppose that's sensible, given that he would have to step across the path of two shadow panthers to get to me.

The beasts are highly alert now, judging by the increased speed of their heartbeats, but they remain in their dark corners. The angels may have intended to harm me when they put me here, but the panthers form an obstacle that won't be easily overcome.

I take my time opening my eyes, staring at the shadowed stone beneath me for a long moment before I attempt to slowly look up.

As soon as I lift my head slightly, Dominus says, "So you're not dead, after all." His speech is followed by the sound of a metallic object clanging against the cage bars as if he's drawing a baton across them. I can't yet lift my head high enough to see what's making the sound, but I catch a flash of light that indicates it could be his hammer.

"Pity," he says. "You will soon wish you were."

My stiff muscles scream when I exhale and force myself to unfurl. The simple movement of raising my shoulders and breathing deeply inward sends shooting pain down my back and through my ribs.

A glance at the wound on my shoulder—the redness and gunk visible around the makeshift bandage—indicates that, despite the regular rain, it's crusted with blood and most likely infected.

What I can see of the rest of my body is covered in yellowing bruises, a progression of color beyond black and blue that could mean I've been in this cell for up to five days.

Dominus stands alone in the dark corridor, heat waves glimmering around him so that I can make out his form. He's wearing jeans and boots but no shirt, and he's clean shaven now. His dark-brown hair appears to have been trimmed and it's far neater than before, but it still falls farther than the bottom of his ears.

He's holding his hammer loosely, a testament to his strength that the heavy weapon seems to weigh nothing in his grasp. The hammer's hilt is pointed toward the bars—confirming it was the source of the clanging noise before.

Golden scales, as luminescent as Callan's, glow across his broad chest like transparent armor, and he's even taller than before—at least seven feet—although his eyes remain juniper-green, cold and hard.

Atrox said he and his brother would come back for me once I was weak enough not to fight them.

"You're here for my dragon," I rasp, my voice nearly disobeying me by not making any sound at all.

Dominus shakes his head, a slow movement, while his smile grows. "I'm here to kill you."

A chill passes through me. "Atrox changed his mind about keeping me alive?"

"Oh, no, he wants you alive," Dominus says. "He sent me to bring you to him. The angels reported that you're on the brink of death and my brother believes that means it's the right time to draw out your dragon."

"Then... why?" My lips purse and my forehead creases in confusion.

Dominus lowers his hammer to the ground, but it doesn't feel like any less of a threat resting there.

"Atrox thinks he can tame you, but he didn't see the look in your eyes when he was tearing Callan's body apart." The shimmers of heat glow brighter around Dominus's fingertips. "You were willing to do anything to save Callan. That kind of love is powerful. Dangerous. You can't be allowed to live."

I don't waste more breath on questions, focusing on reminding my limbs how to stretch—but not so far that I'll extend them beyond my safe spot. I need to make it to my feet before Dominus carries out whatever plan he has for me.

"Your brother disagrees," I say, finding strength in my voice this time.

"The Atrox I knew would have killed you already!" Dominus roars, little flames finally bursting to life around his face and torso. "He would have crushed your body and burned you to ash without a second thought."

"And yet..." I finish rising to my feet, drawing back my shoulders despite the pain racking my body and the alarming weakness in my legs and arms. "He hasn't."

Dominus's biceps flex and the cage bar he's gripping creaks, as if it's going to crumple beneath his powerful grip. "He's determined to control you. To dominate you."

Standing up was definitely a bad idea. I can't hide the tremble in my legs or the hunch of my shoulders as I try to remain upright. The only thing giving me strength right now is the knowledge that Dominus and Atrox are at odds with each other about keeping me alive. Disagreement means division. I can use that. Assuming I make it out of this cage alive, since Dominus has declared he's here to kill me.

"So you've decided to rid yourself of the problem I pose," I say. "What will Atrox do when he finds out you defied him?"

"He won't know it was me," Dominus replies with a smirk. "I will tell him that I arrived here to do as bidden, only to find that the panthers had gotten free of their chains and mauled you to death."

Another shudder racks my body and I cast glances left and right, listening carefully to ascertain that the beasts haven't moved from their corners.

Zadkiel said that the panthers' chains are unbreakable, and that the lever that can open the clasps was melted into place to guard against any accidental release. But there are different ways to break chains.

Dominus's cold smile grows. "I will carry whatever remains of your body and lay the pieces at my brother's feet. And then we will be done with you. He will finally focus on conquering this world, piece by piece. Starting with the Dread clan."

Dominus leans closer to the cage bar he's gripping while the light glimmering around his body intensifies.

"These chains aren't strong enough to defy my hottest flame," he threatens.

He takes a deep breath before he purses his lips and blows his breath out again, directing the air neatly between the cage bars. Blue flames—the hottest kind—flow from his mouth in a narrow stream that burns across the cage floor on my right.

It illuminates the ground as it travels from the front of the cage to the back, lighting up the gray stone and the water troughs that I suspected were located at the side.

Dominus directs his fire like a knife, moving his head to control its path and pausing both times the flames reach the metal rings to which the two panthers' chains are attached.

Within seconds, the clasps begin to melt.

The metal won't hold.

The moving flame is bright enough to cast illumination across the panthers themselves.

The quiet panther opens its silvery eyes and stares at me. All it has to do is run toward me, and it will pull the chain away from its molten anchor. The restraints won't constrain it now.

Dominus gives me a smile. "Time to die, little bird."

CHAPTER SEVEN

*F*ear is like fire burning through my body.

I'm weaker than I've ever been, and I have nowhere to run. No way to survive.

The quiet panther's heartbeat is louder and faster within my hearing as it leaps away from the fire burning at the edge of the room. Its silver claws flash as it flies through the air at me while I remain crouched, my instincts screaming at me to move.

But... to where?

The quiet panther's chain breaks apart. The beast is mere heartbeats away from reaching me. I'm aware of Dominus's laughter as he turns to face the left-hand side of the cage. The two panthers on that side are already straining at their collars and swiping their claws at my back.

I have no choice but to throw myself toward the quiet panther, aiming to slide beneath it. It's evidence of my failing strength that I misjudge the gap I intended to slip through. The claws on the beast's hind feet rake across my left shoulder and down my arm as it sails over me. Only my armband stops it from taking off my hand.

I can't stop my scream of pain, although alarmingly, I also can't feel the agony of the new cuts as badly as I expected. It's an awful sign that my body, and all of my senses, are shutting down.

I barely have time to take stock of my state of health. New blood streams down my side—blood I can't afford to lose. My vision is blurring. My heart rate is low. My adrenaline is gone.

The panther's chain, now loose at the end, snakes past me, making a slapping sound against the stone when the creature lands, skids, and turns so fast that I don't have a hope of evading it again.

The other three panthers are now also free, and they're all coming at me. The quiet one leaps at my front and the other three attack from my side.

It takes me a single, cold moment to recognize the fact that failing a miracle, I won't make it out of here alive.

A scream sounds within my mind, and I have enough mental acuity left to recognize that it isn't my own voice screaming at me.

Get up!

Heat suddenly burns through me, a warmth I desperately need, filling my frozen muscles with a burst of energy.

My right hand drops to the chain that has nearly completely sailed past and my fingers close around the end of it. At the same time, I throw myself against the wall, back first, where I release my wings, using them to propel me off the surface and give me the height I need to leap up toward the bars on my right.

My right hand closes around one of the bars right above Dominus's head, near to the front corner of the cage. As fast as I can, I slip the chain around the bar. At the same time, I neatly plant my feet between the bars against Dominus's chest—all before he can jump away from the side of the cage.

Using his chest as a springboard, I snap my wings closed and somersault backward. The quiet panther's chain makes a grating sound as it loops around the bar.

I have no seconds to waste. Dominus is already reaching for

the chain, and I suspect he's strong enough to snap it with his bare hands—or he could melt it, but that comes with the risk of melting a hole in the cage, too. Not to mention, the panthers haven't exactly sat quietly waiting for me to finish my task.

The quiet panther has adjusted its trajectory and leaps toward the corner of the cage where I looped the chain, while the others snarl and snap, but I'm not aiming to escape their leader now.

I've timed my descent and my trajectory perfectly—slightly above the quiet beast and at an angle that will pull it into the corner since the chain is still attached to the collar around its neck.

As I fly past, my left hand punches down, hitting the top of its head while I swing the chain in an arc around the beast's neck. Using my punch as leverage, I manage to twist, planting my feet against its back and completing the noose around its throat.

All I have to do is throw myself back into the corner of the cage with a scream of effort, my feet planted on either side of the beast's spine.

The chain around its neck tightens. The panther rears up, its front paws slashing the air while its back arches where I push my feet into it. I pull its head back with all my might.

It can't reach me with its claws or its teeth and the more wildly it thrashes, the more it keeps the other panthers at bay.

Heat fills my blood and glimmers of light flicker around my hands and face. My scream is a command, but I hardly recognize my own voice. "Stop fighting me, dark one, or I'll snap your neck."

The panther suddenly freezes, its ears twitching before it gives a whine. The tension in its back eases a moment before it sinks slowly to the ground, hissing softly through its teeth as it moves.

The other panthers take a step back, also snarling softly. Their growls turn into low, keening sounds.

I don't trust their submission for one second, so I maintain the tension on the chain, even though my muscles are now screaming for relief.

"What the fuck?" Dominus's incredulous curse sounds from outside the cage.

Without taking my eyes off the panthers, I respond in a low rumble. "One wild creature always recognizes another."

Dominus paces back and forth for several furious moments before he says, "Fuck it."

He grabs the cage door and snaps the lock right off it before he lifts the latch and wrenches the door open.

The hard scales protecting his skin glint as he storms into the cage. The panthers don't sit idly, their keening cries becoming sounds of rage again, but they're no match for Dominus's size and strength.

He punches the first panther that leaps at him, knocking it into the other two. The three beasts skid across the cage and scramble to get up. In the meantime, Dominus reaches around the quiet beast, as if it poses no greater threat than a butterfly, and plucks me off the wall.

He throws me over his shoulder, knocking the wind out of my chest, and I barely have time to let go of the chain so that I don't break the panther's neck.

It leaps at Dominus, but his free hand closes around its neck and he flings it into the others just as they're recovering.

Within seconds, he storms from the cell with me, spinning and slamming the door shut, dropping the latch into place just as the quiet panther leaps at him again. The creature knocks into the bars, the chain unraveling from around its neck when it drops to the ground and shakes it head.

Dominus stops for a moment and roars at the panthers through the bars, a dragon's shout. Three of the panthers flinch and yelp, but the quiet panther remains at the front of the cage, seemingly unmoved by Dominus's roar. Its snarls turn into a confused whine as its silver eyes settle on me.

I can barely lift my head to keep the beast within my sights and my matted hair covers my face. I have no strength to raise my arms and push my hair out of the way and it means I can't see the cage or my surroundings anymore.

The power that helped me survive the panthers' attack has drained away and now, I have nothing left.

There's a clang of metal and I assume that Dominus is somehow securing the cage again. He must succeed because he quickly scoops up his hammer and strides along the gloomy corridor, carrying me across his broad shoulder.

The central stairway's bright light hits me when we exit the prison.

I'm aware of the presence of angels, possibly all of the Roden-Darr, judging by the number of feet I count as Dominus climbs the stairs. Their scent of muddy lilacs is so strong that for a few moments, it dulls Dominus's ashy presence. They're standing guard along the way, each one acknowledging Dominus's approach by tapping their poleaxe as he passes.

I try to keep track of how many stairs Dominus takes, counting ten, which puts us about halfway up the stairway and around the location of one of the training rooms by the time he finally pauses.

"You will remain out here," Dominus says, presumably to the angels. "We can't predict what's about to happen and it would be senseless for any of you to lose your life in the course of this task."

"Understood," the nearest angel says. "We will not intrude."

A door opens and Dominus carries me into another brightly-lit space. What little I can see around my hair reveals a black marble floor threaded with silver. The way Dominus's footfalls echo tells me that the room is vast, with a high ceiling.

My greater concern is the drops of blood that continue to rapidly fall from my side, leaving a trail in our wake.

The door closes behind us, and the scent of burning embers increases as another set of footsteps approaches.

My head immediately fills with Atrox's presence. A burning field. Trees turned to dust. Stone incinerated to nothing more than charcoal.

His command is quieter than I was expecting. "Place her down."

Dominus slides me off his shoulder and supports my head as he lowers me to the floor. He pulls my legs and arms straight and shoves the bulk of my hair out of my face before he steps back, leaving me lying there.

I'm sure that the care he took positioning me without allowing my head to hit the floor is purely motivated by Atrox's wish to keep me alive.

I stare up into Atrox's eyes as he crouches beside me. He's in full human form, no sign of his scales or wings, and he's dressed in casual clothing. Like his brother, he's clean-shaven and his hair is freshly cut. Even though his irises are cold, juniper-green, it's like looking into Callan's face. Just while he's angry.

His glare flashes from the new wound on my left shoulder to his brother. "Why the fuck is her arm bleeding?"

"The panthers took a swing at her when I pulled her from the cage," Dominus says without blinking.

I intend to contradict him, but Atrox is already nodding, as if he accepts his brother's explanation.

"Then we need to work quickly before she dies," Atrox says.

He rises to tower over me, holding out his hand toward Dominus. "The hammer."

Dominus hefts the weapon in his hands before handing it across to Atrox.

"I will fight you," I whisper up at them, although my assertion is aimed more at Dominus, since he didn't succeed in killing me before.

Atrox lowers the hammer to my side before crouching to me once again.

"You're in no position to fight anything." He takes hold of my chin, harder than I expected, given his quiet tone, making me wince. "If you fail to submit to this process, you will die. The wound on your right arm is infected. The new wound on your left is draining you of what little blood you have left. Your body is shutting down. You may as well be dead already. Only your dragon can heal you now."

"If your theory is correct," I whisper. He hypothesized that my ability to heal is connected to my dragon and that bringing out my dragon will finally allow me to harness my healing power. Part of me welcomes the possibility, but there's another part that fears what will happen if my dragon chooses to destroy my mind just as Atrox destroyed Callan's.

Atrox gives a confident nod, as if there's no doubt. "I'm sure of it."

"Or maybe you'll kill me in the process, and you'll never know who my dragon was," I murmur.

I can't help but notice the fleeting smile that passes across Dominus's face. I don't have to read his mind to know that he's hoping this process will be the end of me.

"Well, then you'll be dead," Atrox says flatly.

His lips press into an uncompromising line. He lifts the hammer off the floor and moves to stand five paces away on my right.

Dominus rounds me to take up position on Atrox's right-hand side, also at a distance of several paces from me.

"Remember, brother," Dominus says. "To wake her dragon, you must harness the light magic in the hammer and draw out the beast's shadow first. If it is our enemy, you must use the magic in the hammer to crush it before it can gain strength."

Atrox is nodding. "But if it's our ally, her dragon must choose of its own accord to tear her body apart and bring her close to death so that her angel's mind will leave her body. That's when her dragon will have the chance to take over. I know this. I've lived it."

I close my eyes, banishing the memory of the way that Atrox, when he was still in dragon shadow form, ripped his claws through Callan's back and closed his jaws around Callan's shoulder, covering the floor with blood. Based on what he just said, it was the action of bringing Callan to the point of death that separated Callan's mind from his body and allowed Atrox to take control.

Callan fought back hard, and I tell myself I will do the same, but the horrible reality is that I'm already weak and dying. It won't take much for my dragon to dominate me.

In fact...

In my fight with the panthers just now, I'm sure it was my dragon's voice I heard and their fire I felt. If being near death allows a dragon shadow to start to take control, then that could be what I just experienced. I don't mistake my dragon's need to keep me alive for concern for my welfare. If I die, they die, too.

Atrox plants his feet, and his biceps bulge beneath his shirt sleeves as he raises the hammer above his head. A look of intense concentration fills his face before he rams the weapon down onto the floor.

At the same time, he shouts, "Wake up!"

His roar is drowned in the *boom* the hammer makes as it hits the floor. A massive ripple of energy flows through the marble beneath me from my right side to my left, and my body suddenly fills with unexpected warmth.

Far from pain.

It's practically euphoric.

My eyes fly wide because I *know* this feeling.

I felt it every time Callan was near me. It's like the sun has come out and shines down on me, banishing all of my pain and fear. Expelling all of my rage.

It's as if Callan himself stepped into this room and now sits beside me. The same fierce calm and warmth that he always made me feel overwhelms me. It blocks out the brothers' ashy scents and eases the tension in my mind and body, bringing with it an overwhelming peace.

Tears fill my eyes, blurring my surroundings.

"Callan," I whisper as Atrox lifts the hammer, preparing to ram it into the floor again.

Another explosion of sound tears through my hearing while the ripple of magic that flows through me makes my heart expand with yearning and hope.

If the hammer is emitting light magic, which has the same effect as Callan had on me, then how strong was the light magic in Callan?

And could such powerful magic ever be extinguished?

I'm conscious of the cracks appearing in the marble floor, but I'm even more aware of the fissures forming within my own heart. They aren't painful or destructive, more like an egg that needs to crack to release what's held inside.

New light. New life. New *hope.*

"*Wake up!*" Atrox roars, his voice echoing up to the ceiling and around the room as the light magic flowing through the space picks up the sound and amplifies it.

With the next fall of the hammer, my back arches, and a cry leaves my lips. Tears spill down my cheeks.

I'm sure it must appear to the brothers as if I'm in pain.

Deep in my chest, a force is growing, and it feels like the first time I saw Callan when his shadow had dropped over me at the theater. I was huddling behind a seat and his mere presence gave me the gift of peace for the first time in my life.

"Fire dragon!" Atrox shouts, sweat gleaming across his face and forearms and soaking the front of his shirt. "Reveal yourself!"

At the next hammer hit, light explodes from the weapon in opaque golden waves that envelop everything around me, filling the space with sunlight so bright that I can't see beyond it.

Atrox and Dominus may as well not exist.

The energy within my chest rises upward, taking shape in the air above me, delicate wisps of power that dance and swirl.

The silhouette of a dragon shadow begins to form, taking on

shape and color. Amber scales flicker within the pulses of magic flowing across us.

My dragon settles into the space around me, and even though there aren't any obvious signs, I sense that her nature is distinctly female. Her body is so large that it spans my side and curves around my feet while her tail rests around my other side and curls up beyond my head. Her wings are tucked in at her sides, but what really surprises me is that her head rests on my chest.

Her shadow form is completely weightless but somehow comforting. Her eyes are like molten lava, not golden like Atrox's eyes in his shifted form, but amber like a fierce flame, and they glisten as she quietly observes me.

I sense her mind, her intelligence, and her quiet calm, although there's also an edge to it, a sensation of controlled strength. As if she is capable of both reason and violence.

My greatest surprise is that I'm not afraid of her, and nothing in her demeanor gives me cause to be.

I'm also aware that the peace I feel in my heart has extended to every part of my body. As she finishes taking shape, my body continues to flood with strength. A quick glance at my left shoulder tells me the blood has stopped flowing, and the pain of the infected wound on my other shoulder has eased completely.

I breathe deeply and without pain for the first time in days.

Atrox was right.

My ability to heal is connected to my dragon. I desperately want to check my wings and see if my feathers have regrown, but I'm reluctant to move from this spot where she rests peacefully next to me.

Until a matter of days ago, I didn't know she existed—that she was part of me—but I was prepared for her to be my enemy as Atrox was Callan's enemy. I was ready for her to try immediately to tear me apart like Atrox destroyed Callan.

Now that she's here, quietly resting her shadow head on my chest, I'm certain with every part of my being that she won't be the ally Atrox and Dominus are hoping for. Which means they will want to kill her.

For now, the cocoon of light magic continues to surround us, and it must be creating some sort of barrier between us and the male dragons, but I'm sure they'll find a way through.

Fear for my dragon is rapidly flooding me.

My voice is still hoarse, but I force myself to speak. "You have to hide yourself," I say to her. "Otherwise, they'll destroy you."

She gives a soft exhale and wisps of flame leave her lips— shadow flames that I can see but not feel.

"The only creature strong enough to destroy me is you, Asper Ashen-Varr," she says, her voice ethereal.

I stare up at her with wide eyes, not daring to stir. "You have nothing to fear from me."

"Don't I?" she asks.

Before I can reply, a furious roar from my right makes me jolt. It reaches us through the thick wall of golden light that encircles us and cuts us off from the brothers. I recognize Atrox's voice, although I can't make out what he's saying.

My dragon doesn't seem perturbed by his rage. She lifts her head from my chest and rises to her feet. While she stands over me, her focus settles on the point from which Atrox's shout originated.

I slip out from under her towering form to place myself at her side, slowly drawing myself upright and bracing for the inevitable attack from the brothers.

The air is warm and somehow comforting as I turn to the side and release my wings, stretching them wide.

My heart leaps to see that the gaps are filled with new feathers, although these ones are darker with an amber sheen across them.

I can fly again!

My relief is so strong that I vibrate with it, wishing I could enjoy this moment, but the dragons are upon us.

Atrox bursts through the lightstorm, his golden scales gleaming across his chest, his eyes pure gold, and his wings held slightly outward. He rages toward us with Dominus close behind him, also partially shifted.

Both dragons jolt to a stop at the edge of the lightstorm, their chests heaving and their eyes rapidly widening as they take in my dragon.

Dominus's whisper is so hushed, it's barely audible. "It can't be…"

His focus flies from my dragon to his brother, who has frozen to the spot.

The hammer slips from Atrox's fingers onto the floor with a *thud* that I feel more than hear. His lips are parted as if in shock and despite the glistening gold of his scales, the color has drained from his face.

He stares at my dragon while he speaks reverently and with a quietness I wasn't expecting. "Viviana."

My dragon's eyes suddenly brim with glistening tears. "Atrox, my soulmate."

CHAPTER EIGHT

I jolt away from my dragon, my wings lifting me off the floor before I land a few paces away.

My chest feels like it's clamped in a vise that's slowly squeezing tighter.

Viviana was... *is*... Atrox's mate.

My dragon... is my enemy's *soulmate*.

The anxiety now raging through me drives me into a crouch, my wings curving at my sides, any joy I felt at their healing overshadowed by this new knowledge and the possibility that this means my dragon is my adversary, after all.

Atrox abandons the hammer on the floor and crosses the distance to Viviana. He stops in front of her, appearing consumed by her when she lowers her head to his.

She touches her shadow nose to his and then turns her cheek to the side of his face, and that's where they stay for a long moment, their eyes closed as the light continues to rage around us.

I remain frozen where I crouch, icy cold despite the warmth of the light magic that continues to illuminate the scene in front of me.

Despite all of Atrox's threats, despite what he did to Callan, in this moment, I'm witnessing a part of him I never dreamed could exist. The gesture he and Viviana are showing each other is the same one that I showed to Callan on impulse.

I didn't realize what importance it could have until I saw Solomon Grudge's son, Micah, greet Sophia's dragon the same way. It was a gesture of connection and faith, of two dragons finding each other.

But in those moments when it felt so right for me to touch my cheek to Callan's, I didn't know what I was doing.

It was pure instinct.

Now it's apparent that the dragon living within me was Atrox's mate. And Atrox was living within Callan, and now I have to ask myself...

Was Viviana reaching out through me and trying to connect with Atrox?

My lips part as I take a rushed breath, my chest suddenly rising and falling too rapidly. My emotions are swinging from one extreme to the other, but more than anything else, I feel vulnerable in my heart as well as my body.

Were my feelings for Callan ever really my own?

When he first stood in my presence and I felt like the world held hope and peace, when I felt as if the sun had come out, were those *my* feelings?

I remain where I am, the sensation of ice within my chest contrasting sharply with the torrent of heat swirling around the room. Even though my wounds have healed, I realize how dehydrated I am when I feel the burn of tears behind my eyes but only a hint of moisture fills them.

Light magic continues to lick across the air while Atrox presses his cheeks to Viviana's, his eyes remaining closed for a long moment before he says, "I thought I'd lost you forever."

She takes a shuddering breath. "You could never lose me."

He opens his eyes, studying her face, his gaze running across her glistening scales before the faintest smile touches his lips. It reminds me, too painfully, of the way Callan would look at me.

A strange contrast now to see his features so calm while his eyes remain pure gold in his partially shifted form.

"I have so much to tell you," Viviana says. "About the day I died and about what happened to our light. There's much you need to know."

Atrox stiffens a little at the mention of their 'light'—whatever it is. His focus flashes to me for a moment before he resumes speaking with Viviana. "I want to hear everything, but you have to guard your speech in front of the angel," he warns her. "Be careful what you say."

Viviana also diverts her attention to me, but her gaze lingers longer than Atrox's did. "Asper Ashen-Varr should know the truth of the angels' treachery. She has no loyalty to them that would cloud her judgement."

But Atrox shakes his head. "She should know about their treachery, yes. But not what they stole. From what I've observed of Callan's' life, there are very few supernaturals who still know of its existence. We have to keep it that way or we'll never win this war."

Before Atrox and Dominus threw me in the cage with the panthers, they spoke of an object that was stolen from them. I'm also struck with the memory of Solomon Grudge telling me about the night he took me from the Sentinels when I was a baby. It wasn't me he wanted. He said that the Sentinels were keeping *two* precious things in that same location: one was me and the other was something very valuable to all dragons. He described it as an object with the power to heal the dragons.

At least this mysterious object now has a name. Of sorts. The 'light' doesn't tell me a lot, but it indicates that it's connected with light magic.

Viviana sighs and warmth shimmers around her mouth, mingling with the heat waves radiating around Atrox. "Then I will speak of it only as our light," she says. "Even though it's so much more."

While they converse, I scream at myself to move. I'm healed

now. My left wing is whole once more. Viviana hasn't threatened me, and Atrox is unusually subdued in her presence. Dominus, on the other hand, is glaring at me across the distance. He won't let me go easily, and if Viviana's shadow behaves like others I've seen, then she'll come with me, which will cause Atrox to retaliate.

I prepare myself for Dominus's attack as I edge back toward the lightstorm.

I only make it three paces before a tugging sensation pulls at my chest. I try to step back farther, only to find that the pulling sensation suddenly feels like a taut chain, forcing me to stop right where I am.

From ten paces away, Viviana's gaze flickers to me. Her voice sounds within my mind, startling in its clarity: *You're tethered to me, Asper. The force of the light magic around us right now gives me the rare opportunity to dictate our actions. You can't leave unless I also choose to go.*

My jaw clenches and I'm forced to take a step back toward her to ease the pain in my chest, while my sense of being caged increases.

Easy, Asper, she says into my mind. *You need to hear what I have to say as much as Atrox does.*

Atrox has narrowed his eyes at me. "Can she step beyond the light?" he asks Viviana, to which Viviana shakes her head.

Seeming satisfied that I'm not going anywhere, Atrox draws Viviana's attention back to himself. "What happened the day you died?" he asks quietly.

Viviana's jaw clenches. "The Celestial Ascendant herself visited me with a legion of her strongest Sentinels. She claimed she wanted to make sure that the light was being safely guarded." Her voice is strained. "When I showed her where our light was being kept, she attacked and cornered me. I never dreamed she would try to steal it. If she had been alone, I might have gotten past her, but with an entire legion of Sentinels at her side, I was beaten down, caught in a net..."

I smother a sigh as I listen to her story. The Roden-Darr caught Callan and me in a net, too. Isaac had subdued me with his soul light for long enough that they could throw the net over us. Unlike the other Roden-Darr, Isaac's soul light was pure and strong enough to force me to fall asleep.

Viviana shudders. "I couldn't fight back... So when the Celestial Ascendant struck my heart with her spear, it was over."

Her head sinks toward Atrox's broad shoulder.

"Sentinel spears are deadly to all creatures." Atrox is pale and he speaks through clenched teeth. "What of the former Avenging Angel? What part did she play in your death?"

Viviana's gaze flickers to me again as they speak of my predecessor. "Eva Ashen-Varr arrived just as the Celestial Ascendant and her Sentinels were leaving me to die."

"She struck the final blow," Atrox finishes for her.

Viviana shakes her head. "No," she whispers, a tremor rippling across her scales like a shiver. "She was enraged. Screaming with fury at what they had done. I had never seen her so angry. She tried to capture the Celestial Ascendant, but the Celestial Ascendant's Sentinels got in the way and Eva's Roden-Darr were still too far away to help her.

"Even the Avenging Angel is not immune to the poison on a Sentinel's spear, so they were able to drive her back and the Celestial Ascendant escaped. I begged Eva to go after her and protect our light, but she wouldn't leave me as I died. She tried to use her soul light to save me."

Viviana bows her head, part of her chin resting on Atrox's shoulder. "It was too late. The poison had done its work."

Atrox is shaking his head with disbelief. "But the Avenging Angel was the one who killed you. We were told—"

"No, my love." Viviana's whisper is firm. "An Avenging Angel is incapable of harming an innocent creature. She does not wish to kill."

"Then we hated her for the wrong reasons." Atrox recovers from his surprise, his expression becoming hard. "But *this*

Avenging Angel is not bound by such limitations," he says with a pointed look at me. "Asper Ashen-Varr is more deadly than any other before her."

Viviana doesn't contradict him. "She is."

Atrox exhales heavily. "Asper's power called to me, and I didn't know why. I couldn't let her go. Couldn't kill her, and it didn't make sense." His gaze softens as he returns his attention to Viviana. "Until now."

"My presence, even though she wasn't aware of it, has given Asper strength beyond that of other angels." Viviana nods as she speaks. "The angels call it 'corruption' because they don't understand it."

She pauses, her gaze holding Atrox's before she continues. "But I am not the only source of her strength. And I am not the only reason you were drawn to her. She has another source of power."

Her gaze is piercing as she stares at her mate. "Before she was stolen from her crib, Asper Ashen-Varr spent the first few months of her life in the presence of our light. She absorbed its power while her mind and body developed. It's the reason my soul was able to survive within her. Without the power of our light, her strength as an Avenging Angel would have consumed me. Then when Solomon stole her, I was able to use the moonlight to anchor myself within her soul."

My forehead creases as she speaks. *Absorbed its power?*

Atrox has become very still and now scrutinizes me with a look of caution.

A few paces away from him, Dominus is also staring at me. He has remained silent and kept to the side, but he takes a step back as he appraises me.

"What does this mean?" Atrox asks Viviana.

Viviana lifts her head from his shoulder, her scales glimmering and her amber eyes alight with flames. "It means she is a source of our light."

CHAPTER NINE

*T*he color drains from Atrox's face. "That can't be true."

Viviana remains firm. "You've experienced the signs." She studies him, watching the shifting expressions on his face.

He begins to shake his head.

"*Callan* saw the signs," she insists. "He said it himself: Asper is like the night sky when the rain has stopped, the sky is clear, and—"

"The moonlight is pure," Atrox finishes for her, repeating what Callan said to me when he and I spoke about how Sophia's dragon had appeared.

He eyes me across the distance between us.

"Callan's clan member, Sophia, didn't have a dragon until she met Asper," Viviana says, as if proof of her claim is still required. "It was Asper who brought her dragon to life. Just as Callan and his sister, Zahra, couldn't shift parts of their bodies at will until they met Asper. Callan may not have understood what was happening, but he recognized that it was a marvel. That *she* is a marvel. Our light lives within her and it—"

"Enough!" The outburst comes from Dominus, who finally makes a move, beginning a slow pace back and forth behind

Atrox, forcing his brother to swivel to keep him in his sights. "Our light has only one true source. If the Avenging Angel absorbed some of its power, then she is an abomination and a danger to us. She must be killed."

Viviana's expression hardens. "Asper is a desperately needed gift, Dominus Audax."

"A gift?" Dominus's voice is filled with contempt. "This angel is nothing but a threat to us."

Viviana spins back to her mate, speaking only to Atrox. "Our light is the very heart of our power. We feared what would happen if it was stolen from us. Everything I've seen through Asper's eyes has proven that our fears have come to pass.

"Dragons can no longer fully shift. Most can't have children. Some are afflicted with half-formed dragon shadows that are mere shades of who their dragons should be. Many lose their minds. All have been deprived of a true relationship with their beasts. We're dying out. Just as the former Celestial Ascendant wanted."

Atrox's response is quiet but firm. "A goal that Asper Ashen-Varr has assisted in fulfilling. She has killed more dragon shifters than any legion of angels or Sentinels before her."

Viviana takes a step back from her mate, her dragon's face filled with agony, as if her heart were bleeding. "I felt each of those deaths in my soul," she says. "I lived them because I have been conscious for all of Asper's life.

"I was there at her birth, and during the moments when Solomon Grudge stole her from her crib. I felt moonlight for the first time when she did, and the pain of the lash when she dared escape the cage the angels placed her in. I have heard the bones of dragon shifters *crack* beneath her hands and watched their malformed shadows return to the ether, where they can't find rest until our light is returned to us."

She swings away from Atrox and back to Dominus with a growl. "And I kept her heart beating when shadow panthers would have torn her apart."

Dominus blanches, since Viviana could reveal his lie about how the panthers attacked me. Hell, *I* want to reveal it, but what Viviana's saying now feels more important.

She doesn't give Dominus a chance to speak, asking what seems to be a pointed question. "Why are you not in your full dragon form, Dominus Audax?"

He glares back at her. "My dragon form eludes me."

Viviana's eyes narrow to amber slits. "Even you, the last of the old dragons to walk this Earth in your original body, can no longer fully shift. Our light has been hidden from us for so long that our power has faded until we are like dying animals gasping our final breaths. Our people are starving for a power they don't even know existed. We need Asper—"

Dominus dismisses her, turning to Atrox instead. "Brother," he says. "It's clear that Asper Ashen-Varr, the Cruel One, has poisoned Viviana's thoughts and placed false memories in her mind."

Atrox considers his mate carefully, his lips pursed in apparent thought.

Viviana shakes her head vehemently. "My mind is my own."

I find myself sinking further to the floor as I process what she has said—the answers to mysteries: the reason why Callan was able to shift different parts of his body at a time and why my flames triggered Sophia's dragon to appear.

The furrow in Atrox's brow eases. "My mate speaks the truth. Our light exists within this angel." His focus swivels to me and his gaze glides down my body in a look that reminds me painfully of the way Callan looked at me the day we stood naked in front of the mirror in his dressing room and I was trying to get him to see his partial shift.

Dominus is quick to change tact. "Then Viviana must take control of whatever light lives within this angel. Asper's body must become a vessel for Viviana to occupy."

Atrox is nodding as he turns back to his mate. "This is your chance to live, Viviana. To reclaim your life. You must destroy Asper's mind."

I brace for Viviana's response, my heart pounding in my chest as I ready myself, trapped where I stand but prepared to fight her with everything I have.

Her voice reverberates through the floor and all the way through my body. "My life will not be secured through blood and violence."

I stare at her, not quite believing what I'm hearing.

Atrox's lips part in surprise at her vehemence, and then his brow furrows as deeply as Dominus's.

Viviana holds her head high as she takes another step back from Atrox, a tower of dragon strength standing between me and the dragon brothers. I'm stunned that it suddenly feels like a protective stance.

Her expression softens, and tears well in her eyes as she faces Atrox. "Eons ago, the angels killed me, but they may as well have torn out *your* heart, Atrox. I feel your pain and I understand how it fueled your choices. But I can't destroy this angel."

Atrox's expression is stony. "Can't or won't?"

"Both," she says, her voice softer. "Asper carries our light, and I swore always to protect it. But more importantly, I can't overcome the light within her. Not in my shadow form."

There isn't any lie in her speech and I'm struggling to process the emerging, and astounding, fact that my dragon's motivations are more complicated than I expected. She has her own heart and soul and convictions, and she remains true to them, even though it means denying her mate what he wants. And giving up her chance to live free of my will.

But she is not without pain. I feel her agony within my own chest. The same pain I feel at losing Callan.

While Atrox's breathing increases with his frustration, his brother's eyebrows are drawn down and his lips are twisted in anger.

Dominus snatches up the hammer, whisking it away from Atrox's side. "If Viviana can't destroy the angel, then we must."

Viviana advances on him so suddenly that the tether between me and her pulls me with her. Wisps of flame emit from her mouth and even though she is nothing more than a shadow, I feel the heat of her fire as if it's burning around us.

"You have a choice, Dominus Audax," she says to him in a low growl. "You can put down that weapon and accept that I won't destroy this angel, or you can use the hammer's magic to crush *me* so that I might never return. Which will it be?"

Dominus's cold gaze falls on me a second before he returns it to Viviana.

My eyes widen when he lifts the hammer and prepares to slam it onto the floor.

"No!" Atrox moves faster than my eyes can follow, leaping toward his brother and snatching the hammer from Dominus's hands a moment before the weapon would hit the ground.

Atrox rolls to his feet, gripping the hammer's hilt, his wings spread slightly and wisps of fire seething through his lips as he growls at Dominus. "Think carefully about your next move, brother."

Dominus takes a heavy step back, a storm growing in his expression, but all he does is lift his arm and point at Viviana. "That dragon is not the Viviana we knew."

While Atrox rises to his feet, Viviana whispers, "None of us are what we used to be. We are all changed."

At that same moment, the rushing lightstorm around us suddenly quietens and my attention is drawn to the way the streaks of light seem to narrow like ribbons unfurling.

Atrox spins to the light with alarm. "Viviana! The light is fading. So is your chance!"

She shakes her head. "I won't do it. I won't kill her." She darts forward to brush her nose to his. "I might not see you again. My soul may be anchored to Asper, but only immense surges of light magic can bring me out. Otherwise, her angelic power subdues me."

"What about moonlight?" Atrox asks, desperation entering his voice.

She shakes her head. "The moon's light does not carry enough power to sustain me against the force of her angelic nature. I'm sorry…"

Atrox's eyes widen. "Wait. Viviana! No—"

He reaches for her, but his hand merely swipes through her fading shadow body.

She tucks her wings as she disappears from view, her glistening silhouette turning into streaks of energy that mimic the dying ribbons around us.

I hear her voice inside my mind one last time. *Be warned: Your body has healed, but it has not recovered from your ordeal. Your strength will leave you once my shadow fades. Prepare yourself for Atrox's wrath.*

Then she's gone, and I'm shocked when it feels like the floor drops out from beneath me and my body is being tugged and swilled around and around in a dizzying spin. The floor rears up at me as the strength in my legs fails and I hit the ground on all fours, trying to clear my head and get my bearings.

I look up in time for my view to fill with the fire dragon raging toward me.

CHAPTER TEN

*A*trox grabs my arms and wrenches me upward, his golden wings curving around my sides. There's nothing I can do to fight back.

It seems that even though my wounds are healed, the effects of five days of dehydration and starvation can't be magically erased. Now that Viviana's energy is gone, I'm as weak as I was when Dominus carried me into this room.

Atrox's eyes are pure golden, his jaw clenched, and his hands dig into my arms—even harder than when he's in human form because they're covered in tough scales.

He pulls me right up to him so that my feet drag and his face is in mine. "Give her back to me!" he roars. "Give me Viviana!"

A well of grief rises up within me, and I'm not sure if it's because I'm reflecting the sorrow he's experiencing beneath his rage, or because his sadness is dragging up my own.

His grief is so strong that it masks his ashy scent and fills my chest with the scent of lilies. White lilies. The kind that the Serene Commander would put around the Cathedral each time an angel died hunting a dragon. That was before she gave me the task of killing them.

Despite my weariness and my inability to fight back, the

scent of lilies clears my chest enough that I find the strength to scream right back at him. "Give me Callan! Give me back the dragon I love!"

Atrox drags in a harsh breath at my scream, his golden eyes burning into me, his heartbeat ragged. His forehead slowly creases as he continues to search my face. "We have both lost."

I shake my head, a slow side-to-side, my voice low and vehement. "We are nothing alike."

He gives an angry snort, and an equally quiet response. "We are exactly alike. You will see. I will show you."

Dominus chooses that moment to approach. He doesn't retrieve the hammer that Atrox dropped to the floor, but the scent of burning ash clinging to him warns me that his anger is still at a tipping point.

"Brother."

As soon as Dominus demands Atrox's attention, Atrox wraps his left arm around my waist, his grip painful where it squishes me to his chest. He tucks his wings and twists to Dominus. The tightness in Atrox's jaw and around his eyes tells me that the friction between the two brothers could ignite.

Dominus stops a few paces away. He's even more shrewd and careful than Atrox and he must read the signs that his brother's mood is volatile.

He speaks more softly than he did when Viviana was present. "Surely, you must realize that the angel is a threat to us," he says. "She has poisoned Viviana's mind and turned her against us. Even if what Viviana said is true, Asper Ashen-Varr had no idea before now that she carried our light inside her. She must be destroyed before she learns how to harness it. Brother, we must trust that Viviana will be born to another dragon shifter in time. One who will not control her mind."

Atrox's arm tightens even more painfully around my waist, and I point my toes and rest them on his feet to take some of my weight and ease the burn at the base of my ribs. "You have misinterpreted Viviana's intentions, brother," Atrox says. "She was giving us the missing pieces of the puzzle."

Dominus's eyes narrow and his brow furrows. He tips his head, as if he's taken aback and he doesn't follow. "How so?"

"Magnus Grim was protecting the Book of Light Magic when I fought him," Atrox says. "He was Solomon Grudge's dragon. I suspected that he might have led Solomon to the Book of Light Magic, but it wasn't confirmed until Viviana said that Solomon took Asper from her crib. He found our light." Atrox's golden eyes peer down at me where I'm clasped to his chest. "The day he took Asper from the Sentinels, he thought he was stealing back our light. Isn't that right, Asper?"

I don't see any reason to lie. "There were two glowing silos. He reached into the wrong one. I was stolen by mistake."

Atrox nods, a slow smile growing on his face. "He mistook you for our light because you absorbed so much of it."

I remember the way Solomon told me he was certain he'd chosen the correct silo of light—right until the moment when his hands closed around me, and he pulled me out. He didn't have time to reach into the other silo because the Sentinels were already upon him.

Dominus appears skeptical. "If Solomon Grudge had the book, why didn't he try to read it again to find our light?"

"Because the book is volatile," Atrox replies. "Magnus Grim wouldn't let me near it because he said it had become too dangerous for anyone to read."

"Solomon managed it," Dominus says.

"Yes." Atrox nods. "Magnus Grim's presence must have shielded him enough to succeed. But I would wager he only had one chance. He may have tried again and failed—or never risked it again because it was too dangerous."

"Where does this leave us?" Dominus asks.

"The Grudge must have the book." Atrox is nodding to himself. "If I were Solomon, I would have hidden it somewhere but told my son where to find it in the hope that another dragon would one day be able to read it."

Atrox's gaze passes over me. "A dragon with enough light within them to withstand the book's rage."

Dominus's focus passes from Atrox to me. He doesn't seem to miss Atrox's meaning. "But, brother, even if Asper can read it, she could lie to us about its meaning."

"I think Asper realizes by now that we are stronger than the dragons she fought in the past," Atrox replies. "She can't defeat us. She must realize the harm that could come to the dragons she cares about if she defies us." His gaze bores into me. "Don't you, Asper?"

I glare up at him, but I can't deny the truth in his claim. Callan was stronger than any other dragon, but he chose not to use his strength for his own personal gains. Atrox won't make the same choices.

Atrox seems to take my silence as acquiescence. "Give me a day with her, brother. Then we'll leave. In the meantime, I need everything the Roden-Darr have on the Grudge. Anything that might lead to their location."

He'll need all the luck in the world with that. Solomon Grudge, his son, and his closest clan members successfully hid from the angels for years. They completely eluded me—I didn't even know Solomon Grudge existed until Callan told me about him.

But Atrox won't be deterred. He and his brother have waited eons for this chance. Atrox won't give up. The gleam in his eyes tells me that.

When Dominus retrieves the hammer and turns to leave, Atrox stops him.

"Brother, I'm not a sentimental fool," Atrox says. "I love Viviana, but if it comes to it, I won't hesitate to kill this angel. Once we have our light, we'll have the power to fully shift again; the power to burn our enemies to ash. We'll also have the power to right the wrongs of the past, and I'll bring Viviana back again."

With a nod, Dominus turns and strides away.

Atrox waits for the door to close behind Dominus before he shifts back to his human form and swings me up in his arms.

I can't ignore the taste of sour lemon in my mouth that arose when Atrox promised his brother he would kill me if necessary.

"You lied," I whisper as he settles me against his chest.

His jaw clenches. "Viviana is everything to me. Dominus never had a mate. His rage is about his lost power. My rage is for my mate's life." Atrox's expression is hard. "But don't mistake my intentions, Asper. You are not her, and I will hurt you in any way necessary to get what I want."

He carries me across the room, and when we emerge into the brightly lit central stairway, Dominus is already at the top of the steps and disappearing into his quarters.

The Roden-Darr are gathered around the doorway, and Zadkiel appears flustered, his cheeks ruddy and his wings ruffled. At first, I wonder if Dominus said something to rile him up, but he blurts out, "Master, there's news from outside the veil."

"Tell me," Atrox says without pausing, proceeding up the stairs with me in his arms while Zadkiel hurries to keep up.

"The Celestial Ascendant has arrived at the Cathedral. She has decreed that the Scorn dragons are responsible for the slaughter of the Roden-Darr at the power station."

Atrox pulls to an abrupt halt. "You said she would place the blame at the feet of the Grudge dragons, not the Scorn."

"Apparently, the only dragon whose body was recovered from the site was Sienna Scorn. The Celestial Ascendant doesn't know that Solomon Grudge was ever there."

Atrox stiffens. "His body was gone?"

"It was."

Callan wasn't conscious when Sienna Scorn killed Solomon, but the Roden-Darr must have filled Atrox in on the details of what happened at the old power station before they brought Callan and me to the veil.

Atrox's eyes narrow. "Someone else got to the scene before the Celestial Ascendant did."

"Possibly Solomon's son," Zadkiel suggests.

Atrox nods. "That would make sense. Micah Grudge was driving away from the power station when Callan arrived. Micah may have come back for his father."

Only to find that his father had been killed. I remember the argument that Solomon and Micah had in the vehicle as they were driving to the power plant. Solomon ordered his son to leave him behind, but Micah didn't want to do it. If Micah had stayed, perhaps he could have protected Solomon's back and prevented his death.

My heart squeezes in my chest. When Solomon died, I may have lost a half-brother I never knew, but Micah lost his father, and his clan lost their leader.

Zadkiel continues. "We debated telling the Celestial Ascendant that Solomon also died there, but she had already formed her view of the scene. We didn't want her revisiting the evidence or questioning how the Roden-Darr really died."

Atrox grunts. "Indeed. Does she still believe that you're loyal to her?"

Zadkiel appears more confident. "She doesn't know that your brother is free or that you have taken Callan's place."

Atrox purses his lips in thought. "This could end up working in our favor, after all. My initial hope was that the Celestial Ascendant would place the blame at the feet of both the Grudge and Scorn and be forced to divide her attention between them. But now she'll be busy focusing on the Scorn, leaving us free to hunt the Grudge."

"Yes, Master Atrox," Zadkiel says, but he continues to shuffle, and his face is no less ruddy than before.

Atrox narrows his eyes at the angel. "Then what's the problem?"

"She has ordered us to leave the veil tomorrow and hunt the Scorn. Once we leave, she will be personally scrutinizing us. It will be difficult to assist you."

Atrox gives a low, unhappy-sounding growl. "You will have to tread carefully." He seems to shake off his ill temper. "Do what she wants. Hunt the Scorn. As long as you keep her eyes firmly misdirected toward them, you will serve our purpose."

Zadkiel finally relaxes. "Thank you, master. We won't let you down."

Atrox continues up the stairs, and once again, Zadkiel hurries to keep up.

"In the meantime, I need your strongest medicine," Atrox says. "Bring clean clothing for Asper, along with food, and leave it with the medicine in the atrium inside the door to my quarters. I want angels posted along this stairway at all times. If she emerges on her own, then she's trying to escape. Otherwise, I am not to be disturbed. Under no circumstances are you to enter my quarters beyond the atrium without being invited, as I can't guarantee your safety around her once she regains her strength."

Zadkiel gives me a wary glance before he nods. "Understood."

"Also, I want every piece of information you have on the Grudge. Everything you've found out about them, no matter how small or seemingly unimportant. I'll expect a full report before tomorrow afternoon. After that, my brother and I will also leave the veil."

Zadkiel doesn't respond as quickly this time, seeming to chew on his words before he asks, "May I ask your plans, Master Atrox?"

Reaching the top step, Atrox turns to Zadkiel, who keeps his distance from us.

The other angels have followed us and have gathered on the lower steps, each of them with their eyes upraised to Atrox, waiting for him to speak.

Dominus was the one who gave the rousing speech to the Roden-Darr about how they could serve the brothers and find purpose following them.

Atrox's response is far simpler, but the Roden-Darr hang on every word. "Once we are able to transform fully into dragons again, we will burn out the evil that has taken root among the angels and restore the light," he says.

He has told them nothing, but they nod their heads anyway.

"You will leave me now," he says to Zadkiel.

After giving Atrox a deep bow, Zadkiel turns and hurries back down the stairs, shouting orders at the other angels.

As Atrox reaches for the handle of the silver door, I eye the empty space between the doors that sit on either side of the top step.

Zadkiel warned that leaving the stairs means entering the dark space between Earth and the heavenly realm—a place from which escape may never be possible—but right now, it's my only option.

I prepare to use the last of my energy to release my wings and leap from Atrox's arms, but before I can twitch a muscle, he clamps them more tightly around me. His arms are like iron, and I don't have a hope of fighting him.

"Only death lies that way," he says, his biceps pressing against my ribs.

"How do you know?" I rasp, struggling to breathe now that he's squishing me. "You've never thrown yourself into darkness."

"Oh, I have," he says. "Not *that* particular darkness, I'll give you that. But I've waded through fields of blood for what I believe in, and I'll continue to do so. No matter whose bones I crush along the way."

His voice lowers as he delivers a quiet promise. "I may not wish to kill your body, Asper, but I won't hesitate to crush your soul to get back what's mine."

CHAPTER ELEVEN

*T*he open space at the top of the steps becomes an ever-diminishing promise of freedom—no matter how dangerous—as Atrox carries me through the silver door.

I promise myself that as long as he's keeping me alive, I won't waste an opportunity to watch for ways to escape, but I need to be stronger first.

Once again, I'm reminded of how hard it is to do nothing. *To wait.* Even if it's the smart thing to do.

Atrox strides quickly along the short corridor at the entrance to the room. I wish I could appreciate the atrium's soft and silvery lighting and the large, silver roses painted on its ceiling. Because of the waterfall of silver petals at the end of the corridor, I still can't see inside the room. Which means it's impossible for me to know what threats might lie beyond it.

The energy pouring from the cascade is immense. I gasp and close my eyes when Atrox carries me through it. He makes a low, grumbling sound in the back of his throat, indicating that the energy within the waterfall also has an impact on him, although I'm not sure if he feels it the same way I do.

It brushes across my skin like soft feathers, somehow momentarily soothing my exhaustion. The reprieve doesn't last long, my bone-deep tiredness returning the moment we step through the barrier.

But then, the cascade blocks off every sound from the stairway and I can no longer sense the angels we left behind, and the beauty of my surroundings calms me.

An enormous bedroom with a high ceiling is situated directly in front of us while a wide archway on the far side leads to a stone balcony. Beyond it, the sky is a dark blue and moonlight shines across the balcony. The four corners of the room are lit with softly glowing lamps.

I had no idea it was nighttime, but then, the passage of time has eluded me.

The far-left wall and the ceiling are painted in the same fashion as the corridor with soft, green vines curling around roses, except these flowers are varying shades of pastel blue and pink, as well as silver. The floor is some sort of pale-gray stone, but it's a soft enough color to feel welcoming.

A large, four-poster bed sits to the left, covered in glistening silver bedding that appears plush and soft, while an ornate wooden desk rests against the far right wall, along with a dressing table and a mirror.

There is a closed door in the corner on my left, and another door on the wall behind us, both with silver filigree around their top edges. Either could be a closet or a bathroom.

Atrox's helmet and armor rest in the farthest inner corner of the room, floating in place like a silent guard.

Beside it, bolted tightly to the wall with multiple chains, is my glaive. My heart sings to see it and the weapon responds to my presence, thrumming against the wall and causing vibrations that hum through the air.

I sense its anger as it tries to free itself, but the chains have been cleverly crossed over with metal caps across each end of the glaive to prevent it from slipping free.

Atrox watches me carefully as he carries me into the room.

"Your weapon is mine now. As is the gold that makes up your feathers."

My forehead creases because I can't see the feathers anywhere, but then I spy a locked case sitting on the desk. If my feathers are in there, I can't sense them, but the glance Atrox gives the case indicates that's where he's keeping them.

"If my weapon was now yours, you wouldn't have to chain it to the wall," I say, glaring back at him with what little energy I can still muster.

I take comfort in the nearness of my blade.

It may be imprisoned like I am, but it's not defeated.

I won't be, either.

Atrox huffs as he continues to carry me toward the bed.

The air becomes crisper the closer we get to the balcony, and the lilting sounds of bird calls reach me across the distance.

I was worried that this room might contain threats, but far from it.

The peace I feel now that I'm here... It's as if Callan has stepped into the room with me, instead of Atrox. All the calm he always gave me somehow pours from every part of this room and the environment beyond it.

This place belongs to an angel with the purest of hearts. It hits me hard that it was supposed to belong to *me*. A private sanctuary. Intended to be mine alone.

Once again, I would be tearing up right now if I weren't so thirsty, but at least there's no danger that I'll reveal this sadness to Atrox.

He pauses beside the bed, his arms clamped around me. His green eyes narrow as he focuses on my cheeks, as if my tears might have fallen without me knowing.

"My brother thought we should break your body, but I should have known better." His hold around me is unbearably tight. "I should have learned through Callan's experience that opposition by force only makes you fight harder."

I squint up at him, wary of where he's going with this line of reasoning.

He continues. "Callan kept my fire under control far longer than I believe any other dragon shifter could have. It may surprise you to learn that I respected his strength."

Atrox slides one hand further up the back of my head, tangling his fingers in my matted hair. "I also respected his intelligence. He discovered, far earlier than I would have, that *kindness* neutralizes you."

Beatrix said she thought Callan was the smartest damn dragon who ever had the nerve to wrap an angel around his little finger. I asked her if she thought Callan was using me, but she shook her head emphatically and declared that Callan was as wrapped up in me as I was in him.

Even though Atrox is talking about kindness, I have no illusions that he intends to show me any real mercy. He's made it clear that he'll do whatever he has to, and the cold gleam in his juniper-green eyes tells me that treating me well is nothing more than a necessary tactic.

"You only speak of kindness because you have a reason to keep me alive now," I whisper. "You want Viviana."

"True," he acknowledges. "But I never lied about wanting you by my side, Asper. Your strength would be an asset in this fight. Now that you've experienced the cage into which I can throw you, you might want to reconsider your position."

He adjusts his hold on me and I prepare for him to drop me onto the bed. "There's one more thing you should know: You may have believed that my heart is made of charred coal, but I knew love once, and because of that love, I also know *hate*."

"You hate *me*," I say with certainty.

"Yes." He takes his focus off me only long enough to give the bed a pointed glare. "It's important that you know: I don't fuck what I hate."

Right. I'm glad we got that sorted out.

"Don't fight me," he says, finally shoving me onto the bed.

A quiet sigh fills my throat even as the force of his shove causes me to bounce hard against the mattress. His command is like telling a bee not to buzz or a leaf not to fall in winter.

I may have only a little energy left in me, but there's no way I'm going to submit meekly to whatever so-called *kindness* he intends to show me. I lift my right leg into the narrow gap between us just as he leans down to me. I don't have enough strength to kick him, but I use my leg as a wedge to keep him at bay.

He responds far too cleverly for my liking by simply pivoting so that my leg slips to his side and I lose my leverage. At the same time, he aims a flat-handed shove at my shoulder with his other hand, his goal appearing to be to pin me against the bed. I knock my armband against his arm and sweep it to the side, managing to slither off the edge of the bed before he can catch me.

He gives a sigh of exasperation when I hit the floor and can't even make it back to my feet. "For fuck's sake. You'll fight your-self to death."

He grabs me around my waist and hauls me upward.

I can't pretend to give up. Not even to save myself. "It's not in my nature to stop fighting."

He laughs softly. "I value your honesty, Asper." He grips me hard around my waist, crushing my ribs so much that I'm worried they'll crack.

This time, when he pushes me onto the bed, he doesn't take his hands off me, using every available part of his body to pin me down—a knee against my chest, a hand on my sternum, another pressing my face to the bed—switching up his hold as fast as he needs so that he can wrench the blanket over me. He lifts, shoves, and even rolls me over so fast that I don't know up from down, even though I'm fighting back as hard as I can, trying to punch and kick him with all my might.

Until I can't anymore.

I find myself lying on my stomach, wrapped so tightly in the silver blanket that my arms are pinned to my sides and my legs are pressed together. The blanket reaches up the sides of my neck and all the way down to my feet. The sound of ripping material reaches my ears, and then the blanket tightens even further around my shoulders, followed by my chest, and finally my legs. I imagine that he's torn the blanket at the edges to make knots and keep it tied around me.

His weight lifts and his footfalls sound. His body comes back into view as he passes around the bed. Without a word to me, he prowls around the room, picking up objects and testing their weight and studying their form.

At first, I'm confused about what he's doing, but then I realize he's taking me at my word. I won't stop fighting him and I'm likely to use any loose objects in the room as weapons.

I could break the ornate wooden chair at the desk and use its parts as clubs—that's if I could reach it. Likewise, I could snatch up the porcelain vase from the desk and break it over his head, not that I think it would do much damage.

Anything that appears heavy, that could be broken or has a sharp edge, he carries to the balcony's edge and throws it over. The vase goes first, together with a large ornament of an angel that also appears to be made out of porcelain—or whatever equivalent of it exists in the veil. The vase and ornament fall soundlessly for long seconds before my sharp hearing picks up the faint crashes as they hit the ground far below.

After that, he works faster, seeming to have made the decision that anything smaller than the chair could be a danger.

Finally, he considers the chair itself, but after a brief study, he leaves it beside the desk. He also leaves the case on the desk that I believe contains my feathers.

At that point, the sound of the door opening within the atrium reaches me and Atrox disappears through the silver cascade. I strain my ears, but even with my sensitive hearing, his voice is muffled. It seems that the cascade is sound-dampening.

He returns quickly, holding a tray of items while several

pieces of clothing are neatly slung over one arm. I catch sight of bandages and little bottles of varying colored glass before he places the tray on the desk and leaves the clothing on the chair.

He brings me a small sapphire-colored vial first.

With little effort, he turns me, one-handed, onto my back. The knots press painfully into one of my shoulder blades and my lumber region, although the one behind my legs isn't so bad.

Scooping his big hand beneath my head to lift it, he places the vial at my lips. "Drink."

I press my lips together, wary of what he's trying to give me.

"It's medicine. To heal any remaining infection and ease your pain," he says. "If I wanted you dead, I would have killed you already."

Given the truth of that statement, I part my lips and swallow the liquid that sloshes into my mouth.

"All of it," he orders me.

"Where did the angels get it?" I ask when the vial is empty. "They don't need medicine to heal."

"I asked Zadkiel the same thing. Apparently, it's the tears of a unicorn," he says. "This vial was confiscated from a witch who was hunting unicorns for their healing powers. Luckily for you, the tears never age, although they aren't a miracle cure for exhaustion."

Neither was the appearance of my dragon.

I breathe a little easier as the liquid warms my throat and chest, and I realize just how cold I was.

"You need to rest," he says before he slides off the bed and heads to the closed door in the corner of the room and disappears into what appears to be a bathroom.

He must be very confident that I won't break these bindings to leave me alone like this. Even so, I take advantage of his absence to try to move, willing myself to lift my left shoulder and roll, but I barely have the strength to wiggle.

Maybe if I try to bounce...

But my stomach muscles are tight and cramped and my

breathing is harsh just from trying. When I can't move an inch, I don't even have energy to scream.

I'm too tired.

So tired.

I have nothing left.

Finally accepting my captivity, I drop my head back to the soft surface, turning my cheek to the cool sheets. They feel like they're made out of the softest silk, a substance like nothing I felt in the outside world. If ever something smelled like clouds, it's these sheets.

Once again, I'm reminded of the purity of the angel who once called this bedroom hers. If it weren't for my parentage and the dragon that sprang to life within me, I would have had this life.

My moment of quiet is broken when Atrox returns, holding a towel and a flask of water, into which he pours the contents of one of the vials from the tray.

He straddles me and leans forward again to lift my head. "Water laced with nutrients," he explains, raising the flask to my lips. "Go slowly. I don't want you throwing up on my bed."

His bed?

If my mouth weren't full of liquid, I'd retort. This is more *my* bed than his.

It takes me long minutes to make it through the entire flask, after which, he fills it again and bring more water to me—into which he also pours another vial. Together with the medicine he first gave me, I finally feel my body responding, my muscles easing, and my exhaustion becoming less sharp. More like I'm floating.

When I finish the third flask of water, Atrox remains straddling me. He reaches for the cloth, and I discover that it's wet when he uses it to wipe my face.

"You're filthy," he says, wrinkling his nose. "Tomorrow morning, I'll give you a bath."

"I don't give a fuck about baths," I retort, happy to find that my voice is stronger than before, although I picture just how mangy my hair has become and how disgusting my clothing must be now.

He ignores my response, studying my forehead where Dominus struck me with the hammer on my first day in the veil.

"This cut was made with light magic," Atrox says, running his fingers across it. "You're lucky it didn't crack your skull, but it's forming a scar."

"Give me as many scars as you like," I say. "They won't define me."

He scoffs as he folds the towel over and uses the clean side to wipe the parts of my neck that are accessible to him. "Callan told you that." His upper lip curls with disgust. "Fucking lies. Our scars mold us. We are nothing if not the sum of our experiences. My original form bore many scars."

He stops cleaning me to point at his forehead, then his left shoulder and right arm. He continues to point to multiple parts of his body, brushing his fingers across his skin as if he were tracing the pattern of scars he used to have.

"My scars were inflicted by supernatural creatures who wanted our light for themselves," he says. "They used magic that defied my usual healing abilities, but I prevailed. I killed them all."

He stares down at me. For a moment, I glimpse disappointment in his eyes, and it reminds me of the look Callan gave me when I refused to ask for his help when we first arrived at his new home. I'm not sure why Atrox feels that way until he continues.

"When you first revealed to Callan how the Serene Commander treated you, I was sure you would be my ally," Atrox says. "I thought that you, of all creatures, would understand my anger."

I can't deny that I *did* understand it. I recognized it and felt it in my own heart. I glimpsed Callan's dragon when he'd burst into flames at my touch. The second time I'd tried to leave his home, and Callan's gold bands had caught me, his body collided with mine and I sensed that his dragon was in control.

While the heat of the fire raged around us, the beast told me he wouldn't let me go. He told me to stop fighting and give in to the fact that I was his now.

I knew, even then, that Callan's dragon's intentions were simple: Trap me and keep me.

And... so help me... my wild heart responded with anticipation and *want*, not fear.

A trickle of dread rises within me now as I wonder how much influence Atrox had over Callan in those moments. Did Callan make those choices for himself or was Atrox making them for him?

Did Callan really want any of this?

"You wouldn't let me go," I say, my voice wooden, my body stiff.

I try to shake off my growing fears about the extent of the influence that Atrox and Viviana may have had over Callan and me, reminding myself of every moment when Callan *was* in control. Too many moments for all of his decisions to have been dictated by Atrox.

Atrox presses his lips together, and I sense his rising fury in the heat that grows around him. He pitches the towel to the floor before he presses his palms against my shoulders and leans over me again, forcing me to stare directly into his eyes. "Tell me, Asper, if I hadn't killed the dragon you love, would you have welcomed me at your side?"

My response is almost an immediate *no*, but I'm surprised by the sour taste that fills my mouth, a tang that warns me an instant rejection would be a lie.

I have to ask myself, if Atrox were someone else's dragon and he had come to me and offered to destroy the Serene Commander, would I have accepted his offer?

The likely answer is *yes*, but I'm also reminded of the list of

Atrox's crimes that were meticulously recorded in the Book of Angelic Monsters—crimes of murder and destruction that have been confirmed by my senses and my need to end him.

"It's not only Callan's death you have to answer for," I say.

Atrox's eyes narrow dangerously as he peers at me. "What do you think you know about me, Asper Ashen-Varr?"

I recount to him what I read in the Book of Angelic Monsters: the names of his victims and the places he destroyed.

"That is the angels' version of things," he says. "I only killed the supernaturals who aided and abetted in Viviana's murder and the theft of our light. We trusted the angels. They were supposed to be our allies. Do you believe they're above rewriting history to cover their crimes?"

I exhale quietly, remembering the conflicting information Sophia and I read about her dragon, Bella Vorago. One book said Bella was killed after being led astray by Atrox, but the Book of Angelic Monsters didn't mention her as one of his victims. In fact, it didn't mention her at all. It's an omission that now feels deliberate. "I suppose you can tell me the truth about Bella Vorago, then."

Atrox gives a heavy sigh. "Bella Vorago died trying to find our light. As soon as she joined me in my fight, the Celestial Ascendant accused her of crimes she didn't commit. Bella died for what she believed in. Just as many dragons did. Even Magnus Grim gave his life for what he thought was just and true."

It's an interesting view for Atrox to take of the dragon who killed him.

He lifts off me as if the conversation is over, but instead of leaving the bed, he pushes me up toward the pillows so that my head rests on one of them.

I'm startled when he drops beside me, pushes me onto my side, and wraps his arms around me from behind, pulling me into the crook of his shoulder.

He's positioned me so that I'm facing the balcony and the

gorgeous night sky, as if he doesn't want me to forget that he could still throw me over the edge.

"Sleep now," he tells me, but his voice is softer than before, and his fingers are warm as they brush the back of my neck.

For a second... he sounds exactly like Callan.

I'm suddenly staring at a view I can no longer focus on.

He plants a kiss on the back of my neck, right where Callan would drop kisses against my skin.

The gesture makes me jolt. "What are you doing?"

"I'm crushing your soul," he replies, his voice remaining soft and low. "Just as I promised I would."

The way he's holding me is achingly similar to those moments when Callan could touch me, moments that seemed like small miracles and are even more precious to me now that I won't have them again.

I try, and fail, to keep my voice deadpan. "You assume I loved Callan so much that simply holding me and kissing me the way he did will hurt me."

"You did love him," Atrox murmurs at my ear. He rises up a little so I can see his face again. *Callan's* face. "And it *will* hurt you. The more I remind you of him, the more pain I'll cause you. Just as you now cause me pain by reminding me of Viviana."

I search Atrox's eyes, seeking any hint of cinnamon brown in his irises that might indicate Callan's mind and soul still exist, trapped within Atrox's mind somewhere.

I want to ask Callan if he was ever truly free to make his own decisions. I need to know if his choices were his own. He gave me choices, but now I desperately wish I'd made it clear to him that he had choices, too.

He was free to let me go, and I wouldn't have hunted his clan.

As I continue to search Atrox's expression, my chest fills with the scent of lilies. Grief and mourning dominate the underlying acrid scent of ashes, and *now* tears fill my eyes, sadness that only builds the longer he stares down at me with a storm in his angry, green eyes.

I refuse to allow myself to imagine that, for the briefest moment, the depth of Callan's presence shines through, his intelligence and reason, as if he's going to return at any moment.

"Hope is one of the most painful emotions of all, isn't it, Asper?" Atrox asks, trailing his fingers down my cheek before he lowers himself back to the bed behind me. "I feel it too. And that's how I can be certain that it will hurt more than anything when I tear your hope away from you. Again and again."

He promised that he would do worse to me than the angels ever did. If there was one cruelty they never showed me, it was to give me false hope.

I close my eyes against the pain in my heart.

Atrox may be in Callan's body, but he isn't Callan.

There is no calm or peace to be found in Atrox's arms.

CHAPTER TWELVE

I sleep fitfully, waking up throughout the night, and each time, I try to release myself from my bindings before exhaustion forces me back to sleep again.

The biggest obstacle is that I have nothing to cut through the blanket from the inside. My golden bracelets and my armband don't have any sharp edges and the way Atrox has tied the knots at my back makes it impossible for me to maneuver my arms to get my hands out at the top.

My glaive rattles against the wall, but it can't get to me, so at one point, I cast my mind toward Atrox's armor instead.

I coax it to come to me. The plates ripple in the air and move slightly, but the helmet is resistant. It remains exactly where it is, and the sense of resentment pouring off it fills me with sudden remorse. I tore one of the horns off it, and it seems the gold is wary of my intentions now.

Damn. The only time I've previously torn gold into pieces was with the gun that Sienna Scorn used to kill Solomon Grudge. I commanded that weapon to shatter, and it did, killing Sienna in the process. I have no regrets about that. It was a heartless weapon that had caused countless deaths and I didn't want it to ever be used again.

When I try again to call the armor to me, none of the pieces budge. It seems that I've used up my one and only chance to connect with that gold and I well and truly burned my bridges.

Extending my senses outward, I'm once again aware that the silver cascade at the entrance to the room is acting as some sort of barrier. I managed to hear and sense through soundproof walls at Callan's home, but the barrier formed by the silver cascade is absolute. I have no way of knowing what's happening beyond this room.

As the stillness extends around me, I turn my thoughts inward.

Viviana said that it would take another immense surge of light magic to draw her out. When I search for her now, sifting through my thoughts and seeking her warmth, I can't find her at all. She may as well not exist.

I try to think through my dragon traits—the ones that I have separate to her.

I can control dragon's gold that doesn't belong to me; I have the strength of a dragon shifter; and I can swallow dragon's fire. I can survive their fire, too, as if I wore transparent scales over every part of my angel body.

But I can only heal when my dragon is triggered: my throat when dragon's fire roars past it; my skin when dragon's gold lashes it mid-transformation; and my body when my dragon shadow appears.

I also can't create fire of my own. Not yet, anyway. Possibly not ever.

If there was ever a truth to the name the Serene Commander gave me—*Lana*, a piece of string—it's in my nature. I'm a tangled ball of power made up of a single thread that feels impossible to unwind. I don't know where my ends are. I can only follow the thread through the tangle for so long before it becomes too entwined and knotted.

Viviana said that their 'light' was at the heart of a dragon's power. She said that without it, their dragon traits are being stifled, and the dragon species is dying out.

It dawns on me that what I'm discovering about myself—my mishmash of powers and not-powers—must be the same agonizing path walked by other dragon shifters. Discovering that they have a fraction of the power they should, or sometimes not knowing to what extent they will *be* a dragon and waiting for more traits to appear.

Sophia's cry reverberates around in my mind with more force than it did when she first spoke it: *The only reason I'm safe around you is because you only kill real dragons. I can't shift. I don't have wings. I barely warrant the title of dragon shifter.*

I exhale a shuddering sigh. I am now on the same path she walked.

I stare at the beautiful night sky beyond the room, but I don't see it as my thoughts swirl in a deepening mire until exhaustion claims me again.

~

"Not-Lana."

Callan's voice is quiet.

His lips are like whispers against my cheek.

"Will you come with me?"

I gasp and my eyes flash open, hot tears spilling from them. I try to reach out, needing to get to Callan and tell him that I will go with him. *Always.* But my arms are squished to my sides and my hands won't budge.

It's a good sign that I can cry again, but being able to shed tears isn't my greatest concern right now.

Atrox leans over me, his fingertips resting on my left cheek, coaxing me awake. He's dressed casually in sweatpants and a T-shirt, but I don't mistake his casual attire or leisurely body language for a relaxed frame of mind.

"There you are," he says, brushing my tears away while he gives me a cold smile. "You aren't as pale this morning."

My mind is far more alert than yesterday, and my body doesn't feel as heavy. I attempt a cautious wriggle, finding that my strength is much closer to normal. So much stronger, in fact, that if I'd been this strong yesterday, I might have been able to free myself from these bindings.

I can't beat myself up for yesterday's physical weakness. I survived it, and that's what matters.

Atrox doesn't wait for my response before he lifts my head and raises another flask to my lips. "Water," he says. "Drink."

When I'm finished, he scoops me up and carries me toward the bathroom—an awkward exercise, given how tightly I'm bound. He has to twist sharply sideways to get through the door.

"I prepared a bath for you," he says.

True to his word.

The bathroom is large enough for an angel to fully spread her wings. A clawfoot bath sits on one side of the room, which has a marbled floor and walls—ivory with silver threads through it. A tall, silver water spout sits separately to the bath, its spout positioned over the edge.

Steam rises from the surface of the water, which fills the bath at least two-thirds.

Atrox lays me down on the floor in the center of the room, his arm cushioning the back of my head before he rolls me over onto my stomach. The sound of ripping material reaches me before the bindings loosen.

I groan with relief and prepare to jump to my feet, but he isn't taking any chances, his arm snaking around my stomach before I can make a move. Wrenching me up against him so that I'm facing the bath, he says, "You can get in on your own or I can put you in, clothes and all."

As much as I want to fight him now that I'm feeling stronger, I need the chance to assure myself that my wounds are healed and assess any physical weaknesses before I determine my best course of escape.

"I'll get in on my own," I say. "Back off."

He gives a low chuckle, seemingly unmoved by my tone. Slowly, he places me down on the floor, allowing me to find my feet before his arm slips away from my waist.

I wait a moment for him to move away. I have no illusions that he'll leave me alone. Even if there are no windows and only one door, which he could easily guard, he'd be a fool to let me out of his sight.

Quickly, I peel off the dirty and broken bodice and slip out of the pants. I remove my armband but keep my bracelets on. Keeping my back to Atrox, I remove my underwear and step immediately into the steaming water.

It's like sliding into a part of heaven. The warm water eases my tension, and the steam carries the calming scent of lavender.

I rub gently at the caked-on blood on each of my shoulders to ascertain that neither bears an open wound and there's no stinging that might indicate a returned infection. When I press my fingers to the cut across my forehead, it also seems to have healed—although Atrox is right; the surface feels uneven in the way of a scar. My bruises look like they've faded, although it's a little more difficult to tell the color of them beneath the water.

Atrox doesn't take his eyes off me as he closes the door and takes up position leaning against the opposite wall.

Satisfied that he's keeping his distance, I grab the soap, briefly submerge my head to wet my hair, and then set about cleaning myself as best I can without standing up and giving Atrox an eyeful of my body.

He watches me the entire time, his arms folded over his chest, the crease in his forehead and the intensity in his eyes growing, and I can only imagine what he's thinking about.

I don't know the details of what he and his brother are planning. He was incredibly vague when he answered Zadkiel's question about it.

When I'm finished, the water is filthy and I'd give anything for a clean tub of water with which to rinse myself, but I suppose I'll just have to live with it.

It's only then that I scan the room for towels. Several sit on a stool in the far corner of the room.

Atrox follows my gaze to them before he retrieves two and brings them to me.

He drops one towel on the floor beside himself and unfolds the other, holding one corner in each hand, indicating that he intends for me to get out and step into it.

I pull my hair forward to cover my breasts before I stand up. After allowing the water to fall off me, I step carefully from the bath and into the offered towel.

He seems amused by my efforts to cover myself. "You forget, Asper, I've already seen every part of your body."

I stiffen a little since I was trying to ignore that fact.

He folds the towel around me before he sets about rubbing the soft material across my back and arms. His efforts are unhurried, and he pays attention to every droplet of water that lingers on my shoulders—an endless task while my hair is dripping—before he descends to my stomach, hips, and legs.

He dries me off in the same way that Callan dried me after he'd taken me to his new home. Slow and gentle.

Tell me what you need, Callan murmured. *Ask for what you want.*

The towel falls away from my legs and Atrox drops it to the floor before he rises upward again. Pursing his lips, he exhales gently across the top of my head. A caress of warmth soaks into my scalp. It's the same method Callan used to dry my hair.

Once again, Atrox is reminding me of what I've lost.

"Viviana had black hair like yours," he says, focusing on my dark tresses where they frame my face.

Or, maybe, he's reminding himself of what *he* lost.

Before I realize what he's doing, he cups the back of my head and his fingers tangle in my hair.

It's a careful touch, not an aggressive one, and it takes me off guard.

Damn him for reminding me of Callan in this moment. Damn him for taking Callan's face and his body. For stealing his hands.

"You hate me," I say. "Remember?"

The heat in Atrox's eyes only grows. "What was it you once asked Callan?" He pauses before he answers his own question. "Is it possible to feel both hate and need at the same time?"

His free hand brushes my now-dry hair away from my face as he searches my eyes with the same intensity with which I'm searching his, as if he's looking for signs of Viviana while I search for Callan.

Does he see her?

His head lowers to mine, his lips oh-so-close to my own.

When he closes his eyes…

He could be Callan. Carefully brushing his hands down the surface of my tangled hair. Stroking the back of my neck and trailing his fingertips down my back.

"I changed my mind about you," he whispers before he repeats back to me what I once told Callan. "Enemies can fuck as easily as friends."

CHAPTER THIRTEEN

*M*y heart hurts to hear what I once said. I believed it at the time, and it's still fundamentally true, but there was much more between Callan and me than the heat of our bodies.

I stiffen in Atrox's arms as I remember how Callan called his dragon 'a beast.' I knew even then that this creature was as far from a mindless beast as I'd ever encountered. Atrox's impulses aren't random. He has a purpose right now, just as he had a purpose when he wrapped me up last night and dropped a light kiss against the back of my neck.

My jaw clenches as my guards fly back up. My voice is low but carries a warning. "They may fuck, but they're still enemies."

Atrox opens his eyes. *Resentful* green eyes. "So they are. But do we have to be? You want Callan, and I want Viviana. There's no reason we can't be them for each other."

My eyes widen as I consider if there's any thread of genuine vulnerability in what he's asking, but I can't be sure. I can't know for certain that this isn't part of his game.

I respond with a simple, "We aren't them."

With a shrug, he slides his hands away from my body.

"What of dragons?" he asks, abruptly changing the subject. "You've only experienced life from an angel's perspective, not from a dragon's. Aren't you curious to explore that side of yourself?"

My forehead creases. *Where's he going with this?*

Without waiting for my answer, he reaches up to the hook behind the door and retrieves underwear for me—underpants and a bra—along with a black dress. The dress is sleeveless but long and with a slit up one leg. When he hands it to me, it feels like it's made from the same sort of silky material as the sheets.

I turn my back and pull the clothing on as quickly as I can. Retrieving my armband, I slip it onto my left arm.

"You must be hungry," he says, reaching for me. "I know I am."

His golden wings extend as he moves, but in a controlled fashion so they don't hit the walls. His golden scales rush across his skin, and his eyes become pure gold again. He's an ominous and dangerously beautiful sight as he wraps his hand around my wrist and his body blocks the exit.

He isn't stupid. He will have watched me check my old wounds and he must know that escape is at the top of my mind, but until this moment, he kept me talking. Immersed me in memories of Callan to subdue my more aggressive impulses.

Oh, kindness, how you defeat me.

"Come and eat," he says, spoken as an order more than a request as his hand tightens around my wrist.

"I will when you get out of my way," I say, challenging him to let me go.

"Put escape out of your mind, Asper," he says. "Even if you make it past me—which you won't—the Roden-Darr won't let you leave. And even if you get past them, you won't make it past my brother. If you try, he will kill you." A ruthless smile flashes across Atrox's golden features a second before he whisks me back up into his arms, this time pulling me straight toward him so that my arms slip to either side of his neck and my legs wrap around his hips.

"Give in to what your dragon wants," he murmurs, his lips brushing mine.

I gasp with rage at the contact, but he spins toward the door before I can retaliate.

He strides into the bedroom and heads directly toward the sunlit balcony. The sound of bird calls greets me again—a low, keening melody like last night—and so does the sound of my glaive rattling against the wall.

Atrox's arms are tight across my back, and they tighten even more when my gaze flashes to the silver cascade that obscures the entrance to the room.

I consider my options quickly, but while he's partially shifted and keeping me in this position, I'm unlikely to get away from him. I need to wait until he lets go of me. Then I can free my glaive and my feathers, then free myself from this place.

All I need is a little more patience.

I spy a table laden with fruit and crusty bread out on the corner of the balcony, and I expect Atrox will head toward it, but instead, he veers toward the center of the balcony.

In the next moment, he steps into the sunlight flooding the balcony and I gasp as I suddenly feel like I'm floating outside of myself.

Pure warmth beats down over my skin, the rays of light carrying an energy that makes my entire body buzz. It's not ordinary sunlight—it can't be because we're in the veil—and it's intoxicating, making me want to tip my head back and experience its full warmth. It heats the scent of lilies that continues to mask Atrox's ashy aroma and transforms it, filling my chest with pure *power*.

Atrox's eyes gleam down at me and his voice rumbles in my ears. "Do you feel it?" he asks me. "This sanctuary belonged to the strongest angel—stronger even than the Celestial Ascendant herself. The environment here is filled with power."

His hand tangles in my hair again. "The dragon inside you makes you even stronger than she was." His gaze burns me. "Dragons were once the strongest creatures in the land. No other supernatural race could stand against us. We were envied for our might, our speed in the air, and our sheer fucking ferocity."

He extends his wings fully and they catch the light, sending sparkling rays across the air and intensifying the energy in the light that continues to beat down on us.

There's a vast environment beyond the balcony. A green field spreads out far below us and a forest sits beyond it, stretching as far as I can see. There are dark patches within the forest, but they're much too far away to see properly. The balcony seems to jut from a rock face that soars upward as well as down, and the sky is the purest blue.

"I'll show you the exhilaration of what it means to be a dragon, Asper." His wings beat and he lifts off the ground. "And then you'll understand why you should stand at my side."

We shoot up into the air so fast that the breath is knocked out of me. My instinct is to release my own wings so that I don't fall, but Atrox growls a warning.

"Don't attempt to fly. Not unless you want to rip your wings apart all over again."

The air rushes past me as he angles sharply downward, wraps his wings around me, and dives over the balcony's edge.

We speed toward the field far below us, and the rock face passes at a dizzying speed. The rush of air warms my blood and my heart pounds as the ground rears up beneath us.

Atrox pulls out of the dive at the last minute, unwrapping his wings and soaring across the field below us. We're so close to its surface that I could reach back and touch the tips of the tall grass. I don't dare try since we're moving at too great a speed and even a small object at this velocity could cut through my skin. Whatever healing ability I experienced, it only lasted as long as Viviana's shadow was with me.

I also heed Atrox's warning against releasing my wings. Even if I wanted to, the force of air against my body is too great to avoid damage to my feathers.

The grass ripples on either side of us as we pass over it, and I glimpse the way the fronds part in streaks when what must be small creatures are disturbed by our sudden appearance. They're hidden by the grass, so I can't see what they look like, but their rapid heartbeats drum in my ears as they race away.

Atrox beats his wings and—*unbelievably*—increases our speed. "Imagine what it was like to soar over fields like this in full dragon form. When we retrieve our light, we can have that again. We can rule the other species. As we should."

I catch a glimpse of his gleaming eyes, but his focus is firmly fixed on the forest that lies ahead of us. He soars upward away from the surface of the field and toward the top of the trees at the edge of the woods.

I sense the lifeforms within the forest. Some must be large like deer, judging by the energy they're emitting and the thuds of their hearts. Some are small like rabbits, and they scurry through the underbrush when we reach the treeline.

"I'm hungry," Atrox says as we pass over the lush canopy below.

My instincts prickle because he said the same thing before we left the balcony, despite walking straight past the table laden with the food.

My chest and thighs feel suddenly warmer and I'm aware of the heat waves shimmering around his body, nearly indistinguishable from the heady rays of the false sun that hangs in the sky above us.

He passes so low across the treetops that his wing beats send tornados of wind gusting through their branches. The canopy is thinner in some places, allowing me to see the leaves on the forest floor kicking up and swirling wildly as we fly by.

With a suddenness that takes my breath away, Atrox soars

upward and stops. After the rush of flying and the immense force of his speed, our abrupt stillness feels unnatural.

Instinctively, I release my wings, and it forces Atrox to open his arms. I dart backward, putting enough distance between us that he can't reach out and grab me.

Despite how far we've traveled, I estimate that we're still only about a quarter of the way across the forest. The vast field of grass stretches out beyond the treeline all the way back to a mountain that I can now fully see. I can just make out the shape of the balcony carved high into the side of the rocky cliff face.

I never imagined that there would be such an enormous landscape behind the Avenging Angel's silver door.

Atrox doesn't retaliate and he doesn't appear concerned that I've darted backward, his shoulders relaxed, his wings beating slowly as he hovers opposite me.

"You can't outfly me, Asper," he says. "Not in this angel form that you cling to."

"I'm not 'clinging' to this form," I say. "I don't have a choice."

"Maybe." He appraises me with his gleaming, golden eyes. "Or maybe, when we retrieve our light, you *will* have a choice. Who knows what transformations will happen once our light is released into the world once more." He edges closer to me. "What would you choose, Asper? Angel or dragon?"

"Neither." It's a cold but instant truth. "I want to be free of all of this."

He laughs, a harsh sound over the gentle breeze. "To live a quiet life filled with mundane problems? The boredom would kill you."

I sweep my wings and maintain the distance between us. "I'll never have the chance to find out."

His laughter fades as his attention flickers to the trees below us. We're hovering high enough now that our wing beats don't disturb the canopy, but even so, something has shifted in the air. The intense warmth has become a sort of charged energy that prickles my arms and the back of my neck.

I listen carefully, picking up the quiet thuds of multiple heartbeats that blend nearly imperceptibly into the breeze. I estimate that they're larger animals, maybe the size of horses, and they're remaining very still.

It feels like the forest is holding its breath.

Atrox smiles again, but this time without any shred of humor. "It's time to hunt."

CHAPTER FOURTEEN

*A*trox beats his wings in a powerful sweep, aiming downward into the forest before he tucks his wings and dives into the canopy.

I blink at the space he leaves behind.

I'm shocked that he left me alone. Recovering quickly, I focus on flying back to the balcony and fighting my way free of this place as fast as I can. He wasn't exaggerating when he said that I can't outfly him. I'll need as much of a head start as I can get.

I spin and thump my wings, rising rapidly into the air.

An unearthly scream sounds from within the forest behind me, making me pull up sharply midair. I've never heard anything like it, a sound of fear and rage that makes the hairs on my arms stand on end.

Atrox said he was hungry. He told me it was time to hunt. He's been talking about how dragons dominated the land since before we plunged off the balcony. In his original dragon form, he would have hunted animals for food in forests just like this one.

But *this* land... It's intended to belong to the Avenging Angel, who was pure and never killed any living thing.

I'm intensely torn about what to do, but my instincts are clear to me, even if they war with my need to escape.

I may not belong in this place, but death doesn't, either.

I can't fly away. Not when I could try to stop him.

My muscles tense as I listen carefully, waiting for another crash to betray Atrox's location.

The sound of violently rustling leaves reaches me from the distance to my right. I sweep my wings and launch myself in that direction, aiming for the sounds of the struggle. As soon as I reach the spot, I tuck my wings like he did and drop through the nearest gap in the canopy.

I land on the mossy ground, my bare feet sinking into the bright-green debris that covers the forest floor. I don't have time to admire the immense height of the trees or the breadth of their mahogany-colored trunks as I spin to locate the glints of gold in the distance that tell me Atrox is moving fast through the forest.

My feet fly as I race after him, running beneath the broad branches and brilliant, emerald leaves that form the thick canopy overhead. I dash between trees and across fallen branches, my still-matted hair beating against my back.

In the distance, there's another crash and I push myself to go faster—only to jump with fright when a beast with a hide the color of the green leaves that cover the forest floor leaps across my path.

I swallow a cry of alarm, astonished that it was so quiet, I didn't hear its approaching footfalls, and its hair so perfectly camouflaged that I didn't pick it out until it was right in front of me.

It's the size and shape of a horse, its body majestically sleek, but with one distinct difference: antlers the color of mahogany rise from either side of its head like those of a stag.

It's moving so fast that I barely have time to process its beauty and agility before I'm forced to veer wildly to the right so I don't collide with it. It leaps to the side, racing away into the woods. Within seconds, it has blended into our surroundings and I can no longer distinguish it from the trees.

But the scent of fear it leaves in its wake is thick and sharp within my chest.

Up ahead, I catch sight of a narrow clearing and the wide expanse of Atrox's golden wings.

The antlered horse he's chasing shoots across the clearing, but Atrox aims for the spot ahead of it, his timing impeccable as he crashes down onto its back and knocks it to the ground.

The horse screams and struggles, kicking up earth and debris around them. Atrox uses his wings to full effect, ramming the tips of his wing bones into the ground on either side of himself to pin down the horse's body. Its emerald-green hair is sleek with sweat and its brown eyes are wide, its hoofs scrabbling and digging turrets into the mossy ground as it tries to escape.

Atrox grips its neck in his hands, preparing to break its bones. The beast must be strong because it nearly wrenches itself free of Atrox's grasp. In response, Atrox grabs one of its antlers.

I'm running so fast that I don't see for certain, but the moment Atrox touches the antler, it glows an icy blue and Atrox quickly lets go, as if the contact was painful.

I burst through the trees toward them.

Atrox's focus snaps to me. His golden eyes are feverishly bright. "Come, Asper!" he shouts. "Take the kill. Know what it is to be the most powerful creature. To dominate all others and hunt without limits!"

I don't stop running, hoping that Atrox won't suspect my intentions until the last minute.

With every heartbeat, this clearing is disappearing from my vision and all I can see is Sienna Scorn leaning over Solomon Grudge moments after she shot him in the back. She could have killed him with a single bullet, but instead, she chose to cause maximum damage while keeping him alive because, according to her...

Only a slow death can satisfy a hunter's heart.

I launch myself forward, and at the same time, I release my wings to gain air. As I shoot toward Atrox, I drop my hand, grab the middle of his left wing bone, and wrench his wing up off the horse.

The force of my collision knocks him backward. His hold on the horse slips and, without his upper wing holding it down, the creature darts back to its feet.

Its footfalls are frantic as it crashes across the clearing and then it's camouflaged within the forest once more. I don't see any more of it because Atrox retaliates with full force. He retracts his wing, swiveling as we fall, and his arms wrap around me before we crash into the ground.

He's strong enough to adjust our landing, turning us midair so that I land on my back beneath him. I retract my wings a split second before his right fist smacks the ground at my side and he would have crushed my wing bone—whether or not he intended to.

His face is filled with fury and the feverish light in his eyes fades as he stares down at me, pinning me to the ground.

"You can't stop me, Asper," he says. "Dragons kill what they want. It's the natural order of things."

Have you ever seen a dragon hunt a thunderbird? That's what Dominus asked me. He wanted me to know that he was hunting me in that moment, but his question suddenly rings with a harder truth. He told me that thunderbirds were nearly as large as dragons, that their hearts were powered by lightning, and when they beat their wings, it sounded like thunder.

And yet dragons killed them.

My hand closes around the nearest fallen branch, which I smack across Atrox's head. He takes the blow with a mere flinch and continues to glower down at me.

"No," I say. "You won't kill what you want. Not in my forest."

A deep laugh rumbles through his chest. *"Your* forest? Everything you see around you belongs to me now, Asper. The trees, the fields, the horses—even the little creatures I can crush within my fists." He stares at me. "Including you."

There's only just enough space where we landed in the clearing to accommodate his wings as he gives them a sweep and rises off me to land on his feet a few paces away.

I hurry to crouch on the mossy ground while he surveys the forest in the direction that the horse fled. The horses have proven that they can fully camouflage within the forest and move so quietly that their footfalls are barely discernible, but they can't hide their heartbeats. If Atrox's hearing is anything like mine—and I'm certain that it is—then that's how he's tracking them.

Now that I'm in the middle of the forest, I can hear three of them to our far right and two on our far left.

Atrox's anger at my interference does not seem to have abated. "You think you can save them," he says, the muscles in his biceps flexing and heat waves growing around his face and chest. "But I could burn this forest to ashes, and everything in it, with a single breath."

My eyes widen when he inhales deeply and the clearing fills with burning heat that rivals the force of the false sun. Except that the sun's rays are exhilarating and Atrox's fire is destructive.

"No!" A cry leaves my lips as the first flame bursts from his mouth.

Without thinking, I leap across the distance between us, spreading my wings to gain speed. My left hand connects with his shoulder and I use it as a pivot point to propel myself into the path of his flames.

His fire burns across my face, neck, and chest, scorching heat that fills me with fear, even though I know I've survived this fire before. But the times I've withstood this inferno, Callan was the one breathing it. It was wild and untamed, but it came from him.

Atrox's fire, like his intentions right now, carries malice so sharp that I feel it in the very depths of my soul.

And still, I throw myself into the heart of danger, as is my nature.

Without a moment's hesitation, I cover his mouth with mine.

Flames like molten lava pour from him to me for the seconds it takes him to react to my sudden presence.

He wraps his arms around my waist, crushing me to his chest, even though my wings are still beating behind me.

His fire fades, but the heat of his mouth does not, his lips seeming to take everything from me as his grip around my chest forces me to stay right where I am.

His kiss is like flying into the sun. It's destructive and demanding and it's cracking my heart because there is nothing of Callan in it.

I press my hands against his chest and beat my wings as hard as I can, attempting to push myself away from him now that the immediate threat of his fire is gone.

He doesn't let me go. My gasp is smothered against his mouth when he turns me toward the nearest tree and presses me up against it, wings and all.

His groan tells me that he isn't in control and he's forgotten who I am. "Viviana."

The force with which he's holding me and pressing me against the tree's trunk makes it difficult to move my arms, but I manage to slide my right arm upward. Freeing my hand, I push my palm against his chin and shove his face to the side, forcing him to break the contact between our mouths.

I drag in a breath. "Let me go."

His eyes are glazed, but he rapidly refocuses. It's apparent that he sees me as *me* again when he says, "You gave Callan your light. Because of you, he could shift at will. Your light will do more than that for me. You will give me the power to fully shift again."

I shake my head, my hand still wrapped around his chin. "I won't help you."

"You don't have a choice. Viviana wasn't lying about why I was drawn to you. You carry power that you can't control."

I've reached my limit. I've had as much as I can take of what he wants from me. "Let me go!"

I wrench my left hand free and knock my fist against his cheekbone. The force of his grip eases just enough that I can get my leg up between us, attempting to kick him off me. He takes a step back, attempting to absorb the impact and retain his hold on me, but I fight him with an uncontrolled frenzy.

I've already learned that his scales protect him from my fists, but I beat my hands into him anyway, my only goal to free myself. The force of my thrashing takes us past the edge of the clearing and into a thicker gathering of trees, their bases concealed by bushes. It will be far harder to fight him in this confined space.

I catch Atrox's cruel smile before he finally lets me go, shoving me away from himself and into the nearest tree. The wing bone of my right wing hits its trunk and I'm knocked off-balance, spinning to the side of the tree and landing heavily on my knees on the other side of it.

I snap my wings closed and prepare to jump back to my feet.

The sight in front of me makes me freeze.

I've landed on the other side of the thick patch of bushes at the base of the tree and the ground here has been burned out.

My knees sink into ash that covers the forest floor in a rough circle in front of me. Scorch marks extend up the trunks of the surrounding trees.

Directly in front of me, within reaching distance, a pair of mahogany antlers lie in the gray ash.

They're beautiful in their complexity, each with three strong points, and each point longer than the one before.

I guess there was a part of me that hoped this was the first time Atrox had hunted in this forest. The first time that he had used his fire against the beautiful creatures that live here.

Not so.

This was never my home, won't ever be my home, but I feel like I should have been here to protect this forest and the animals that call it home.

In the next moment, Atrox lands at my side, an agile predator. He barely pays attention to the ash and the antlers as he reaches down to grab my arm. "There's a dragon inside you, Asper," he says. "Viviana was one of the gentlest dragons, but even she knew the call of the hunt just like every dragon does. It's in your nature to *crave* the kill. You just won't acknowledge it."

"Never the innocent," I say, unable to tear my gaze from the antlers. "Only the darkest hearts."

"What makes darkness?" Atrox demands to know. "When does light become dark? I was hated because I was willing to do what other dragons wouldn't to prevent the annihilation of our race. I bloodied my hands when they wouldn't."

Maybe so.

Maybe he had his reasons, and they were justified.

But I won't be a casualty in his war.

As he pulls me roughly upward, I snatch up the nearest antler.

As soon as I touch it, the antler's color changes from mahogany to icy blue, and pain screams through my hand. It's a cold burn, the antithesis of Atrox's fire. The contact with the antler feels like it's cutting through my hand, but it's my only weapon and I don't let it go.

My aim is perfect as I drive the antler's tip against Atrox's chest right at the location of his heart. I'm not sure if it will have any impact, considering that his scales are impervious to even dragon's gold.

My eyes widen when ice radiates out from the point of

impact on his chest, and he gives a roar of pain, lurching backward and letting go of my arm.

I'm aware that I'm screaming with the pain of contact with the antler, but there is no agony in the world that I won't suffer to defeat this dragon once and for all.

I launch myself after him before he can regain his footing, releasing my wings to gain air.

I drive the antler toward his neck.

There's nowhere in this very small clearing for him to retreat and his left hand has flown to his heart, exposing his neck on that side.

Colliding with his chest, I wrap my legs around his waist once more. For the briefest moment when my chest connects with his, I feel the ice that remains across his heart, the brittleness of his scales.

With a scream of effort, I drive the antler into the side of his neck.

It breaks his scales, sending tentacles of ice across his throat and drawing blood.

His eyes fly wide and he gasps for breath, bumping into the tree behind him as he struggles to breathe. My knees and calves knock against the tree's bark where they're wrapped around his waist.

I show no mercy, drawing my arm back and ramming the weapon into his heart again.

This time, his scales crack apart, the weapon's tip drives inward, and blue ice spreads all the way up to the blue burn across his throat.

He drops to his knees and his wings snap closed as he collapses to the side in the ash.

Getting my legs out just in time, I push him onto his back, where I straddle him, still holding the antler despite the pain screaming through my arm and the awful blue ice now covering the entirety of my hand and my forearm.

It will only take one more blow to end him.

The shallowest breaths rasp between his lips as he looks up at me with an expression of disbelief.

He attempts to speak, and I expect more threats, or maybe another assertion of his strength or expression of his certainty that he will always win.

Instead, he rasps, "I should have... remembered... what Callan discovered. You never... put your own safety first..."

Atrox reaches up and covers my freezing hand with his warm palm, easing some of my pain. He draws my hand closer to him, and I don't fight him because he's only taking the weapon closer to his own face.

He purses his lips, takes a last ragged breath, and exhales it gently across my hand, breathing the warmth of his flames over my frozen fist.

It's so much like something Callan would do that hot tears burn behind my eyes and my heart suddenly feels like it's being torn apart.

I drag in a deep breath, inhaling the intense scent of lilies that gathers around him. The scent of sadness.

I exhale it with a cry of grief, a wail that wrenches out of me.

In the brief moments that I met my mother, she told me that I have the strength to do what needs to be done, no matter how much it hurts me.

But I don't know if that's true.

My hand shakes, the weapon's tip is an inch from Atrox's throat, and I'm desperately trying to convince my heart...

He isn't Callan.

Callan is gone.

Atrox's eyes close, and his head tips to the side, cushioned in dust. His voice is faint as he whispers, "You have to end me."

I swipe at my wet cheeks, trying to see through my tears. His assertion makes my brow furrow with confusion over the fact that he's asking for his end.

"Do it, Lana."

Impossibly, the scent of lilies fades and a deep peace washes over me. It's the same undeniable calm that I always felt in Callan's presence.

My heart is in my throat and my eyes are wide as I force myself to unclench my fist enough to drop the antler onto the ground. I tell myself I can grab it again if I need it. My hand is blistered and discolored, and I hold it to my chest as I lean forward over Atrox, although he doesn't stir.

I press my left palm to his lower cheek, turning his face back to me slightly while he continues to lie still.

He drags in a ragged breath, suddenly deep enough to expand his chest and press against my thighs.

His eyes open, but only the slightest.

I'm frozen as I stare down at him, my tears dripping onto his face.

His irises are cinnamon brown, the color of Callan's eyes—a color I haven't seen since Atrox destroyed him.

The ruby heart charm on my bracelet suddenly comes to life, emitting light in regular beats, as if it's mimicking my heart and conveying its rhythm to the man I love.

I struggle to speak as pain and hope collide within me. "Callan?"

CHAPTER FIFTEEN

I wait for his response, my whole body suddenly shaking, and I don't know if it's because I'm afraid I'm wrong, or because I'm struggling with the hope I'm feeling.

His next exhalation is soft and his cheek presses into my palm as if my touch is giving him strength.

"Not-Lana," he whispers. "Atrox isn't gone. You have to end me before he takes over again."

As soon as Callan speaks the name he gave me, I know it's really him. I can't repress the cry that leaves my lips as I lean forward and press my cheek to his.

"You're alive." Tears pour from my eyes, and my voice is barely coherent. "You're alive."

His arms rise to slowly wrap around me, his palms warm as they press against my back, a touch I feared I'd never feel again.

"I thought I'd lost you." I sob in his arms, all of the grief I've been repressing rising up in a wave to overwhelm me.

He's quiet, his cheek pressed to mine while the ice across his chest slowly seeps through the front of my dress, reminding me how wounded he is.

He speaks slowly, his breathing labored. "I'm not *me.*"

I draw back but only enough to see his face. I swipe again at my tears with my left hand while my right fist remains clenched against my chest.

"You are," I say vehemently. "You will be." I press my left palm to his cheek again. "You can fight him. You're stronger than he is."

Callan's expression softens. "I'm trying, but..." He pauses and his smile is faint but gentle. "The longer you stay with him, the stronger he becomes."

My brow furrows. "What are you saying?"

His hands stroke my back. "There's light in you, Lana. Just like your dragon claims. It gives you strength, but it also spreads to the dragons around you. Slowly, but surely. Every time you open up your heart a little more, you give some of your light away."

I quickly put the pieces together. "So... every time he reminded me of you... I made him stronger."

Callan gives the barest nod. "I could feel it." His gaze brushes across my face, his brown eyes taking me in from my awful, matted hair to my tear-streaked face. "I felt your sadness and I felt your love."

Fresh tears spring to my eyes and I can't stop them falling.

"Not-Lana," he says, his palms pressing gently against my back as if he wants to ease my pain. "I might not have another chance to tell you that I love you."

I try to catch my breath, needing to respond, but he continues with even greater vehemence. "It's killing me that my hands, my voice, and my memories are being used to hurt you."

"Then show me how you want to use them," I say, a wave of pain and hope and need overwhelming me as my mouth crashes against his.

I'm in agony, both physical and emotional, but my body is screaming at me to connect with him while I can, to remember what it feels like to be touched by Callan without Atrox's malice.

Callan responds with a deep groan of need, a sound that makes heat pool between my thighs.

He rises off the ground beneath me, his hands branding me through the thin material of my black dress, grazing up my hips and torso to rest beneath my breasts before he drops back down.

Holding my injured arm tightly against my chest, I adjust my position where I straddle him so I can tug at the waistband of his sweatpants. He helps me push them down before he slides my dress up around my hips.

I rip at the inner seam of my underpants so hard that the stitching snaps and the material gives way, allowing me to fit my body to his.

The first thrust makes me scream, a desperate need bursting into life within me.

He grips my hips, steadying me as I grind myself onto him again. My movements are wild and my dress pools around me as I ride the waves of intense pleasure that mingle with the pain of knowing I can't hold on to this forever.

His groan is nearly my undoing. When he strokes his hand across my stomach to my center, the first brush of his thumb against me draws another cry to my lips.

My heart is both breaking and mending with all that he's giving me, and all that I'm giving back to him, even though I know it can't last.

It's impossible to delay the burst of molten pleasure.

Impossible to hold back the crash.

I drop forward as I come, my good hand planted beside his head, my cries smothered against his mouth as I kiss him as hard as I can.

He joins me in the crash, his hands tightening on my hips and his deep groan thrumming through me.

Against my will, a sob leaves my lips.

I don't want this moment to end. I refuse to separate my body from his. I can't face what has to happen next.

He's breathing hard. His hands rise to my face, coaxing me to look at him. "If you won't take the life from this body, then you need to escape while you can."

"No!" It's an instinctive response, and not a rational one. I attempt to slip my left hand beneath Callan's head while I unfurl my right fist so I can reach for his other shoulder. As if I could lift him and carry him. "If I'm going, you're coming with me."

"Not-Lana—"

"I won't lose you!" My cry is sharp, and it carries the weight of all the desperation filling me.

Already, I can sense the faintest emerging aroma of lilies around him that tells me Atrox isn't far away. Somehow, I drove Atrox away from Callan, but it's not permanent. He will return and when he does, I can't imagine the scope of the wrath he'll storm down on me.

I refuse to pick up the antler once more and drive it into Callan's heart, so my only choice is to take this chance to escape. I must take advantage of this headstart to fly back to the balcony. Once there, it's only a short distance across the room to the steps and the darkness that I'll have to leap into.

I tell myself all of that, trying to rationalize what I need to do next, trying to convince myself that it doesn't hurt my heart, doesn't make me want to scream with rage.

The greatest cruelty is losing Callan again, and it's tearing me apart.

"I can't leave you."

His gaze is gentle, but it burns with conviction as he lifts me off him, separating our bodies. "I want you to do the one thing I know you'll struggle to do: Protect yourself. Not my clan. Not the Grudge. *Yourself.*"

My jaw clenches, but I force myself to exhale. Force myself to straighten my dress—a clumsy attempt with one hand—while he fixes his own clothing.

Then I take a deep breath, committing to memory these last precious moments with Callan.

I can't promise that I'll do what he asks, but I can promise that I'll try.

Quietly, I say, "I'll find a way to destroy Atrox without hurting you."

His forehead crinkles gently, but I hurry on.

"Protecting you *is* protecting me," I say, my voice choking. "It protects my heart."

I press my lips to Callan's, a soft kiss, as I memorize the shape of his mouth and the taste of sunshine that he brings to me.

When I draw back, the icy color of the damage to his chest is fading, and a hint of gold is entering his irises, a warning that Atrox isn't far behind.

"You have to leave the bracelets," Callan says. "You can't take the chance that Atrox will be able to track you through them, just as I could."

My heart is already breaking, shattering that I have to abandon these items that represent the connection between Callan and me. My right hand is too injured for me to operate the clasps on the bracelets, so I close my eyes and speak with the jewelry through my bond with the gold.

Please let go of me as I must let go of Callan. Please know that I will come for you just as I will come for him.

I'm grateful when both bracelets *click* softly and drop onto Callan's chest. Despite Atrox's threatening emergence, the ruby heart's glow remains strong, beating now in time with Callan's heart.

Still, his presence is fading, and Atrox is taking control again.

"Go, Lana," Callan whispers.

With a sob, I force myself back to my feet, pausing only long enough to use my dress to scoop up the antler, since I might need it again.

I spread my wings and prepare to fly, looking back only once to see Callan struggling to rise from the bed of ash that Atrox created. His forehead is thick with sweat and I sense the mental war going on inside him.

I *will* him to win it, and I wish that there was some way I could help him. I promise myself that I will find a way. Now that I know his mind, heart, and soul have survived, I will destroy Atrox and restore Callan's life to him.

I fight the agonizing fracturing of my heart as I sweep my wings and rise into the air, forcing myself not to look back again because I want to remember Callan as himself.

Flying as fast as I can, I remain aware of the environment behind me and conscious that Atrox could come after me if Callan can't keep him at bay for long enough. I keep the antler securely wrapped in my skirt, gripping the material with my left hand.

My heart is in my throat the entire way back to the balcony and by the time I reach it, my breathing is rapid and I'm shaking again. I snatch up a piece of fruit from the table, realizing how starving I am. Biting into its crisp flesh, I discover that it tastes a lot like an apple. I devour it quickly as I head straight for my glaive, where it's chained to the wall.

My weapon strains against its restraints, although it doesn't rattle as fiercely this time, as if it senses I might be able to free it now. The chains are made of ordinary metal, which means I can't command them at will. They're also attached to the wall with thick nails, but if I can just loosen the metal cap that's securing my glaive to the wall at either the top or the bottom, then I'll be able to slide it free.

I need something to use as a crowbar.

My focus falls to the antler wrapped up in my skirt. Its sharp tip and icy magic made it effective against Atrox, but I'm not sure of its strength or density. Despite my uncertainty, I don't have any other good options immediately at hand, so I race to the bed, grab the blanket to protect my skin this time, and then open my skirt to drop the antler onto the blanket.

I sense its icy power through the material, but it doesn't

burn my good hand as I slip it behind the bottom chain, test its strength, and finding that it doesn't immediately snap, I pull downward with all my might.

The chain groans. The nail creaks. And then the fastening breaks free. I quickly drop the antler to the floor before I reach up to slip the metal cap away from the bottom blade of my glaive.

Now it's free to slide down the wall behind the chains.

The gold sings as I wrap my left hand around it and I close my eyes for a moment, absorbing my glaive's joy at returning to me.

I place it down on the table only long enough to open the ornate box inside which Atrox indicated he'd placed my golden feathers. I don't need them to fly now, but I'm not leaving them here with him.

The latch at the front of the box is securely fastened but not locked. As soon as I open it, my golden feathers soar upward in a brilliant cascade before they circle me, flying around and around. Before I met Callan, I never would have dreamed that gold could *feel* emotions. Now, the joy that this gold is emitting brings warmth to my aching heart and makes me feel as if, somehow, the world is just a little bit better.

I'm about to shut the box when I spot a book in the bottom of it. It's titled *Angelic Monsters*, the same title as the chronicles of the Roden-Darr in Callan's library. I don't have time to look inside it, but I also don't want to leave it behind.

I hurry to the second door in the wall, hoping to find a closet behind it. There isn't a lot within it—just a few sets of clothes—but I grab one of Atrox's large, long-sleeved shirts. It's an awkward task working with only one hand, but I manage to wrap the book up in the body of the shirt, and I use the sleeves to tie the shirt around my waist, wincing when I have no choice but to use my damaged hand to tie the knot.

My feathers follow me from the closet back to my glaive, floating in the air like fireflies. I consider the dropped antler with some regret. I wish I could take it with me, but I only have one good hand, and I'll be using it to wield my glaive.

Just as the thought passes through my mind, five of my golden feathers swoop down to the antler and scoop it up off the floor. Working in unison, they raise the antler to my eye level and present it to me like a gift.

"Well, then," I murmur, biting my lip as gratitude floods my heart. "Thank you."

I pause only a moment longer, knowing I have no time for sentimentality. This place was meant to be my home, and even with the lingering sense of Atrox's presence, I can appreciate that it's beautiful and ethereal.

Retrieving my glaive, I hurry through the cascade of petals that conceals the entrance to the atrium at the front of the room.

Once I've passed along the corridor, I pause at the silver door. Now that I've stepped beyond the cascade, which was creating a barrier between the Avenging Angel's room and the rest of the veil, I can sense the angels guarding the central stairway.

When I close my eyes, the energy of their silhouettes shimmers within my senses. I discern that there are two angels standing guard in the middle of the top step, and one in front of each of the doors for several steps down. They're all holding their spears, and I remind myself that I will need to avoid the cut of those weapons at all costs.

I have no other way to leave the veil than to leap off the central staircase into the dark space between Earth and the heavenly realm. The top step provides the largest gap to jump through and it's also the most direct route from my room. Just a few steps away.

It makes me wonder at how oblivion was placed so close to the Avenging Angel's quarters, as if to remind her that darkness is a choice that remains close.

I take a moment to center myself. My right hand is too badly injured for me to use it unless absolutely necessary. But I take comfort in the weight of my glaive in my left hand, the presence of my feathers in the air around me, and the knowledge that my wings are healed.

I push open the door, ready to fight the angels, who immediately spin in my direction. One of them is Zadkiel and the scent of betrayal hits me just as his focus lands on me.

He gives a shout of alarm, and all of the angels on the stairs launch into action.

Just as I leap forward, using my glaive to deflect the swing of Zadkiel's spear at my neck, Dominus Audax bursts through the opposite doorway, his hammer in hand.

Suddenly, my escape will be far more difficult than I hoped.

CHAPTER SIXTEEN

*D*ominus roars at the angels. "Stand clear! The angel is mine."

Zadkiel and the other angels instantly obey. They twist and leap down toward the next lowest step, working in unison so they don't bump into each other in the small space. I thought they might simply spread their wings and lift into the air, where they could form a barrier to stop me from flying away, but it seems Zadkiel's warning against flying around the steps was a serious one.

No sooner have they moved out of the way than Dominus storms into the space they left behind.

He has been thirsting for the chance to end me ever since I broke his chains and freed him. But *my* only goal right now is to escape, and by telling the angels to back away, Dominus has done me a favor.

He's a mountain of rage bearing down on me, his hammer lifted and ready to swing at me. "Where's my brother?"

I have no intention of answering him. I don't waste a second, and I don't stop moving, making it to the left-hand edge of the top step in the heartbeats it takes him to reach me. The power within the golden hammer makes the air sing with magic, a buzz of immense power that I now recognize as light magic, and it's perfectly aimed to crush my head.

I drop to my knees to avoid his swing, but I'm not so confident that he won't adjust his aim in time, so I lift my glaive defensively, my left arm raised. Sure enough, his reflexes are startlingly quick, and the hammer collides with my glaive.

An unexpected shot of energy races through my arm, beneath my armband, and up to my weapon, and the point of impact between the hammer and the glaive explodes with golden light. My forearm burns and the heat in my palm is immense. It's just like the burning sensation I experienced when Atrox first put me in the cage with the panthers, and I dragged my fingernails down his scales.

It's the same energy that radiates from Dominus's hammer.

Except that this time, the energy came from me as well as from his weapon, the two powers colliding so forcefully that I'm knocked back toward the silver door.

Dominus also loses his footing but remains on his feet, skidding into the doorframe behind him.

He recovers quickly and powers toward me once more, but my freedom is within my reach. The antler wrapped in golden feathers hovers at my eyeline while every muscle in my body prepares to launch me into oblivion.

My mental cry reaches the golden feathers as I throw myself sideways. *Strike!*

The feathers shoot forward, and Dominus's momentum is against him. The antler turns icy blue on impact with his torso, piercing his shirt and driving into his chest below his left collarbone.

He gives a shout of pain. The feathers scatter from the antler's hilt before he can grab them. His palm lands around the antler instead and his roar only increases as he struggles to remove it.

I'm aware of the angels racing toward him—and toward me

—but the cold oblivion of the empty air on my left is already embracing me.

I throw myself into the open space, holding on to my glaive as tightly as I can and casting a mental scream at the feathers to stay with me. Preparing to release my wings, I plummet for a second through the bright space at the top of the central stairway until a rush of cold air spirals around me.

It's suddenly as if vines made of ice have wrapped around my neck, my waist, and my thighs, and they're wrenching me down at a pace I can't fight.

The feathers return to me, plastering themselves against my arms and legs wherever my skin is exposed, a mere heartbeat before I plummet into darkness.

The cold is so intense that I black out for a moment, regaining consciousness to find myself floating in a vast, dark space. It's even more oppressive than the environment within Dominus's prison. I try to sense the parameters of the space around me, but my mind feels like it could be shattering beneath the force of the sheer impossibility that I'm in a place that has no beginning or end, no corners or edges.

The silence makes it somehow worse.

There is no breeze, no movement of air, and yet...

I sense that I'm not alone.

A figure takes shape in the distance, moving toward me. I can sense it more than see it, because it seems—*impossibly*—to be making the dark even darker.

From what little I can make out of the approaching form, it appears to be male, tall, and wearing a long, black robe that produces the first noise I've heard in this place.

Swish-swish. It's like someone swilling their hand through water. Muffled somehow.

Every instinct within me screams at me to move, but... *move where?* I don't sense a solid surface beneath my feet. There's nowhere to go. It feels like I'm merely suspended in space, dangling from nothing within nothing.

It's not until he's much closer to me that I can make out a black crown that sits, not on his head, but around his eyes, as if he's sightless.

His voice reaches me across the distance, a menacing, wraith-like hiss. "Your magic is not mine to take, but take it I will."

I shrink away from him—or at least, I *will* my body to, even if thinking it has no effect. "Who are you?" I ask, alarmed to find my voice is weak and breathy. "*What* are you?"

"I am the keeper of dark magic," he says. "When magic dies, it must be claimed. I am charged with ensuring that all dark magic returns to me."

"I'm not dead," I whisper. "And I'm not a creature of dark magic."

I sense him smile in the darkness as he creeps closer. "As I said, your magic does not belong to me, but the natural order has been disrupted and your power must go somewhere. As for being dead..." He shrugs. "Neither are they, yet here they are. Lost in the ether."

They?

Just as I wonder whom he's talking about, a low growl reaches me through the darkness. I spin to the sound, relieved to discover that my body obeyed my mental command this time but startled by the ethereal shapes converging on me from all sides, each of them appearing like smoke in the air.

They are dragon shadows. But misshapen ones. Just like the twisted shadows of the dragon shifters whom I killed before I met Callan.

My chest floods with the sharp scent of mindless rage pouring off them. Viviana spoke of dragon shifters' malformed shadows returning to the ether, where they can't find rest. Now it seems that I have willingly thrown myself into the ether with them.

As the keeper of dark magic creeps closer, and the dragon shadows storm around me, I call on my wings and sense them extending before I tip my head back, seeking to fly to safety above the tumult.

It's like swimming up through oil.

My wings beat, my legs kick, and my arms drag at the air, but I move what feels like mere inches.

I try to reach the source of light magic Viviana said existed within me, the same light that seemed to explode through me when I fought Dominus just before. I try to call on it and chase the shadows away, but I don't know how to control it. I try, also, to call on Atrox's fire, but I don't know how to control that, either.

The golden feathers plastered to my arms suddenly glimmer at the corner of my vision, but I sense immediately that it's because they're reflecting a light from a source above me.

I seek this new light through the gloom while I claw at the air around me and kick my legs harder, trying desperately to rise away from the growling shadows and the dark magic keeper, who is almost upon me.

With a scream of effort, I rise a little higher.

Just as the keeper reaches me, a stronger burst of light washes across me, originating from a point above my location. As soon as the light touches me, the keeper turns his face away —all gray and aged—his robes billowing around him.

When I look up again, it's like looking up from the bottom of a pond, and the light radiating through it is my lifeline.

With a heave of effort, I swim toward the bright rays, and then, suddenly...

I'm surrounded by actual water.

I break the surface and gasp for air, realizing how close I must have been to drowning.

The sounds and smell of Philadelphia fill my senses, and I make out the gray underside of a bridge that passes across the river. I'm also aware that I'm right at the riverside and that two figures are crouched beside it.

One of them reaches into the water and pulls me out onto a

small concrete platform, turning my head so I can cough out the water before they rest my head down on their lap.

I struggle to make out their features because the light is so bright in my eyes and it's making my thoughts fuzzy.

One of them speaks. "Asper? Dearest?"

I spoke to my mother for the shortest time at the old power station before the Roden-Darr captured me, but I could never forget her voice.

"Melisma?" I ask, my voice sounding as terrible as I feel. I try again. "Mom?"

She leans closer as I remain lying on the riverbank, water pouring from me. Her black hair falls forward across her shoulder as she crouches close to me and her face comes into view. The aura around her shimmers like sunlight reflected off sunflowers.

"You're okay," she says. "We've got you. You're safe now."

I peer up at her, my brow furrowing because the light continues to shine down onto me, and it's not my mother's lap that my head is resting on.

Squinting through the brightness, I make out the stern features of an angel I didn't think I'd see again.

His pure-white hair falls to either side of his face, framing his high cheekbones and highlighting the gray color of his eyes, which remind me of storm clouds. His skin is flawless and his features are immaculate.

He's beautiful, and he was meant to serve me.

"Isaac?" My voice slurs and his name comes out all garbled.

Like the first time I met him, his perfect lips are pressed in a stern line. And like the *last* time I saw him, his palm is extended toward me, his soul light subduing my senses and making my thoughts sluggish.

His palm lowers to my forehead, his soul light draws closer, and then soothing warmth fills my mind, blocking out all of my worries and drawing me down into a different kind of darkness.

"Rest now, Asper," he says before my consciousness fades.

CHAPTER SEVENTEEN

$\mathcal{I}$ wake with a start, immediately aware that I'm resting on a soft surface with a pillow beneath my head while my right arm—the injured one—feels constricted.

A low ceiling made of gray stone looms over me. I'm facing a solid brick wall, also gray but visibly damp. A lamp is attached to it and casts a dull glow around me. My surroundings instantly remind me of the cell I used to live in under the Cathedral. In fact, this room is so similar in appearance that I jolt upright with my heart in my throat.

Surely, my mother wouldn't have brought me back there.

My head spins as soon as I sit up, and I'm forced to lie right back down again, although I manage to turn over so I can face the other side of the room.

Isaac comes into view, half-risen out of a chair beside the bed. His white hair is tied back, and he's dressed in a gray T-shirt and sweatpants that look a little loose but somehow emphasize his chiseled frame.

His gray eyes are like rain clouds as his shadow falls across me. "Easy, Asper. Don't rip out the line."

I gasp as my arm pinches at my sudden movement. My focus shifts to the head of the bed, where an intravenous pole holds a bag of fluids. It's attached to my right arm, around which a bandage is wrapped. The bandage and the apparatus are the source of the constricted sensation.

I seek the door in the opposite wall behind Isaac and relax a little when I see that it's wide open. A sign that he might not plan to keep me here against my will.

My mind eases even more when I locate my glaive propped in the far-left corner of the room and my armband and golden feathers resting in a pile on a shelf next to the door.

I can call them to me at any moment if I need them.

Of course, that's assuming Isaac doesn't intend to use his soul light on me again.

I stare uneasily at his outstretched hand. "Where am I?"

He seems to read my apprehension and lowers his hand, but he doesn't answer my question. "I'll get your mother."

"No, stop."

My request sounds more like a command, but even so, I'm surprised when Isaac obeys me.

My surprise quickly pales in comparison to my need for answers. Not least of which because the way Isaac avoided my question about my location reminded me too much of Solomon. That dragon's cryptic responses meant I was waiting for a conversation with my mother to unearth the truth about my heritage. And the consequence of that was that I learned more about myself from my most formidable enemies—Atrox and Dominus—than I did from people who might care about me.

"Danger is coming," I rasp. "I need to warn the Grudge, and I have to tell the Dread—"

"The Grudge are safe, and the Dread have gone to ground," Isaac replies, quickly returning to my bedside. "Danger will have a hard time finding them."

"Not when the danger I speak of already knows every location where the Dread might hide," I say, trying again to sit up.

The room spins in a nauseating whirl and no amount of gripping the sheets with my left hand makes it any better.

"You're in no shape to warn anyone." Isaac's palm on my upper shoulder is surprisingly gentle. "Tell me what you need and let me take care of it for you."

I stare up at him, my forehead creased as he urges me to lie down again. I lower myself to the bed on my right-hand side, my left arm curved across my chest while my bandaged arm lies uselessly wedged at my side.

Tell him what I need?

His request reminds me too much of Callan. My eyes fill with angry and unwanted tears. I'm having a very difficult time reconciling Isaac's demeanor now with the angel whose hatred felt like hot coals in my mouth when I first met him.

I'm also struggling to put into a few words why the Dread mustn't trust the dragon who looks like Callan. All I can say is, "I need to protect the Dread."

His palm remains firm on my shoulder, stopping me from rising again.

"You need to rest," he says, as if he's genuinely worried about me. "Your mind is still healing. And I would guess it's been a while since you ate anything."

The fingertips of his free hand brush my cheeks. "You can't see yourself to understand, but the circles under your eyes are black with fatigue, your skin is sunken around your face, and your body is covered in bruises. You must take care of yourself now, Asper, or you won't be able to help anyone."

Distrust rises to the forefront of my mind, but then a more worrying thought drives it away. *What if I'm still stuck in oblivion and this is some kind of strange and deceptive hell? A dream of what my life would have been like if I hadn't been born with dragon blood running through my veins.*

Although his description of the state of my body would be accurate. I've survived for days without food and I can sense my body lapping up the hydration from the intravenous drip. A sheet is covering much of me, but the bruises on my left arm are undeniable.

"You're alive," Isaac says, his gaze clear and strong as he demands my attention. "Your priority now must be to make yourself stronger for the fight ahead."

I can't deny the pull of the bed beneath me, but I'm struggling to accept the way Isaac is treating me. Caring. Worried.

"I saw you die," I say, my brow fiercely furrowed as I seek the side of his head where Zadkiel struck him. The way his hair is tied up, it's hiding the spot.

His expression becomes guarded. "You saw me bludgeoned and left for dead."

He turns his head and pulls out the hair tie to reveal the wounded patch before tying it up again. "I'm only alive because your mother found me in time. She came back to the power station when Solomon Grudge didn't come home."

"She rescued you." A cruel sort of hope rises within me because if Isaac survived against all the odds, then perhaps Solomon did, too. I try not to let my hope show when I ask, "What of Solomon Grudge?"

Isaac becomes very still before he shakes his head. "I'm sorry. Your mother said he had already passed when she arrived."

It's as if a dagger pierces my heart again, those little shards of grief rising up to shatter me. I sink back onto the pillow, trying to breathe through my emotions while I stare at the ceiling, not seeing anything now.

As the hope drains out of me, a heavy anger fills its place.

Oh, anger, you will always be there to glue the pieces of my heart back together.

I squeeze my eyes closed. "Am I a prisoner now?"

"No," Isaac says softly.

I exhale my held breath but continue to lie where I am, my eyes closed as I fight the burn of tears. "Then why did you knock me out to bring me here?"

"My soul light can be used to subdue an enemy, but it can also be used to heal a friend," he says, more softly still. "Your mind was fracturing. You jumped into the oblivion between Earth and the heavenly realm, did you not?"

I give him a small nod of confirmation.

"It's a miracle that you survived. In this instance, I used my soul light to guide your mind back to your body."

I remember the way I'd swum toward the light that was spearing through the water. Isaac's light.

"How did you find me?" I ask.

"Because you were near the entrance to the veil, and I was coming to free you," he says.

My eyes fly open. Hot tears roll down my cheeks as I stare up at him, wishing more than ever that I could rise into a sitting position. "Why would you help me?"

A soft smile grows on his lips and his eyes glow a little, but not with cold light. It's warm, and I imagine it's merely a hint of the pure soul light he carries within him, since he's the strongest and purest of all the Roden-Darr I encountered.

His beauty takes my breath away as he carefully extends his white wings. He curves them around his sides as he crouches at the side of the bed so that he's at eye level with me.

"Maybe I spent too much time in this world," he says, with a defiance that seems to carry the conviction of his beliefs. "You warned me that I should be careful your corruption didn't rub off on me."

My lips part in surprise at the vehemence in his voice and the way he holds my gaze. Isaac proved in the past that he was one of the few angels who could look me in the eyes. For other angels, my corruption hurts their souls. Isaac told me that it's painful for him to look me in the eyes too, but he does it because it's his duty. He was created to follow me and fight beside me, no matter the cost to himself.

"Something's changed in you," I whisper as I stare back at him, and he doesn't even flinch.

"I caught your fury. And when I have the chance, I will destroy the beasts that did this to you."

His rage hits me like a spark to tinder. When I first met him, his anger was directed at *me*, but now, his presence evokes the clash of swords in my ears, the feeling of a muddy battlefield beneath my boots, and the roar of battle, but on that field, Isaac is now standing in front of me like a shield.

I try to breathe. "What are you saying...?"

He kneels at the side of the bed and places his left hand on its edge, palm up.

I gasp when a tendril of light rises from his palm like a glistening ribbon.

"I don't expect you to trust me," he says. "All I ask is that you give me a chance to earn your trust."

When I don't immediately object, he continues. "I was created to be your soldier. My heart and soul were molded in the purest fires of the heavenly realm. Will you accept the loyalty I wish to give you and allow me to stand at your side?"

He quickly adds, "I ask for this chance only for as long as you are willing to give it. You may renounce me, if you ever feel I am not worthy of you."

It's a solemn request, spoken quietly, and my instinct is to reach out immediately and take the light he's offering, but I hesitate.

"Do you understand what I am?" I ask.

He gives me a small smile. "An Avenging Angel with the ferocity of a dragon. You are a *Drago Ashen-Varr*."

A dragon-angel.

My lips twitch. "You just made that up."

His smile becomes a grin. "Do you like it?"

"I do." But my own smile fades. "But it's dangerous at my side. I have more enemies than friends."

"Which is why you need another friend," he replies.

I consider the ribbon of light warily, but not because I'm afraid for my own safety. "If I accept your loyalty, what does that mean for you?"

"It means I'm bound to you until I die, unless you renounce me sooner—"

"No." I immediately lean away from him, unable to accept the weight of responsibility his vow brings with it.

"The way I should have been bound to you when you were born," Isaac continues firmly. "You asked me why I'm doing this, and it's because betrayal cuts deep. I should have realized that the Celestial Ascendant couldn't be trusted when she failed to summon me the moment you were born."

He looks me directly in the eye. "Yes, when she finally did bring you to me, I rejected you. I didn't understand that you were a dragon's child and that your nature was different because of it. I believed what she told me—that your angelic heart had been corrupted. Rejecting you was my failing, not yours."

"You said my desire to kill is my corruption. That an Avenging Angel should be pure above all others. How can you stand with me now?"

His wings curve further inward. "What I failed to consider is that light must balance itself. Dragons are creatures of light magic, just as angels are. Because you carry both dragon and angel power, you carry more light than any other. But to balance that, you must also carry darkness."

While he continues to hold his left palm upward, the bright ribbon of power twining in the air above it, he dares to reach for my uninjured hand. Slipping his palm beneath mine, he wraps my hand in his.

It's an unexpectedly comforting gesture and it takes me by surprise that he would give it—and, more surprisingly, that my instinctive response is to lean in and accept his support.

His eyes shimmer, but he doesn't look away. "I saw your power as corruption. But I should have realized that it's a heavy burden, and I should have been there to help you carry it."

I drag in a ragged breath, overwhelmed by the sensation of a weight lifting from my shoulders. A load that might not be mine to carry alone anymore.

I don't try to fight the burn of tears in my eyes as I reach carefully toward the ribbon of light he's offering—the light of his loyalty. Turning my hand palm up when the ribbon brushes the tip of my pointer finger, I accept the way it twines around my fingertips and flows across my palm.

It shines a little brighter before it settles against my skin and disappears into the surface of my hand. It's a soothing sensation, a lot like the brush of the silver cascade that concealed the entrance to the Avenging Angel's quarters back in the veil.

"Now my strength is yours," Isaac says.

He makes it sound simple, and it's the simplicity of his vow that means so much to me. It means having someone to guard my back and fight beside me without fear of betrayal. When the Dread dragons offered me their help—when Felix fought Sentinels for me, and Beatrix stood between me and a room full of Scorn dragons, and when Sophia sheltered me from the rain —I struggled to accept their friendship. When Callan asked me to take a chance with him, I struggled to believe that I wasn't alone. But all of them brought alive the hope within me that I might not have to walk my path in solitude, and now...

I've embraced that possibility.

Isaac rises to his feet. "I need to get your mother. She didn't want to leave your side, but I promised I would get her as soon as you woke up."

His hand lingers around mine for another moment, waiting for me to release him, which I do, although reluctantly.

"I will also ask for more information about the Dread," he says. "Since their wellbeing is clearly of concern to you."

He folds his wings and turns away, but I call out softly. "Don't hide your scars, Isaac. Wear them boldly because you survived them."

He casts me a crooked smile as he immediately reaches up to remove the hair tie, allowing the white strands to fall around his face. He stretches his neck and rolls his shoulders, as if he's shaking off the remnants of the betrayal from his brothers before he continues to the door.

Pausing there, he reaches out to touch the edge of the shelf on the wall beside the door. It's where the pile of my golden feathers rests. "It's lucky that you exited the oblivion near the entrance to the veil, but even so, I wouldn't have seen you floating in the river if not for your golden feathers."

He brushes the surface of the nearest ones and I'm grateful when they don't shrink from his touch.

"Three feathers flew over to me and guided me to your location." A small smile grows on his face. "The other feathers kept the Book of Angelic Monsters dry. Dragon's gold is not inherently good or bad, but the loyalty it shows you can't be dismissed."

He hovers beside the shelf for a moment before he seems to make a decision. "Asper, you must rest—and I do need to get your mother—but first I would like to bring you the Book of Angelic Monsters because there's something in it that you need to see. Among other things, it might help explain why I've offered you my loyalty."

"Okay," I say cautiously.

When he lifts the book from the shelf, it's clear that the feathers have wrapped around it so tightly, it looks like the cover is made of gold.

When Isaac returns to my side, he says, "After we pulled you from the water, some of these feathers lifted off the book and it fell open to the back page. That was when I knew, without any doubt, that my path had to change."

He places the book onto the bed beside me, the gravity in his expression making me wary. *What could possibly be in here that would turn this angel's heart?*

I run my left hand across the book's cover. The golden feathers rise off it at my touch, each one slowly unfurling and rising into the air before wrapping around a section of my left arm. The gold conforms to my skin, comforting and cooling against my bruises.

Carefully lifting the book's front cover, I read the inscription on the first page:

I, Eva Ashen-Varr, make this record, a true account of my actions. May the light give me strength.

I'm tempted to flip directly to the back of the book—where Isaac indicated I should start—but I don't want to read it out of context.

I don't remember all of the entries in the Roden-Darr's account, but Eva's are even more richly illustrated.

Her account seems to follow the same order, starting with a description of her battle with the witch who drained the life force of a human village, then with the wolf who was attacking other supernaturals, followed by her efforts to imprison the nest of vampires.

On my quick reading, Eva is as honest about her struggles as the Roden-Darr's account was, detailing her fight against the darkness she felt when she fought another supernatural.

Finally, I reach the entry about Atrox Imperator. My heart sinks. Not because I'm reminded of his strengths, but because of the way her entry deviates from the one I read in the Roden-Darr's version.

She describes Atrox as a possible threat, but it's clear at the time she made this entry that he hadn't yet committed any of the crimes listed in the other book. The entry is short and she ends it with a note that she will watch him carefully.

On the next page is a drawing of a woman. It's the first entry I don't recognize because this woman was not included in the Roden-Darr's book.

The drawing is in black ink, so I can't tell the color of her hair or her eyes, but her wings are feathered. Angelic wings. She holds her head high and wears intricate armor on her body and a band across her forehead that is adorned with jewels.

She holds a spear like a Sentinel's, but it's larger.

Beneath her image, Eva's handwriting is ragged...

For too long, I've shut my eyes to true evil. Now I must face a critical truth: An Avenging Angel does not discriminate.

It should not matter what species a creature is. Even an angel is not above justice.

Even an angel who claims purity as a shield.

It's the last entry. Eva didn't make any others. Certainly nothing more about Atrox.

The remainder of the book consists of blank pages.

Returning to the image of the angel, I stare at her picture for a long moment before I ask, "Who is this?"

"The Celestial Ascendant," Isaac answers. "The one who ruled in Eva's time. You can tell by her jeweled halo."

The gravity of his response is unmistakable.

Even when he was against me, his belief in the ability of the Avenging Angel to judge guilt was unwavering.

He looks at me with the same certainty now.

Quietly, I repeat back to him what he told me when I first met him. "An Avenging Angel has the capacity to feel nothing but loathing for the guilty. She can't be swayed by threats or bribes. Or emotion."

He nods. "Or the fact that the guilty person is her leader."

I try to bring moisture to my lips. "This entry was made before Atrox became a threat, which means it must have been before the dragon's light was stolen."

"And yet, even then, Eva Ashen-Varr sensed the evil that had taken root in the ranks of angels," Isaac says.

"She was going after the Celestial Ascendant." I close the book carefully. "But would the Roden-Darr of her time have supported her?"

Isaac gives a heavy exhale. "My own actions prove that the Roden-Darr are not immune to being manipulated by the Celestial Ascendant, and the actions of my brothers show that we are not invulnerable to malice."

I wish I could speak with Eva now and tell her to trust her

instincts. To act before it's too late. It could have been within days of her making this entry that the Celestial Ascendant stole the dragon's light and blamed Eva for Viviana's death, assuring that the dragons would go after Eva. Assuring that Atrox would become the angels' enemy.

Somehow, knowing how Eva felt toward her leader brings me peace.

I went after the Serene Commander, intending to orchestrate her death. I fought a legion of angels. Despite my reasons and my convictions, I harbored doubts about my actions. I believed that my ability to hunt angels stemmed purely from my corrupted heart.

That *I* was the one whose heart was rotten because what sort of monster would hunt angels?

But now I know. It takes a monster to hunt monsters.

CHAPTER EIGHTEEN

$\mathcal{I}$ saac strides back to the door, preparing to leave, but I stop him once more. "Isaac?"

"Yes?"

"You asked me what I need," I say. "Can you tell me if these walls are fireproof?"

I'm conscious that I swallowed Atrox's fire in the forest, and I won't contain it forever. I know how to identify some of the warning signs now, which will help, but I still need a safe place where I won't endanger anyone.

A crease forms in Isaac's forehead and a curious gleam enters his eyes. "Why?"

I keep my explanation to a minimum. "Because I inhaled Atrox's fire and at some point, I'll breathe it out again. I need a safe place to do that."

Other than the brief widening of his eyes, he focuses on my request. "I'll find out if there is such a place."

"And I need you to watch for the warning signs," I add. "You'll taste ash in the air if it's about to happen."

"Then I'll return as quickly as I can to watch over you," he promises. "If I notice signs of fire, I'll move you immediately."

I wish there were a way for him to stay and find out where a fireproof room might be, but he can't be in two places at once, so it's a risk I'll have to take. "Thank you, Isaac."

He gives me a brief nod. "I've broken my promise to your mother for long enough. I'll tell her you're awake."

His gaze lingers on me for another moment before he disappears through the door.

When he's gone, I check myself over as best I can. I'm not surprised to find that it's all bad news. My bruises are blue and aching, although the fresh color indicates I wasn't asleep for long since they haven't progressed to yellow. My right hand, of course, is thickly bandaged from my fingertips to halfway way up my forearm, making it very difficult to use that hand.

And my body generally continues to defy my will.

I try again to fight my way into an upright position, but it's no use. It's only when I allow myself to sink fully back to the bed that I realize Isaac didn't answer my first question. *Where the hell am I?*

I take a fresh look at my surroundings, noting once again the moisture on the surface of the walls. The slightly musty smell in the air and the dampness indicates that this room is underground, like my cell under the Cathedral. But the bricks are neatly put together and appear manufactured. In fact, they look like they may have been constructed by humans.

Rapid footfalls sound beyond my room and the fact that I can't sense who it is from a distance confirms how dull my senses are.

My mother rushes into the room. She's carrying a tray with multiple bowls on it, one of which sloshes dangerously because of her pace.

"Asper!"

The relief in her voice makes my heart squeeze.

As she hurries toward me, the scent of chicken soup and vegetable stew wafts ahead of her, along with her own summer afternoon scent. She's wearing the same worn-out sleeveless T-shirt she did when I first met her at the power station and crinkled jeans. Her appearance is a far cry from the bright armor she used to wear when she was lauded as the strongest warrior angel in the Serene Commander's legion.

Placing the tray of food at my feet, she quickly checks me over.

I don't object to her touch when her fingertips lightly brush my face before descending to my bandaged arm.

Appearing satisfied that I'm okay, she leans back again. "You need to eat. You're dangerously malnourished."

She reaches for a spare pillow at the bottom of the bed and sets about elevating my head before she reaches for the bowl of chicken soup.

I can't deny the hollow in my stomach as I inhale the delicious scent of warm broth when she lifts the spoon to my lips. I also can't hold off my questions, speaking between sips. "Where am I?"

She begins to speak, but in the next moment, there's another set of rapid footfalls nearby.

My tension returns when I inhale the scent of a forest intermingled with darker notes that evoke the sensation of a wolf hunting prey. I wouldn't say that a single mouthful of broth has returned my senses to full strength, but there's no escaping the anger in those footfalls.

Micah Grudge storms into the room. He's the same height and build as his father was—over six feet tall and broad-shouldered. His light-brown hair is scruffy, his cedar-brown eyes are narrowed, and the tension in his jaw is undeniable. So is the scent of lilies, and the grief it conveys, as he strides to the side of my bed.

Less than a week ago, he lost his father.

Before that, he was my enemy.

Now I know we have far more in common than I ever dreamed.

"Tell me where the Dread are hiding," he snarls at me.

My defenses fly back up. "If you think that the Dread had anything to do with your father's death, you're mistaken."

"I *know* they didn't," Micah snaps back. "I also know you have knowledge of their hiding places. If you value your life, you'll tell me where they are."

My mother has stiffened beside me, staring up at Micah, her lips parted and her cheeks pale with sudden outrage.

I also stare up at him for a rage-filled second before I give a harsh laugh. "'Value my life'?" I ask. "You think I'm afraid of *your* anger or what you could do to me?"

He bares his teeth and I suppose I must be sharing some of that light Viviana said I carry with me because his pupils shift to jagged slits, reptilian like his father's used to appear. "Think carefully, angel," he says. "And choose wisely."

"I won't reveal where they are," I snap back. "I will never endanger them like that."

My mother's glare is sharp enough to cut through dragon scales, but her voice is remarkably constrained. "Micah. Perhaps if you explain why you're asking."

Micah returns my mother's glower with a more fearsome one of his own before turning it on me. "The Dread and the Scorn have gone to war. I need to find Sophia and bring her to safety."

"War?" I jolt hard enough that I would have knocked the soup bowl out of Mom's hands if her reflexes weren't so quick. She whisks the food out of the way, even though I can't sustain my upright position for more than two seconds. "But the Dread and the Scorn are allies!"

Mom shakes her head. "Not anymore. The Scorn believe that Callan deliberately led Sienna Scorn into an ambush with the angels at the power station. They believe Zahra sought an alliance to get Sienna to lower her guard—and that she intended to take over the Scorn as soon as Sienna was dead."

"Fuck," I whisper, my heart sinking at the mess that the scene at the power station has created. "Meanwhile, the Celestial Ascendant believes that the Scorn were responsible for killing the angels there. Sentinels are being sent after the Scorn from tomorrow—" I check myself. "No, wait, how long have I been here?"

"Half a day," my mother replies.

"Then the Sentinels will soon arrive," I say.

Mom reaches for the bowl of soup, eyeing me warily in case I make any further sudden movements. She lifts the liquid to my lips, seeming determined to make me eat.

Micah narrows his eyes, but this time, he appears deep in thought. "The Sentinels will slow the Scorn down, but they won't stop them. The Scorn are trained assassins and know how to move in the shadows, *and* they won't hesitate to put human collateral in the way to save themselves."

My thoughts whirl. Beatrix and Felix are trained fighters. So is Callan's sister, Zahra. But Zahra's daughter, Emika, is only five years old and that makes her—and her mother—vulnerable. As for Sophia, she was a quick learner when I was training her, and her water dragon is strong, but she still has a lot to learn.

Solomon's death proved to me that even the strongest dragon can be taken unawares by a bullet from a Scorn assassin's gun.

I take a deep breath and try to calm myself enough to drink the soup my mother is insistently holding to my lips.

I remind myself of how well guarded and shielded Callan's home is. Also that Isaac assured me the Dread were safe. "The Dread are hidden," I say. "And Callan's bodyguards are the toughest humans you could meet. If you can't find them, then the Scorn won't, either."

Micah's mother was a wolf shifter, and that part of him survived, making him an anomaly among dragons. If the Grudge do, indeed, have the Book of Light Magic then that might have something to do with how Micah's wolf survived. It also gives him an acute sense of smell, stronger even than mine, which he used to find me on at least one occasion.

"That would be true, if the Dread weren't trying to find Callan," Micah says.

There's such a storm in his eyes that I pause mid-sip, my heart sinking. "They're searching the city?"

He sighs. "One of them is. The others have stayed hidden."

"Which one?" I ask, fully expecting him to tell me it's Callan's sister, Zahra. She became alpha after Callan renounced his position. She and Callan didn't always agree, but at the end of the day, they would fight for each other's safety.

Micha's growled response surprises me. "Sophia," he says. "Twice, I've tracked her through the city at night, and both times, I've killed a Scorn assassin who was about to take her out. Each time, she slipped away from me before I could get to her. Next time, I might not be there to save her."

"What about Beatrix and Felix?" I ask, worry growing in my heart.

"The Lamonte cousins?" Micah's curled upper lip indicates how much he dislikes them. I don't really blame him, since Beatrix and Felix don't make good first impressions. It's only once they came to trust me a little that they revealed just how fiercely loyal they can be.

"They haven't been seen," Micah responds. "The rumor is the Scorn targeted them first."

I try to catch my breath as fear shoots through me. "Killed?"

"Unknown." Micah looms over me and for the first time, I sense the flicker of darkness around him, the hint of his dragon shadow, and I hear the echo of its roar in his tightly-controlled voice. "I need Sophia here. I need her safe. You will tell me where she is, or so help me—"

"No." I glare up at him. "I won't break my word."

But I won't ignore the danger, not least because the threat of the Scorn is nothing compared to the danger that Atrox and

Dominus pose to the Dread. A worse danger because Atrox already knows all of the Dread clan's hiding places.

I need to get to Sophia and Zahra—and Beatrix and Felix because I refuse to believe that anything has happened to them —and warn them about Atrox as soon as I can.

"I will go to her," I say. "If Sophia agrees to come here, then I'll bring her—"

"I'm coming with you," Micah says.

My mother's voice cuts across us like a whip.

"Stop. Both of you." The corners of her mouth are turned down and her eyes are fiercely bright. "Asper isn't going anywhere."

She turns her gaze on me and the full force of her worry hits me for the first time, as if she's been hiding it since she entered the room. "You were barely alive when we pulled you from the water. Barely breathing. No color in your cheeks. Completely depleted. You can't move from this bed until you're stronger."

She steadfastly raises another spoonful of broth to my mouth and all I can do is stare down at it, the reality of my situation finally sinking in.

I've been hurt before, but not like this.

I can barely lift my head off the pillow and my mother is spoon-feeding me, for fuck's sake.

"Fuck," I whisper.

Micah studies me far more quietly than he did before, and I sense the fury draining from him, revealing the emotion he was concealing beneath it.

Cold-as-ice fear.

"I can't lose another person I care about," he says, his hands lifting and then dropping, as if he doesn't know what to do with himself. "I won't."

On the few occasions that I interacted with Micah before now, he struck me as far more impulsive than his father, more prone to rash decisions, leaping into a fight before thinking, but he's no less protective of the people he cares about.

I give a tired sigh. "If I tell you where Sophia is, what do you think is going to happen when you get there?" I ask him. "The last time she saw you, your father absconded with me, Callan came after me, and then we both disappeared. As far as she's concerned, you're as much her enemy as the Scorn. If she attacks you out of fear, then best case, *you* get hurt. Worst case, she does. In neither of those scenarios will you succeed in protecting her."

I watch his expressions change—denial at first, and then frustration.

"The only way you're getting past the bodyguards and into her home without anyone getting hurt is if I'm with you," I say before I quickly accept the next spoonful of soup. "I'm sorry I can't take you there right away. Please believe me when I say I would give anything to be strong enough to leave this bed already."

My mother watches our interaction, and when Micah remains silent, she says, "Doing nothing is hard."

I glance at her since it's like listening to Callan.

"You have to trust that Sophia is strong enough to protect herself," she says. She follows that with a stern look at Micah. "And since Asper isn't going anywhere, this gives us the chance to talk about the past, clear up misunderstandings, and focus on the problems that we're now facing."

Micah's expression remains obstinate for all of two seconds before he capitulates. Blowing out a breath, as if he can expel his fears, he gives Mom a nod. "Okay."

Mom returns her attention to me, and her voice is softer. "To answer your initial question, Asper, in case you haven't already guessed, you're with the Grudge clan."

I guess I'm not surprised that she would bring me here, since she was friends with Solomon Grudge. I suspect—but don't know for sure—that she was hiding with the Grudge clan for years after she falsified her death. It *does* surprise me, though, that Micah allowed her to bring me here.

The last time I saw him, he was driving the vehicle that took me to the old power station, where Solomon intended to do me the mercy of allowing me to meet my mother before he killed me.

He made it clear that my mother knew nothing of his intentions to end me, and I wonder now if Micah told her the truth. *Possibly not.*

"Why did you allow this?" I ask him.

Micah's jaw clenches and I taste his renewed anger on my tongue.

Hot coals.

The kind of hatred I was expecting from Isaac.

The white-haired angel chooses this moment to re-enter the room. He's carrying two chairs and gives me a quick, reassuring nod, which I hope means he's located a safe place for me to breathe fire.

The friction between him and Micah is as strong as it is between Micah and me, but neither man says anything to the other.

Isaac seems to quickly take note of my mother's position perched on the edge of the bed before he places one of the chairs—which I suspect he intended for my mother—beside Micah instead.

He positions the other chair between the end of my bed and the left-hand wall and quietly sits on it. I notice for the first time that he isn't wearing his gold watch—the innocuous shape his weapon can take. I wasn't awake for the aftermath of the slaughter at the power station, but I suspect that Zadkiel would have taken Isaac's spear with him.

Ignoring the offered chair, Micah narrows his eyes at all three of us. Wherever I am right now, the Grudge have successfully used this location to hide from angels and other supernaturals for decades.

Now, there are three angels within it.

I don't have to imagine how Micah feels about it, since the heat of his anger says it all.

He repeats my question back to me. "Why did I allow it?" he asks. "In the last few days, I've learned that my grandfather's blood runs through your veins. You're my father's sister. My aunt. You're a fucking Grudge dragon."

His jaw clenches but his speech becomes quieter. "Despite the fact that you hunted your own people, you're the only blood relative I have left. You're family."

CHAPTER NINETEEN

*M*y emotions are in turmoil.

Ever since Magnus Grim told me I'm the Grudge King's daughter, I've been fighting for my survival. I haven't had the chance to think about what that means for the Grudge clan. Or how I can ever reconcile the fact that I'm one of them with the way I hunted them.

While my mother reaches for the next bowl of food, I give a soft exhalation into the silence. "I'm not sure that I can ever atone for the past, but I want peace between us, Micah. Your father—my brother—believed that the future of the Grudge clan depends on you. I do, too."

I take a deep breath. "Which is why I want to warn you. There's a far worse danger coming for this clan than any Scorn assassin."

Micah's brow furrows. "What are you talking about?"

There isn't a good place to start, so I jump right in. "I'm talking about the Book of Light Magic and a dragon named Atrox Imperator."

I wasn't sure how much Micah might know about Atrox or the dragons' history, but the way the blood drains from his face tells me he knows enough.

He flashes a quick, worried glance at my mother.

She slowly places the spoon back in the stew, and Isaac rises out of his chair, stepping toward us both. He extends his wings and curves them slightly outward as if he would wrap us both up and protect us that way.

Melisma's blue eyes are wide, and her voice is a worried whisper. "Are you telling us that Callan's dragon has taken control?"

"You knew?" I can't keep the accusation from my voice. "You knew who Callan's dragon was."

"I tried to warn you," she says quickly. "At the power station."

I sigh as I recall the way she'd urgently told me to get as far away from Callan as I could. "But how?" I ask. "How did you know?"

She grimaces. "Magnus Grim warned Solomon, and Solomon warned me and Micah. It was after Solomon met Callan for the first time at the Cathedral. Callan's dragon shadow was fully visible, and Magnus Grim recognized Atrox."

I could never forget that night at the Cathedral. I lured Solomon into the angels' stronghold with the intention of killing both him and the Serene Commander. I thought I could end the war between angels and dragons, but I had no idea how deep the rivers of war ran.

I remember the way Solomon glared at Callan and then, for the briefest moment, Solomon's dragon shadow flickered darkly around his form. It was the first time I sensed Magnus Grim's immense power. A beast that could rival Callan's.

I also recall the way Callan's dragon shadow—Atrox—lurched forward, its teeth bared, as if it had been waiting in anticipation for Solomon's dragon to emerge.

Fuck. The hatred between them was right in front of me back then. I just didn't know what it meant.

But my attention is now on Isaac since he didn't seem surprised by the news about Atrox, either—despite the fact that the Roden-Darr believed Atrox was securely imprisoned in the veil. "And you, Isaac: How did you know?"

"I didn't," he says. "Not until your mother told me after she saved me. When I first met you at the park, I knew the damage any fire dragon could cause, and for that reason, I wanted to stop you from joining with Callan, but I never suspected that his dragon was the beast I thought we'd imprisoned. I didn't believe Melisma at first. After all, who had we imprisoned in the veil all these years if not Atrox himself?"

Isaac looks to me, as if he's still baffled, and I'm not surprised. None of the Roden-Darr knew about Atrox's brother. Neither did the last Avenging Angel. Chances are that Magnus Grim didn't, either. The dragon brothers had hidden their secret incredibly well during their lifetimes and used it to their advantage.

"The fire dragon imprisoned in the veil is Atrox's twin brother, Dominus Audax," I say.

My mother is sickly pale. "There are two of them?" She's suddenly shaking so hard that she has to put down the bowl of stew. "When Isaac told me Atrox was imprisoned in the veil, I was sure that his predecessors had simply made a mistake and caught a lesser fire dragon. Maybe they didn't want to admit it because it had been a failure on their part. But if what you're saying is true and there's another dragon of Atrox's strength... This is very bad news."

I stop myself from mentioning that, of the two brothers, Dominus is actually the more volatile one. My mother is in enough shock as it is.

"I thought I had all the pieces of the puzzle," she murmurs. "But it seems I didn't."

Isaac is nodding. "I also have pieces, not the whole picture."

Micah prowls toward me in a way that reminds me so much of his father. Right down to the forest scent. I don't know who Micah's dragon is, but that's a concern I'll have to put aside for now.

He stops right beside the bed, inches from Isaac's wing. "I only know what Magnus Grim could tell me, and while that seemed like a lot, it's clear there were things he didn't know, either."

At Micah's declaration, my mother turns to me with a hopeful look. "Then maybe, between us, we can put everything together so we have the knowledge we need to overcome this threat."

With renewed determination, she picks up the bowl of stew. "Asper, will you start by telling us what happened after you were taken from the power station?"

I hesitate as they wait for me to speak.

Too much happened.

Too much to talk freely about. The reality is that I barely know these people. I don't know what happened to my mother in the past, how she met my father, and why she left me in the care of the Serene Commander.

I've accepted Isaac's loyalty, but it hasn't yet been tested and I can't trust that his ties to the Roden-Darr and their ways won't cloud his judgement at some point.

And as for Micah Grudge, he's hardly my friend. He and his clan tried to kill me. I killed them. There's too much history there for us to be easy allies.

But...

The secrets of the past have been the poison of my life.

Secrets prevented me from finding out who I am and what I'm capable of.

I can't keep perpetuating the same secrecy now. It's time for all the happenings of the past to come to light, even the ugly things that will hurt to speak about.

So I start from the moment that Isaac used his soul light to subdue me at the power station, and I tell them everything that happened in the veil after the Roden-Darr carried me and Callan away in their net.

My mother listens intently, feeding me at just the right

moments when she seems to sense that I need a distraction to bring my emotions back under control.

Micah finally sits in his chair, a myriad of expressions passing across his face as he reacts to my descriptions of Atrox and Dominus, their strength, and characteristics.

When I describe the appearance of my dragon—Atrox's mate, Viviana—and recount what Viviana said about the dragon's 'light' and her belief that I somehow absorbed some of it, my mother becomes particularly still, while Micah leans in, seeming to absorb every word I speak.

Finally, I relay to them that Atrox and Dominus believe the Grudge have the Book of Light Magic and they will hunt the Grudge to find it.

When I finish, my mother, Isaac, and Micah are all quiet.

I swallow the last mouthful of stew and wait for one of them to break the silence.

Micah is the first to speak. I expect him to tell me how he plans to protect his clan, but it seems he's taking my mother's wish for knowledge seriously.

"Magnus Grim told me about all of the dragons he knew in his time," he says. "*Viviana Incendia* was the last dragon to guard the mythical dragon's 'light.' That is, until she was murdered and the light was stolen and hidden from us. As far as Magnus Grim knew, Eva Ashen-Varr, the Avenging Angel, was responsible for Viviana's death and for taking the light. But I guess that wasn't true."

Micah folds his arms across his chest. "The way Magnus explained it, when the light was hidden from us, it was like the sun was taken away and our oxygen was limited."

I nod, since Viviana described it in a similar way.

"What I don't understand is how Solomon and Magnus lived symbiotically without Magnus destroying Solomon like Atrox tried to destroy Callan," I say. "And how do you control your dragon shadow when other dragons can't?"

"It's all about communication," Micah says. "Think of it like a soundproof barrier between a dragon shifter and their beast. We can't communicate through it, no matter how hard we try. But if you find a way to take that barrier down, then conversation can flow freely between them, and so can power.

"My father taught me how to communicate with my dragon and to share his power. That's how I control his shadow," Micah says. "My dragon can resist the pull of moonlight by connecting with my mind. And, in return, I can—in theory, at least—harness all of the aspects of his physical strength through my connection with his mind."

Micah adjusts his position in his seat a little. "I'm still working on that. Dad could choose to shift different parts of his body, but I can still only call my wings and scales both at once."

"But how did Solomon learn to communicate with Magnus Grim in the first place?" I ask. "Were they just unique in that way?"

Micah shakes his head emphatically. "My father was only ten years old when Magnus first appeared, and his experience was like every other dragon shifters'. Magnus was able to speak with him for a few brief seconds before the barrier rose between them."

Micah's eyes gleam. "But Magnus... Fuck, he was smart... He was ready with his message, and he used those seconds wisely. He told my father two things—one was where to find the Book of Light Magic, and the other was that my father must not tell another soul about its location.

"Dad had to wait another twelve years before he was strong enough to travel into the forests located to the west of Portland, where a territorial war raged between witches. He was captured but managed to escape. He found the book right where Magnus said it was hidden: in the heart of a tree at the edge of a deep ravine. It was when he was traveling back through Portland that he met my mother and brought her back with him. She was a member of the Western Lowland pack—one of the two strongest packs in that city."

Micah stops speaking. He's lost both of his parents and the scent of lilies and grief only increases, but he squares his shoulders and continues.

"Until my father read the book, his relationship with Magnus Grim was as disjointed as every other dragon shifter's connection with their dragon. The book showed him how to communicate with Magnus, and also where to find the light."

"Which is why Atrox wants it." I've finished my food and my stomach feels full for the first time in days, but there's a hollow feeling now in my chest.

"So we come back to the dragon's light," I say. "Do you know what it actually is?"

My question is for Micah, but my mother's hand suddenly twitches where it's resting on mine.

She was quiet during Micah's account of his father's journey, but I consider her carefully now. "Mom?"

"I know what the light is," she says. "I've seen it."

CHAPTER TWENTY

I wait for my mother to continue, but she's quiet.

"No more secrets," I murmur. "We need the answers you can give."

Her hand tightens around mine and when she finally speaks, her voice is bitter. "It's difficult to speak of betrayal. But more so when you're a pawn in its game."

"What happened?" I ask softly.

Her shoulders hunch. "I was once the Serene Commander of the Philadelphia Order."

I startle a little at this news, but it matches Melisma's reputation and why the new Serene Commander thinks so highly of her.

"Two years before you were born, the Celestial Ascendant—the current one—came to me and asked for my help," Mom continues. "She said that the war between angels and dragons had gone on for long enough and she wanted me to help build peace between our species. It was a great honor to be singled out like that."

Mom gives me a rueful smile. "Your father, Edmund Grudge, was a cautious man. It took months for me to find him. Longer for him to trust me. Eventually, he opened his home to me, and I saw how close-knit his clan was. I witnessed the faith that they had in each other, the way they worked together as a community, and I fell in love with how much they cared for each other. It was a kind of faith and love that should exist between angels, but we've lost it somehow..."

Isaac is nodding quietly, as if he agrees.

Mom shakes her head with a sigh. "I also witnessed the Grudge clan's pain. Their power was deteriorating, and several members of their clan had already chosen to exile themselves because they had become a danger to their families."

"They chose to leave their clan?" I ask.

Melisma nods. "Just as other Grudge dragons have chosen to do since then, until there are only a handful left."

"And my father?"

"He'd separated from Solomon's mother years before. I never dreamed I could love anyone the way I fell in love with him." She bites her lip with a smile, but it quickly fades. "I wanted to help him and his people, and I believed that's what the Celestial Ascendant had sent me to do, so I told her what I'd learned and sought her counsel. I was naïve to believe she had the dragons' wellbeing in mind.

"On the day I found out I was pregnant, she mounted an attack on the Grudge. I managed to warn Edmund in time for his clan to go underground. When the Celestial Ascendant and her Sentinels arrived at his home, he and his clan were already gone. She was furious."

My mother falls silent, her gaze far away, and I sense both sadness and remembered relief, followed by pain. "She punished me by confining me in one of her own personal pockets of the veil—a place where nobody would find me. She said we would wait to see if my baby was a dragon or an angel. Some days, when she was particularly spiteful, she would tell me she hoped it was a dragon baby because then I wouldn't survive the birth."

Melisma lifts her chin, as if in remembered defiance. "I was only two months into the pregnancy when my stomach started glowing like there was a little sun growing within me."

She gives me a smile and I can only listen as she continues. "I was sure you were an angel. Either way, it was clear you were no ordinary child. You should have seen the Celestial Ascendant's face when she sensed your power and realized you were the long-awaited Avenging Angel."

My mother gives a sudden but gentle laugh. "Oh, but how I struggled to get any sleep with such a bright light radiating from my body all through the day and night."

I hold my breath as I listen to the story of how I came to be, sensing my mother's shifting emotions from sparks of joy to moments of pain and finally to bitter betrayal.

"When you were born, she took you from me," Melisma says. "She told me she would keep you surrounded by pure light until she could be certain that any dragon within you had perished."

The corners of my mother's mouth turn down. "She told me I'd never see you again and she made me a hateful promise... That you would be raised to hunt and imprison your own kind." Melisma takes a deep breath. "And then she imprisoned *me*. For seven long years."

My lips part with surprise. "Seven years..."

"Apparently, she told my legion that she'd sent me on a special mission. By the time she released me, your father had died and things had gone terribly wrong for you. You were under the care of the new Serene Commander—a former Sentinel—and you were being kept isolated from other angels.

"The Celestial Ascendant warned me never to speak with you. She reminded me that she knew who your father was. She made it clear that you were now an outcast, labeled as corrupted, and your existence was barely tolerated. All she had to do was let it slip that you had dragon heritage, and she would doom you to the deadly cut of a vigilante Sentinel's spear in your sleep."

Melisma stares down at our now-clasped hands, falling silent for a long moment.

"You didn't try to defy her?" I ask quietly, even though I'm certain I already know the answer to my question, since I don't remember a single conversation with my mother. Just seeing her from afar.

She raises her eyes to mine. "I did what I thought would protect you: I stayed away. When the Serene Commander sent me out to hunt dragons, I looked for Solomon instead. It took me years to track him down, and even then, he was the one who found me. But by then, he was a different man than when I knew him."

Tears shimmer in her eyes as she casts a long glance at Micah. "He'd lost everyone but Micah. His family had succumbed to their beasts. His wolf mate had died giving birth. He said he'd failed to save any of them."

She returns her attention to me. "I tried to tell him about you, but he refused to believe me. He said that if you were a dragon baby, then I would have died like all the other non-dragon mothers. He didn't believe that it was different with you because your angelic power was stronger than your dragon." Her shoulders hunch. "There was too much pain in him..."

I close my eyes as I remember the look on Solomon's face when he pinned me against the wall of the Cathedral after I'd stolen his gold.

He murmured: *I didn't believe her. But now, I think she was telling the truth.*

My mother takes a deep, shaky breath and manages to continue. "Eventually, I couldn't keep up the façade at the Cathedral anymore. I needed to get out, so I asked Solomon to help me disappear."

"You turned your back on me," I say, knowing my speech carries a deep accusation, but I need to speak the truth. "You left me in a cage."

She takes a quick, sharp breath. "On the night I left, I went to get you and take you with me, but you weren't there."

"You came for me?" My eyebrows rise in surprise, but then my brow furrows. "I was always in my cell. It was only after you 'died' that the Serene Commander started sending me out."

She shakes her head. "Your cell was empty that night."

My heart is sinking as I recall the only time I left my cage without permission. "Was it when I was fourteen?"

"You would have been about that age."

It must have been the night I broke out of the Cathedral and stepped into the outside world for the first time.

My need to hunt had awakened and I couldn't deny its pull.

All I can manage is, "I escaped that night."

"I'm sorry," my mother whispers. "I failed you. Badly."

Tears burn behind my eyes because fate has been against me. It was against me from the moment that Solomon stole me from my crib. Possibly from the moment my parents fell in love.

But I can't change the past and I can't hold on to the anger that could fester at my mother's choices.

I lean forward and press my cheek to hers. If she loved a dragon, then she'll understand this offering of forgiveness.

She accepts the gesture, and we remain like that for a long, quiet moment.

When I draw back, a small spark of awe has entered her eyes. "When Solomon heard that Callan Steele had captured you, he was certain it would be the tipping point in the war between the dragons and angels. We waited to hear who had survived—you or Callan. But then days passed, and there was no news of your death or of his."

She shakes her head, as if this were unbelievable. "For the first time in years, I dared to believe that maybe there was hope after all." She lifts my hand in hers, and presses it to her cheek. "My daughter. A dragon and an angel with the strength to rise above the past and make things right."

"The only way to make things right is to find the dragon's

light," I say, as if it were simple. "But, Mom, you haven't told us what it is."

She pauses again, and I taste an unexpected tang in the air around her. Not lies. Not secrecy.

Fear.

"Mom?"

She speaks at a whisper. "When the Celestial Ascendant forced me into captivity while I was pregnant, she had a choice to make. Her most private chambers were the only place where she could keep me without being discovered. But it was also where she was keeping the dragon's light." Mom's lips move, but only the barest whisper comes out. "Have you ever stood too close to a fire?"

I can honestly say that I have. Every time Callan's flames nearly destroyed me, but I don't have the chance to say so before she raises her eyes to mine.

"I never dreamed that dragon's gold could radiate with so much rage."

My eyebrows rise in surprise. "The light is made of dragon's gold?"

"An orb of gold," she says. "But not like the usual dragon's gold. Not like your feathers or your glaive. It was alive in a way I never imagined gold could be. Its power nearly tore me apart."

My mother trembles as if she were facing the fires of hell itself. "I truly believe that it was only because I was pregnant with you that the orb allowed me to live. If you hadn't been a dragon's child, I have no doubt that the energy in that gold would have burned me alive."

Her blue eyes are luminescent as she raises them to Micah. "Solomon blamed himself for not retrieving the orb, but even with Magnus Grim's power to protect him, I'm not sure he would have survived touching it. By the end of my pregnancy, its power was so fierce that the Celestial Ascendant had to shroud it in a column of pure light to contain it."

Micah's face has fallen, and his shoulders have slumped. "It sounds like the orb is as dangerous now as the Book of Light Magic."

"Tell me about the book," I say, knowing that it's the last piece of information I need to understand what I'm up against.

"Nobody can safely read it," he says. "It nearly killed Dad and since then, it's only gotten worse. Stepping near it is like risking a lightning strike. If you've never been hit with pure light magic, you won't be able to imagine how dangerous that is."

My hand flies to my forehead, where Dominus clipped me with his hammer. The surge of magic had paralyzed me.

Micah continues. "My father had no choice but to wrap the book up in layers of gold and place it in multiple steel boxes, each bigger than the last. Then he sealed it in a separate room in our vault. To open those boxes invites death."

"Then maybe we should let Atrox take it," Isaac suggests. He's remained quiet throughout the conversation, but it's clear he hasn't missed a thing. "Suffer the death it will bring him."

My focus is drawn to my glaive across the room and then back to the feathers wrapped so lovingly around my arm. The feathers don't know rage, but my glaive does. It's made from gold that was filled with anger when I first touched it. It could have turned on me, but instead, it recognized the anger in me. We understood each other, forming a bond because of our shared history and intentions.

The Book of Light Magic isn't made of gold, but the way Micah describes it tells me it's dangerous because it's capable of *feeling*—just as dragon's gold is.

"Atrox might be able to calm it," I say, speaking my fears aloud. "He seeks the book to find the orb. Not for the purpose of peace like Solomon did, but for the purpose of vengeance. He wants to burn the world and recreate the time of dragons. He wants to take his original form and sweep across the sky, burning and hunting and destroying. He wants his mate back.

"He carries enough rage in his heart to match the book's

anger and, I daresay, to match the orb's fury, too. He could bond with them in a way that no other dragon could."

Micah follows my line of sight to my glaive, as if he's remembering the moment it formed in my hand and its blade nearly cut through his father's wing.

With complete certainty, I say, "With the book, and then the orb, Atrox could turn the world to ash."

Micah slowly rises from his chair, and once again, he reminds me of his father. "The Grudge clan has hidden the Book of Light Magic for over twenty years. It's in the safest place it can be."

His chest lifts with his deeply indrawn breath. "We'll stay hidden. Allow the storm to pass over us. The only way Atrox, or his brother, can find us is if they track one of us back here, which means that nobody can leave." He gives me a pointed look. "Or if they do, they can't come back."

"That includes you," I say quietly.

His jaw clenches. "Then I'll have to trust you to look after the Dread."

He sounds stoic and resigned. He's saying all the right words. But the tension around his eyes and the way his heart is pounding, as if he's fighting the urge to break something, betrays how much this responsibility is tearing him up inside.

I'm glad I'm able to sense heartbeats again, but that small happiness is well and truly overshadowed by the fact that my recovery won't be fast.

Staring at my bandaged hand, I speak carefully, trying to subdue the hope I feel. "If I could pull down the barrier between Viviana and me, I could heal my body faster." I raise my eyes to Micah's. "Can you teach me how to speak with her and draw her out?"

He gives it thought before he shakes his head. He sounds genuinely regretful when he says, "I'm sorry. The way we learned to connect with our dragon can only be done mid-shift. There's the smallest moment when the barrier drops. You have to identify that moment and seize it. But unless you can shift some part of your body to take on dragon characteristics—wings or skin—then this method won't work for you."

I knew it was a long shot. Viviana herself said it would take a massive surge of light energy to bring her out again.

I try to shake off my disappointment. "I understand."

My mother has remained tense beside me, bringing us back to the problem at hand. "While the Grudge are keeping the book safe, what of the storm that's already raging over this city?"

She looks at each of us in turn. "The Scorn hunt the Dread. The Sentinels hunt the Scorn. And all the while, Atrox and Dominus will tear apart anyone who gets in their way—"

"No," I say softly. "I won't let them."

Raising my eyes to my mother, I say, "I was born to hunt. So I'll hunt."

I'll hunt the man I love.

CHAPTER TWENTY-ONE

ears glisten in my mother's eyes. "You can't fight the dragon brothers alone."

I look to Isaac. "I won't be alone."

Before Mom can point out that two angels hardly makes an army, Micah clears his throat.

"Okay, then we have a place to start," he says. "We'll protect the book while Asper hunts the hunters."

I nod just as I pick up the sound of footfalls outside the room. A moment later, the older dragon shifter, Leon, looms in the doorway. His wavy, brown hair is speckled with gray, his skin is light brown, and his voice always reminds me of a rusty engine. His scent is filled with spices and the dryness of a desert.

He has a calm presence, but I'm not fooled. He's as dangerous as every other Grudge dragon.

He quickly takes in the room before he addresses Micah. "You need to get out there. The clan's... *unsettled.*"

The way he says 'unsettled' sounds like an understatement.

Micah spins back to us. "Melisma, my clan is accustomed to your presence here. They trust you, but the same can't be said for Asper or Isaac." His next direction is for me. "Don't stray from this room without permission or they'll take it as an act of aggression." He follows that up with a glare at Isaac. "And you, no more wandering around."

Isaac shrugs, his expression unreadable. "I needed chairs."

I can't help but smile at the way that Micah seems to have taken to the role of alpha, even though he once expressed doubts about his clan's willingness to follow him. They may be unsettled right now but I have no doubt Micah will pull them into line.

He's already at the door before I call out to him. "Micah?"

"What?"

"Your clan needs you to lead them, so fucking lead them."

His scowl clears and a smile grows on his face that reminds me of a wolf before it takes the first bite of its prey. "You sound just like Dad."

Micah's gone before I can murmur. "Yeah, well, he was my brother."

I listen to Micah's and Leon's footfalls, counting their steps to judge the distance along the corridor outside my room before a door closes and then all sound stops.

"So I *am* a prisoner," I say, noting the way Isaac is already closely watching the door.

"Rest," my mother says to me, a firm command before her expression softens. "I know this doesn't feel like a welcoming place, but I'm glad you're here. I'm grateful that we could finally talk."

She clears her throat, wiping at her eyes as she rises off the bed. "I'll bring you a fresh change of clothes and more food soon. In the meantime, I need to help Micah. The Grudge don't do things democratically. Ever since Edmund died, they've lived harsh lives and rely on violence too often to solve their issues."

At that, Isaac drags his chair across the room to position it between the door and my bed, taking his seat like he's guarding me.

"Okay, then," I murmur.

Mom presses my shoulder in what I'm sure is intended to be a comforting gesture before she hurries from the room, her footfalls heading in the same direction as Micah's.

I listen as she opens the door I've discerned is at the end of the corridor, then it closes and there's silence again.

"You can't stay here any longer than absolutely necessary," Isaac says, keeping his voice low as he speaks aloud my own thoughts. "Not when the enemy's claws are already scraping at your door."

He could be referring to the Grudge or to Atrox and Dominus. Either way, I agree with him.

"Did you find me a fireproof room?" I ask him.

"This room could withstand fire," he says, indicating the room I'm in, "but not for an extended time." His eyes suddenly gleam and I'm not sure why he's looking at me so intently. "The safest place to contain a fire is the vault."

The vault...

I consider him carefully. "You mean the vault where the Book of Light Magic is hidden."

He nods.

"There's no better room to withstand a firestorm?" I ask.

He shakes his head in a slow, side-to-side motion.

"How do you know this? Surely, they keep the vault locked."

"I know because I looked inside. And yes, they keep the far side of the vault locked—that's presumably where the book is contained—but not the main compartment. There's no reason to keep the front of the vault locked because there's nothing in there. Maybe they once had gold and jewels, but not anymore. You won't destroy anything if you breathe fire there."

I speak his name carefully. "Isaac?"

"Yes, Asper?"

I pause because I suspect what he's not saying: that I should try to read the book.

Viviana said that I might have a chance at surviving the book's volatile nature because some of the dragon's light exists within me. To read the Book of Light Magic is to know where the orb is hidden. To reach the orb first would turn the tide.

But how to survive the book's rage, let alone the orb's power?

If the book and the egg are somehow connected, then my angelic nature could add fuel to the orb's rage.

"*Your* soul light is a powerful, calming force," I say to Isaac, choosing my speech carefully. "Do you think you could use it to keep the Book of Light Magic calm enough for me to read it?"

"Maybe." He's quiet for a long moment. "You spoke of Atrox's rage—how he might use it to constrain the book—but you failed to mention your own."

It's my turn to become quiet.

When I first encountered Dominus, he knew who and what I was. I asked him how he knew. He told me what Zadkiel had told him. That looking into my eyes was like standing in the heat of flames and being burned alive; all Zadkiel felt was a terrible need to tear the world down.

That's how I'd felt most of my life.

I considered anger to be my greatest sin, but also my greatest strength, and I embraced it. I used it to fuel my actions and shield myself from the consequences of my choices.

Since I met Callan, I've experienced more than anger. I've felt hope. Real hope. And friendship. And the power of *calm*. I shook off the cage around my heart and I defied the possibility that I might never feel love.

"I still have rage," I say. "But I've also experienced love."

Maybe, if Callan hadn't spoken to me in the forest, I would have nothing left but anger now. But even the feathers clinging lightly to my arm remind me of the way he cared about me.

"I have too much love in my heart to feel the kind of rage I believe would be necessary to subdue the book," I say, which I imagine would require a burning, mindless anger.

"Then maybe Atrox needs some love in his life," Isaac replies. "To render him vulnerable to the dangers of reading the book."

No matter how much I scrutinize Isaac's features, I can't tell if he's joking or serious. Even if his suggestion is serious, it would be impossible to bring about.

Atrox loved Viviana, and I'm not her.

"Love can only burn to ash on the surface of a hot coal," I say.

Isaac makes a humming sound as if he agrees before he leans back in his chair.

I sink into my pillow and try to rest.

An hour later, my mother returns with food and fresh clothing just as she promised. She helps me change and I welcome the jeans and shirt she offers me, even if they're both a little threadbare. She also helps me brush my teeth and my hair, although some knots are too tricky to untangle, and she helps me to use the bathroom. After that, I'm able to sit up on my own and feed myself, so that's a good sign.

She tells me that the unrest within the Grudge is settling down, but she describes it as being like a simmering pot that could just as easily boil over.

She kisses me on the forehead before she dims the light. Her gesture takes me by surprise, but I accept it, knowing that all too soon, I'll be strong enough to leave and I don't know how long it will be before I see her again.

I try to sleep, but the decision about reading the book rests heavily on me. Just by removing it from its protective casings, I could risk death. Worse, I might endanger the Grudge clan. Especially if I can't put the book safely back into its boxes again.

But if I succeed, then I'll have the knowledge I need to find the orb...

Which poses its own danger.

With a sigh, I remind myself that there's nothing I can do about that yet, and I try to get some sleep.

~

I wake to Isaac's hand on my shoulder.

His white hair frames his beautiful face in the dim light, and his voice is low but urgent. "Asper?"

I try to catch my breath, tasting heat on my tongue and exhaling the scent of burning ash.

The fire tastes different this time. Not so much like a field burning beneath a fiery sun, as like the heat of the sun itself. It's slower somehow. Less like a wildfire and more like a hot ember.

"Do you wish to stay here or go to the vault?" Isaac asks.

"How far is it?" I manage.

"It will take me two minutes to carry you there."

I close my eyes and press my uninjured hand to my chest. My heart rate is still steady. My breathing is calm. The heat at the back of my throat is mild. A slow burn. It's unexpected but should give me time to get to the vault before the full force hits me.

"I can make it."

Isaac immediately disconnects the intravenous line and scoops me up into his arms. I send a quick mental command to my glaive, armband, and feathers to stay here, and I sense my glaive's anxiety, but I'm grateful when it obeys me.

Isaac's heart beats steadily in my ears and his arms are strong around me. I should be focusing on the fire that's heating my throat, but instead, I study the shape of his jaw as he moves me across the room.

He was created to serve me and, although he once vowed to imprison me, he's now carrying me when I can't carry myself.

A month ago, I never would have accepted this gesture.

I would have crawled to the vault if I had to, just to prove I didn't need anyone's help.

Now, I allow my head to rest against Isaac's shoulder and find myself relaxing into his hold with a trust I never imagined I'd feel. My mother may smell like a warm summer afternoon, but Isaac reminds me of fall, when the leaves are turning to burnished amber. It feels like loss, but with the promise that new life will spring up again.

Within seconds, we've left the room and I can finally see what's outside it: a corridor made of motley bricks with a gently arched ceiling. A metal gate sits ahead of us, much like a cage door, while behind us, I glimpse the wooden door that I heard Micah and my mother step through earlier.

Isaac turns his back to push open the gate and proceeds through another corridor to the right. "Hold on. It's uneven ahead," he murmurs before he descends down a set of bumpy stone steps that let out to an atrium with multiple arched corridors leading off it.

He takes the corridor to the right, quickly striding along it until we reach another set of stairs, at the bottom of which is another atrium. This one has a single doorway on the other side.

"How did you find this place?" I ask, heat shimmering around my face when I speak.

He doesn't shrink away from the near-flames. He sounds a little sheepish when he replies. "When your mother brought me here, I was unconscious for three days. When I awoke, I was told to stay in my room. Just like you were." The corners of his mouth hitch up. "Of course I didn't."

"So you already knew about the vault before I asked you to find a fireproof room?"

He smiles down at me as he strides through the doorway into the vault, which is open, just like he said it would be. The walls appear to be lined with steel, while a solid, metal door—this one presumably locked—is situated in the opposite wall.

A table, also metal, rests in the middle of the room and there are several steel shelves on the walls.

All of them are empty.

Callan told me that the Grudge never owned a lot of gold. When Solomon first tried to kill me, he and his clan members tried to use golden bands against me, along with a web-like clip that was intended to force my wings to close. The web became my armband, and one of the bands became my glaive. I subdued the other bands, and it appears the Grudge didn't bring them back here. Or, if they did bring them back, they didn't put them in the vault.

Isaac props me on the edge of the table, and I'm very happy to discover that I have no trouble staying upright.

On the downside, the heat in my throat is increasing.

"You can't stay," I rasp, tiny wisps of flame leaving my lips. "You won't survive my fire."

"I'll be right outside." He hurries to the door and heaves it closed.

The light from the lamps outside the vault is blocked off and then I'm alone in the dark.

I press my hand to my heart again, expecting to find it racing. Talking with Isaac was a distraction, but I need to prepare myself mentally and emotionally for the oncoming fire.

I inhale. Exhale.

My forehead creases in confusion.

I open my eyes to watch the glowing ribbon of flame forming in the dark in front of me.

It's a gentle plume that narrows when I purse my lips.

The other times I've exhaled the flames, they've screamed out of me, but this fire is remarkably constrained. More so than ever before.

Breathing across my fingers, I swill my hand through the air, swishing the little flames back and forth and feeling the warmth on my skin.

It's even more unnerving because it was *Atrox's* fire I swallowed, and I thought it would inevitably tear me apart, but if anything... the flames are decreasing in strength.

They feel... suppressed somehow...

On my next exhale, they've lost their amber hue and are mere shimmers of heat in the air, leaving me in near-complete darkness.

My thoughts churn as I wonder if Viviana's appearance has something to do with it. I can't sense her, hear her, or communicate with her, but maybe something changed within me when Atrox drew her out so that I can... somehow... control these flames now.

To test my theory, I take a deep breath and, instead of trying to constrain the fire, I blow out an exhale as hard as I can to see if the flame's intensity increases.

My eyes widen when not even a whisp of fire escapes, but mid-exhale, a sharp pain strikes through my chest and my heart squeezes as if it's caught in a clamp.

I suddenly find myself gasping for air. Trying to finish exhaling. Trying to inhale.

Desperate to breathe at all.

Can't... breathe!

I slide off the table onto the stone floor, landing on my knees in the darkness, registering how cold the floor is but unable to gasp with surprise.

My head spins and all I can think is that I need to get to the door. If I'm not going to release a firestorm, then I need Isaac's help.

Sweat breaks out across my entire body as I make myself move, making me want to rip off my clothing, which is suddenly clinging to my damp skin.

Now my head fills with heat and smoke, but it's as if it's trapped within me, unable to release, and the pressure is unbearable.

Down on my hands and knees, I crawl toward the door, sweat dripping into my eyes and making my vision blurry until I look up, register that the door handle is different, and realize...

Wrong door!

I've reached the other side of the vault, not the entrance I was aiming for. I press my palm against the steel surface, trying to turn myself around, but the moment I touch the door, a shock runs through me.

Oh... hell...

The Grudge might have thought they could wrap the Book of Light Magic up in gold and steel and contain its energy, but the power running through the surface I'm touching is irrepressible.

It's sharp and sudden and it's like it was waiting for a chance to surge.

The force around my heart squeezes more tightly with every passing second, and the power swelling beneath my palm won't let go of me.

It's suffocating me on my own fire.

I press my forehead against the door's surface as a shudder runs through me. Within that contact, I feel the rush of wind, the thump of wings in the air, the crackles of flames, and the *crunch* of bones snapping between sharp teeth.

Atrox's golden eyes suddenly burn within my memory, along with his voice roaring at me. *Take the kill, Asper! Know what it is to be the most powerful creature. To dominate all others and hunt without limits!*

Instinctively, my wings release, spreading wide, their tips nearly hitting the walls on either side of me. In the dark, my black feathers shimmer with astonishingly bright gold, an opalescent coating on each one that glistens like...

My eyes widen.

My feathers are gleaming as if their surface is covered in translucent dragon scales. I noticed the change in color after I first experienced Callan's fire. Now, the transition of my feathers is unmistakable.

Viviana said it would take another surge of light magic to draw her out and if ever I needed her strength, it's now when the power from the Book of Light Magic is surging through me and won't let me go. Micah said there's a moment mid-shift when the barrier between a dragon shifter and their dragon falls and they can communicate. It's that moment that I need to find now.

Slowly retracting my wings and desperately trying to ignore the fact that I'm unable to breathe, I close my eyes and count the increments in seconds, sensing the tightness within my back, feeling the shift in my muscles, the sensation of retraction.

I picture Callan placing his palms on Sophia's shoulder blades and helping her withdraw her wings for the first time, and I imagine him pressing on my back now, the strength in his palms helping me to distinguish the sensations within my body.

Just before my wings would retract fully, the clamp around my heart eases.

It's the briefest relief, but it's all I need.

I scream within my mind. *Viviana!*

At the same time, the energy beneath my palm surges and I can't tell if I'm drawing on it or if it's trying to dominate me, but my back arches and a ripple of power explodes through me.

It expands across my chest in bursts of light, building into the form of my dragon shadow. Viviana's amber scales flicker in time with the energy bursts, her enormous body filling the space on either side of me and around my back, her tail whipping to my right while her head descends on my left until she's eye level with me.

Her molten eyes glisten brightly enough to burn me.

"I'm here, Asper," she says, her voice growling in the darkness as she bares her teeth. "Now fight back and *breathe!*"

I thump my bandaged right fist against the door. Once. Then again. *Harder.* Hard enough to dint the surface.

Come on, you fucker, I scream at the book within my mind. *Give me more.*

I accept the next surge of the book's power into my body, and then, finally, I can exhale.

CHAPTER TWENTY-TWO

*B*lue flames pour from my mouth, billowing across the steel in front of me.

I bask in the intense heat, welcoming it as the pressure within my chest and around my heart releases. My flames cut right through the door, the pressure blowing it back into the room behind it, where it careens across the floor.

I push to my feet, taking in the room while the firestorm rages around me with every breath I exhale.

A crimson storm swirls in the middle of the room in front of me, a tornado of power rushing around a golden object that floats midair in the storm's center.

Micah said that the book had been placed inside multiple steel boxes, but it looks like only the golden wrapping remains clinging to it. A quick, alarmed glance at the sides of the room reveals metal shards embedded in the walls, as though the book blew the steel boxes apart.

The furious ruby light now whirling around the book strikes out toward me, hitting the ground mere inches in front of my feet, and I flinch before I realize that my fire is keeping it at bay. It can't seem to strike through the flames.

My fire and the book's energy appear to be two powers that repel each other.

Viviana's shadow remains at my side, her tail reaching the wall to my right as she lowers her head and growls at the book as if it were another beast.

"Did I do this?" I cry to her. "Did my presence somehow release the book?"

She gives a definitive shake of her head. "The storm within this room has been raging for days. I can sense the layers of energy it's been building. The book was breaking free before you arrived. These dragons were foolish to believe they could contain its fury within mere metal."

The gold still clinging to the book's surface is peeling up at the edges like curling paper. Slowly, the molten gold drips from the book to the floor, forming a golden puddle.

I'm even more grateful now that my glaive, armband, and feathers didn't follow me here or they would be destroyed in this heat—a heat that I can withstand because of the fire dragon I've carried within my heart all my life.

All the while, the storm of angry light continues to rage around the book.

How do I step into a storm like this?

A memory of Callan returns to me like a shot through my heart. The shadows deepened across his features as he pointed out that my greatest strength is also the aspect of my nature that worried him the most.

I am single-minded. Focused only on my goal, not on my own safety.

Resolve settles heavily around my heart.

How do I step into this storm?

I just do.

Ripping the bandage off my right hand, I check my palm and fingers to find them perfectly healed now that Viviana's strength is flowing through my body, enabling me to repair my burned skin.

I open and close my fist, satisfied that I have full use of my hand before I extend my wings fully, black and glistening at my sides. They cut right through Viviana's shadow, but she merely shrugs at me, a gleam in her eyes.

I roll my shoulders and remind myself of the strength of my muscles, the speed of my wings, and the heat in my flames.

Taking a deep breath, I cast out of my mind any fear of the book's fury, holding the heat in my lungs and letting it build for a few precious seconds.

Then I leap into the storm.

I release my flames and, at the same time, beat my wings to give me speed, my arms outstretched while my flames billow around my flying form, a layer of protection.

The crimson rage strikes at me, biting energy that wants to rip me apart as I fly into its center.

I collide with the book, my hands closing around its melting gold covering as I hit the floor. Instantly, I sense the pain in the metal, but also the agony in the book's heart.

Off! I cry to the gold before it can burn my hands.

In answer to my cry, the final molten gold splashes away across the floor.

At the same moment, the book lashes out with the full force of its pain, but not at my torso this time. It flashes across my wings and knocks me to the ground. I retract my wings but refuse to let go of the book, desperately inhaling so that I can summon more flames to protect myself.

In that second, the crimson energy curls around my chest and strikes my back and ribs and it's like Dominus's hammer all over again. A surge of light magic shoots through me and I'm sure I'm screaming, but if the book thought I would let go of it, well...

The difference this time is that Viviana's healing energy is flowing through me. As I push up to my knees, I exhale across the book's surface, breathing out as hard as I can.

Blue flames scream across my arms and hands, hitting the

book's surface and billowing through the space around us, driving back the crimson energy.

I can finally see the words on the front of the book: *Light Magic.*

I'm already on my knees, so I push the book down onto the stone, my fire forcing its furious energy to recede again from around me.

My instinct is to hold my breath as I open its pages, but that's the last thing I should do. Continuing to inhale and exhale flames that keep the furious energy at bay, I open the book to its middle, not knowing what to expect.

The paper is thick parchment, its edges ragged, but it doesn't contain words.

An image of a golden dragon leaps from the paper into the air in front of me. Although the image is small, it's clear from the battlefield around the dragon that it's a huge beast. Larger even than Viviana, Atrox, or Magnus Grim in their shadow forms. Fire bursts from its mouth and pours across the battlefield, while people wearing armor run beside and behind it. Two more golden dragons swoop from the sky, pouring flames down onto the opposing army.

At the head of the rival force is a woman with amber hair who rides a gorgeous, white horse that zigzags between the bursting flames. A diamond crown glitters on her head. The army at her back must be supernatural, because bright streams of burning power pour from their hands as they try to cut the dragons down.

I can't tell if the supernaturals opposing the dragons are witches or fae, but it strikes me with sudden clarity that the army fighting beside the dragons is human.

Human!

They fight with only their weapons and the strength of their bodies, and even though I'm outside the battle, I can smell the ash and blood. My ears ache with the shriek of fire, the clash of weapons, and the churning mud.

I tear my eyes from the book for long enough to seek Viviana where she remains at my side, the crimson storm swilling through her shadow form.

"What is this?" I cry above the rushing tornado, pointing to the image.

The history of light magic, she says, speaking directly into my mind, and it's a relief that I can hear her over the din of the book's energy. *You must read on. Quickly now.*

Uncertain if I'll see anything useful in this image, wondering if I should turn the page, my hand presses to the ragged edges of the book just as the woman wearing the diamond crown drives her horse toward the first dragon and leaps from the saddle. She gains air as she lifts a sword above her head and aims it at the dragon's neck.

The image freezes and I jolt as a streak of the book's crimson energy lashes toward me, cutting through the image like a ruby river as it aims for my face.

I exhale just in time, pushing the energy away, although the book's events are now blurred and glitching like an old television.

The image suddenly clears, but it's apparent that I've missed something because the dragon is unharmed, the attacking woman with the crown is now crouched on the ground in front of the beast, and a new figure—a human woman—is leaping forward in the dragon's defense.

The human woman holds a weapon with a double-blade at the top. It has a humble-looking wooden handle, but when she lands and drives the handle into the ground, magic explodes across the space in front of her, knocking the Queen and her army back across the muddy battlefield.

The power in that simple weapon astounds me. It's even stronger than Dominus's hammer.

In the next moment, the book's crimson energy lashes out, this time powerfully enough to flip multiple pages before I can stop it.

New images leap from the page.

A white pedestal sits on a carpet of silver flowers. A golden orb rests on top of the pedestal. It isn't perfectly spherical; rather, its shape is slightly misshapen in the way of a raw nugget of gold.

I lean in closer because it has to be the orb.

A woman stands beside it. She has flowing, black hair, loosely braided, and bright, amber eyes. Her hand rests on the edge of the pedestal, her fingertips mere inches away from touching the orb. I'm not certain that she's Viviana until a male voice says her name, "Viviana," and she breaks into a smile.

I see only his outline as he scoops her up into his arms, and then the image freezes again, energy crackling through it.

Even though the image is fractured, a dragon's roar rises from the book's pages, a shout that's filled with pain, and my heart aches as I allow the pages to flip with the next energy surge.

When I glance at Viviana, her eyes are filled with tears, and I have no doubt it was Atrox's roar of pain I just heard.

My fire has lasted much longer than I thought possible—has extended far beyond the release of the flames I swallowed—which must mean it's now coming from me and my connection with Viviana.

It's *my* fire.

But I'm not sure how much longer I can sustain it, and I'm nowhere close to discovering where the dragon's orb is being kept. All I've seen so far is the past. Not the present.

I plant my palms on the book, willing it to recognize the light that Viviana claims is within me.

"Show me!" I cry, even though I'm not sure if the book can understand me. "Show me where the light is."

The images crackle and blur and suddenly, I'm watching a scene I remember, but it makes me more confused.

I'm looking down from above into Emika's room—the one she was in when the Roden-Darr attacked her home. I recognize the walls decorated with her drawings and with fairy lights before I focus on Emika herself. In the image, she's curled up on her bed, just like she was when I flew into her room. Her hands are pressed to her ears, her eyes are squeezed shut, and the Sentinel with red hair and porcelain skin towers over her. His soul light flows from his palm around her face while he holds a dagger in his other hand.

His voice reaches me through the mire of my confusion.

"Don't be frightened, little dragon," he says to her. "I'm here to save you."

Why is the book showing me this?

Within the image, Emika suddenly opens her eyes. She looks up at me while I look down at her, as if she sees past her room and right into me where I sit in this vault, reading this book.

She fixates on me in a way that didn't happen when I rescued her from the red-haired Sentinel. Her face is framed by her short, straight, black hair, and I'm drawn into her large, angular eyes. Cinnamon-brown like Callan's.

I blink and the frame of the image changes, widening to reveal that she's no longer five years old.

She's at least twenty, if not older, and she holds her head high, her straight hair blowing across her cheeks while golden armor sits across her chest.

The silhouette of a dragon rises up behind her. I can't clearly see its face or body, but its wings extend to either side of her, wider than I imagined any dragon's wings could. They're the color of rubies and they flicker in the wisps of fire smoldering around Emika's torso.

Her chest rises and falls with a deeply indrawn breath, as if she expects it to be her last.

"Hello, angel," she whispers.

CHAPTER TWENTY-THREE

"*E*mika—?"

I lean toward her, but the book's crimson energy explodes across my view, flooding Emika's image and striking at my face and chest so sharply that I'm thrown backward.

I try to hold on to the book, but the blast rips it from my hands. It lands several paces away while I manage to get my feet under myself before I hit the stone floor.

Pain from the burst of power tears my senses apart, but Viviana's shadow engulfs me, her healing energy a buffer against the agony.

Her voice roars inside my mind. *Asper! Get the book!*

I struggle to rise and fight my way through the wash of crimson energy, trying to reach the book, surprised when its power doesn't rip my body to shreds. Even more surprised to realize that the book's power is fading.

My fire is depleted, but so, it seems, is the book's energy.

I slump forward across it as the storm fades so fast that it leaves my ears buzzing. I gasp for breath, trying to slow my heart rate, grateful that the light magic isn't striking at me anymore.

But what does this mean for the book—and what the hell was that last image?

Can the book show the future of light magic as well as its history?

The crimson light vanishes, and silence falls.

I spin to Viviana, all of my questions on the tip of my tongue, only to realize that as the light magic fades, so does Viviana's shadow.

I extend my hand toward her as her silhouette disappears. "Viviana!"

Her voice reaches me from what sounds like a great distance. "Find Emika! Her dragon is…"

I hold my breath as Viviana's voice fades. "What?" I whisper. "Her dragon is… what?"

I wait in the silence, hoping her voice will sound again, but she's gone, and I don't have the answers I need.

What's more, when I lift myself off the book, I find that its pages are dull.

Hurriedly, I flip through the thick parchment, only to see that the pages are blank.

They're *all* blank.

As if it burned itself out.

It's now pristine. Unblemished. A blank slate. Not even charred like the walls of this room.

"No…" I turn more pages, desperately hoping to see something. *Anything!* But the magic is well and truly gone.

I sink back to the floor, pressing the book to my chest, fighting the bone-deep frustration I feel. I survived reading it, but I'm no closer to knowing the location of the dragon's light. I connected with Viviana, only to lose her again. And as for finding out how to destroy Atrox so I can have Callan back…

The book has told me nothing.

Fucking nothing!

A scream works its way up through my chest, tearing my heart apart as it rages past my lips. The agonized sound bounces off the blackened walls. Of all the times I might have wished for fire to pour from my mouth, it's now when my heart is burning up.

I'm done suppressing my grief.

I'm tired of having power that only hurts me.

I would give my strength away in a second if it meant I could live a life with Callan that was free from all this.

Letting out my pain with a deep moan, I drop my head into my hands, the book wedged against my chest, hot tears streaming down my cheeks.

I rock forward with another cry, letting it all out until my throat hurts and my voice is hoarse.

As my scream fades, I register the sound of the door bursting open behind me and the rush of air at my back that can only be caused by beating wings.

The scent of fall leaves reaches me a moment before Isaac comes into view, visible through the cracks between my fingers.

He took a big chance bursting in here, given the threat of fire, although he doesn't touch the ground, and I guess that's because the floor's still sizzling hot and glowing like embers. It's not as if there's a crystalline fire extinguisher here to cool things down like there is at Callan's home.

His voice is quiet. "Asper?"

I lift my head out of my hands. "That's not my name."

He studies my face, following the tear tracks down my cheeks. "What do you wish me to call you?"

"Call me 'Lana,'" I whisper, tears leaking from my eyes. *Lana* is simple, but *Asper* is cruel. "I would like to be insignificant."

"That seems impossible." His voice remains gentle as he looks around the room from the puddle of gold only a few paces away to the burned walls, to the book I'm clutching.

I hold the book up, offering it to him, but he shakes his head. "That isn't for me to take."

"It's blank," I say. "It destroyed itself." I struggle to my feet. "I may have had a hand in that. I don't really know." The book is lighter now that it's blank. Easy enough to hold in my right hand, which drops to my side. "I don't really know anything."

Except maybe that I need to find Emika.

I peer at Isaac where he continues to hover at my side, his wings beating air that makes the stone glow hotter with the influx of oxygen.

I'm suddenly struck with another memory. It was after I killed the red-haired angel in Emika's room. It was the second time I saved her life, and I counted both of those times as the only truly good things I've done in my life.

I asked Isaac why the Sentinel would have tried to kill Emika, and Isaac said...

"Tell me, Isaac," I start carefully. "Why would Emika's dragon have the power to change the world?"

He freezes in the air before his wings continue beating again. I watch him and wait for the taste of sour lemon on my tongue that will tell me if his response is a lie.

"Because of something the Celestial Ascendant said to me before she ordered me to go to Zahra Steele's home."

"The Celestial Ascendant sent you there?"

He nods, a single downward motion. "Sienna Scorn told us the location of Zahra's home, but it was the Celestial Ascendant who sent me."

I narrow my eyes at him.

He continues. "As far as I knew, I was there to determine what kind of dragon had been reborn through Emika Steele and report back to the Celestial Ascendant for further orders. I didn't know that she had ordered one of my brothers to kill her."

"Why would the Celestial Ascendant be worried about Emika's dragon?" I ask. "She's only a child. What could be more of a threat than Callan's fire dragon?"

Isaac presses his lips together, his gray eyes stern. "One of the old ones."

My forehead creases, but the intensity of his expression makes me wary. "'Old,' as in...?"

"A dragon from one of the original bloodlines. A beast from the time before dragons could shift and they still had the power to dictate the laws of destiny."

Callan and I spoke about the old dragons when he first captured me. They'd lived on a mountain range he called 'the Crystal Peaks.' I also knew the stories because the Serene Commander told me. One dragon in each generation was gifted with the knowledge and responsibility of making sure humans and supernaturals respected the old laws. That dragon was the Vanem Dragon. The 'dragon of light.'

I read about the last Vanem Dragon in the books in Callan's library. His fire was fueled by the power of old magic and his wisdom was practically mythical. He was the one who'd tempered the chains that bound Dominus in the veil. The chains I broke.

Isaac continues. "That was in the time when humans fought beside dragons with weapons of light magic that could decimate our world today."

When I first opened the book, it showed me a battle where human warriors had fought with dragons—enormous, golden dragons larger even than Atrox. Those weapons might devastate our world, but so could those dragons.

"What did you ascertain?" I ask Isaac, unable to raise my voice above a whisper. "Is Emika's dragon one of the old ones?"

Isaac takes a deep breath. "As you know, the only way to identify a dragon shifter is to expose them to moonlight and see if a dragon shadow forms. Of course, it has become apparent that the Grudge have learned how to overcome that. But as I understand it, they still need moonlight if they want their dragon shadow to appear."

I nod, since even Magnus Grim hadn't appeared or spoken to me until we were standing within moonlight and Solomon could be said to have had the strongest symbiotic relationship with his dragon of any shifter I've encountered.

"Or they need a surge of light magic," I add, considering the way Dominus's hammer caused both Atrox and Viviana to appear. My forehead creases. "But why are you telling me things I already know?"

"Because the moment I stepped near that child, a dragon shadow began to form." Isaac's eyes burn mine. "Without moonlight or any other obvious influx of light magic."

He gives a shake of his head. "I may not be certain that her dragon is an ancient one, but it isn't like any other dragon."

I'm quiet as I reconsider what the book showed me: the old dragons fighting alongside humans; the orb being protected by Viviana; and then Emika.

Maybe it was trying to tell me something after all.

If the Celestial Ascendant thinks Emika is a threat, she'll try to hurt Emika again. The danger to Emika is even higher now that the Roden-Darr are returning to the city.

I may not have any of the answers I seek, but I know one thing for certain: I won't let anyone hurt that child.

CHAPTER TWENTY-FOUR

I stride back along the dim corridors toward my room with Isaac close on my heels.

I suspect—but don't know for sure—that it's the middle of the night now. It also seems that the vault is located far enough away from wherever the Grudge dragons sleep that none of them were disturbed by the energy storm.

Isaac assures me that the vault door was so thick that he couldn't hear anything through it, and it was only when I was in there so long and he became worried that he took the risk of bursting in.

When we reach my room, I quickly retrieve my glaive, slip on my armband, and call my feathers. I don't have a bag to carry the two books—the Book of Angelic Monsters as well as the Book of Light Magic—so I take the sheet off the bed and form a makeshift sling out of it. I also offer it to my feathers and they cascade in on top of the books. The whole thing is now heavier than I'd like, but I'll have to make do.

I stare forlornly at the slippers my mother brought me, wishing for sturdy boots.

Since Isaac carried me to the vault, I didn't put the slippers on before I left this room before, which is just as well because my shirt is singed, my jeans are burned through at the knees, and I have no doubt the fluffy slippers would have gone up in smoke during the firestorm.

They'll fall right off my feet if I need to fly, but they're all I've got for now.

"I'm ready," I say, and Isaac gives me a nod before he sets off through the door.

His footfalls are incredibly quiet and I'm grateful that he's dimmed his soul light, turning himself into a dark spot within my senses. When I was hunting the Roden-Darr, I could locate them from far away—farther than they could sense me. I came to recognize the tactic they would use where one would make himself bright while others would go dark in an attempt to draw me in and then overwhelm me. It worked once and I swore I'd never be taken in by it again.

I prowl along the corridor behind him until we reach the solid door through which Micah disappeared earlier.

Placing my hand on Isaac's arm, I urge him to wait while I close my eyes and expand my senses. These walls are no more difficult to 'see' through than the soundproof walls in Callan's home and I make out five forms in separate rooms to the far right, along with my mother's sleeping form to the far left.

The dragons register as humans in my senses, but my mother's angelic aura is easily detectable.

All of their heartbeats are slow and steady, confirming that they're all sleeping.

To my knowledge, there are only five Grudge dragons left: Micah, Leon, and the three others who were in the alley beside the Cathedral the night I first encountered Solomon.

I'm confident we can creep past them, although my heart aches a little that I'm leaving my mother behind without saying goodbye.

I tell myself I'll see her again soon, so goodbyes aren't needed.

I release Isaac's arm and give him a nod.

He pushes open the door and we slip through, moving fast along the next corridor to the larger room beyond it. It appears to be a communal dining room with multiple wooden tables and chairs within it and doorways set at intervals along each wall. I don't have time to stop to admire the elegant woodcraft in the furniture.

Isaac leads me across the room and through another door, quietly closing it behind us before we enter a second long corridor, this one also with multiple doorways along it. I have the sense of a vast maze of interconnected corridors and rooms, and I imagine what it might have been like when they were teeming with a community of dragons.

They're all empty now and the silence is eerie.

Eventually, Isaac leads me through a final door. This one is sealed from the inside and requires unlatching to pass through.

I find myself standing at the bottom of what looks like a mine shaft. High above us, I can just make out slivers of moonlight that *might* be shining through some kind of a trapdoor, but it's hard to tell.

We've remained quiet the whole way so far and I'm reluctant to break the silence in case sound echoes and carries.

When Isaac carefully releases his wings, I do the same, flying up the shaft after him. Somehow, I manage to keep the fluffy slippers on my feet while Isaac reaches a narrow platform that's only wide enough for one of us.

He balances there while I coast the air behind him.

The slivers of light I saw from the bottom of the shaft are in fact shining through very small cracks and tiny holes in what looks like a wooden door. It's only as high as Isaac's waist, so we'll both have to crawl through, and the gaps between the wooden planks reveal what looks like stone covering the other side.

Isaac fully retracts his wings before peering cautiously through one of the small holes. Seeming satisfied that the way is clear, he unlatches the door and pushes it open, also with great caution.

Moonlight floods the air around me and I follow quickly onto the narrow platform, putting away my wings before I crouch and hurry through the opening.

When Isaac closes the trapdoor behind me, the stone surface blends perfectly into the wall and only a few rust-colored sections of stone could be used to distinguish it from the wall around it.

I'm surprised to find myself in weirdly similar surroundings to the underground, except that the wide corridor stretching out in front of me is—oddly—not so well kept as the ones I left behind. Moonlight beams down through a broken, arched ceiling and the floor is uneven. There are also far more cage doors here...

No. *Prison* doors.

Well, what do you know?

Keeping my footfalls silent—an easier feat than I thought it might be in the fluffy slippers—I hurry along the corridor, more confident of my whereabouts now. If I am where I think I am, then there should be an open courtyard right ahead. The humans will have locked the outer doors to prevent unauthorized access, but they won't count on beings who can fly right out of the open-air yard.

Exiting through a creaky prison gate into the open area, I allow myself to smile as I confirm I'm standing at the center of a dilapidated penitentiary.

From the outside, the place looks almost like a castle made of old stone, complete with multiple turrets. According to human history, it was once a grand old prison that housed some of their worst offenders. Now, it's a tourist destination.

The irony is that I've flown over this location many times and even stepped within its walls on several occasions. Even more ironic, the Cathedral is only a twenty-minute walk south from here.

It's the perfect hiding place, easy to come and go during opening hours due to the influx of people as well as outside of hours, given that the open prison yard allows for simply flying out under the cover of darkness.

Who would guess that dragons would choose to build their home under a human prison?

Once Isaac reaches my side, I spread my wings and fly up to the nearest turret, landing on the cool stone.

From here, I can see out across parts of the city. Rainclouds are gathering in the distance, and they'll provide cover for us to fly more freely, but until we reach them, I need to plan the safest path for us to run across the rooftops.

Isaac lands on the turret beside me and quickly puts away his wings. His white feathers make him more visible than me at night, while my black wings blend in, although the white sheet I'm using as a sling is probably a bit like a white flag in the dark and my glaive catches the moonlight.

Now that I've oriented myself, I point south. "Callan's last home is that way. It's the best place to start. We'll need to take the long way around the Cathedral so we don't draw attention. Once we get close to Callan's home, you should hang back. The dragons won't welcome your presence."

Assuming they haven't already moved on.

Zahra already relocated after the Sentinels had attacked her home, so I don't know where she lives now. But Sophia, Beatrix, and Felix were settled in Callan's home. I both hope and dread the possibility that they're still there. Hope because otherwise, I'm not sure how I'll find them. And dread because then Atrox can find them too.

Isaac doesn't object to my suggestion that he keep his distance. "I'll watch your back," he says, closing his eyes for a moment before he opens them to study the street ahead. "There are humans about but no Sentinels nearby. However, Atrox and Dominus could be anywhere."

I nod. "Other than their scent, we have no way of locating

them. We have to assume that any being who presents as a human could be a dragon."

I point out a possible path along the rooftops and we fly quickly to the nearest one, staying low and running the distance. It's awkward with the books banging against my thigh and my glaive in my hand, but by some miracle the slippers stay on my feet. Small mercies.

We draw to a stop on a rooftop east of the Cathedral to catch our breath.

I close my eyes and reach across the distance with my senses to determine any possible threat from the angels. "There are seven Sentinels guarding the Cathedral's perimeter," I murmur, recognizing the bright energy of the Roden-Darr. "Which means two are unaccounted for."

I narrow my eyes at our surroundings, but I don't locate the other two Roden-Darr.

Isaac also gives me a shake of his head.

"We'll need to keep our eyes out for them," I say before we resume our path along the rooftops, veering west in the direction of the river now that we've skirted the Cathedral.

Finally, we reach the edge of the rainclouds where the moon is obscured and the shadows are deeper. A few spots of rain touch my face, but the threatening downpour hasn't yet arrived, and we're able to use the extra cover of darkness to take to the sky.

Five blocks from the bar that gives access to Callan's home, my instincts buzz, and I alight on the roof of a nightclub, keeping to the shadow cast by the taller building beside it. The muffled *thud-thud* of music thrums through the air, reminding me of the night Callan took me to the Hollow Rose, the nightclub he owns. Or *owned*. He may have sold it out of an abundance of caution.

Crouching and wrapping my wings around myself to protect against the wind, I wait for Isaac to stop beside me.

"We've picked up a tail," I say, my voice low, although I

needn't have worried about speaking softly because the wind whips my words away.

Our follower is keeping to the shadows of the rooftops across the street on our left. If I hadn't spent my life honing my instincts, I probably wouldn't have noticed them.

Isaac nods. "I see them. It's most likely a dragon since I don't detect an obvious aura."

"Agreed." I narrow my eyes in thought. "But which clan?"

For a moment, I wonder if it's Atrox, but his silhouette is much larger than this being's lithe form.

Isaac hums in the back of his throat, his shrewd gaze following the furtive figure. "Would you recognize a Dread dragon?"

"Maybe. But I didn't meet all of them," I reply. "It could definitely be a Scorn dragon, but they don't tend to hide from me. They're more likely to attack."

Such is their confidence, despite my reputation.

Now that they've gone to war with the Dread, with whom I'm aligned, I can safely assume they'll have even more reason to come after me.

I might need to get up close to confirm if it's a Scorn dragon, though, given that the only telltale sign of their clan is the insignia they etch into their weapons and I can't see the detail of the sword across their back from this angle.

As I wait to see what our follower does, my forehead creases. I'm confused when they continue on their way, despite the fact that we paused.

"Unless they aren't targeting us," I say, my heart thrumming as I quickly reassess the situation.

My focus shifts to my right. There's another furtive figure slipping through the shadows of the rooftop across the street far off to our right. A third figure darts from the shadows of a rooftop ahead of us, heading in the same direction as the others.

None of them seems to have seen us, and I suppose it's lucky that we stopped where we did—concealed by the taller building behind us, which would have impeded the view of the ones coming up on either side of us.

The one ahead is dressed completely in black, which makes it difficult to identify any part of their features, but they're carrying a sword in a harness across their back. For a brief second, I catch sight of the dragon insignia on its handle.

"They're Scorn," I whisper. "They're hunting someone. We need to know whom."

The trouble is that their target could very well be a Sentinel, in which case my preference would be to let them fight it out, but I don't sense a bright spot up ahead—or a dark spot, for that matter—which would indicate they're tracking a Roden-Darr.

Isaac gives me a quick, acknowledging nod. "I'll take the one on our left, but you need to be aware that I can't kill them."

He means he *won't* since it's not in his nature to kill, but I accept that. "Use your soul light to full effect," I say as I slip the makeshift sling over my head and place the books down on the rooftop. I hate to leave them here unguarded, but they'll impede me in a fight.

I ready my glaive as I continue. "I'll take the one on the right. We need to catch the one up ahead as fast as we can."

Isaac darts away from me and I quickly take off to the right.

Out here, in the cold of night, things seem so much clearer.

In those few wind-swept moments as I race across the rooftop and leap from its edge, I could be my old self.

Simple Lana.

A hunter of hunters.

CHAPTER TWENTY-FIVE

I release my wings as I jump from the rooftop's edge, catching the air with a strong beat and propelling myself higher so that I sail in an arc toward my target.

The wind howls around me and the clouds have darkened, giving me the perfect camouflage from above.

My target has stopped in the center of the rooftop ahead and has dropped to a crouch, reaching for their left boot and tugging at the straps on it. They haven't covered their face—which is a bit unusual for a Scorn assassin—but at this angle, I can discern their strong jawline and broad-shouldered physique, which indicates that they're male.

He seems to be having trouble with his boot. A softly-exclaimed *"fuck"* reaches me, and apparently not because he's realized I'm bearing down on his position.

He's definitely not like the experienced Scorn assassins I've tackled before, who are as twitchy as shadow panthers and never forget to look up.

It gives me enough pause that I don't go for the quick kill.

Dropping my glaive to free up my hands, I pluck him off the rooftop and fling him across the flat surface.

He rolls awkwardly but glides back to his feet, crouching

defensively, but not in time to deflect my next attack. My fist connects with his face, he falls backward, and I land on his chest, straddling him.

Now that I can see him up close, I'm surprised.

He couldn't be more than fifteen. Just a fucking kid.

Of course, age doesn't necessarily determine threat level in a clan like the Scorn, but all I inhale is the scent of cloves. I certainly don't taste copper on my tongue, which means he's a thief but not a murderer.

Not yet anyway.

I grab the fist he aims for my throat, blocking him without trouble.

"You're *her*," he says, although he doesn't try to hit me with his free hand, which is also a little surprising. "If you're going to kill me, make it quick."

His focus flickers to my glaive where it lies only ten paces away before he stares up at me with defiant eyes. Smart enough to be afraid, but brave enough to face me.

"I always do," I reply. "But I'm curious. Is the Scorn clan so desperate that they're sending out their children now?"

A muscle in his jaw twitches. "I'm not a child."

He's barely more than one. I switch topic. "What's wrong with your boot?"

"Too fucking small for my foot," he replies.

"Not enough room for your dagger?" I ask.

He narrows his eyes at me, but I catch the slight hitch in his breathing and the pinched skin around his mouth that tells me he's in actual pain, and not from my punches. Talking about his boot seems to have reminded him of it.

I release him, sliding backward faster than he can react, and pull off his shoe.

He grits his teeth, but not in time to stop the throaty moan that escapes. I crouch where he could easily kick me if he wanted to, but I'm confident of my ability to evade any attack.

I'm also a little shocked at what I see.

His foot is bloody. At first, I think it's because he was inexpertly trying to conceal a dagger in a too-small boot and he's cut himself, but there's no flash of metal within the shoe I'm holding. No weapon.

The cuts across the bottom of his foot are clean and sharp. Definitely made by a blade and the angle indicates he didn't make them himself. Some cuts appear partially-healed, while others are still bleeding, indicating that his ability to heal is slower than other dragons.

My focus flashes back to his face. "Who did this?"

Now that he's free from my grip, he propels himself backward, leaping to his feet—although he keeps his weight off the injured leg.

He's tight-lipped as he stares back at me. "Fuck you."

I ignore his angry response. Something isn't adding up here and my instincts are prickling. "What's your name?"

"Dane," he snaps.

I consider the rest of his body, fully covered in black jeans and black long-sleeved shirt with a high collar. I wonder if there are other wounds I can't see. "The Scorn don't tolerate dissent, do they, Dane?"

I'm fishing. It's only a hunch. But Sienna Scorn once tried to solve the problem of Beatrix and Felix by sending them out on a mission that she was sure would get them killed. I find myself wondering if history is repeating itself here with this teen and whoever his new leader is.

"Fuck you," he says again.

I've definitely hit on a truth. The problem is that I don't have time to figure out what's going on with this dragon. I want to trust Isaac to deal with the other two Scorn dragons before they reach their target—if they haven't already—but I can't abandon Isaac to fight both those battles alone.

I put away my wings as the wind continues to whip around us. A few more spots of rain land on my cheeks.

The longer I stare at Dane, the farther he inches away from

me. He takes a step back, hopping a little. The pasty color of his cheeks tells me he wants to get as far away from me as possible, but I still have his boot.

"Why haven't you killed me?" he demands to know.

I'm silent for only a moment, but he rallies before I can respond, hopping toward me now instead of away. "They sent me out here to die, so get on with it!"

There isn't a hint of sour lemon on my tongue. He isn't making it up. It's confirmation of my suspicion that he's somehow at odds with his leader. Whatever he did to piss the new leader off, they didn't expect him to come back tonight.

My dilemma now is what to do with him. If I let him go, I suspect his clan will kill him some other way. But I can't exactly take him with me.

"You aren't going to kill me... are you?" His forehead is creased, eyes narrowed, shoulders tense, voice uncertain.

"I'm still deciding."

He shakes his head, his shoulder tension disappearing. More confusion now. "Nah, you would have done it already. Why show mercy?"

"I only kill killers," I say. "You aren't one."

"Maybe I will be," he retorts, seeming to gain a little confidence the longer I don't strike back. "Maybe I'll take out every fucking Dread until I find the one who killed Sienna."

I study the shadows that pass across his face with the shifting clouds above us. "What was Sienna to you?"

"Sienna was the only reason Gisela was safe," he says.

"Gisela?" Not a name I recognize.

"Her daughter."

Oh. The pieces suddenly click. I remember the teenage girl with blue-black hair and high cheekbones. She served us at the party Sienna Scorn had thrown during the forging of the alliance between the Dread and the Scorn. Sienna loudly introduced her daughter as a fucking waste of her time because she doesn't have a dragon.

But now that Sienna's dead... *Damn.*

Sienna may have belittled her daughter in front of others, but without her mother, Gisela will be an easy target.

"The Dread didn't kill Sienna," I say, without a shred of remorse. "*I* did."

Dane's eyes widen and then narrow. I sense his growing anger and don't miss the twitching of his hands, his primal need to attack warring with his intelligence, which must be telling him to run the fuck away from me.

Give him a few years to build up strength and skill and I have no doubt he would be strong enough to fight me. But he's not there yet.

I shove his boot back at him. "I'm guessing your clan sent you out here to die because you tried to defend Gisela. The upside is that they won't expect you to come back alive. So you have a choice: You can either fight me and most certainly die; or you can make use of your 'dead' status to help your friend. Which will it be?"

His comeback is instant—and I can't help but feel a little respect for him.

"Nothing is more important to me than Gisela's safety."

"Good," I say, keeping my expression deadpan as I wave my hand pointedly at the side of the rooftop. "Fuck off before I change my mind."

With a rebellious glare at me, he releases his wings and takes off into the sky, his injured foot still bare.

"Good luck, kid," I whisper after him, but I don't have time to waste now.

I quickly retrieve my glaive, calling it to me now that Dane isn't watching, before I scan the rooftop two streets over, finding it dark. A sliver of fear creeps into my heart when I don't immediately locate Isaac. He's strong—the strongest of the Roden-Darr—but Solomon was strong too, and he wasn't immune to an assassin's golden bullet.

I launch myself upward and fly into the dark sky and toward the rainclouds that are now more like *storm* clouds.

There's a sudden burst of light, and I finally spot Isaac three rooftops over. My fear for him settles, since his light will subdue his opponent. Although it carries another risk. Whatever battle he fought with that Scorn dragon, it must have been stealthy and as quiet as the wind allowed. I certainly didn't hear it. But his light will alert the third Scorn that the game is up.

I seek the final dragon, spotting them up ahead where they've suddenly crouched, drawing their weapon as they now face in Isaac's direction.

A second later, they resume their previous path, but much faster now. They've seen him, but his presence hasn't deterred them from their original path.

Gripping my glaive, I soar after them.

My heart stops when I spot the figure standing in clear sight at the edge of a rooftop three buildings ahead of me.

Even though her back is to us, there's no mistaking her cerulean-blue wings.

Sophia!

Her fair skin is luminescent in the dark, her long, brown hair tied up into a high ponytail that exposes the side she shaved. She's dressed all in black, which would make her harder to see if it weren't for her radiant wings, which are like a beacon. Her dragon is the water dragon Bella Vorago, and her power more strongly flows through Sophia when rain is near.

I expect her to turn, to sense the danger behind her, but her wings remain curved at her sides and she crouches down, her focus fixed on something in the alley below her.

She doesn't give any indication that she's aware of the Scorn dragon who's now prowling up behind her, only one rooftop away.

Micah said that Sophia was taking risks, but *damn*, this is fucking reckless.

I beat my wings against the gusting wind and fly as fast as I can. I'm aware of Isaac now soaring silently toward me from my left, but he won't reach her any faster than I will.

There's a flash of metal as the Scorn dragon pulls out their sword. They've made quick progress and now they're a mere few steps away from her.

An awful, sickening feeling fills my stomach as I realize that no matter how fast I push, I won't reach Sophia before her attacker does.

Fuck! I shouldn't have spent so much time with Dane.

Damn those moments of curiosity and compassion!

Sophia's still leaning forward, as if something in the alley is incredibly important.

Important enough for her to lose her life.

CHAPTER TWENTY-SIX

*N*ot if I have breath in my body.

I reach deep and give a savage beat of my wings, plowing forward, nearly close enough to safely use my glaive as a spear without fear of hitting Sophia.

At the same time, the assassin holds their blade high, their other fist about to close around Sophia's shoulder, as if they intend to swing her around before they stab her.

I'm only a heartbeat away from releasing my glaive when—

Whoomph!

Another figure shoots across my path from the right. A wall of muscle knocks into the Scorn dragon, wipes them out, and plummets into the alley with them as if the newcomer intends to use the Scorn dragon as a cushion when he hits the ground.

Sophia seems to lose her balance, her wings catching the wind, before she also drops into the alley below.

I pull up sharply, astounded at the newcomer's speed, let alone the fact that I had no idea there was another hunter in the mix.

Then the scent of a prowling wolf reaches me through the rainy air as I touch down on the edge of the roof.

Micah.

I lean over the edge in time to see him break the Scorn dragon's neck with his bare hands.

Sophia has landed near the closed end of the alley. She poises like a coiled wire ready to lash out, one arm outstretched, remaining half-crouched as Micah lifts himself to his full height.

Quickly scanning the rest of the alley, I look for whatever demanded Sophia's attention before. My brow furrows when all I see are a few trash cans. Nothing that could have concerned her so much that she didn't notice the Scorn dragon creeping up on her.

Of course, whatever—or *whoever*—she was watching could have taken off as soon as Micah plummeted into the alley. I can't dismiss the possibility that there could be other attackers prowling around. Not least of which the two Roden-Darr, who weren't at the Cathedral.

I take a moment, remaining crouched up high, my heart still in my throat as I scan the surrounding rooftops, deciding that it's wisest if I stay on guard up here since I trust Micah to keep Sophia safe in the alley.

The wind swirls through the alley and carries Micah's voice up to me. "Are you okay, Sophia?"

I jolt when she lets loose a near-scream of what sounds like some serious frustration.

At the same moment, the rain clouds open up and needle-sharp water pelts down on me. I can't help but wonder if her dragon's power over water is responsible for the sudden downpour. It has the effect of covering Sophia's cry, so she doesn't draw the attention of the few passersby out on the street—especially since they're all suddenly running for cover from the downpour.

The rain instantly soaks Micah, flattening his hair against his head and drenching his shirt and sweatpants, making his clothing cling to his muscled form. All while a water-free dome forms around Sophia, allowing her to remain dry.

"Back the fuck off!" she shouts, striding right at him. The corners of her mouth are turned down and her large, green eyes flash with fury. "You think I don't know you've been 'rescuing' me." She makes air quotes as she advances on him. "You think I'm some helpless dragon who needs your assistance? Don't you get it? I *wanted* to get caught!"

My eyes widen with surprise at her declaration.

Micah stands his ground, appearing completely baffled—and he's not alone in this. I blink down at her, certain that I must have misheard over the rain.

Micah's forehead creases fiercely. "You wanted... Huh?"

Her arms rise in a gesture of frustration. "I was luring them in, and it was working until you showed up. *Again.*"

She stops so close to him that her water-free dome covers him, too. The final water gushing off his body forms a large puddle on the uneven asphalt around his feet.

With an exasperated sigh, she says, "I'm the *bait*, Micah."

Micah's confusion clears, but his brow rapidly furrows. "You can't be bait for Scorn dragons. They're more likely to put a bullet through your head from a distance than capture you alive."

Too true.

"Oh, no, they won't," she says, her voice seething with rage. "Because my ex-husband is now part of their ruling Cohort. Did you know that? Tyler is one of them now. And he hates that he can't control me. So I can pretty much trust that the Scorn are going to keep me in a fuckable condition until they take me to him."

Micah's expression is suddenly blank. "What then? What was your plan?"

Her teeth are gritted. "My plan was to get inside their clan and kill every one of those assholes who had anything to do with Callan's disappearance."

I expect Micah to respond with his own rage. Maybe frustration. But he's surprisingly quiet as he glances back at the

Scorn dragon lying in the alley behind him. "The angels don't have to lift a finger for dragons to die. We're busy enough killing each other."

A soft sound behind me tells me that Isaac has landed there. He hands me my makeshift satchel with the books inside it, which I quickly pat to confirm that the feathers have covered the paper. Hopefully, in time to keep the books dry.

I suspect Isaac heard what Micah said because he quickly backs away to where he can't be seen from the alley.

I need to get down there. Micah must have seen me when he shot past me and collided with the Scorn dragon, so he shouldn't be alarmed if I drop into the alley beside him.

Just as I'm about to leap downward, Sophia's face crumbles, and it makes me pause. She's standing close to Micah and the friction between them is changing, softening to something else —something I don't want to interrupt.

"I can't stay home and do nothing, Micah," she cries softly. "Callan's gone. Lana's gone. Tyler's joined the Scorn and taken half the Dread with him, including my mother. Most of them probably only went because they're afraid. I mean, the angels have hunted us for forever, but only Lana was able to kill us. But other dragons?"

She gestures at the Scorn's body. "Other dragons can finish us." She presses her hand to her chest while her wings unfurl from around her body and fan the air. "My heart hurts. Callan and Lana were my family, and then they were taken away from me."

Tears sparkle in her eyes, and the water resting at Micah's feet begins to rise in reverse raindrops. He doesn't even seem to notice, transfixed by Sophia as she continues. "I know that what I'm doing is reckless. And stupid. But I just... can't... stay still. Can you understand that?"

"I can," he says earnestly. "I do understand."

She leans toward him, not quite touching, while all of the anger and frustration seems to drain out of her. "I heard about your father." Her green eyes are luminescent as she turns her face up to his. "I'm sorry for your loss."

I wanted to fly down there, but now I realize, with a pang in my heart, that I'm not the one Sophia needs right now. I need to stop listening and give them space.

I have no doubt Micah saw me when he tackled the Scorn dragon, although the downpour is most likely masking my presence from Sophia, and I have to trust that he'll tell Sophia that I'm up here.

But first, they need time.

I close my ears and turn my attention to our surroundings again as I back up and join Isaac a few paces away. The rain has plastered his white hair to his face, his shirt and sweatpants to his muscular chest and thighs, while the raindrops sparkle on his skin and wings. He manages to appear both bedraggled and ethereal.

He hands me the fluffy slippers with a crooked smile.

The damn things are waterlogged. There's no way I can put them back on my feet, but I don't want to leave them behind. They're Mom's slippers, and I left *her* behind. These sopping shoes are my reminder that I need to make my way back to her.

I bite my lip as I set the slippers and my glaive down on top of my satchel. We can't stay above the alley longer than completely necessary. Visibility isn't good in the rain, water runs down my face and the back of my neck, and my feet are turning to prunes, but I tell myself I can guard the alley for the next few minutes. I'll be able to resume my mission soon enough: Find Emika and figure out where the orb is being kept. Even if freeing Callan seems increasingly impossible.

Micah must have told Sophia that I'm here because there's a sudden upward rush of water from the alley. Both of them ascend to the rooftop, somehow avoiding colliding with each other's wings.

Sophia sets down faster than Micah, who hangs back. She

brings the water-free dome with her as she rushes toward me. "Lana! You're alive!"

Fresh tears fill her eyes and the relief on her face nearly kills me as she closes her arms around me, her hug warming my heart. I inhale her scent and it's like the crystal-clear water that rushes down the side of a mountain.

"I'm so sorry, Sophia," I murmur, my eyes suddenly burning. "I couldn't get back to you sooner."

She pulls back, her dragon's power making her glow. "It's okay now. You're here—"

She glances past me and the fear that crashes over her face makes my heart stop.

Her wings snap closed, and she whirls toward Isaac, at the same time attempting to pull me away from him. "Sentinel!"

"It's okay!" I try to get her attention, acutely aware of the tension in her muscles, as if she's going to leap at him. She was a fast learner when I was training her, and there's a hard edge to her expression now that wasn't there before, as if she's had to fight some hard battles since.

"Isaac is my friend," I say, my voice urgent. "He won't hurt you."

She doesn't take her eyes off him, but her question is for me, a new wariness in her expression. "Explain to me why one of the angels who attacked Zahra's home now stands at your side."

Her distrust is warranted, but it makes my heart hurt. She may have deliberately put herself in the path of Scorn dragons— even if her purpose in doing so was incredibly rash—but she won't easily accept Isaac's presence. He and the other Roden-Darr invaded Zahra's home and Emika was nearly killed.

My heart is sinking with every breath I take. It was difficult to build up trust between her and me, but it seems it will be painfully easy to tear it down.

I quietly berate myself for not anticipating her response to Isaac's presence. I should have asked him to wait in the shadows while I explained the situation to Sophia.

I want to tell her that I would never harm her, but my history is against me. I've killed dragons. She knows it. That fact will always lie between us like a festering wound.

As I struggle to speak, Isaac raises his hands, palms up, and veers around me while keeping his distance from Sophia. Every cautious step he takes is muffled by the pounding rain.

"My life is bound to Asper now," he says. "Please know that I will never harm you."

"Your word means nothing to me," Sophia snaps at him. "Your sole purpose is to hunt and kill dragons." Her chest rises and falls rapidly, fear in her voice, but also pain. "You came into my life like an unexpected light in the dark and then you disappear for a week without a word and—lo and behold—you turn up here with a Sentinel in tow!"

Okay. She's definitely not speaking to Isaac now.

I stand my ground while the rain pelts down on me, its needles sharper than the rain in my cage. Sharp enough to cut through my chest and drive their points into my heart.

I can't lose her trust now.

Before I can speak, she asks, "Where's Callan? Why isn't he with you?"

I try to exhale. I don't make a move toward her because I don't want her to fear any aggression. "He's trapped," I say quietly, barely audible above the rain. "His dragon is in control of him, and I have to save him."

Her eyes slowly widen and the fury drains from her face. "His fire dragon is in control?"

At my nod, Micah steps up beside her, brushing her arm lightly. At his touch, she leans in toward him.

"You're wary of trusting the word of a Sentinel," he says. "I would be, too, but what about trusting *me*?"

His quiet question brings a furrow to Sophia's brow. Her lips part with surprise when it seems to finally dawn on her that Micah isn't attacking Isaac—and doesn't remotely appear as if he intends to.

Micah steps fully into her space, his upper arm connecting with hers as he positions himself at an angle that will partially block Isaac from her view.

"This Sentinel—Isaac—is alive because I granted him amnesty," Micah says. "I had the chance to kill him when he was injured, but I didn't."

Her wide eyes flash from Micah to Isaac and back again. "You let him live?"

Micah nods. "His people betrayed him. They tried to cave his head in with a lump of gold. He won't harm you, Sophia."

Micah's statement is clear and confident, and he follows it with a savage smile. "Not least because I'd kill him before he even got close." He inclines his head toward me. "That's assuming Asper didn't kill him first. She won't let anything happen to you, either."

I allow my heart to feel the warmth of Micah's unexpected statements, although I worry about how Isaac might feel right now.

The white-haired angel merely nods. "I accept this truth," he says. "I would expect no less if I were to hurt someone Asper cares about."

Sophia's fear slowly bleeds away, her shoulders slump, and she exhales heavily. It seems that Micah's promise carries a lot of weight. Probably because he's already proven he will protect her. Also because he's a dragon, and she could expect him to hate Isaac. For him to trust Isaac will mean a lot to her.

Sophia's expression beseeches me for answers. "How can we help Callan?"

I don't know and it's killing me.

I swallow hard. "I need to see Zahra. I can explain everything once we get there. Can you take me to her?"

Sophia blows out an exhale. "I can take *you*, but the Sentinel can't come with us. Zahra will kill him on sight."

I take the threat seriously, although, as much as there's been a lot of talk about ending Isaac, I know without a doubt that any dragon would struggle to kill him. Even me. His soul light is too powerful.

But... *fuck*. I know she's right about Zahra, and I don't want to start my interaction with her with a fight.

I turn to Isaac, who tips his head as if he's waiting for my verdict.

"What if he was in chains?" I ask, watching carefully for Isaac's response to this suggestion. I haven't tested the limits of how far he's willing to go for me. Submitting to chains might be a step too far.

"Hands, feet, *and* wings," Sophia replies. "It's the only way."

Isaac is deadpan at the suggestion. "Whatever it takes," he says quietly.

My worry eases.

Bending to my makeshift satchel, I unravel the sheet to reveal the feathers. Many of them are plastered around the books, but some are still loose.

I hesitate. These feathers are filled with the strength of the wind and have never been used to trap anyone, although they've wrapped themselves against my arms and legs from time to time.

Placing my hands gently over the top of them, I bow my head, needing them to obey me, but knowing I can't force them or I'll break their trust.

Clearing my thoughts of all other worries, I reach out with my mind and whisper to the gold:

Will you wrap around Isaac's skin like you wrapped around mine?

Will you protect him from harm by taking on the appearance of chains?

My heart leaps when the feathers immediately fly upward, soaring in a graceful arc toward Isaac, wrapping themselves end-to-end around his wrists and ankles. Beautiful feather-shaped chains. He doesn't resist when they draw his wrists toward each other, binding them in front of him. But I quickly whisper another command: *Leave his legs for now. He needs to be able to fly.*

"What about his wings?" Sophia asks, pointedly arching her eyebrows.

"We can't carry him," I say. "I'll apply a clip once we arrive."

After a moment of consideration, she capitulates. "Yeah, okay."

She spins, comes face to face with Micah, and then grinds to a halt before she would collide with his chest. "Oh... fuck."

His eyes gleam as he gives her a wolfish grin. "I guess you forgot I won't be welcome at Zahra's home, either."

She chomps her bottom lip, looking up at him and making no move to step out of his personal space. "Zahra knows you've been killing Scorn on my behalf, but it doesn't matter what you do. She won't trust a Grudge dragon."

"That's fair enough." He shrugs his big shoulders and shakes the water out of his hair, sending little droplets through the air. One lands on Sophia's bottom lip, and she pulls it into her mouth, a touch of color rising to her cheeks.

Watching their interaction closely, I'm reminded of the way Sophia's dragon shadow bumped noses with Micah. There's a bond between them, even if neither of them is acknowledging it yet.

"She doesn't trust me, either," I interject, hoping I'm taking a step in the right direction. "But she'll have to fucking get over it. Micah's coming with us."

I pin the Grudge dragon with a glare. "After all, he can't go home now, or he'll risk being followed by a Sentinel and bringing slaughter to his clan's door."

Micah gives me a hard stare. "Endangering my clan is the last thing I'll do."

"Good. Then you're coming with us."

I may have the Book of Light Magic on me now, but Micah doesn't know that—the golden feathers are concealing it within my satchel—and neither do Atrox or Dominus. They'll be searching for the Grudge, and I won't risk any further harm coming to that clan. Even if they have no love for me, my mother is hiding there, and I won't risk her life.

"You *want* a Grudge dragon to come with us?" Sophia purses her lips as she scrutinizes Micah, Isaac, and me, pointing at each of us in turn as if she's cataloging us. "A Grudge dragon, a Sentinel, and an Avenging Angel. And you're not trying to kill each other."

I guess we're an unexpected sight. All three of us gathered in peace.

She shakes her head in disbelief. "What the fuck is going on here?"

I try to soften my voice, but somewhere within me, Viviana's fire is burning, and my voice is a growl. "Take me to Zahra and I'll tell you everything."

CHAPTER TWENTY-SEVEN

*D*awn is breaking across the horizon by the time we reach Zahra's home. Sophia leads us along a circuitous path, and we stay within the shadows as much as possible, walking when we need to and flying when we can.

We touch down behind a bakery in a part of town that's quiet right now but will be busy once the city wakes up. Other than Sophia, we're drenched by the time we arrive, although I'm the only one shivering since Isaac and Micah seem to be able to regulate their body temperatures.

"Through here." Sophia gestures to a door in the service alley that has a sign on it announcing that it's private property. "I'd ask you to finish binding the angel already, but I don't want to risk human attention."

I expect we'll walk through the back of the bakery, but instead, the door opens directly into a small atrium with a single elevator.

"You need to bind the angel... uh... Isaac now," Sophia says, pausing in front of the elevator door. "Zahra can see everything from this point on."

I try to quiet the chattering of my teeth as I open the satchel a crack so that the remaining loose feathers can float out.

I need a clip, I whisper to them in my mind. *Can you form that for me?*

The feathers continue to float in the air in front of me, a little more slowly, and I sense they're less willing to comply this time. After all, I'm asking them to stop Isaac's wings from flying —the exact opposite of the purpose for which Callan created them.

I close my eyes, clear my mind, and try again.

Will you bind his wings so that he might live to fly again?

This time, the feathers respond, their shapes elongating— not into a fine spiderweb like the clips I've seen before, but into a thicker web.

Quickly placing my glaive and slippers onto the floor, I turn to Isaac. He's already taking a knee, his hands still bound, but his ankles are yet to be tied. When he leans forward, I reach for the base of his shirt and slide the wet material up to his shoulders, exposing the muscles across his back.

I press his shoulder blades at the points from which his wings usually extend, and the feather-clip glides through the air and settles down across his spine, adhering to his skin.

He inhales a sharp breath but doesn't protest. I know first-hand how uncomfortable the clip can be—and how limiting it is not being able to call on my wings when I need them.

"Thank you, Isaac," I say to him as I draw his shirt back down.

As soon as he stands up, I send a message to the feathers already wrapped around his ankles to bind his legs. The final loose feathers soar down to create a chain that extends a short distance between each shackle so that he'll be able to shuffle along.

"Is this enough?" I ask Sophia, unable to keep the tension from my voice. I'm trying to balance Isaac's wellbeing with the need to keep Zahra from lashing out. He has sworn loyalty to me, and his welfare—mental and physical—is important to me.

"Yes." Her response is surprisingly small. Maybe she didn't

think Isaac would submit so willingly to being bound. "Thank you."

Sophia enters a security code into a panel by the elevator doors and, once we step in, she hits the button for the lowest level. She stays as far away from Isaac as she can in the small space, hardly taking her eyes off him, while the rest of us drip puddles onto the elevator floor.

Nobody speaks.

I'm holding my glaive in one hand, my sodden slippers in the other, while my satchel rests across my shoulder, and my teeth chatter into the silence. So loudly that Sophia casts me a worried glance.

In the elevator's harsh light, the circles under my eyes are probably more visible, along with the new scar near my hairline. I find her staring at it—the first time she's taken her eyes off Isaac since we entered the elevator—before her focus shifts to my bare feet and then the slippers I'm clinging to. Certainly not my usual look.

Isaac leans toward me as we ride the elevator down. "Your temperature is dangerously low," he murmurs to me. "You need to get warm as soon as you can. You haven't fully recovered from your ordeal."

"I will," I promise him, although I have no guarantees.

It all depends on the reception we get from Zahra.

With his hands bound, Isaac can't wrap his arms around me, or draw me in to his chest, but he stands close enough that I can lean against his side and take a little warmth. Not much, since his clothing is also cold and wet.

My move isn't lost on Sophia, whose expression is increasingly perplexed when she considers Isaac. He hasn't made a single aggressive move toward her, and the longer he remains calm, the more he seems to baffle her.

The elevator lets out into another small room with a metal door on the other side. A security panel sits on the wall beside the door, very similar to the security measures beneath Callan's last home.

Sophia types in another security code and then presses her palm to the scanner. When the door opens, she leads us into the corridor behind it, which is narrow and illuminated with strip lighting along the ceiling.

"Zahra had this home set up for the worst-case scenario," Sophia explains, speaking across her shoulder after the door closes behind us. "She calls it her 'burn building.' She bought it in secret and didn't tell anyone. Not even Callan. She only planned to use it if her life got ripped apart. She didn't want Emika to live with all this security unless it was absolutely necessary."

Sophia waves her hand at the corridor. "When Callan disappeared, Zahra went nuclear and brought us here."

"Who is *us*?" I ask.

"Me. Beatrix. Felix. And Emika of course."

I breathe a sigh of relief to hear they're all safe, especially Beatrix and Felix, whom Micah said the Scorn had targeted first, but a new worry settles in my stomach. "What about Callan's human bodyguards?"

Callan formed a strong bond with his human friends when he joined the human military and fought in a human war. When he left the army, he asked them to work for him. Their well-being is just as important to me as the shifters'.

Sophia shakes her head. "She didn't even bring her own bodyguards. She didn't want to risk that someone would be careless with this location. Which is why..." Sophia glances at the three of us. "She's going to go ballistic when she sees I've brought you here. You need to be prepared."

"Noted," I say. I'm fearful for Callan's bodyguards if Atrox returns to his home, but all I can do now is hope they're safe and promise myself that I'll try to reach them as soon as I can.

It's slow-going along the corridor since Isaac can only

shuffle along, but we eventually reach the other end, where there's another security door.

Sophia takes a deep breath, as if to steady herself, before she activates the door. We step into another softly-lit atrium and across to the elevator. Sophia presses the button for the fifth floor and it's a short, tense ride up.

The moment I step out of the elevator into the wide hallway outside the apartment, I sense the energy from within the home we're about to enter.

It's emerald-green within my senses, the color I associate with anger, and it's quickly becoming stormy gray.

Danger.

Sophia's warning that Zahra will go ballistic could prove to be an understatement.

"Isaac," I whisper, a sudden burst of adrenaline making me feel unnaturally warm. "Stay behind me at all times and don't be too proud to back away from the fight."

He gives me a small smile. "My pride isn't important."

Not so, it seems for Micah, who stands his ground at Sophia's side.

There's very little warning before the door ahead of us bursts open and Zahra storms out. She's adorned in gold jewelry that perfectly accentuates her light-brown skin and cinnamon eyes, but I doubt she's wearing so much gold because she's trying to look beautiful.

All six bracelets rise off her wrists, and her golden necklace breaks into three segments, each forming sharp blades with pointy tips. They quickly zip into place in the space around her.

Three of them point at me, three at Micah, and the final three are aimed at Isaac—although, since he's taken my advice and is staying behind me, they're slightly off to the side and could just as easily impale me as him.

"What the fuck, Sophia?" she snaps. "You bring a Grudge dragon and a Sentinel into my home?"

I'm a little heartened that Zahra doesn't include me in that immediate list of enemies.

Sophia quickly steps in front of Micah and keeps her response short and clipped. "I can explain. It's important. You need to hear me out."

Zahra doesn't wait for more. Her steely-eyed gaze clashes with mine. "Where's my brother?"

I begin to speak. "If you'll let us come inside—"

"Like hell I will." She approaches me slowly, her eyes narrowed, her footsteps those of a predator. I've fought her before, and I know her to be a formidable opponent. One of the best. Especially when she's afraid for her family. She'll fight with everything she has.

"Callan went after you and the next thing we know, there's been a massacre," she says. "Sentinels. Sienna Scorn. Solomon Grudge. All dead. Callan was gone and so were you. Now. Tell me. *Where the fuck is my brother?*"

A burst of heat within my heart makes me snap right back at her.

"Don't make me slap you with my soggy slippers, Zahra," I say, watching every flex of her muscles, anticipating the command she'll send to her golden blades. "Let us come in and I'll tell you everything you want to know. Along with a few things you'll probably wish I never told you."

Her jaw is tense and her cheeks are flushed with anger. "I don't trust you, Lana."

"We've established that," I snap. "But I thought we agreed that trust is irrelevant to our relationship. You just need to be prepared to accept my help. In this instance, you need the information I can give you."

The golden blades shiver in the air, a constant threat, and I'm aware of Sophia, Micah, and Isaac all backing away from both of us now.

I'm grateful that they're getting out of the way. My connection with dragon's gold feels so natural to me that I'm not afraid

I'll be hurt, but I *am* worried about collateral damage if the blades veer off course.

Within my mind, I murmur to Zahra's gold. *Return to your mistress's wrist.*

It's a gentle command, but it's firm and clear as I test how much force it will take for her gold to obey me.

The weapons shudder in the air, making a humming sound, but continue to hover beside Zahra. I imagine that Zahra's commands must be screams within her mind, trapping the gold between our two wills.

As well as fearing that others could get hurt, I don't want to damage the gold. The last time I took that risk, I tore Atrox's helmet apart, and it ended up backfiring on me.

"Zahra, you should know that in exchange for the information I can give you, I need something in return," I say, trying to distract her from her rage.

To the gold, I whisper within my mind: *If your mistress will not let you return to her, then come to me.*

Be mine.

"What do you want?" Zahra's voice betrays the strain on her mind. Her focus flickers to her gold, a little crease of confusion forming in the center of her forehead when the blades edge in my direction, but gently, as if they intend to glide right over to me.

I hide my smile.

She would have no idea that I can control her gold—hell, I didn't figure it out until *after* I last saw her—and she must be wondering why her gold is disobeying her.

"First, I'd like you to lower your blades, or I'll be forced to take them away from you," I say. "Second, I need to speak with Emika's dragon."

"You *what?*" My first request seems to have washed off Zahra, while my wish to speak with Emika's dragon causes her to stare at me incredulously. "There's no way in hell that I'll let you speak with my daughter."

"Not your daughter," I say, very softly. "Your daughter's *dragon.*"

"You can't..." The crease in her forehead has burrowed deep. "You can't speak with someone's dragon."

Right then, a little voice sounds from within the doorway behind her. "Mama?"

Zahra whirls to the door.

Emika stands there. Her straight, black hair is tousled and she blinks her large, angular eyes as if she's adjusting to the light. Her irises are the same perfect cinnamon-brown as Zahra's and Callan's. A family trait that makes my heart squeeze.

"Emi!" Zahra exclaims softly. The golden blades that were skimming the air whip back to her wrists immediately, forming harmless bracelets and a necklace once more. "You're supposed to be in bed."

"No, Mama," Emika whispers in her soft, little voice, shaking her head earnestly. "My dragon is awake."

When Zahra crouches to Emika, I make out two other forms standing in the space behind the little girl. Beatrix and Felix Lamonte are both tall and slim, their cheekbones high and their hair dark. Felix is a silent predator, his longer hair swept back in his customary sleek bun, while Beatrix is wearing just as much heavy eye makeup as the last time I saw her.

They're both drawn, their shoulders tense. On edge as they hover behind Emika as though they're ready to pull her away from danger at any moment.

She's the only child born to the Dread in five years. She's precious to everyone.

In the doorway, Zahra reaches for her daughter while trying to keep me in her sights at the same time. "Emi? What do you mean... your dragon's awake?"

Emika's expression is far too solemn for a five-year-old. "My dragon wants to speak to the Avenging Angel."

CHAPTER TWENTY-EIGHT

$\mathcal{T}$he blood drains from Zahra's cheeks, leaving her ashen. "Emi...?"

Her daughter turns her gaze up at me and I'm suddenly filled with ice. Not from fear, but from the sensation of my feet sinking into snow and a frosty wind brushing my body. In my mind, intricate snowflakes waft across my path while a bright sun shines in the sky, and ahead of me, a mountain peak beckons me to fly to it.

I shiver, and Isaac draws closer to me. I remember the way he described Emika's dragon as something *ancient*. An 'old one.' Also the way Callan described the ancient dragons as living on a snow-capped mountain range called 'the Crystal Peaks.'

I sense those mountains now.

The first time I met Emika, she said her back hurt because her wings were clipped. They wanted to fly. I feel the same need in her now. A powerful instinct, even as young as she is, to let loose her wings and take to the dawn sky without fear of the consequences. To search for that mountain range that's been lost to time.

Zahra whisks Emika up into her arms, searching her daughter's face for a long moment before she whispers, "Okay. You can all come in."

She whirls to me, still hugging Emika. "If any of you so much as *twitches* in the wrong way, I'll kill you. I won't risk my daughter's life. Do you understand?" She casts a scowl in Micah's direction. "That includes you, Grudge. I don't give a fuck if you've saved Sophia's life. That doesn't make us friends."

"Understood," he says.

There's an unsettled air over all of us as we step inside Zahra's home, but it eases a little once we enter the homely environment.

When Sophia said Zahra called this place her 'burn building,' I expected it to have a harsh and austere appearance.

Far from it.

The lounge area that sits to the right is complete with plush couches. A dining area sits to the left with a simple wooden table and chairs. A welcoming fireplace is built into the opposite wall.

Like in Callan's home, the walls are completely blocked off from the outside world with no external windows that could let moonlight in, but this room doesn't appear to be fireproof like his had to be.

Beatrix and Felix stand to the side and, up close, I can see how fatigued they both look. They have rings as dark as mine beneath their eyes and their shoulders are slumped. I inhale their respective scents, finding them sharply similar. The tang of sour lemon tells me they're both tricksters and liars. It's mixed with the heavy scent of cloves that indicates they're thieves. But what gives me pause is the new taint of copper that coats my tongue.

A week ago, despite all their talk and reputation for ferocity, they hadn't killed anyone.

Now... they look defeated. There are shadows in their eyes where there wasn't darkness before.

It takes me a mere heartbeat to inhale more deeply and

realize that the taint of copper is mingled with the scent of sun-warmed grass—a protective essence. It tells me they've killed, but in self-defense, or in the defense of another.

There was a time when Felix would have blown me an obnoxious kiss across the air, but he remains unmoving as he looks me over, his focus lingering on the cut at my hairline, and a worried crease deepens in his brow.

Beatrix appraises me from my head to my toes, a similar concerned expression falling across her face. She's one of the prickliest people I've ever met, and I'm not a hugger, but I really want to wrap her up in my arms right now.

As I approach, a glimmer of her old self appears and she gives me a sudden, snarky smile. "Nice slippers, Night Sky."

I tip my chin at her. "I'll get you a pair."

It's the closest we'll get to hugging.

Isaac steps in behind me, and the crease in Beatrix's forehead deepens, although it eases a little as she contemplates the solid bindings around his wrists and ankles. "I didn't take you as the sort to keep a pet, Lana," she says to me, continuing to conceal her anxiety behind snark.

Isaac has been incredibly patient, but now he bristles. "I wear these chains, not because I am a threat to you, but because you fear I am. I do this out of respect for my leader. I am nobody's *pet*," he finishes with a snarl.

Beatrix's lips part as she draws a quick breath, blinking at him. She's tall, but he's taken a step into her space and manages to loom over her.

He glares down into her face, his outrage slowly fading as he contemplates her dark eyes, gorgeous face, and the softening curve of her lips. He suddenly appears a little bewildered by her.

A full smile creeps onto her face as she looks up at him and then looks him up and down with new appreciation, from his dripping hair to his muscular chest.

"You could be *mine*," she says, biting her lip with a little gleam in her eyes that truly sparkles like her old self.

At that moment, Sophia slips in behind us. She pauses, taking quick glances between us. "I'll get towels and blankets. You all need to get warm," she says before she hurries away across the room.

Micah lumbers up behind us but doesn't say anything as he moves to the left side of the room where the dining table is located, apparently waiting for Sophia to return. I guess it doesn't seem like a good idea to sit on Zahra's plush couch in wet clothing.

Ahead of us, Zahra has carried Emika to one of the lounge chairs. She straightens before she points at Isaac.

"Your prisoner can sit there," she says to me, indicating a wooden chair on the right-hand side of the fire. It's a location that will be fully visible from all other points around the room. I suppose she wants to keep him well within her sights.

"Isaac isn't my prisoner," I reply as I take his elbow and guide him to his allotted place. "As he said, these chains are purely for your benefit." Reaching the chair, I ask, "On that note, will you allow me to unbind him?"

The angry flush of Zahra's cheeks is my answer.

I sigh. "I didn't think so."

Isaac takes his seat.

I pull off my satchel and place it, my glaive, and the slippers beside his chair. Then I fetch another wooden chair from the dining set. I'm not unhappy to pull it up next to Isaac so close to the fire. I desperately need the warmth.

Beatrix takes the armchair on my left while Felix silently leans up against the wall behind me, as is his way. He may appear to be dismissive, but I learned that he sees and hears and catalogs everything.

When I turn back to Isaac, a flash of gold catches my eye.

A row of golden bullets sits neatly on the mantelpiece above the fire, and they make me freeze.

As far as I know, the Dread don't use golden bullets. Only the Scorn do.

I take another look at Beatrix, Felix, Sophia, and Zahra. They can heal quickly, which means they don't sustain scratches or bruises as evidence of their battles, but the bullets are telling a story that would match with the haunted looks in Beatrix's and Felix's eyes.

"Scorn bullets?" I ask, my throat tight.

"Zahra dug them out of Felix and me," Beatrix says, absently rubbing her shoulder as if that was one of the places she was hit. She gives herself a little shake and pastes a smile on her face. "I plan on making a pretty necklace out of them. I just need a few more bullets to complete it."

"They went after Beatrix first," Sophia says, returning with a pile of towels and blankets so large that I can barely see her face. She speaks matter-of-factly, but she can't hide the tremble in her hands when she passes me several towels and one of the blankets. "That's how we knew the alliance was over."

"It hardly began." Zahra's voice is constricted as she finally takes her seat on the central lounge chair and pulls Emika close to her side. "After the massacre at the power station, Tyler was quick to make his move. Callan suspected Tyler was building networks within the Scorn, but I didn't realize just how much of a traitor Tyler was until then. Whatever he said to the Scorn, they came right after us for Sienna's death."

Sophia's lip curls with disgust. "He saved his own skin." She passes a towel to Isaac, who manages to wipe his face and legs with his hands tied.

She returns to Micah, sitting with him at the dining table.

I find my own hands trembling, but not with fear. My old friend, *rage*, raises its ugly head. That cold need to hunt that drives all other worries out of my mind and makes my decisions seem simple. Masking how complicated my path really is.

Life or death? Good versus evil? It's never that straight-forward.

I focus on drying my hair as fast as I can, pushing my

emotions into my hands as if I could contain the fury rising within me. But beneath it is a deep sense of responsibility.

I was the one who killed Sienna Scorn. I brought this on the Dread.

Zahra breaks my thoughts with a huff. "You need a hot shower and some dry clothes, Lana. You won't get warm that way."

I stare at the towel scrunched in my hands. Placing it on the floor, I pull the blanket around my shoulders and huddle inside it.

I made the decision to kill Sienna in a split second of justifiable rage. I thought I could save Solomon, but I didn't. I never considered what the long-term consequences might be for the Dread.

When I look back up, I find Zahra waiting for my response. Emika is nestled into her side, the little girl giving a yawn. It's not yet dawn and she should still be asleep. On the other side of the room, Micah and Sophia sit apart from everyone else. Beatrix is closer to me while Felix is behind us.

Zahra and Emika are like an island in the middle.

They're all disconnected. Missing the glue that used to bind them together.

They need Callan as much as I do.

"Warm or not warm, it doesn't matter," I say, dismissing how cold I feel. I've survived much worse than this. My instincts are telling me that nothing can warm me now that I've sensed Emika's dragon. Even now, the distant whisper of a snow-filled mountain breeze lingers in my ears and the sensation of sinking into an icy drift covers my feet.

"*Callan* is what matters," I say.

He's the thread that connects all of these dragons to each other, and me to them.

"His dragon has taken control of him," I say. "A fire dragon with more power than any beast you've ever encountered. Worse, he has a twin brother. Another fire dragon, who is even more dangerous. Vicious. Violent. Together, they're unstoppable."

I sense the Dread dragons holding their breath, each of them leaning forward—except Emika, who pushes out of her mother's grasp and slips to the rug between the couch and fireplace.

"It's Atrox Imperator," Emika says quietly. "And Dominus Audax. The fire dragon brothers."

I nod, trying to hide my surprise, but I can only assume that Emika's dragon has given her that information. Behind her, Zahra's mouth has fallen open in surprise, and in the background, Sophia has half-risen out of her seat. She will have read about Atrox in Callan's library and will understand the threat.

"I have to find a way to free Callan from Atrox's soul," I say. "Otherwise, I fear what will happen—to other dragons, supernaturals, and humans."

"My dragon wants to speak to Asper now," Emika says, sitting cross-legged in the middle of the rug in front of the fire, facing me.

Zahra is on the edge of her seat, as if she'll pull Emika back into her arms, and I have to respect her need to protect her daughter. Cautiously, I give Emika a nod, taking the blanket with me as I slide off my seat and onto the rug in front of her.

I have no idea what to expect, but I startle when the firelight flickers and the flames pull toward Emika's position, surrounding her shoulders and rising into the air at her back.

Zahra gives a cry, and I feel her fear as the flames dance and sway at Emika's back. Just as Zahra's launching from her seat, Emika releases her wings.

They're ruby red and disproportionately large compared to her small body, nearly pulling her backward under what must be an immense weight. She grits her teeth and remains upright. Her wing bones are as bright as crimson stones and the membranes between them are so radiant that they cast flashes of ruby light around the room.

Zahra jolts backward to avoid being impaled, sitting heavily on the lounge again, her hands gripping the material at its edge.

Crimson light swirls and dances within the flames around Emika. Slowly, they take shape in front of me, except that I can't make out her dragon's form until I realize...

It's so large that I need to *lean back* to see it. Further and further until I can finally make out its full shape.

Oh... hell...

The beast's shadow barely fits within this room. Its head rests in the air above Emika's position, its body taking up the entire space behind her. Its red wings are tucked into its sides but would extend far beyond the walls if it extended them. Its legs are thick and its claws gleam. Every scale on its body catches the light flickering around it. Flames smolder within its mouth and its brown eyes make me feel incredibly small.

Incredibly inconsequential.

Its tail curves all the way around behind me, its nearness intensifying the breathtaking power rippling off it in waves.

The other dragons have frozen in place.

Sophia and Micah are sitting directly within the dragon's body. Sophia's hair whirls around her face and her hands clench her chair. She's trembling violently, as if she's being buffeted in the dragon's power.

It only takes a second for Micah to snap into action. He scoops Sophia up, colliding with her so fast that her legs wrap around his waist. He spins with her, extends his wings, and, with a single beat, propels them both out of the danger zone.

At the same time, Felix darts away from the wall he was leaning against, a space which the dragon's tail now occupies. A wind I can't see plucks at his body, throwing him to the side, but he moves with it, ducking and rolling. He runs at lightning speed, meeting Micah as they both head straight for the safe zone in the center of the room—the couch where Zahra is located.

Felix leaps lithely over the back of the lounge chair and slides into the space on Zahra's right.

Micah rounds the chair and drops into the space on her left. Sophia continues to cling to him, her head tucked into the crook of his neck, her shivers violent.

"C-C-Cold," she whispers as Micah rubs her back and arms.

Beatrix has shrunk within her armchair, but, like Isaac behind me, she's sitting next to the curve of the dragon's tail and not directly within his shadow.

Now wedged between Felix and Micah, Zahra remains on the edge of her seat. She's half-risen as if she's about to leap toward her daughter and whisk her out of here once and for all. "Emi!"

Something stops her in her tracks.

Maybe it's because Emika is so calm.

The little girl tips her head back, gazing up at her dragon with a trusting smile, and the dragon dips its head, brushing Emika's cheek with his.

I'm certain this beast is male because I recognize him from the books in Callan's library. One of the most powerful fire dragons, whose flames were fueled by the power of old magic. He was responsible for keeping the old laws, one of the wisest of dragons.

Old one doesn't come close to describing this beast.

I struggle to speak. "But you're..."

Isaac slips from his chair to shuffle into place beside me, the ruby light making his white hair appear crimson. His normally gray eyes have turned the color of bloody steel. Unlike the Dread dragons, his face is filled with awe, not fear.

He bows his head. "Vanem Dragon."

CHAPTER TWENTY-NINE

The Vanem Dragon's power is breathtaking. Frightening. Overwhelming. So intense that I hold my breath in case this dragon's mere presence is enough to pull Viviana from the shadows.

She doesn't appear and I'm forced to close off my senses before I'm drawn into the stream of the Vanem Dragon's energy, which is so hot, it feels icy even through the layer of blanket I clutch around my shoulder.

While Emika remains quiet where she sits on the rug, the Vanem Dragon acknowledges Isaac with a slow dip of his head before he turns his mesmerizing gaze on me.

His voice sends shivers down my spine and the impact on the other dragons appears to be the same, given the way they tremble.

"Asper Ashen-Varr, Daughter of the Grudge King," he says, a deep rumble that resonates through my heart. "Thief of gold and fire, vessel to Viviana Incendia, who is soulmate to Atrox Imperator. You have a weight on your shoulders that you must carry alone."

His description of me only makes that weight feel heavier.

Isaac bristles a little beside me, but the Vanem Dragon swings to the Sentinel.

Smoke wafts from the dragon's nostrils. "Isaac, first of the Roden-Darr," the dragon addresses him. "Your heart is in the right place, but this task is not for you. Asper Ashen-Varr must carry this responsibility alone."

I try to find my voice as I rise from my crouch and take a knee, bowing my head. Questions rest on the tip of my tongue, but within my heart is a truth I've had so much trouble admitting. "But I can't... do this alone. I need help."

Smoke spirals around me, brushing my arms, as the Vanem Dragon exhales a sigh. "This conversation is for you and me only, Asper Ashen-Varr. It will be up to you how much you share afterward."

His words are clearly audible for everyone in the room and on my left, Zahra finally jumps to her feet. "Wait a minute—"

Isaac attempts to reach for me even with his hands tied. "No—"

Neither is faster than the Vanem Dragon.

He exhales with force, his energy rushing around and behind me, swirling in a tight arc that blows both of them back into their seats and then thickens around me and Emika. The wash of power spreads back across the dragon's body, but no further than needed to create a tight barrier of ruby energy around me, her, and the dragon's head.

When I inch back toward the barrier, its energy sizzles at my approach and I don't go any further.

"Ask your questions, Asper Ashen-Varr," the Vanem Dragon says quietly, arresting my attention. "I will answer as many as you need."

I look up, feeling insignificant compared to the might of this beast. "How can you appear without moonlight?"

"Ah," he says, a gentle rumble. "Dragons are creatures of light magic, are they not?"

I nod.

"The moonlight contains light magic, so their shadows can manifest in it."

Again, I nod.

"But, as I'm sure you know, I am one of the old ones. I have no ability to shift into human form. I am not born of light magic." He lowers his head to mine, and I can see the years in his eyes. "I am *old* magic."

I digest this for a moment. "If you're old magic, and the dragon shifters are the descendants of you and other old dragons, how did they transition into shifters?"

He breaks into a gleaming smile. "An excellent question. But to answer it, I must begin elsewhere. A question I'm sure you think isn't important enough to ask." His power intensifies. "It begins with humans."

I force myself to focus amid the wash of ruby light that swirls now with ice. "The Book of Light Magic showed me that humans once fought beside dragons."

He nods. "We were once their defenders, living in harmony, and in turn, they fought beside us. Humans may seem like frail creatures, but the power in a human's heart is beyond measure."

I recall the human woman striking down the fae queen, and then also, the image from one of the books in Callan's library showing Sophia's dragon, Bella Vorago, using her power to put out a fire in a human village.

"There is a synergy to the dragon-human relationship even now," the Vanem Dragon continues. "Dragon shifters keep human bodyguards. I wonder if there is still a deep instinct within our kind to seek human help. Of course, there were humans who feared us even then, but they did not covet our power like supernaturals did."

His jaws snap together, and shadow-flames leak from between his lips. "There is nothing like envy to destroy a race of supernaturals. Even in the time of the Twilight Queen, it was apparent to us that dragons needed a way to survive without being hunted by other supernaturals for our scales, our wings, our teeth, our claws, our *fire*."

His voice grows in strength as he speaks and the ice in his flames beats against my face, torso, and thighs, where I continue to kneel in front of him, the blanket draped over my shoulders. "So we created a source of light magic that would ensure our survival."

"The orb," I whisper. "I need to find it. The dragons... my people... are dying without it."

It's the first time I've thought of the dragon shifters as *my* people, but it feels natural to describe them that way now. "They need its power—" I begin to say, but the Vanem Dragon emits a burst of flames that swirl around me.

"No," he snarls. "They do *not* need its *power!*"

My eyes are wide in the face of his sudden rage. I've said something wrong, and I have no idea what.

He growls at me. "In the wash of history, in the violence, and the envy, and the bloodshed, the fundamental truth about the orb's nature has been lost. I suspect the truth may have even been deliberately suppressed by those who didn't want it to be known."

He inches forward, his scales shimmering. "The most important truth."

My heart is pounding in my chest. I wait for him to continue as his brown eyes burn down on me.

"The orb's purpose was not to give power to dragons," he says. "It was to keep dragons in balance."

Balance? My forehead creases as I think that through, but I can't be sure what it means. "What are you saying?"

He exhales another sigh. "As the world changed around us, we needed a way to temper our power and ensure that every new generation of dragons is capable of not only surviving, but thriving. We needed the ability to adapt so we could live in harmony with the changing world."

"Adapt... how?" I ask.

"The orb gave dragons the power to evolve," he explains. "Each new generation could be born with traits that ensured our survival. Such as the ability to take human form. Or the ability to walk among humans without detection from other supernaturals."

He pins me with his burning gaze. "Even, if necessary, *limiting* our ability to shift into full dragon form. After all, a dragon of my size could never walk modern streets now without drawing the full wrath of the human military. We foresaw that our connection with humans could be broken and this is the consequence."

I take a sharp breath. "Atrox believes the orb will allow him to take his full dragon form again. He thinks its power…" I stop myself before I draw the Vanem Dragon's ire once more. "He's wrong, isn't he?"

His eyes gleam. "He is."

"Then… if I find the orb and return it to my people, what will it do?"

The dragon draws a deep breath. "There are only two things I'm certain of. The first is that the energy in the orb has turned to darkness. I can sense it in the vibrations of this world. Unless you find a way to calm it, it will destroy everything around it. Including the veil it's contained within. Even now, I suspect the Celestial Ascendant has lost control of it. It's only a matter of time before it becomes a destructive force that can't be subdued."

My thoughts shift to the Book of Light Magic. It was like a bomb waiting to detonate and I shudder to think what would have happened if fate hadn't brought me to it in time.

The orb could be a thousand times worse.

"And the second thing you're sure about?" I ask.

"If you can calm it and bring it out from the veil, the orb's fundamental purpose will ignite."

"Which is?"

"It was created to ensure that we never lost our dragon

hearts. No matter how we evolved, we would still have dragon souls," the Vanem Dragon says more softly. "Ever since the orb was hidden, new dragon souls can't be born to match our evolved bodies. And the old souls can't find rest."

"Like Atrox, Dominus, Viviana..." I hesitate to ask. "Have you been reborn before?"

He nods. "Three times. But each shifter I was born to was not strong enough to contain my mind. My presence drove them to self-destruction." Shadows form in the Vanem Dragon's eyes. "I believe this generation of dragons calls it 'succumbing to the beast.'"

"The old dragon souls are killing them," I whisper, remembering with a sharp twist in my stomach how the shadows of the Grudge dragons I killed were misshapen. Dark malformations.

"Only the strongest minds can sustain the energy of the old dragons for any length of time," the Vanem Dragon says. "And eventually... they all crumble."

"Minds like Callan's," I whisper. "And Solomon's."

And mine. Apparently.

But not forever, it seems. Just longer than others.

My father, the Grudge King, somehow had the ability to fully shift, but even he wasn't strong enough to withstand his beast's power.

"My father could shift into his full dragon form," I say. "But some shifters don't even have dragons. Many can't have children."

The Vanem Dragon blinks away the regret in his eyes. "Without the orb, dragons have not been kept in balance. Our powers have become unpredictable. Too many dragon shifters have been destroyed as a consequence."

"What will happen to the old souls if I liberate the orb and bring it back beyond the veil?" I ask, a flicker of hope coming alive within me.

"The old souls will be extinguished," the Vanem Dragon

replies. "New souls will be born. As they should have been all this time."

Hope is a shot of energy that drives me back to my feet. It's so intense that I can hardly speak. "Atrox will be destroyed?"

"Yes," the Vanem Dragon says. "You will liberate Callan Steele and every other dragon shifter who struggles beneath the weight of an old soul. They will be graced with new souls that match their strengths and personalities. They will be able to live long and healthy lives."

An enormous weight lifts off my shoulders and my eyes burn with tears because, *finally*, I have a way forward. I have a way to stop the pain that has clouded the shifters' lives and to bring Callan back.

The Vanem Dragon is watching me carefully. "Asper," he says, and the heaviness in his voice threatens to suck all of the joy out of the heart.

"What is it?" I whisper.

"There's something else you should know."

I stay very still, as if even breathing might break me.

"I see the orb's rage in your eyes," he says. "Such a connection could only come to exist if you were exposed to it before you were born."

I nod cautiously. "My mother was imprisoned alongside the orb while she was pregnant with me."

"You carry its light within you," he says. "You've enabled the dragon shifters to draw on it to their betterment."

His gaze flickers to Emika. I'm surprised to realize that she's fallen asleep at his feet, her chest rising and falling evenly, her upper wing resting across her torso.

"Even this child is stronger because of her moments in your presence," the Vanem Dragon says. "But you also carry the orb's anger. A rage that is a self-perpetuating poison. No trace of that energy can be allowed to survive if the orb is to return to its original state."

My lips part as fear trickles through me. "Then... how do I rid myself of it?"

He shakes his head slowly. "I'm afraid it's threaded through your entire body."

I study the gorgeous swirls of ruby energy floating through the air around me and the way they mingle with the smoke and fire from the Vanem Dragon's mouth.

"That's why I have to carry this weight alone. Isn't it?" I ask, lifting my chin. "It's not because I have some sort of special strength or power that others don't have, but because I'm not coming back from it."

The Vanem Dragon's eyes are leaking. Silvery trails of dragon tears. "I'm sorry, Asper Ashen-Varr, but whoever retrieves the orb will be torn apart by its rage. Even if you manage to calm it..."

I lift my head. "My own rage must die with me."

CHAPTER THIRTY

*C*allan once described me as single-minded. Focused only on my goal. He said I don't think about my own safety.

Well, now is not the time to start.

"What about my mother?" I ask, a sudden fear racing through me. "She was exposed to the orb's rage, too."

The Vanem Dragon gives me a reassuring look. "But she is not part dragon, is she?"

At the shake of my head, he continues. "Then she would not absorb any part of its light or its rage. Neither would the Celestial Ascendant."

This rage...

I've been given so many reasons why the angels can't look me in the eyes. The Serene Commander told me I was corrupted. Then she told me I was incapable of love. Isaac told me it was because of my desire to kill, a desire that does not belong to an Avenging Angel. My mother told me I'm simply something that has never existed before. But she also told me how painful it was for her in the orb's presence. How much it felt like being torn apart.

"Angels feel pain when they look in my eyes," I say. "Could that be because of the orb's rage?"

The Vanem Dragon gives this some thought before he replies. "Angels are far more sensitive to dark magic, and there is no magic so dark as light magic transformed to darkness. Angels are built to detect and combat darkness. I'm not surprised that they would be affected by the rage in you."

"My mother isn't," I whisper.

Again, the dragon gives this thought. "She was exposed to the orb for an extended period of time, wasn't she?"

"You're inferring that she was desensitized," I say.

He nods, and I bury my sigh. I wonder for a moment why the Serene Commander isn't the same. But then I remember that she guarded me as a baby when the orb was shrouded in a silo of pure, angelic light. She wasn't exposed to its raw power like my mother was.

I suppose I wanted to believe that my mother was somehow immune because she loved me.

As if love could overcome rage.

I wonder now if the Celestial Ascendant will be able to look me in the eye since she would have spent time in the orb's presence. There's a part of me that hopes she can.

I want her to look at me when I kill her.

My heart sinks because I face a bigger problem first. "None of this matters, since the orb is hidden in a pocket of the veil and I don't know where to find it."

"But you do," the Vanem Dragon says, sounding startlingly certain.

I can only blink at him. "Um… No. I really don't."

He gives me a gentle smile. "If we trace its path, you were housed with it as a baby, then when an attempt was made to steal it, the Celestial Ascendant moved it to a new location, yes?"

I incline my head in the affirmative. "Apparently. Or Solomon would have tried again."

The Vanem Dragon bears down on me. "If you were the

Celestial Ascendant, where would you hide an object where you could be guaranteed it would be guarded by your fiercest angel and no dragon would ever be foolish enough to retrieve it— even if they knew where it was?"

He's staring at me so hard that he's boring holes into my mind.

Guarded by her fiercest angel? Well, for a long time... that was me. But surely, he couldn't mean...?

The pieces are clicking together, but I can't acknowledge how close the orb was to me all this time. I shake my head vehemently. "No."

"Yes," he growls.

My breathing is suddenly ragged and my teeth grit so suddenly that they *clack* harshly against each other. "In the Cathedral. Behind my cell."

The Vanem Dragon inclines his head.

A wash of frustration and intense disbelief floods me. The Celestial Ascendant hid the orb in a pocket of the veil behind my cell in the Cathedral.

I was the perfect fucking guard dog all these years.

"How could I not know?" I ask. "If the veil was right there all these years, how did I not sense it?"

"Don't be angry with yourself, Asper Ashen-Varr," the Vanem Dragon says. "The veil exists on another plane and is undetectable to humans and supernaturals, no matter how powerful they are. Only the Celestial Ascendant knows the locations of *all* controlled pockets of the veil, but otherwise, each separate location is known only to the three Sentinels who guard it. Likewise, the Avenging Angel's territory is known only to her and her Roden-Darr."

I try to exhale some of my frustration, but it's difficult. "If you're right, how do I get inside the veil? It's not as if it opened to me at any stage."

He's nodding. "Entry into the veil can only be gained in limited ways—the easiest is if the territory belongs to you. The

Celestial Ascendant can, of course, walk in and out. Just like the Avenging Angel's realm would open automatically to you."

I make a mental note to ask Isaac exactly where my part of the veil is, although it's far down my list of priorities now.

"The second way is if you can gather three creatures of old magic at the entrance," the Vanem Dragon continues. "But even then, there are further securities."

I huff. "Creatures of old magic don't exist anymore."

The Vanem Dragon arches an eyebrow at me.

I gulp. "Do they?"

He gives me a sharp-toothed smile without confirming either way. "Another way is with brute force. I believe that may be how Solomon gained access."

"Brute force? You mean... blow it up? Punch through it?"

He gives a chuckle. "You need a powerful object of light magic and then, yes, you use it to break the entrance down."

One object of light magic immediately comes to mind. "Dominus's hammer."

The Vanem Dragon nods. "That's one option."

"The Book of Light Magic is another," I add. "Although it's burned out now."

The Vanem Dragon nods. "I believe that would have been how Solomon gained access."

I narrow my eyes at the dragon since there seems to be more.

He casts an unexpected glance in the direction of my waist, and it takes me a second to realize he's looking at my right wrist.

"The last time Emika saw you, you were wearing a bracelet with a ruby charm," he says.

I left both of my bracelets with Callan. I asked them to let me go, and I promised that I would come for them.

The Vanem Dragon gives me a soft smile. "You must have worn those bracelets many times when Callan's fire raged across you. And at the same time, your heart was beating through the stone. A symbol of the connection between you. You created an object of light magic. I sensed its power when Emika was near you."

My lips part in surprise, but I'm quick to face the hard reality. Both the hammer and my bracelet are in the possession of Atrox and Dominus.

"Are there any other options?" I ask.

"I'm only aware of one other object of light magic—more powerful than any other—but it is lost to my sight. If it still exists, it's hidden well, as it should be. To unearth it would only invite death."

I don't waste time asking what it is, although the weapon used by the human woman in the battle the book showed me comes to mind. I take the Vanem Dragon's warning seriously. Besides, there are already two magical objects within my reach. Finding them merely involves doing what I knew I'd have to do anyway.

"Then it's time for me to hunt Atrox and his brother," I say.

The Vanem Dragon lowers his head to mine. Even though he isn't flesh and blood, I feel the contact in the tingle of his energy, the wash of power spreading all the way up to my scalp and down to my bare toes.

"You must not fail, Asper Ashen-Varr," he says to me in a throaty growl.

"I don't intend to," I reply, reaching up to press my palm to the surface of his shadow nose. The glimmer across the surface of his scales sparks at my touch, brightening and then fading when I remove my hand.

He gives me a solemn nod, and I try not to think about the fact that *not failing* means ensuring that every shred of the orb's rage is destroyed.

Including the rage that lives within me.

"I will lower my energy barrier and leave you now," the Vanem Dragon says. "Be prepared for your friends to be in a state of agitation."

"Wait!" I lurch forward. "If all of the old souls are extinguished forever, that will include you."

"I've lived my life, Asper. I welcome the chance for my soul to rest." He tips his head, a gleam in his eyes. "I hope never to see you again, Asper Ashen-Varr, and I mean that in the best way. But you must not delay. Go quickly now..."

Light bursts around his silhouette, the barrier behind me drops, and the Vanem Dragon is gone in an instant.

His absence is so sudden that I blink at the empty space.

"Emika!" Zahra cries, leaping toward her daughter, anxiety written all over her face.

"She's sleeping," I say, keeping my voice low as Zahra kneels beside her daughter. "She was safe with us."

The narrow-eyed glare Zahra shoots me tells me I should back away now.

Right into Isaac's chest. His bound hands dig into my lower back and I whirl to him, my heart squeezing at the worry in his eyes as he looks me over.

I wrap my hands over his. "I'm fine. I know what I need to do now."

Get Dominus's hammer—or, failing that, the bracelet—and infiltrate the Cathedral. It seems so simple, but any number of things could go wrong. Particularly the fact that, if I'm forced to rely on the bracelet, Atrox will be able to track me through it.

"Night Sky?" It's Beatrix's voice and it wobbles a little.

With my hand still resting on Isaac's forearm, I whirl back to the room.

Beatrix stands closest to me, her hand outstretched as if she would touch me. Felix is close behind her, and Sophia and Micah are on the front foot beside him. Even Zahra looks up at me now that Emika is safely cradled in her lap.

"What did the Vanem Dragon say to you?" There's both awe and terror in Beatrix's voice. "Will you tell us?"

I'm caught between wanting to protect these dragons and giving them the power to choose their own path. The Vanem

Dragon told me I have to retrieve the orb alone, but he didn't specify that the other dragons couldn't help me get there. The last time I decided to go out on my own—the night I thought I could beat both Solomon Grudge and the Celestial Ascendant—I ended up making things worse for the Dread.

But having them come to the Cathedral would simply continue this war. Even if I can liberate the orb and change their lives, they would still contend with the full force of the heavenly realm, which won't take kindly to any sort of attack on Cathedral grounds.

I close my eyes and take a deep breath. I won't make those decisions for them anymore. They deserve the chance to choose for themselves.

If there's anything good I'll take to my grave, it's the beauty of being given a real choice. A real chance to decide my own fate.

"The Vanem Dragon told me how to free Callan from his dragon." My focus flickers to Micah. "He told me where to find the dragon's light. That's what I'm going to do now."

The hopeful looks the others give me become puzzled when I mention the light—they don't even know that it exists—but Micah lurches toward me, a savage growl in his voice, every bit the alpha his father wanted him to be. "Tell me where it is."

"The Cathedral."

The breath sucks between his teeth. "Fuck."

"Micah, you have to realize that to attack the Cathedral will bring the might of *all* angels down on the dragons," I say. "No matter how strong you are, you won't survive the full force of the heavenly realm."

Sophia is shaking her head. "Wait. Back up. What is the 'dragon's light' and why is it so important?" She glares at Micah. "And what does it have to do with Callan's dragon?"

I give Micah a hopeful look. "You have to tell them everything. About the light and what happened to it." I swallow hard. "You have to tell them who and what I am. All of it."

I let go of Isaac to prowl toward Micah, my focus pinpointed because I know that if I even glance at the others, I'll give in to the urge to tell them everything myself.

"Give them the chance to decide what they want to do," I say. "All I ask is that when it comes to the Cathedral, you'll consider the consequences very carefully."

"What are *you* going to do?" he asks me.

"I need to find Atrox. Then I'll infiltrate the Cathedral myself. I have a good chance of getting inside without bloodshed or battle because I was once a prisoner there."

Micah catches on quickly. "You plan to turn yourself in."

"The Cathedral is currently defended by Sentinels who are secretly working for Atrox," I say, "along with a legion of warrior angels who are allied to the Celestial Ascendant. They all want a piece of me. If Isaac escorts me there as his captive, they'll let me in."

I half-turn back to Isaac, catching the deepening furrow of his brow.

"And after that?" Micah asks.

"I'll do what your father couldn't. I'll bring the light back into the world." I take a step toward him. "I know what you're thinking. You want to come with me. I won't stop you. I want everyone in this room to have a choice.

"But if you decide to storm the Cathedral—even if you think you're helping me—you have to understand that there will be consequences for decades. Angels live long lives, and they don't forget. If you want your people to have a chance, please consider leaving the responsibility on my shoulders. If I'm the one who attacks, I will be to blame. Not you."

Micah looks like he's going to argue, but I'm not finished. "Doing nothing is hard." I cast a piercing glance at Sophia. "But paying the price will be harder. Watching your *children* pay the price will be intolerable. Please think about that before you make a decision."

A muscle in Micah's jaw clenches. He takes a moment.

Appears to chew his thoughts. But the tension finally leaves his shoulders, and he nods quietly. "I understand."

"Okay, then." I exhale, trying to expel some of my worry.

With the briefest thought, I reach out to the golden bullets on the mantle, taking in their cold nature. They're formed from dragon's gold that was taught to feel nothing, except the need to obey basic directional commands. Go here. Go there. Follow that path.

Well, now they will obey *me*.

Rise.

Each golden bullet glitters as it lifts from the mantle. They're all slightly squished, which must be a sign that their owners didn't have the same skills as Sienna since she managed to shoot two bullets through Solomon's chest without the gold compressing on impact.

I retrieve the makeshift satchel and coax the golden bullets to land inside it next to the books. Then I scoop up my glaive.

Zahra's huff stops me in my tracks.

Her lips press in a displeased line. "If you're going into battle, even as a prisoner, you need a proper satchel. And a harness for your weapon." She arches her eyebrows at my bare feet. "Definitely some boots."

I simply shrug because I can fight just as well in bare feet.

Her expression softens and becomes puzzled. As if I baffle her.

In response to Zahra's comments, Sophia darts across the room. "I'll get some boots."

"Oh. Okay." I was ready to leave and now I hover awkwardly in the silence, settling a little when Isaac nudges my shoulder. I hate that he's still bound, but I don't want to cause further friction by releasing him.

Beatrix and Felix wait opposite me wearing shadowed expressions. They must be burning with questions, and I keep expecting them to speak, but all they do is exchange glances. Silent communications.

I break up their exchange with a quiet suggestion. "If you need to help someone, please consider finding Sienna Scorn's daughter, Gisela. She's in danger from her clan. Just like you once were."

Sophia returns then, holding a pair of black boots, a supple denim jacket, and a duffel bag. "I don't have a harness, but we're about the same size in clothing, and you can have my bag," she says, handing me the items.

I quickly shove my glaive into the duffel bag, which is long enough to accommodate enough of the glaive so that when I zip the bag up, only the glaive's top blade will stick out.

I pause as I consider the books within my makeshift satchel. I don't want to take the Book of Light Magic to the Cathedral, so I pull it out and hand it to Micah.

His brown eyes widen as he takes it. "It's peaceful, but how?"

"I'm sorry," I say. "It's blank."

He peers at me and I have the distinct impression that if we were standing in moonlight, his dragon shadow would make an appearance. Sometimes I forget that, unlike the other dragons, he can communicate with his beast.

"Maybe," he says. "Maybe it'll wake again."

"I hope so," I whisper before I pull on the jacket and boots, grateful that they fit well enough.

I bite my lip as I consider the slippers. I'm not sure why, but I blurt out, "Those are my mother's."

"I'll get them back to her," Micah offers.

"You found your mom," Sophia whispers.

I give her a small smile. "Thank you for the boots."

She steps into my space and hugs me. "Come back alive, Not-Lana."

I bite my lip again, chewing hard to stop the burn of tears when she lets me go.

Taking Isaac's arm, I escort him back across the room before I let the tears fall. He shuffles along as quickly as he can, and we make it there within seconds.

Closing the door behind me, I blink away my tears and hurry to call the feathers away from his wrists and ankles, and the clip away from his back, freeing him.

"Will you tell me what the Vanem Dragon said?" Isaac asks.

"I'll tell you everything on the way. But we need to move."

I'm surprised when the door opens behind me, and Felix slips out. He keeps his distance, but his dark eyes are shadowed. I once thought he had a cruel beauty. I still do, but now I see it as a shield that he wears.

"Felix?"

His voice is mesmerizing, a hint of his serpentine dragon. "Remember that you have allies, Lana," he says. "We may not yet understand what's going on, but you don't have to do this alone. There are ways for us to help you without dooming our people."

I remember the way he slipped through the darkness and took out Sentinels so that I wouldn't be captured—all without me knowing. I remember the fact that he shed blood for me, fighting in the shadows.

My heart constricts and so does my voice. "Thank you, Felix, but this time, I do."

Isaac has already pressed the button to call the elevator and when the doors open, I back toward it.

"Don't come after me, Felix," I say. "Don't come anywhere near the Cathedral. All dragons have to be kept innocent of my actions. Keep your clan alive, keep them safe, and I promise everything will be better."

A promise I'm determined to keep.

CHAPTER THIRTY-ONE

The morning sunlight sparkles through the treetops by the time Isaac and I alight on the rooftop of a building near the park where I first met him.

In the distance, the rush of the river is a soft lull. The streets below us are damp from the rain overnight, but the rooftops are quickly drying out. I had to take Sophia's jacket off to release my wings, but now I pull it on again, grateful for the warmth.

Humans are already busy going about their day, and we made sure to land where we won't cast shadows across the street below us that might draw attention. Dropping to street level in the darkness of the nearest alley, we cross the road and head into the park. Its trees are lush with leaves, but there aren't enough of them to provide any real cover, so we head to the thicket of trees on the far side—the same location where I first fought this angel.

He spins to me when we get there. "Will you reconsider?"

I give him a firm shake of my head as I hand him the duffel bag. "I need you to stay here and keep everything safe. Atrox and Dominus don't know you're with me. It's better they don't find out."

The park is ideally placed for me to return to it and head quickly to the Cathedral once I have either the hammer or the bracelet.

I send a silent request to my glaive, the feathers, the bullets, and my armband to remain with Isaac. I expect my glaive to rattle and protest, but, like my feathers when Isaac brushed his hands across them, my weapon seems calm in his presence.

If I had any remaining doubts about his loyalty, they disappear now.

"Asper." He snags my arm before I can turn away. "I'm only staying here because you asked me to. I need you to be careful."

It took me time to recognize the importance of asking for what I need, so I acknowledge his concern. He is such a mix of ethereal beauty and stormy emotion that I find myself stepping into his space. I reach up to press my palm to his cheek and give him a crooked smile. "I'll try."

I swing away from him and hurry across the park.

Now that I'm not carrying a weapon in a bag in broad daylight, I can blend more easily into the stream of humans on the streets, but I don't intend to stay among them for long.

Finding the nearest service alley, I watch carefully to make sure I'm not observed before I slip off Sophia's jacket and then release my wings, ascending to the rooftops once more.

I quickly tuck away my wings and stay well away from the edge of the roof. It would be so much easier to travel under the cover of night, but I don't have that luxury.

I stop three blocks away in the middle of a row of brownstones with multiple gables across the top. The gables provide shelter and a place to think where I'm unlikely to be observed.

Leaning against the sloping tiles, I take a deep breath and consider my next move. Finding Atrox and Dominus will be nearly impossible. There's no way I can sense them, just as I could never sense Callan. In the past, I always relied on moonlight and dragon shadows to identify my dragon shifter targets

—especially since I didn't know their faces in advance. Hunting them was painstaking and took months.

Now I know exactly what Atrox and Dominus look like, and who they are, but it's not nighttime and they don't cast shadows like other dragons, so as for finding them...

I have to use what little knowledge I have about them and their goals.

I know they want the Book of Light Magic and that they need to find the Grudge for that purpose. But I also know that the Grudge have successfully hidden themselves for decades and Atrox and Dominus will be faced with that fact.

Given that the brothers know nothing of what has transpired between me and Micah in the last twenty-four hours, they could reasonably suspect that the Grudge might take a risk and come out from their hiding place if they were trying to find out how Solomon died. Which would mean the Grudge would be looking for... *me*.

To find the Grudge, Atrox needs to find me. And, well, he'd know exactly where to start: the known homes of the Dread dragons I care about.

Back in the veil, he threatened to harm them. He wanted to use them as leverage against me.

He knows I'll want to warn them about him as soon as I can.

I imagine him paying visits to all of their known homes in the hope that he might catch me with them. But Zahra was smart. She moved everyone to her burn building to keep them safe and Atrox doesn't know where it is. Right now, he'd be coming up empty.

Except... Zahra didn't move everyone to safety.

She left Callan's human bodyguards behind.

Atrox knows I care about those humans, especially about Jada, the woman who helped me when I was injured.

All of which means... Atrox doesn't have to go anywhere to find me. He just needs to return to his last home, where his human bodyguards will have likely remained.

He knows I'll come for them. In fact, he could also reasonably assume that I would be operating under the belief that Sophia, Beatrix, and Felix were still living there too. If I hadn't been so badly depleted when I emerged from the veil, I would have gone there already.

I exhale, squeezing my eyes closed for a moment, and curse softly into the morning air. "Fuck."

I've followed my reasoning as far as it will take me. I've made assumptions to reach conclusions, and some of my beliefs could be wrong. None of it is watertight or certain. But it's a place to start.

It's hard to accept that my best course of action right now may be to simply walk back into Callan's last home.

Of course, there will be nothing simple about it.

I have no idea what I'll find when I get there. A worry flashes through my mind that Atrox could have killed the humans, but I dismiss it. He wouldn't give up that kind of leverage over me. Not before he tried using it against me first.

I rise to my feet, sensing my surroundings, allowing myself to take this moment and feel everything that comes with being part of the world.

The grumble of vehicles along the surrounding streets. The hush of the water in the distance. The hum of voices inside the building I'm standing on. Even the pall of guilt that hangs over the structures around me—low-level guilt, nothing like the oppressive force I experienced in the veil from the Roden-Darr, the prisoners, and Atrox and Dominus themselves.

The sunlight reflects off the nearby rooftops. A bird twitters from a row of trees in the street. A neat line of ants marches around my boot.

Everything seems normal.

And yet...

My instincts prickle and I return to a crouch, pressing my palm to the rooftop near the line of bugs, slowly spreading my fingers across the warm tiles. The Vanem Dragon said he could feel the orb's darkness in the vibrations of the world.

If I close my eyes and stretch out my senses, reaching tentatively beyond myself…

I sense it coming for me, but it's too fast for me to withdraw in time.

A sharp shock of energy strikes my fingers.

I gasp, retract my hand, and shut down my senses.

It felt like the strikes from the Book of Light Magic before it burned out, except that this energy traveled through the surface I'm standing on instead of through air.

I stare, incredulous, across the rooftops between my current location and the Cathedral. The orb's energy somehow made it through the veil's entrance and across ten city blocks to reach me and make its presence known.

Damn.

Whatever darkness has taken hold of it, it's looking for me.

The Vanem Dragon said I had to hurry, but now I feel the urgency in my bones.

I head in the direction of the bar that will give me access to the underground tunnel to reach Callan's home. It's only a few blocks away, but I'll need to be careful, as it won't be as crowded inside and I'm more likely to be noticed. I can't dismiss the threat of Roden-Darr or Scorn dragons. Or even Grudge dragons, for that matter. I'm only certain of my tenuous alliance with Micah. None of the other Grudge dragons have any reason not to kill me.

Staying alert on my way, I reach the service alley at the side of the bar and take the staff entrance.

It's quiet inside. There are no angels in here or other supernaturals, but the bartender glances up as I hurry to the door that leads down into the basement. I remind myself that the humans who work here are paid not to pay attention to anyone coming or going, and I can only hope their paychecks have continued despite Callan's absence for the last week.

I quickly enter the basement and hurry to the door on the far side. Holding my breath, I press my palm to the security scanner beside the door and hope it still recognizes me.

It does.

The door opens to a tunnel, which is similar in appearance to the underground access to Zahra's burn building and passes beneath two blocks. At the end of it, I'll be able to gain access to the basement of Callan's building.

It takes me five minutes to reach the other end of the brightly-lit hallway, during which time I fight off the echoes of the past.

The first time Callan brought me through this tunnel, he referred to his home as *our home*. I truly thought I might have found somewhere I could belong. Somewhere where maybe I could learn to trust and open my heart to others, even risk getting hurt.

Pausing at the end of the tunnel, I prepare myself to open the next door, which will lead to a wide waiting room with an elevator.

Assuming everything still operates like it did when I was last here, there are security cameras in the elevators and at the entrance of each secure floor, which means the human body-guards will be able to see me once I'm inside the elevator—although I'm pretty sure visibility only kicks in once I reach the first floor.

I pat my hair. It still has knots. My stomach's empty again, a dull ache I've become accustomed to. My shirt and jeans are a little water-stained and musty-smelling from the rain, but they're dry. I tug at the edges of the jacket, straightening it. As if that can fix my appearance.

I tell myself that my body has got me through a lot in the past and it will get me through this, too.

Just as I press my palm against the scanner, my instincts prickle. I'm aware of a sudden rush of sound in the room I'm about to enter, but it's too late to stop the door now.

The lock clicks and the door swings inward.

Opposite me, the elevator door has opened and four of Callan's human bodyguards are dropping into position in front of it.

Each of them is pointing a gun at me.

CHAPTER THIRTY-TWO

I freeze in place, quickly assessing the threat level.
High.

Each weapon is a semi-automatic, and I know these humans are trained to use them. Even if I manage to step back into the tunnel in time, it will be hard for them to miss me in the small space.

They're in perfect formation, the two in front crouched on one knee, the two behind standing but with feet planted so they can maintain control of their weapons. All of them stare down their barrels at me.

I recognize each of the four tall, muscular men. Brock stands in the back with Paul. The two crouched in front are Sean and Dermot. Callan told me that both Sean and Dermot are trained as close combat fighters, so I'm not surprised to see them in front.

The last time I saw these men, they helped me. The way they keep their weapons trained on me now tells me things have changed. Drastically.

"Lana," Brock says, a deep furrow in his dark forehead. "Step inside slowly. We're here to escort you upstairs. Callan is expecting you."

His speech indicates he has no idea that Callan isn't himself anymore.

I very slowly raise my hands, my mind working through all the angles. Callan didn't pick trigger-happy, reckless body-guards. They're as intelligent and well-reasoned as he is, so I know they won't get nervous and start a bloodbath.

Even so, I regret leaving my gold behind. I would be far less vulnerable to bullets with my armband and golden feathers to shield me. Ultimately, though, I want to make sure that the humans aren't hurt. They're innocent of all this.

"Tell me what to do and I'll do it," I say to Brock. "I'm not here for trouble."

"Okay, Lana. Keep your hands raised and turn around. Slowly now."

I do as he says, obeying each of his instructions until I'm lying flat on the floor, face-down, no longer wearing my jacket. Brock's knee rests across my shoulders, his hand pressing my head to the ground. Someone else's knee—Dermot's, I think—presses down on my lower back while Paul zip-ties my hands and chains my ankles, and Sean keeps his weapon on me.

It's a far cry from the care they treated me with when Callan first brought me to this home. They carried me onto a medical stretcher and watched over me while Jada helped me. But I'm grateful when they don't stay on me for a second longer than necessary, and Brock pulls me to my feet with less force than he could have.

I take a deep breath of air as my lungs expand, but I remain quiet.

Brock keeps hold of me as he tells me to walk to the elevator. "Sean and I will take you upstairs. Keep following directions and you'll make it through this."

He seems a little surprised that I've complied so far, and it makes me wonder what story Atrox told them.

While Dermot and Paul keep their weapons on me, Brock

and Sean put away their rifles and draw handguns, which will be better suited to the confined elevator space.

They escort me inside and the doors close, but my sensitive hearing picks up the rumbled conversation of the two men who remain behind.

I recognize Dermot's voice as he mutters, "I don't like this one fucking bit."

Then Paul's quiet response. "Something isn't right here."

It's silent inside the elevator as we ride to the tenth floor, but it could be my last chance to ask these men questions. "What did Callan tell you?"

Brock is closest on my left. For a moment, I don't think he's going to answer me, but then he says, "We knew you were dangerous, but nearly getting Callan killed in a drug deal gone bad puts you on another level."

Drug deal...?

I guess it's a story that the humans might understand. Far more believable than dragon shifters, angelic veils, and magical gold.

Sean's gruff voice sounds from behind me on my right. "Doesn't make a lot of sense that Callan would get involved in that shit to begin with. Let alone that you'd leave him for dead."

There's a question in Sean's voice and I want to face him, want to give him answers, but it's better if I don't move an inch more than necessary.

The elevator doors open, and I force myself to focus on what's ahead of me.

The door on the other side of the entry room is closed, its soft, eggshell blue color no longer evoking the calm that it did when I lived here. Extending my senses beyond its soundproof surface, I discern two heartbeats inside the room beyond it, both hearts calm and even, although one carries immense power.

It has to be Atrox. I consider for a second if it could be

Dominus, but the humans haven't mentioned a newcomer, so it's less likely.

The other must be human, possibly Callan's female bodyguard, Jada.

Brock escorts me to the door while Sean paces in an arc that keeps him at the right distance to shoot me if I make a wrong move—without me getting away or knocking into him.

Brock presses the button for the intercom and speaks into it: "We're here."

My heart is in my throat as the door slides open.

The room beyond is just as lovely as I remember it. The entire right-hand side wall forms a narrow, indoor greenhouse filled with plants. The floor is polished wood with fire-rated glass covering it. A narrow wall, somewhat like a column, sits in the center of the space and contains a waterfall. The far side of the room is furnished with a black glass dining table.

Three doors, also painted a calming shade of blue, are located at intervals along the left-hand side wall. The first leads to Callan's room.

I take in my surroundings first because I know that once I acknowledge the people in the room, I'll have trouble focusing on anything else.

Jada is closest on my right, her feet planted, her handgun aimed and ready to fire. Like the human men, she's dressed in beige military pants and a collared shirt. Her dark-brown, shoulder-length hair is loose around her face.

Her scent wafts ahead of her—earthy, real, tainted with death, but warm like soil that seedlings flourish in.

I'm sure it's only because Atrox is standing much farther back that I can feel her presence at all. Burning ash fills my chest as Atrox prowls toward me, closing in on Jada's position where he stops, a towering form. He's far too casually dressed for a dragon like him, his charcoal-black hair a startling contrast with his sharp, green eyes.

I yearn for the calm that Callan used to bring me.

I remind myself that he isn't dead, even if, in this moment, it feels like he is.

Brock moves me forward but stops me a safe ten paces from Jada and Atrox.

I speak before either of them can. "I'm here," I say without dropping my gaze from Atrox's. "You've got me. Just like you wanted."

My greeting won't fit with the narrative the humans have been fed. I can't see the men behind me, but the skin tightens around Jada's brown eyes, a slight narrowing that tells me it's not what she anticipated I'd say. Her lips press more tightly as she glances from my face to my feet and a crease forms in her forehead. She won't miss the evidence of new wounds. I sense her confusion. Her compassion. She never treated me like the enemy. Not even when I turned her own gun on her the first time I met her.

"Callan?" She doesn't take her eyes off me as she speaks, her voice strained and uncertain. "What do you want us to do?"

Atrox directs his response to Brock. "Does Lana have any weapons on her? Metal of any kind?"

"We checked her over," Brock replies. "She's clean."

"Then you can leave her with me," Atrox says.

There's a pause as Jada, Brock, and Sean exchange glances.

"Callan?" Jada asks. "Are you sure?"

His expression softens before he turns to her, a reassuring smile pasted on his face that doesn't quite sit right. "I'm sure, Jada. I have some questions I need to ask Lana before I turn her in to the police. There's nothing in this room that she can use to hurt me. I'll be perfectly safe."

"Okay." Jada sounds even less certain than before, her brow more deeply furrowed.

She doesn't question him again, taking careful steps around me in a practiced arc. I tear my gaze from Atrox to follow her path. I'm not sure I'm doing a very good job of concealing my worry for her. I want to scream at her to run as far and as fast as she can, away from here. She and the others will only live for as long as Atrox believes they're useful.

I close off my expression as her gaze clashes with mine.

If I spook her, it might only make things worse.

Her footfalls retreat with Brock and Sean, the door closes, and then I'm alone with Atrox.

It's shocking how quickly his calm demeanor vanishes.

He swoops toward me with a speed I should have anticipated but nonetheless makes my eyes widen.

With my ankles cuffed, I have limited ability to evade him. I attempt to jump, but he snags my right arm before I can completely dodge him.

"Come here," he orders me, wrenching me toward him, nearly toppling me against his chest.

For the briefest moment, I consider fighting back—headbutting him, or releasing my wings and kicking him with both feet tied—but he could easily overpower me and it won't get me closer to the hammer or the bracelet.

I allow him to pull me close.

His left arm snakes around my waist, and his right hand cups the back of my head as he tugs on my hair and forces me to look up into his eyes.

His gaze cuts across me like a knife. His voice is sharp, demanding an answer while the faint scent of lilies grows around him. "Is she still with you?"

"If you mean Viviana, yes." I don't see any reason to lie. "She sees and hears everything I see and hear."

"And everything you feel," he says, relaxing his grip behind my head with a softening of his expression that seems real this time. "I hoped you'd find me, Asper. I'm glad you did." Tension rebuilds around his mouth and eyes. "But I'm curious why you'd walk in here, unarmed and alone. It seems reckless, even for you."

"Maybe I decided to join you after all," I whisper, walking the fine line between truth and lies.

He chuckles softly. "That's unlikely."

My voice hardens. "Maybe I don't rate my chances of survival while the Grudge, the Scorn, and the Roden-Darr are after me."

All truth. Although Micah is the exception within the Grudge.

"The Dread dragons I care about have gone underground. They can't be found." I allow my voice to wobble, real anxiety about what lays before me showing through. "I have nowhere else to go right now."

Quietly, I'm calculating my next move. There's no sign of the hammer or the bracelet in this room—not that I expected Atrox to leave them lying around—but I need to find out where Dominus is before I abandon all hope of stealing the hammer.

Atrox's eyebrows rise. "I never thought I'd be the lesser of the evils for you."

I lean in closer to him, trying to block out his fiery scent, trying to pretend that he's Callan and convince myself that I can do what I need to do.

"You're the greatest of evils," I whisper. "But I'm a survivor. I know what I need to do to survive."

"You burned your hand using that antler against me in the veil when you thought you wanted to escape me." He gives me a confident smile. "But here you are. You need me. You always have."

His fingertips slip from my hair down the back of my neck and to my shoulder, his thumb brushing the curve at the base of my throat. "I sensed the fire in your core from the first moment that Callan saw you. You were huddled behind that seat at the theater with your knees to your chest."

His voice lowers to a compelling rumble as his other hand rises, stroking up my bare arm. "You weren't hiding. You were holding back."

He lowers his head to mine, his lips hovering near my cheek. "You don't have to hold back with me."

My most basic instincts take over and I lean in to the danger. "I don't intend to."

CHAPTER THIRTY-THREE

*A*trox doesn't release me from his powerful gaze. His hands run down my arms, pulling me so close that my breasts press against his hard chest. This close to him, I expect his scent to overwhelm me, but it's calmer. No longer as ashy. More like heat waves across a dry field than like scorched earth.

He bends his knees, creating a small gap between us, so that he can reach around to clasp my bound hands. "I didn't think zip-ties would hold you, Asper."

I attempt a shrug, which is a little difficult while he's gripping my wrists. "They can't, but I didn't think you'd appreciate me breaking them in front of the humans."

He's so close to me that I nearly miss his challenging smile. "Not so for these chains around your ankles."

He slowly lowers himself to his knees, his hands grazing down my hips before resting on the outside of my thighs while his focus lowers to my ankles.

"Spread your legs as far as you can," he orders me.

I blink at him, surprised at first, then refusing to comply.

He tips his head back a little, a gleam in his eyes. "I'm going to melt the metal."

I tip my chin up. "I don't fear your fire."

He shrugs. "Suit yourself."

Still gripping my hips, he takes a deep breath before he purses his lips and exhales a stream of hot, blue flame across the short chain between the shackles. The metal warps in the heat, which is intense against the inside of my calves, and I reluctantly shuffle my feet outward.

Within seconds, the chain is a puddle on the floor and the bands around my ankles are also warping in the heat waves.

Atrox releases my hips to quickly flick the shackles off each of my legs before rising and pulling me away from the pool of burning metal on the floor.

He crushes me to his chest, one arm slipping up between my bound arms, making my back arch.

"Free yourself," he orders me.

I have no reason not to comply. Flexing my muscles, I concentrate on the tie, brace, and pull it apart with a *snap*.

The broken tie flicks across the room behind me.

Atrox smiles down at me. And... weirdly... it seems like a real smile.

For the briefest, most fucking painful moment, I could almost imagine that his cold eyes soften. That his gaze becomes warm. That his irises become the color of cinnamon.

Stop it, Lana. Don't do that to yourself.

"What are you going to do now, Asper?" Atrox asks me softly.

"That depends," I murmur, rising up onto my tiptoes, slowly bringing my hands forward and pressing them to his chest, molding them to the shape of his hard muscles. "On whether or not we're going to be interrupted." My focus flicks past him. "Where's your brother?"

He pauses, a small crease appearing in his forehead before he replies. "Dominus is out killing angels."

I'm surprised. Genuinely so. "In broad daylight?"

Atrox's hands explore my back as he gives me a grin. "It's amazing how the angels trust the Roden-Darr. They consider them to be incorruptible. Faultless. The purest of Sentinels. In the last day, Zadkiel and his men have lured ten angels to their deaths." Atrox pushes my hair to the side. "There are plenty of dark spaces in this city, even in the daytime. All of the deaths are blamed on the Scorn, of course."

His explanation fits with what I sensed when I searched for the Roden-Darr. Most were at the Cathedral. Two were not. They must be the ones who are out hunting with Dominus. The angels of Philadelphia are not my friends, but I'm both horrified and confused by Dominus's actions, and I'm not sure that I'm hiding my response. "I thought you were going after the Grudge."

Atrox shakes his head with a soft laugh. "We were, but we realized that finding the book will take too long. The Celestial Ascendant is here in Philadelphia, which gives us a rare chance to confront her. If we pick off enough angels, she will be vulnerable. We'll break through the Cathedral's defenses and force her to tell us where our light is hidden."

"You'll get what you want through brute force," I murmur.

This is exactly the kind of action I warned Micah against taking because future generations of dragons will pay the price.

"The Celestial Ascendant thinks she's protected by Sentinels —Zadkiel and his men," Atrox continues. "She won't realize she needs to call for reinforcements until it's too late. After we have our light, it won't matter how many angels come after us. We'll be invincible."

There's so much he doesn't know—that the orb has become a destructive force and that, even if calmed, it won't have the effect he believes.

Even so, there's a part of me that considers—for the briefest moment—if I should let him carry through with his plan. While he keeps the Celestial Ascendant busy, I could slip through the veil and get the orb...

I dismiss that idea. There are too many variables. Atrox and Dominus are too volatile. I can't predict what they would do or what could happen. After all, I was sure they were going after the Grudge and now I discover they plan to take an entirely different approach.

My current plan is still my best option, but I have to get to the Cathedral before Atrox and his brother attack.

Atrox's palm cups my cheek and I'm suddenly aware that I've remained quiet for several long seconds.

"Your mind is working at a million miles, Asper," he says, his voice softer than before. "I can see it in your eyes. Let me carry some of that weight."

It's a confusing offer from a dragon like him. But more bewildering is the way I'm drowning in the touch of his palm, the way his hand molds to the shape of my face and his thumb brushes the corner of my lips. The sudden warmth in his eyes. The trickle of calm that makes me tremble with need.

The need to be calm. To leave all my rage behind. To feel loved. Even if just for a few moments.

A light crease forms in his forehead. He gives himself a small shake before his forehead smooths out. "We won't attack the Cathedral until tomorrow. In the meantime, we have all the time in the world."

Once again, he lowers his head to mine, his cheek brushing my cheek before his lips touch my earlobe. It's the softest caress, but it sends a shot of heat to my core. "Tell me what you need, Not-Lana."

I'm so overwhelmed by how-the-fuck my body can suddenly ache so badly for his touch that I almost miss what he called me.

Not-Lana.

As his lips whisper down my neck, making my heart ache, I seek the color of eyes.

Cold, angry, juniper-green with... warm, molten cinnamon flecks that weren't there before.

I force myself not to react. I want to cry Callan's name, draw him out further, give him control. Give him the choices he gave me. But I don't know if Atrox realizes what's happening and I don't want to alert him to it.

I inhale the mix of his scent, a fiery field like dry blades of grass about to catch fire, but not yet turned to ash. Still capable of life.

Closing my eyes, I brace against the conflicting sensations striking through me and making every part of my body come alive.

Peace intertwined with fury.

Two threads wrapping around my heart.

One that calms me and the other that ignites my rage.

Slowly—as slowly as I can—I turn my face to his, the corner of my lips nudging the edge of his mouth.

He asked me what I need, and now I say, "You. I need you."

His breath catches before he pulls back a little, the corner of his mouth hitching up.

He nudges my lips with his. A soft, toe-curling, moment of skin against skin that belongs only to Callan and me.

His hands smooth my hair while his lips drive my need higher. "Let's get you cleaned up," he says, lifting me up and wrapping my legs around his waist.

I drown in his nearness and the warmth of his body, the press of his hard muscles, and the graze of his chin across the top of my head.

He carries me to his room, activating the security panel to open the door. The smell of food hits me immediately. I'm surprised to see a small table and a chair in the corner on my right, both wooden—flammable things he couldn't have in here before.

He takes me there, nudging the chair around with his foot before setting me down in it, kneeling between my legs, his hands on my upper thighs. "You must be hungry."

"A little," I admit.

Starving, actually. But my need for food is not as important to me as my need for information. From this position, I can see most of the room, including through the doorway into the dressing room. Two items draw my attention.

One is the suit of armor floating in the air—the side of which is visible through the door.

The other is a small, soft ruby glow emanating from the shelf directly visible through the doorway. It has to be the bracelet with the ruby-heart charm. The charm came back to life when Callan reemerged in the veil, and it's still glowing.

He offers me a croissant, and I tear my focus away from the dressing room to accept the food. If he noticed me staring past him, he doesn't say anything, slowly running his hands back and forth along the tops of my thighs before settling up on my hips.

I gobble the food, then reach for the half-eaten apple sitting on his plate. He must have been in the middle of breakfast when his bodyguards alerted him to my arrival. Crunching into the juicy piece of fruit, I devour it quickly before I reach past him for the tall glass of green smoothie that looks untouched. *Callan's* favorite drink.

Atrox arches an eyebrow at me when I gulp it down in one, long go.

When I'm done, I replace the glass on the table and lean back with a sigh.

He watches me with a smile, his hands finding their way beneath the hem of my shirt to stroke the tops of my hips. He leans in slowly while his fingers stroke up to the base of my ribs.

"Mine," he murmurs before he nudges my lips with his.

I need to get into the dressing room and he's giving me the perfect excuse.

Giving in to the taste of his lips, the startling contrast of warmth and fury, I slip forward and wrap my arms around his back. "I need a shower first."

He responds without question, lifting me off the chair and carrying me to the dressing room, which contains an adjoining door into the bathroom.

As much as I want to observe the room, his kiss is intoxicating.

I glimpse the suit of armor, the way the pieces of gold ripple and shift at my presence, along with the glow of the bracelet where it's half-concealed under one of his shirts, as if it had been hurriedly shoved under there.

Also the neatly-folded clothing on the shelf that was mine—black T-shirts and jeans and underwear. Reminders of my life here with Callan.

He takes me straight into the large and opulent bathroom. Again, I catch glimpses of my surroundings. The two sinks with black taps. The gleaming, white-tiled walls. The enormous bath on the left-hand side. The shelves with towels.

He heads straight for the open shower with the two shower-heads that are as large as dinner plates. After setting me down on the tiles, he turns on both showers.

Steam rises up around us and makes me moan with relief as I become warm for the first time in hours.

The sound makes him spin back to me. "You were cold," he says, rubbing my arms.

"I flew in the rain."

"Then let's get you warm."

He helps me remove my boots and then he doesn't take his hands off me as he adjusts the temperature of both taps. Just like the physical connection we used to have to maintain so that his dragon didn't make an appearance. It's a muscle memory, a remembered necessity, a way of being that Callan and I got really good at.

It isn't something Atrox would do.

It's like a trigger and I can't stop myself.

The moment he turns back to me, I collide with him.

I don't dare speak his name, only seize this moment, tugging at his shirt, slipping it up off his head. Pulling at my own. Somehow succeeding in removing it, even though the material gets tangled in my hair and hands. Slipping off my jeans.

Unclasping my bra. Maintaining contact with his arms, his chest, my own muscle memory coming into play until the moment when I'm naked and so is he, and then I collide with him again.

He pulls me back into the warm water, smoothing down my hair, brushing the strands out of my eyes before he lifts me closer, his lips destroying me.

Soul-crushing kisses. Sweet kisses. Demanding kisses. Kisses that make my head swim and my thighs clench.

Every time I want to speak his name, I stop myself, my breathing harsh and ragged like his.

When he presses me back against the tiles, his left hand cupping the back of my head, cushioning me against the hard surface, I struggle to articulate what I want.

All of him. Forever.

White steam fills the space around us, rising around his muscular form, droplets of water clinging to the hard lines of his chest and shoulders, the strong angle of his jaw.

It masks everything around us and the world could simply be us.

Only us.

He presses up against me, his hard length between my legs, and I want to scream with my need for relief, but he makes no move to take it further.

His hands grip my shoulders. "Whatever you came back for, you need to get it and go."

I try to think through the haze of desire raging through my body as I search his eyes. More than anything—even more than my physical craving—I need to untangle the threads in his voice.

Atrox's voice? Callan's?

"I'll delay him for as long as I can," he says. "But it won't take him long to realize that he's missing time. That he can't quite determine if your presence here was real." He pauses, his voice becoming ragged as his gaze passes across my face, and it's as if he's memorizing my features. "Or a fucking beautiful dream."

He dips his head to mine with a groan, the taste of his lips devastating me. Warm. Like basking in sunlight. "Lana. Asper. Not-Lana. Go while you can."

He releases me and steps back into the wash of steam and it's so thick around us now that he disappears. Just like the dream he spoke of.

I jolt after him, my outstretched hands swilling through the steam, coming up empty. I slap my hand across my mouth before I scream into the mist. *No!*

I swipe at the hot tears trickling down my cheeks, unaware until now that I was crying. I don't know when I started.

I can sense his heartbeat as he backs away to my left, hear the soft slap as he presses into the tiles and stays there. Keeping his distance from me.

A soundless scream rends my mind, a scream I can't utter, as I listen to his strained heartbeats and sense the strength of will it's taking him to stay away from me. To give me the chance to leave.

Trying to breathe through the pain, control it, I stumble through the mist to find the other side of the bathroom, fighting every impulse in my body that wants to go to him.

I scoop up one of the towels he left in the doorway and dry myself, hardly able to focus on the room ahead of me.

The shelf containing my clothing is nearest on my right, then the armor, then the bracelet. I fumble with my clothing, taking a black shirt, black jeans, and clean underwear and somehow managing to pull them on.

I latch on to the ruby glow in the distance, the bracelet I need to take.

I nearly shoot right past Atrox's armor, but then I sense...
Pain?

I'm drawn to the helmet—to the horn that I ripped off it.

Dominus reattached it, but when I look closer, it's apparent that he did a bad job of it.

Cautiously, I extend my hand, wary in case the gold reacts to my approach. When it remains still, I close my hand around the base of the horn, twist it around, and nudge it to the side so that it sits back where it belongs.

Seal, I command it.

The gold stays put when I lift my hand away from it, and the pain I sensed in it before is gone.

Hurrying onward, I snatch up the bracelet, pull it onto my wrist, and convince myself that I can run out of here without looking back.

I tell myself to run. The fuck. Out of here.

Forming a fist with my free hand, I thump it against my heart.

Be cold. Be still. Feel nothing.

I gasp a breath.

Don't fucking feel anything.

Then I exhale.

With every step I take, I stomp on my pain and longing until it's beaten down far enough that I can function and focus.

I slap my hand against the security panel, praying the door will open to me, grateful when it does.

My dilemma now is how to get past the bodyguards. I'll be able to sense them from a distance, but I don't want them to get hurt—or them to hurt me.

I prowl quickly to the front door, listening and determining that there's nobody on the other side of it. It's a little unexpected. Activating the door, I step through it and head straight for the elevator. The security cameras in here are concealed and I never thought to ask where they are—if I had more time, I could probably detect their location by sensing the hum of electricity—but I make do with raising my hands at my sides.

If they're watching, they'll see that I'm still unarmed.

I make it into the elevator and press the button for the sublevel that will take me back to the tunnel beneath the neighboring buildings.

Once the elevator starts to descend, I extend my senses, prepared for the bodyguards to have remained in the room that gives access to the tunnel.

I stand to the side of the elevator and brace myself, muscles coiled and ready, picturing the best way around them without anyone getting hurt.

A single heartbeat meets my ears as the elevator stops and the doors open.

Jada stands alone in the center of the room.

I'm prepared for her to take a shot at me, but her weapon is holstered.

She gives me a crooked smile. "I know better than to try to draw a gun on you again."

"You didn't feel that way upstairs," I say, stepping into the room without taking my eyes off her.

"That was for Callan's benefit," she says. "But the thing is... Callan would never order me to pull a gun on you like he just did. So what the fuck is going on?"

"I didn't hurt him or get him mixed up in some drug deal," I say, continuing to edge around her.

She gives a heavy exhale, turning to follow my movements, keeping me as firmly in her sights as I'm keeping her in mine. "I know you wouldn't. You can't fake what you and Callan have. It's real. Hell, I can only hope I find someone to love that much. Which is why none of this make sense."

I'm suddenly struck by the memory of what I saw in the Book of Light Magic—a human woman defending a dragon—and the Vanem Dragon's claim that humans can be powerful allies. That the power in the human heart is beyond measure.

It makes me pause. *Could she help me?*

I dismiss the idea instantly. The danger to her would be too great.

"I can't give you details," I say carefully, even though her brow immediately furrows. "But Callan would want me to tell you this, so I'm telling you: You need to leave. Get yourself and Brock and the others away from here until this situation is sorted out."

She doesn't flinch, although she considers me warily. "Does this have something to do with his new friend, Dom?"

Dom, huh? It sounds like it's short for Dominic. It's certainly a more modern name than Dominus.

"Yes," I say. "He's dangerous, and right now, Callan can't get himself out of this situation."

"Then I need to stay and help."

"No, Jada. You're not listening to me." I try one last time. "You're the *leverage*."

Her expression falls and the color drains from her cheeks.

"The best way to help Callan is to leave," I say. "Right now. Before Dom gets back. Can you do that?"

The tension in her flexed muscles tells me she's torn, but she nods. "I can do that."

I pause for another moment as I reach the black door on the far side. "You were my friend, Jada. I want you to know that I valued that."

"'Were'?" she asks, with a raised eyebrow.

"Are." I activate the security panel, wait only for the door to open, and then I hurry through it.

The bracelet glows at my wrist, a constant reminder that Atrox can track me now and no matter how fast I move…

I grit my teeth, determined that it will be fast enough.

CHAPTER THIRTY-FOUR

I race back to the park with my heart in my throat.

The bright, mid-morning sunlight does nothing to calm me as I sprint through the trees, not even trying to pretend that I'm out for a jog.

Isaac sits on the park bench in the distance, but as soon as I come within range of his power to detect my presence, his head shoots up.

He picks up the duffel bag, hoists it over his shoulder, and breaks into a run, meeting me in the middle of the park, where we veer together to our right, heading for the path along the river that will take us in the direction of the Cathedral.

He doesn't have to ask me if I got the bracelet. His quick gaze takes in my wrist and my new attire.

I don't need to tell him that we have to hurry.

We only slow down a block away from our destination, where we dart into a shallow side alley. It's barely dark enough, but it will have to do.

"Dominus is hunting angels," I say, quickly updating Isaac. "He's using the Roden-Darr to lure them out. He and Atrox plan to attack the Cathedral tomorrow and force the Celestial

Ascendant to tell them where she hid the orb. Once Atrox knows I've come here, they could move up their plan."

"They want to take the Celestial Ascendant unawares," Isaac says, quickly reading the situation. "She thinks she's safe with the Roden-Darr."

"Precisely."

As I speak, I send quick commands to the golden feathers, the bullets, and my glaive. I ask my glaive to accept that Isaac will need to take control of it soon. I ask the bullets to remain in the bag with my armband and not to react unless I ask them to. And, finally, I request that several of my feathers bind my wrists behind my back.

They all comply.

Before we leave the alley, I take a breath. Just a small one. Expanding my senses one last time, inhaling the city air, I step into the sunlight.

Isaac stays close at my back, his hand on my arm, concealing the fact that my hands are bound while we walk the final block to the alley at the side of the Cathedral. We casually steer clear of any humans we pass along the way.

We walk silently along the cobblestones until we reach the door in the brick wall.

The door in the side of the alley is the one I used many times when I left the Cathedral to hunt dragons. There's a hook beside it where I would leave my blindfold once I stepped outside.

I fight the tumult of rage rising inside me when I see that the band of dense material hangs there still.

Isaac turns me to face the door and he only pauses for a second before he reaches for the blindfold. Sliding it free from the hook, he wraps it around my eyes.

The material feels foreign against my skin now.

Without my sight, my other senses come alive.

The firm *rap-rap* as Isaac knocks on the door.

Then the soft *thud* as he places the duffel bag on the ground and the *swoosh* of metal against material as he pulls out my glaive and holds it in his free hand. He will leave the duffel bag unzipped so I can easily access its contents if I need to.

I sense the flurry of angelic power beyond the door, the rush of wings, and the scattered exclamations.

They'll be reluctant to send a legion of angels out here in broad daylight, but it's unclear who will greet us at the door until it swings open, and the scent of a crisp, winter's day greets me.

The Serene Commander.

An overabundance of spring flowers fills the space behind her, indicating that the warrior angel, Aria, hovers close at her back.

A third scent makes me freeze. The smell of muddy lilacs—the scent of the betrayer—indicates that one of the Roden-Darr stands beside Aria. Possibly Zadkiel, unless he's out with Dominus. Whichever Roden-Darr it is, they won't be happy to see Isaac. They thought they killed him.

Behind them within the building, a legion of angels has gathered, their silhouettes shimmering in my mind while the clang of metal confirms they're heavily armed. I count a depleted number of them, which would match Atrox's boast that Dominus has killed ten of them already.

The Serene Commander seems frozen in the doorway. "Isaac Roden-Darr!" she exclaims. "We thought you were dead!"

Isaac must have rehearsed his response at the park because it rolls off his tongue like truth. "I woke with no memory of what happened, only to find myself surrounded by my slaughtered kin. The Cruel One was gone, so I set out immediately to track her down."

"But... Lana was imprisoned in the veil," the Serene Commander says, sounding genuinely confused.

The Roden-Darr standing immediately behind her speaks quickly, false alarm thick in his voice. "She must have escaped after we were called away. This is very grave indeed."

"I've captured her and subdued her with my soul light," Isaac says. "She's compliant and not an immediate threat, but if you please, Serene Commander, I need a place to imprison her as soon as possible. I'm sure you understand how much damage she could do once my soul light wears off."

The Serene Commander's voice is suddenly sour. "Oh, I know only too well."

Her scent recedes a little, so do the others', and then Isaac pushes on my arm. I stumble a little as I cross the step, a deliberate move on my part to give the impression that I'm not in complete control of my body or my reactions.

Some of the tension in the air abates, but the warrior angels ahead of me don't lower their weapons. They surround and follow us along the corridor, the heaviness in the air continuing to indicate their animosity toward me.

They have always feared me, but now I sense the depth of their hatred.

I sided with the dragons.

The Celestial Ascendant decreed that my death by the hand of an angel would be lawful.

It was Isaac's goal to imprison me, but not so for these angels. They tried and failed to end me outside this building in the very alley that I just left behind.

"This way," the Serene Commander says as we head through the labyrinth of rooms and corridors inside the Cathedral. I know them all. I memorized each of them every time I left this place to hunt at night.

A short way in, the Roden-Darr steps up close to Isaac's other side, his foul scent making my stomach churn.

"Brother Isaac, I'm relieved to see you," he says, his voice oily and smooth. "We believed you were killed in the battle with the Cruel One."

"What happened in the fight, Brother Kemuel?" Isaac asks. "My memory fails me every time I try to recall it."

Kemuel must have been thinking hard from the moment we

stepped inside the Cathedral. "The Cruel One was secured in the net, but we underestimated her ability to control dragon's gold. She used her power to lift the remains of Sienna Scorn's gun and hit you with it so hard that you collapsed. You weren't breathing. I'm sorry, brother. We believed you had passed."

"Hmm," Isaac says. "Her control of dragon's gold is powerful indeed. You will need to be wary of it."

"Are you confident she is subdued now?" the Roden-Darr asks, and I feel his eyes on me.

"Very," Isaac replies. "Trust me, brother, I will not make the same mistake twice."

As they speak, I'm suddenly aware that we've taken a turn *away* from the direction of my cell. I clench my fists and slowly tap my fingers against my palms. It's a quiet movement, but it will warn Isaac that something isn't right.

Not that he can do anything about it.

We're heading into the heart of the Cathedral, where more angels join the guard around me until I'm nearly certain that every angel and every Roden-Darr in the Cathedral is now escorting me—ten in front and at least twenty behind me.

When the group ahead splits in half and begins lining up along the walls on either side of me, I sense we're nearing our destination.

The movement of air around me tells me that we're coming to the end of a corridor. Up ahead, a door opens and quickly closes again, and I identify Aria's scent as she hurries toward us.

She falls into step beside the Serene Commander with a hushed, "I reported what was said at the door. She knows Isaac's alive."

Moments later, we come to a stop.

Someone—the Serene Commander, I think—knocks loudly on the door.

It swings open and she says, "Isaac, you will proceed inside."

He hesitates, his grip on my arm tightening like a warning. "This isn't a cage," he says.

The tension in his voice is overpowered by the energy now emanating from the room ahead of us.

Fuck. I thought *the Serene Commander's scent* was pure. I never imagined any angel could have a scent like the one I'm inhaling now. It's so pure, it washes away everything around it.

Can the absence of a scent be a scent?

Within the room, there's a swish of material—a skirt, most likely—combined with soft footfalls that somehow make me think of ice cracking dangerously on the surface of a lake.

I have no doubt I'm now standing in the presence of the Celestial Ascendant.

CHAPTER THIRTY-FIVE

*T*he longer Isaac hesitates in the doorway, the thicker the expectant silence around us becomes.

The Serene Commander's emerging anger is like the thick haze of fog over a meadow, but its impact is dull compared to the power ahead of me.

I listen to Isaac's deeply inhaled breath before he finally urges me forward.

The Serene Commander steps in behind us, firmly closing the door before anyone else can follow us inside.

Kemuel's voice is sharp behind us. "I really think I should come with—"

His objection cuts off when the door seals.

Isaac halts me not more than three steps inside the room. The tension thrumming through his body is like electricity and I *will* him to be calm, although I suspect that his anxiety is not so much about the Celestial Ascendant, but about my reaction to her.

She speaks in lilting tones, the most graceful voice I've ever heard. "Remove the child's blindfold. I want to look at her."

Child?

Maybe, compared to her, I *am* a child, but still...

I quickly squash my anger and cast my eyes downward, concentrating on keeping my expression blank, my countenance compliant, calling on the memory of how fuzzy Isaac's soul light made me feel when he used it on me.

He lets go of my arm to untie the material and slide it free.

I blink slowly and keep looking down while my eyes adjust. I'm immediately aware of the legs of polished wooden furniture, the gleaming floor, and the ornate decoration around the base of the walls.

I always wore my blindfold within the Cathedral and saw none of its interior except the corridor at the top of the steps leading down into my cell. The walls of that hallway are paneled with ivory stone and decorated with gold filigree, so I imagined that the rest of the Cathedral would be just as beautiful.

I don't look higher than the top of the large wooden desk opposite me, no higher than the Celestial Ascendant's waist, but already, I can see that this room is grotesquely opulent. Overdone. Not the simple beauty I expected.

The Celestial Ascendant folds her hands demurely in front of herself. Her fingernails are perfectly manicured and shine like pearls. She's wearing a white skirt with a belt that's adorned with jewels: rubies, sapphires, and emeralds. Her boots are mahogany leather, like a female Sentinel's armor.

"Well, child," she croons sweetly. "What a fearsome mess this is."

I remain silent as she glides toward me, her voice sharpening. "You will look at me when I'm speaking to you!"

My gaze flashes upward.

She halts, her lips parting as she stares back at me without flinching. Her hair is auburn like a glittering sunset, her lips glossy, and her skin tanned. She's radiant. Fearless.

Her presence doesn't evoke the tang of copper, the heaviness of cloves, or fill my mouth with sour lemon. No muddy lilacs. Not even the scent of lilies that would speak of loss.

Nothing at all.

The last Avenging Angel's words return to me with sudden clarity. I *feel* what she meant when she wrote:

Even an angel is not above justice. Even an angel who claims purity as a shield.

There is a shield around this angel, a power that stops me sensing her guilt, but she is not faultless.

If I do nothing else, I will break her shield and discover what lies beneath.

A smile touches her lips the longer she holds my gaze. "Well," she says softly. "What am I going to do with you?"

"If I may, Celestial Ascendant, she needs to be in a cell," Isaac says. "According to Kemuel, she broke through my soul light when we captured her the first time. She could do it again."

The Celestial Ascendant barely acknowledges his concerns. "Oh, but this angel has already broken many things. The laws of nature. The natural order. The hierarchy of angels. She is so monstrous that it's hard to believe I ever held her life in my hands and allowed her to live."

She nods to herself. "I intend to rectify that mistake without delay."

She holds out her hand for my glaive. "Give me her weapon."

Isaac's hand tightens around the glaive's hilt. "Celestial Ascendant?"

She turns her hard gaze on him. "Give me her weapon, drop the bag, and leave." She swings to the Serene Commander. "Both of you."

The Serene Commander is standing at my back, but her surprise is like a rush of cold air as she steps forward. "With respect, Celestial Ascendant, is that wise?"

The Celestial Ascendant scoffs. "Do not fear for me, my dear. She will not overcome me like she overcame you. I'm stronger than you."

The Serene Commander stiffens at the insult. "As you wish."

She bows and spins on her heel. Seconds later, the door opens and closes behind her.

"You too, Isaac," the Celestial Ascendant says more softly. "You've done your duty. Go, eat a meal, and get some rest. I'm sure your brothers will want to hear your story. Don't worry about me. I'll be fine."

"Thank you, Celestial Ascendant," he says, stepping forward, turning my weapon so that it's horizontal with the floor and holding it out to her as she requested.

Go to her, I whisper to the glaive. *Let her know your strength so that she will fear you when you come for her.*

The Celestial Ascendant's perfectly manicured hand closes around the glaive's hilt and her smile grows as she tests its balance.

Isaac steps back and bows deeply to her, but his stormy gaze flashes across me as he turns away from her.

I don't want him to be worried for me.

I have everything I need to kill her.

Within seconds, the door closes behind him, and now it's just me and her.

"This is a beautiful weapon," she says, turning the glaive into the light. "The warrior angels told me that this glaive was formed from a simple band of gold, as if you conjured it with a mere thought." She gives a light laugh that grates across my nerves. "What a preposterous lie. Even the ancient dragons couldn't fashion a weapon like this in seconds."

She gives me no warning. She's barely finished speaking when she swings the glaive at my throat, its blade glinting as it cuts through the air toward me.

The weapon stops an inch from my skin.

I don't flinch. This blade would never harm me.

It stops so suddenly that the Celestial Ascendant's arms shudder and her knuckles turn white.

She grunts with the impact. Her brow furrows, but she continues to push the weapon, her lips twisting and a bead of sweat dripping down the side of her face. "Damn... dragon's... gold..."

With a scream of rage, she wrenches my glaive backward and hurls it at the wall. The weapon stops before it would break the garish, gold filigree, humming in the air like a plucked string, while she glares at it, her chest heaving.

I use those seconds wisely, calling my armband to me, along with the bullets. I also send a quick thought to the feathers to be ready if I need them.

The golden bullets glint and the Celestial Ascendant spins back to me, her auburn hair flicking about her face and her lips forming a surprised circle. "Oh. You're awake."

Strike.

At my command, the glaive slices the air, flying back at her, aiming for her neck like she aimed it at mine. The bullets shoot through the air, each one intended for her torso.

But in the same instant, the golden filigree lifts off the walls around us like puzzle pieces, flying past me and onto her body, forming armor faster than my weapons can reach her.

She ducks and rolls. My glaive spins harmlessly over her head and thuds into the opposite wall. Only three of my bullets hit her, but her armor is already in place, and they smack into it, dinting it and sticking for a second.

She rises to her feet.

The bullets drop off her chest.

"This"—she explains with a gleaming smile as she gestures at the breastplate that formed across her torso—"is angel's gold."

CHAPTER THIRTY-SIX

The Celestial Ascendant lifts her hand and a group of filigree pieces still clinging to the wall behind her rise up and fly in her direction.

They elongate and turn around on themselves, fitting together to form a poleaxe that she deftly catches and swings toward me.

I leap back in time to avoid her attack, extremely wary of this new weapon. If it's anything like a Sentinel's spear, then it could kill me with a single scratch.

Calling my glaive back to me, I welcome its weight in my hand, but I sense it shudder, as if it's trying to shake off the feeling of being held by that angel.

I also sense its rage.

It has a purpose, and so do I.

I prowl left while the Celestial Ascendant prowls right so that we're circling each other in the wide space at the front of the room. Gently, she swings her poleaxe back and forth at her side as she moves, as if she's reacquainting herself with its shape and strength.

"Well, Asper," she says, "what are we going to do?"

"I'm going to finish you," I say, scrutinizing every move of her body, the way she favors her right leg, and the possible weakness in her left arm since she hasn't used it to hold her weapon yet.

"You won't kill me." She laughs, a soft, confident sound. "You can't kill the faultless. Only the guilty."

"You're mistaking me for my predecessor," I say. "There's a dragon in me who fills my heart with enough fire to tear down your shields and find your guilt. Then I will *end* you for the crimes you've committed against the dragons."

"Dragons!" she snaps. "Oh, but they're seductive creatures. Their strength. Their *fire*. It warms the blood and inspires such envy."

As she speaks, I split my focus between her weapon and her armor, trying to get a feel for the nature of her gold. I was once able to hold the Serene Commander's spear without pain, but I wasn't able to make it do what I wanted. I was very surprised at the time when Solomon Grudge used his power to flick the spear out of the Serene Commander's hands. He didn't exactly control it, or use it as a weapon, but he commanded it.

I wonder...

Is angel's gold so different from dragon's gold?

I need to connect with it to find out. I can't sense its emotions across the air or call to it like I can with dragon's gold. Right now, all I can guess is that it's insulated—shielded, somehow—like the Celestial Ascendant's true nature.

"You doomed dragons to extinction because you envied them," I say, wanting to keep her talking.

Her head shoots high. "Of course not! Envy is a sin."

My lips curve into a smile. *So it is. And I'm certain she feels it.* "Why, then?"

"Dragons don't belong in a modern world," she says, the first hint of true passion in her voice. "They are beasts that hunted other creatures—and not just for food, but for sport. They razed whole villages to the ground. Their hunger for blood could never be sated. They had to be annihilated, or they would have destroyed us!"

There's truth in her claims. When I was in the veil, Atrox tried to convince me to hunt with him, to truly understand a dragon's strength and dominance. He killed beautiful animals—a crime I can't forgive—and brought death to the Avenging Angel's haven. Likewise, Dominus boasted about killing thunderbirds, not for food or survival, but for the exhilaration of the hunt...

Atrox told me: *Dragons kill what they want.*

But they are the old souls, who lived in an old world that's gone now. The former Celestial Ascendant may have believed she was doing the right thing taking away their 'power,' but instead, she guaranteed the rebirth of dragons who don't belong in the modern world.

I sigh. "By trying to defeat dragons, you created what you feared: powerful enemies."

The Celestial Ascendant's cheeks flush. "I did what was right!"

My voice grows stronger. "Hiding the dragon's light? Imprisoning my mother? Keeping me in a cage? Contributing to the extinction of an entire species?"

Her lips twist into a cruel line as she pauses opposite me and repeats slowly and with emphasis, "I did what was right."

For the briefest moment, sour lemon coats my tongue.

Her guilt is fleeting, but it's enough. Like a wedge that can be used to push a door open.

I need to connect with her gold, her heart, push her to her limits and force her to reveal her inner thoughts...

"I'm the Celestial Ascendant," she snarls. "Ordained in the heavenly realm. My word is truth."

Even an angel is not above justice.

"Yet I'm here to judge you," I say.

Her eyes flash from my head to my feet, a scathing assessment, but again, for the briefest moment, I sense her inner emotions—this time, the sharpness of fear.

She continues to swing her weapon, but she's gripping it far more tightly as she says, "From the day you were born, I wondered: Who would be stronger—you or me?"

"Time to find out." I leap toward her, holding my glaive in both hands as I swing it at her head in a move designed to test her strength.

She blocks with her poleaxe, ramming it downward, attempting to disarm me. Her move exposes her left side.

I was hoping for that.

I've trained myself to fight left-handed. While maintaining control of my glaive with my left hand, I use my right hand to shove her shoulder—flat-palmed.

My intention was merely to connect with her gold and, in that first heartbeat, I confirm that it's insulated. It's almost like looking through the frozen surface of a river while icy water rushes along the riverbed below. The power in the gold is as immense and alive as the energy in my glaive and my feathers, contained beneath a shield.

But in the next heartbeat, the charm on my bracelet knocks against the gold too, swinging forward with the momentum of my hand.

Crack!

White light bursts across the Celestial Ascendant's chest, originating from the point of contact. The sound of breaking ice is so sharp, it's like a dagger through my mind.

The Vanem Dragon said that the bracelet contained light magic, but *damn...*

In that same instant, the Celestial Ascendant's countenance changes and suddenly, I can see who she truly is.

Her eyes are pure darkness, a void like a cavern in which treacherous creatures thrive. Her skin is mottled gray and putrid, as if her heart has rotted. Her fingers are clawed, and her fingernails are caked with blood and filth, dirt she can't remove.

The exposure of her inner nature is brief, a mere flicker, before her appearance reverts to an illusion of perfection.

But the impact on me is lasting.

My mouth floods with copper, choking me with the sensation of swallowing blood, and my heart feels like it's being stabbed repeatedly with daggers of malice.

Decades of the deaths she caused—not by her personal hand, but as the known and intended consequences of her deliberate choices—draw a scream to my throat.

Some of them are deaths I was part of.

That's all I see before we're thrown back from each other in the force of the explosion.

Neither of us loses our feet, both remaining upright but crouched opposite each other.

In the blast of light magic, I sense Viviana's shadow, a flicker of amber at my side, the hint of her shape, but the burst of magic must have been too short to sustain her presence.

The Celestial Ascendant's lips are parted in shock, her focus flicking to the bracelet.

I've never had so much certainty about what I need to do.

I advance on her, holding my glaive ready while the bullets—and now the feathers—hover in the air around me.

"You kept the light from the dragons," I say. "You knew the pain it was causing them, but you didn't stop. You sent my mother to find them so you could slaughter the Grudge. You gave me to the Serene Commander, who raised me to hate all dragons. My own people." My voice rises. "I killed them for you!"

"Then you're as guilty as I am!" she screams back at me, and with her rage, her eyes turn dark, her skin becomes gray, and her fingers claw. Again, it's only for a moment, but the door is open now.

"I am guilty," I say. "And I'll pay the price for that soon enough. But before I die, I will embrace all that I was born to be."

I leap forward, anticipating the swing of her poleaxe at my torso. Spreading my wings, I use them to maintain my balance as I lean sharply left, avoiding her weapon. Her swing has left her other side exposed, and I plant my left hand on her armor for a brief second as I slide past.

Free yourself.

My mental command is fleeting, but I know the gold heard me when the metal plates ripple, separating briefly before pulling together again. It's not enough time to ram my glaive into the gap, but I'm certain that I will make it happen.

The Celestial Ascendant isn't idle. Her boot kicks toward me hard enough to break my jaw, but I manage to evade her.

Snapping my wings closed, I spin and leap back into the fight. She's fast and strong, but so am I. Our weapons clash and clang against each other. When I try to use my bullets against her, her armor moves across her body and protects her. As we fight, she calls more of the gold from the wall and a multitude of blades slice the air and for a moment, I'm not sure how I can evade all of them.

Just as they would reach me, my feathers wrap over my skin, covering my arms and chest and forming a moving set of armor that protects my body.

I send a quick message of gratitude to them, but that's all I can manage before the fight demands all my attention.

Within moments, gold swirls around us in a brilliant tornado of metal that's answering our commands.

Bullets, blades, and both our weapons strike and deflect. It's so fast and so intense that we're engulfed in a storm of our own making.

My muscles are screaming. My mind is stretched to breaking point. My reflexes fire so quickly that it's pure animal instinct. My most basic need to survive.

But I've fought hard battles my entire life and she's tiring faster than I am, her reactions slower—only slightly—but it's enough.

I take a risk. A big one.

I throw my glaive—not at her, but over her head. It makes a *whooshing* sound before it thumps into the wall behind her.

Her eyes widen with glee. I suppose she thinks she somehow disarmed me. In all the chaos, it might seem so. At best, she probably thinks I've made a mistake out of exhaustion.

Once again, she goes for the quick kill, her axe aiming for my throat while her golden blades prepare for killing strikes.

I step close, right into the danger, and block her arm, wrapping my left hand around her wrist. Her armor-plated chest is wide open, and I shove my right palm against her shoulder, above her heart.

This time, I'm ready for the blast of light magic when my charm connects with her armor.

To her gold, I say: *Be rid of her.*

Just like before, the plates that form her armor part. It's only the slightest separation before the light magic hits her shoulder in another blast of white light.

The Celestial Ascendant is thrown backward.

So am I, but I'm ready this time, sending a final command to my glaive while I release my wings and soar with the current. My feathers can't protect me from all of the Ascendant's golden blades. They nick my arms and legs, causing flesh wounds, but it's a necessary sacrifice to achieve what I wanted.

Opposite me, there's a *thump* and the Celestial Ascendant's backward momentum comes to an abrupt halt. Her eyes fly wide with shock.

The wash of light magic dissipates as the Celestial Ascendant drops to her knees in front of her desk and looks down at her chest, her forehead creasing with faint disbelief.

"Oh," she says.

One end of my glaive protrudes from her chest, its sharpest end neatly aligned with the gap between the plates of her armor. If I were to step around her, I would see just how precisely my weapon slipped through one of the gaps that had formed in the armor across the back of her left shoulder. The glaive impaled her at a downward angle, given force by her own backward momentum in the blast.

She drops her poleaxe to the floor, her arms going limp while she remains on her knees.

Her blades are still hovering in the air around me, but my feathers are greater in number. They wrap around her gold and force it back to the wall, away from me.

She looks up at me as I slowly approach.

My chest is heaving and sweat drips down my face. My muscles want nothing more than to force me to drop to the ground, so I do, but carefully, kneeling a few paces away from her.

"I was watching your bullets," she says, as if she needs to explain how she lost awareness of my glaive.

"Hmm." I fold my hands in my lap.

Her breathing is increasingly shallow. "You haven't asked me... where I hid the dragon's light..."

"I don't need to," I say quietly. "I already know where it is."

"Oh." She's quiet for another moment. "It's angry. It was getting... harder to control, but... it became far worse when you didn't return to your cell these past weeks." Her voice is strained now. "You will never survive it."

"I know that, too."

"We doomed ourselves." Her shoulders are slumping, her head is lowering, and her hair is stuck to her sweaty face.

I can hear her heartbeats slowing down. It will only be moments before they stop altogether.

Just when I consider doing her the mercy of helping her stay upright until her final breath, she gives a spiteful laugh.

"I put it behind your cell," she says, "because I thought... if it's going to destroy everything around it... then at least it will destroy you first..."

Even though she's slumping over, she tries to keep her eyes

on me, probably wishing to witness my reaction to her final taunt.

Her forehead creases a little, as if she's puzzled, when I don't react at all.

"I'm an Avenging Angel," I say softly. "Your death was my goal. Now it's done."

Her lips part, but that's when her heart stops beating, and whatever she was going to say remains unspoken.

CHAPTER THIRTY-SEVEN

I remain in silence for a long moment.

I know I need to move, but I also need to process my fight with the Celestial Ascendant, so I stay, motionless, right where I am.

Finally, the quiet within the room is broken by the soft slither of her gold falling from her body.

I don't let it touch the ground.

Quickly gathering my thoughts, I say to it: *Come to me.*

Without the Celestial Ascendant to counter my commands, the pieces float across to me. At the same time, my feathers peel off the walls around me, releasing the blades that have now become docile, and they glide over to me too.

All of the gold gathers around me: the bullets, the feathers, the blades, and the pieces of armor. Together with my armband, my bracelet, and my glaive, they're all mine now.

A hoard worthy of any dragon.

I rise slowly to my feet while the hovering gold parts for me.

Proceeding to the Celestial Ascendant's body, I step around her, press my boot to her back, and pull out my glaive.

Removing my shirt, I use it to clean my weapon before I straighten out her body and lay my shirt over her face.

"You will see no more," I murmur to her. "All the life you could have lived, and all the love you could have given, is forfeited."

Rising back to my feet, I call the swarm of gold to me, reaching out to brush my fingertips across the pieces. The delicate feathers. The sharp blades. The cold bullets. Some fashioned with love, others with hate.

"What will you become now?" I ask them, speaking aloud this time. "It's your choice."

The gold begins to spin, the pieces whirling together in a new tornado, this one smaller than the one they made when I was fighting the Celestial Ascendant, but no less furious.

Three items begin to take shape as the pieces meld together.

The first is a harness with straps shaped at the back to accommodate my wings while creating a scabbard the perfect size for my glaive. I step into the harness, slipping my arms through each side while the gold glides into place. Then I slide my glaive into it.

The second is a supple breastplate that divides into four separate pieces and slips neatly beneath my harness to cover my chest and lower back and protect my vital organs. As it settles into place around my torso, a pattern emerges across the plates: the shapes of feathers, and I sense where several of my feathers have gone into this piece. The love with which it was made disperses through the armor.

The third item puzzles me.

It looks a bit like a lotus flower with a flat base about the size of my palm and large petals curving up around it. It's made up of alternating feathers and blades and the whole thing is about the size of a small bowl.

I'm not sure what to make of it, but when I reach out to touch it, it flattens itself, the petals folding over the top to form a disc, which zips onto my armor and positions itself above my heart.

It's a little odd, but I gave the gold the choice to become what it wants to be, so I don't fight it.

Last of all, I reach into the duffel bag for the only remaining item: the Book of Angelic Monsters written by the last Avenging Angel. I won't take it with me to the orb because there's no leftover gold to protect it from whatever fires I'll have to face.

I open it to the last entry, place it on the Celestial Ascendant's desk, and back away. It's up to the angels if they read it.

After taking a deep breath, I proceed to the door, listening for who might be waiting beyond it. I expect to hear the heartbeats of warrior angels and Roden-Darr guarding the door, but there's... nothing.

Only a heavy silence.

But... why?

Carefully pushing open the door, I find the corridor empty. Possibly, the Serene Commander ordered everyone away. After all, the Celestial Ascendant dismissed her.

After closing the door behind me, I hurry down the corridor, checking the hallways that lead off from it.

They're also empty.

I stop at the end of the corridor and that's when I sense a sudden vibration in the walls. Crouching to the floor, I press my palm to its surface, attempting to discern the origin of the tremors.

Energy thrums through my hand, but it feels like two different kinds. One is biting and sharp like the dark energy around the Book of Light Magic before I calmed it. The source of that dark energy is most certainly the orb, hidden beneath the Cathedral. It's painful enough to make me withdraw my hand quickly.

The other source of the vibrations feels physical—a literal shaking of the walls—as if the Cathedral were...

My eyes widen.

The Cathedral is under attack.

The next vibration is visible in the walls around me, which tremble as if an earthquake has just started. Fine cracks shoot through the wall to my left, and a mist of plaster falls from the ceiling above me.

Quickly, I calm my heart and extend my senses, immediately discerning the fury of a battle on the Cathedral's western side: the ring of metal on metal, the crack of bones breaking, the shouts and clamor, and the awful chaos of rapidly beating hearts fueled by fear and adrenaline.

My heart sinks as I wonder if Micah and the Dread dragons have chosen to attack the Cathedral, after all. Of course, if it's not them, then it's Atrox and Dominus.

I race down the hallway to my left, my footfalls quiet while the vibrations grow louder.

The next room I pass through appears to be some sort of meditation room. It has a row of windows high up on my left side that allow natural light inside. Like the Celestial Ascendant's chambers, its walls are decorated with gold, but the threads are finer and more tasteful. It's also larger, its floor is wooden, and pastel-colored cushions are scattered across the entire left side.

Reaching the closed door on the other side of the room, I pause there for a cautious moment. Placing my palm on the door's surface, I estimate that it's made of thick wood, possibly to create a sound buffer to protect the serenity of this room.

It doesn't stop me sensing the two heartbeats of the beings rapidly approaching along the corridor on the other side of it. One has a shimmering silhouette that tells me they're an angel—a Roden-Darr, most probably, because they're brighter than the usual warrior angels.

The other heartbeat conveys a deep *thud-thud* that's immensely powerful.

It's either Atrox or Dominus and I won't know which until they burst through the door.

I back away into the center of the room, mentally preparing myself for the battle ahead.

In my heart, I know that fighting either of the dragon brothers could mean the end of me. They're both powerful and strong. They both want me dead. But of the two, Dominus is the one who has no reason to keep my body alive. Viviana may have once been his friend, but his actions in the veil proved he doesn't value her life highly enough to keep me alive. He wants the orb because he believes it will restore his full power and he'll jeopardize his relationship with his brother to get it.

Crack!

The heavy door splits down the middle and the two pieces spiral across the room.

Gold glints in the doorway as Dominus storms through, his hammer swinging. I'm surprised to see him wearing Atrox's armor—all except the helmet—but not surprised that it's splattered with blood.

He halts abruptly, his large form a towering menace as his focus falls on me. Whereas Atrox carries grief in his green eyes, Dominus is cold. A shadow of growth sits across his jaw and his hard lips are set in a cruel line. His wings aren't extended, but golden scales give his skin a sheen that is more than beautiful. It's nearly impossible to pierce his hide.

"Asper Ashen-Varr." He prowls toward me, moving more slowly now, while I stand my ground. "The little bird who keeps flitting into my path."

I recognize Zadkiel hovering in the doorway behind him. He's the dark-haired traitor who tried to kill Isaac. But of course he's leading Dominus in this direction; their plan is to force the Celestial Ascendant to give up the orb's location.

"You brought up your timeline," I say to Dominus, making his brow furrow. "You didn't plan to attack until tomorrow." I narrow my eyes at him. "Not enough dead angels until then."

Zadkiel interjects. "Kemuel sent word that you were here."

Zadkiel's white wings ruffle at his sides and the distance between us isn't enough to stop his muddy lilac smell from wafting toward me. "Time is of the essence."

I'm a little intrigued that they're here because *Kemuel* sent word, and not because Atrox tracked me, but I keep those thoughts to myself.

I give Zadkiel a cold smile. "You failed to kill Isaac. Just as you won't reach the Celestial Ascendant."

Zadkiel's lips pinch, but I don't wait for his response before I turn back to Dominus.

"Where's your brother?" I ask him. "I thought he'd be at your side."

Dominus snarls so savagely that it seems I've struck a nerve. "Atrox's goals have diverged from mine."

I consider the dragon cautiously. Even if Atrox's motivations now differ from Dominus's, there's no path Atrox could take that's good for me. If he were at his brother's side, then at least I'd know what to expect.

Even so, I understand the core differences between them.

"Atrox is fueled by a broken heart and anger about his lost life," I say. "You act only out of a desire for power."

"Power that is rightfully mine!" Dominus snarls. "All my life, I stood in my brother's shadow, a mere reflection of him. Yes, we protected each other. But it was his name that was known. His reputation. His life that mattered." Dominus steps toward me, his knuckles turning white where he grips his hammer. "I want what's owed to me."

"Well," I say softly, planting my feet before I briefly incline my head in the direction of the doorway behind me. "The Celestial Ascendant is that way."

Dominus's gaze rakes down my body, a coldly calculating glance. "You think I will underestimate you." His lips draw back. "But I will not."

"Good," I murmur. "Because I'm going to kill you."

He laughs. "Now, little bird, *you* underestimate *me*."

Taking a quick step forward, he swings his hammer at my head. His reach is long enough that the side of the hammer would have crushed my face if I wasn't so quick.

I've already thrown myself backward, my wing beats giving me enough speed to evade his weapon.

I won't survive a long, drawn-out fight with him. My armor protects parts of my body, but it won't shield me against a hit with his hammer—the light magic will rage right through me. I have my glaive, but it won't pierce his tough scales. I tried controlling his hammer once and found it impossible. I have no guarantees I'll succeed this time. As for my mental state, I'm still recovering from my fight with the Celestial Ascendant.

I need to end this quickly, but it's going to take everything I have.

Drawing my glaive, I focus only on his hammer and not on his other fist.

I don't have time to take a breath, only to act on instinct.

As he chases after me, hefting the hammer back to swing it again, I beat my wings and dart inward, fully retracting them in the next instant. Knocking into his chest, I wrap my legs around his waist and use every muscle in my torso and all my forward momentum to drive my glaive down across his bicep.

My intention was to knock him off-balance, or at best, force him to drop the hammer, but as my weapon connects with his arm, its blade changes shape.

Multiple rows of short, razor-sharp needles form across its entire edge.

My eyes widen as I catch sight of them a split second before they slice right into his scales.

This weapon once saved my life when Solomon Grudge was my enemy. It saved Callan's life when the Serene Commander was about to kill him. Maybe, now, it will save me again.

Beautiful, angry blade.

"Fuck!" Dominus's shout is so close to my ear that it's deafening.

I don't waste my advantage, ripping my weapon backward, tearing flesh and sinew as I move fast.

It was possible to kill the Celestial Ascendant by commanding my glaive from a distance, but to kill Dominus with his scaled skin will take far more force. I'll only have one chance to deliver a lethal strike while he's in shock. One chance to drive my weapon into his throat with enough strength to cause mortal damage before he crushes me with his left fist—which is already flying toward me.

My legs are still wrapped around his waist, my backward momentum as I pull my weapon from his arm pressing the apex of my thighs against his armor. I scream with effort as I propel myself toward him again, trying to complete the swing of my glaive before his fist reaches me.

My weapon rams into the side of his neck.

His left fist collides with my ribs and even my armor can't protect me.

My bones *pop*.

A scream of pain leaves my lips.

But he's stumbling backward, and I force myself to move through the agony, unfurling my legs and spreading my wings. I lift off him and fly backward as fast as I can, leaving my weapon right where it is.

He grabs at the blade embedded in his neck as he tries to speak, blood bubbling through his teeth, before he drops to his knees.

I'm moaning with pain, my own breath coming fast, but I can't take my eyes off him. Not even when Zadkiel gives a shout of rage, seeming only now to realize that his beloved master is on the cusp of death.

The white-winged angel rushes toward Dominus, but I'm merciless.

Cruel like the name that was given to me.

With a single command, my glaive rips from Dominus's throat, spins so that its other point is aimed at Zadkiel, and flies into his chest.

His forward momentum works against him, and my aim is accurate, hitting his heart and stopping him in his tracks.

He's knocked sideways and his reflexes must still be firing because he extends his right hand toward me. I sense the burn of his soul light as it crackles through his arm, but I don't move out of the way because I know it will never reach me.

His heart has already stopped.

His body meets the floor a moment later.

I glide back to the ground as the silence within this room thickens.

Beyond this space, the sound of battle continues, but in here...

The quiet is only broken by Dominus's labored breathing and the soft tap of my boots on the polished wooden floor as I stumble closer.

He presses both of his big palms to his neck to try to stop the bleeding, his forehead creased with disbelief, or maybe determination, but the damage is too catastrophic.

He survived for millennia in a dark prison, and if he'd chosen a different path since escaping it, we wouldn't be here now.

For a moment, I remember the seconds before Solomon Grudge died. The irreversible damage that left him alive for long enough to speak with me but ensured his healing power could not save him.

My heart hurts at the memory of all the things that could have been.

It's painful to speak, but I tip my head to the side as I whisper, "Have you ever seen a dragon hunt a thunderbird, Dominus Audax?"

It was the first thing that Dominus said to me, back when I thought he was Atrox.

He doesn't answer, but even now, the cold in his eyes is like ice around my soul.

His skin is increasingly pale, his broad shoulders hunched, his golden scales slowly receding.

As his life and his power fade, I say, "I am the dragon."

CHAPTER THIRTY-EIGHT

*M*y chest is cold, and pain strikes me with every breath I take.

I force myself to move as fast as I can away from the room where I put an end to Dominus and Zadkiel.

My glaive is back in its harness—cleaned once again. I'm carrying Dominus's hammer, although it requires both my hands due to its weight. My footfalls are quiet.

I may never have seen the path to and from my cell with my open eyes, but I've memorized it, and I follow it now by instinct.

I've only taken two steps into the next room when the charm on my bracelet begins to glow. Not a burst of light magic, but a strong, sharp, crimson glimmer. It's the same glow it made when Callan re-emerged in the forest of the veil.

My breath catches because of the implication that Atrox is ahead, and I prepare myself as I hurry in the direction of the continuing battle. The next corridor I come to is cracked so badly that part of it falls to the floor as I proceed swiftly past it.

Beyond this corridor... is pure, fucking chaos.

I've reached the central atrium, and it's littered with glass from the broken ceiling and debris from shattered furniture. The far walls are charred.

Warrior angels are battling Roden-Darr. They're fighting in the air as well as on the ground. On the left side of the room, I spot Isaac fighting back-to-back with the Serene Commander. I'm sure that's an uneasy alliance, but a necessary one, given that the Roden-Darr are their common enemy.

As if Isaac senses my presence—and maybe, somehow, he does—he spins in my direction.

At the same time, the Roden-Darr named Kemuel, who escorted me into the Cathedral, flies toward me from the other side of the room.

He's carrying a deadly Sentinel spear, but my fight with the Celestial Ascendant has given me the confidence to deal with angel's gold now.

With a single thought, I disarm him, sending his spear into the cracked wall to my right, where it twangs—a sound that's drowned by Kemuel's cry of rage.

I'm about to heft the hammer so that I can fly up to him and knock him down when a blast of light propels him to the floor.

I recognize it immediately as Isaac's soul light.

He runs toward me, his wings tucked tightly to his sides and his white hair matted with blood—whose, I don't know.

His eyes meet mine across the distance. If he's surprised by my armor, he doesn't show it. "Go, Asper! Do what you need to do!"

I hesitate. There appears to be a greater number of warrior angels as there are Roden-Darr, but the Roden-Darr carry deadly weapons.

Making a judgement call, I decide I can spare the seconds it will take to give the warrior angels an advantage.

My eyes narrow, and I send a firm command to every Sentinel spear in the room.

Each one whips out of its owner's hand and flies into the nearest wall. A ripple of shock passes through the throng, but the fighting only stops for a moment. It won't take the Roden-

Darr long to retrieve their weapons—some of them are already trying to do so—but it will give the warrior angels a chance.

Isaac's eyes are wide with surprise, but he roars at me, "Go!"

I want to stay, but he's right. Another battle lies ahead of me —one I have to fight alone—and I still don't know where Atrox is.

The only way I'll end this war is if I reach the orb and change the course of my peoples' future.

Releasing my wings, I rise into the air, holding the hammer close to my chest as I dart between the warring angels. It's difficult to maneuver around them while I'm carrying the hammer, its heavy nature seeming to want to drag me to the floor, and the pain in my ribs worsens with my continued movement.

Finally making it through the opposite doorway, I touch down, fighting the agony in my chest as I stride along the hallway that will take me to the final corridor from which I can access the stairway down into my cell.

The way is deserted, the sound of the battle recedes, but my heart remains in my throat until I reach the ivory-paneled door leading into the final corridor.

Shoving open the door, I stumble along the hall, realizing just how dark it is. When I lived here, I stopped noticing the absence of natural light. The dimness of the lamps set at intervals along the wall were normal to me. The white wall seemed bright. Now that I've experienced the vibrancy of life outside my cell, the darkness of this place hits me hard.

Halfway along the corridor, I stop and lean against the wall, trying to catch my breath. The hammer slips to the floor, its weight finally getting the better of me, and I have to acknowledge that I can't carry it while I'm injured.

I remind myself that I don't need it to open the veil. I have the bracelet.

Continuing onward, I reach the top of the staircase. It's hewn from within the rock walls around it and the ceiling slopes downward, which means I can't see inside the cell until I'm part of the way down.

That's when I freeze, my foot poised above the next step down.

My cage looks exactly like it did when I left it. It's a small space with the barest of necessities. A lidless toilet and a small, tiled area for showering. A simple mattress on a wooden frame. One blanket folded at the end of the bed. A small desk. A lock on the cage door made of reinforced steel.

And, finally, a chair.

On which now sits a figure whose scent carries both the heat of a fire and the warmth of the sun.

Atrox swivels toward me, his angry eyes seeming to devour me as I take the final steps to the stone floor. His focus quickly moves from the golden armor covering my chest and the new harness to the tip of my weapon that will be visible at my back.

His gaze lingers longest on my face.

I'm sure my cheeks must be splattered with blood, but he won't know that his brother is dead, and I'm not going to tell him. I'm grateful now that I left the hammer behind.

"This cage is unworthy of you," he says, making no comment on my appearance.

"It's better than the cage you put me in."

As I speak, threads of dark magic prickle the soles of my feet, all the way through my boots. I have no option but to bear the sharp pain, just as I'm managing the pain of my cracked ribs.

Can he feel the dark energy? If he can, he isn't showing it.

I stop ten paces from the bars of my old cell. "How did you find this place?"

My mind is working fast. The bracelet lets him track my current location, not predict where I'm going to go, so it can't have brought him here.

Upstairs, Dominus said that their paths had diverged, which was why Atrox wasn't with him. But that doesn't explain why Atrox is *here*.

"I asked Zadkiel to tell me where your cell was," Atrox replies without a flicker of emotion as he rises to his feet, his tall, muscular frame making the cell seem smaller.

"Why?"

He shrugs. "I wanted to understand you."

I shake my head at him as I take another cautious step forward. "*Callan* wanted to understand me. *You* want to hurt and destroy me."

"To destroy your enemy, you must first understand them," he replies.

Well, I suppose that makes more sense than the possibility that he cares about my wellbeing.

He pulls the blanket off the end of the bed and draws it to his face, inhaling deeply. "The night sky after it rains," he declares as he exits the cage toward me. "An intoxicating scent."

He advances on me, his smile mesmerizing. I expect him to ask me why *I'm* here, but instead, he says, "I had a dream about you."

I step to the right as he approaches, maintaining an arm's-length distance between us.

He follows me around as I back away from him—now heading toward my cell.

"You were naked in my arms," he says, his voice a low growl that makes my breath hitch.

Callan warned me that those moments in the shower would seem like a dream to Atrox. I search his eyes for the cinnamon-brown flecks I saw earlier, any hint that Callan might be surfacing, but Atrox appears to be completely in control again.

"A dream is only a dream," I say, stepping quickly backward.

"It felt real," he insists, his voice softer. "Too fucking real." His eyes narrow as he prowls after me. "You were at my home—"

"Callan's home," I say. "Not yours."

He continues without missing a beat. "But I don't remember you leaving. I don't remember *allowing* you to leave."

"Maybe I wasn't there at all." I step back through the opening into my old cage and take a quick look at the lock on the door.

Atrox's response is another heated growl, but he doesn't have the chance to say more before I slide the cage door shut, clicking the lock into place before he can follow me inside.

He pulls up abruptly, but he isn't idle. The lock is reachable through the bars, but it means slipping my arms between them and I don't retract my hands in time. He snatches my left hand into his, locking his fingers around my wrist.

"Why the fuck would you trap yourself in there?" he asks. "You know my fire can melt these bars in seconds."

I can only hope that seconds are all I need.

My left palm is turned toward his arm and it allows me to close my fingers around his forearm. It's a gentle movement, my fingers soft against his skin, because right now, I'm talking to Callan.

I don't know if he can hear me, but I try anyway. "I choose this."

A puzzled crease forms in Atrox's forehead. "Choose what?" he asks. "Your cage?"

Deftly reaching back with my free hand, I slip my glaive from its harness and jab it lightly at his chest between the bars. It barely connects and his golden scales ripple across his skin, but his grip on my hand loosens like I hoped.

I pull my arm free, slip my glaive back into its harness, and hurry across my cell to the back wall.

The energy within its surface is biting.

The Vanem Dragon told me I had no way to detect that a pocket of the veil was hidden behind my cell, and the Celestial Ascendant said that the orb had grown far angrier since I last left this place, which would explain why I didn't feel this energy when I was last here.

But now, little jabs of electricity strike my face, arms, and legs—basically everywhere that my new armor isn't protecting me.

I'm aware of the threat to my gold and it gives me pause. When I stepped into the Grudge dragons' vault where the Book of Light Magic raged, the book's energy destroyed the dragon's gold that was wrapped around it.

I don't want the same outcome for my gold.

You can stay here if you wish, I say to it. *But please choose quickly.*

I give it a beat, but my armor doesn't budge, and my glaive remains in its harness. I don't have much time for gratitude, but it warms my heart all the same.

Behind me, Atrox grips the bars, watching me intently. Heat shimmers around his torso, but he hasn't used his flames yet, his head tilted and lips pursed as if he's too puzzled to take action yet.

I want to ask him how he could have stood within my cell and not felt the sharp energy within these walls, but I think I know the answer. Within my body, I carry the orb's light as well as its rage.

I'm connected to it in a way that nobody else is.

This energy that I now feel tingling across my body is triggered by my presence.

It's reaching out to me, and me alone.

I *alone* can feel it.

But I have no doubt that once I open the entrance, its energy will strike outward with enough force that Atrox will feel it, too.

Quickly, I position my right wrist above my left palm and ask the bracelet to drop into my left hand.

I don't know how to use the magic within the charm to break open the entrance into the veil. All it took was contact with the Celestial Ascendant's body for the light magic to burst outward before, and I hope that will work now.

Before I can raise my hand, Atrox's voice interrupts me, his tone suddenly urgent. "It's here, isn't it?"

The heat of his flames bursts around his mouth and the acrid scent of burning metal grips my chest.

His snarl is guttural. "Our light is fucking *here!*"

I'm out of time.

With my heart in my throat, I ram the ruby charm against the damp, stone wall.

CHAPTER THIRTY-NINE

*W*hite light explodes across me.

I brace, expecting to be flung backward into Atrox's fire, but the dark energy radiating from the other side of the wall wraps around my body and anchors me to the spot.

The bricks in front of me becomes insubstantial, dissolving before my eyes, and I can finally see...

My breath catches and a cry rises into my throat at the destruction that lies beyond this wall.

It's a crimson landscape, every inch of it on fire like some kind of new hell.

Hot wind gusts around a vast circle of trees that stretches out in an arc in front of me. Their trunks are glowing red, as if they're burning from the inside out, and their leaves are brown and curling in the heat. A crumbling stone wall sits behind them, a wide gap in the middle of it, but somehow, the trees are still upright, seeming suspended in the moments between being set alight and crumbling into ash.

A flat courtyard fills the immediate space in front of me, its surface made of what might once have been white marble but is now ruby-red and cracked, the fissures filled with what appears to be molten lava.

In the center of the courtyard is a pedestal that holds the source of all this destruction.

The golden orb is hardly golden anymore.

When Mom described this orb, she said she never dreamed that dragon's gold could radiate with so much rage.

Crackling threads of blood-red energy stream around it, making it impossible to see the orb's original form. A storm of energy is consuming it. An energy that seems acutely aware of my presence.

It strikes toward me, coming straight for my heart.

All of this, I take in within the space of a heartbeat while the light magic within my bracelet breaks across me and my muscles react, my instincts screaming at me to move.

I leap toward the danger. Never away from it.

As my wings thump out at my sides, propelling me right at the source of energy, I'm aware of multiple things at once:

Atrox's fire melting the bars behind me and his scaled fists ripping them apart. His voice roaring, but his speech indiscernible above the howling, hot wind.

Viviana's shadow bursting into form beside me, her amber body towering at my side, her teeth bared, as the surge of light magic within the bracelet clashes with the magic within the veil.

And finally, the way the bracelet cracks within my closing fist, the ruby-heart charm shattering with enough force to cut my palm to shreds.

The pieces are torn from my hand as the dark energy within the veil engulfs me. The shards of the ruby heart charm scatter and mix with the energy shrieking through the air.

"Asper!" Viviana's scream reaches me as the wind catches my wings and flings me into a dizzying spin.

Her presence gives me the power to heal, the damage to my hand and my ribs repairing as I force my wings to contract against my body.

My feathers cocoon me for long enough that I can gather my thoughts. I focus on breathing. Focus on the fact that I've stepped into hell and I'm still alive—despite the heat beating at my face and body and despite the anger rising inside me. Or maybe, *because* of it.

Snapping my wings closed, I push my center of gravity down, managing to find my feet and crouch low to the ground. Viviana's form flickers at my side, the power around us seeming to tear through her over and over.

My palms press hard against the hot marble as I raise my focus to the orb. It's ten paces away but may as well be a mile because the force around us is growing stronger with every passing second.

I feel its rage within my bones, and it's as if my basic structure were becoming putty, my edges unable to be separated from the energy around me. Where my hand rests against the ground, my skin is already glowing ruby-red. The strands of my hair appear like ropes made of fire whipping around my face.

Where I'm crouched, I can partially see the stone wall of my cell behind me.

It's closing up fast, but Atrox is flying toward it. He's as shifted as he can be, his shape still human while his skin is covered in golden scales, his eyes are pure gold, and his wings give him speed.

I pray he doesn't make it.

I can't fight him *and* the orb at the same time.

Just as the edges of the opening shrink inward, he tucks his wings, throws himself into a spin, and shoots through the gap.

It closes behind him with a *crack*.

The crimson rage plucks at his body and he may as well be weightless when it throws him across the courtyard into the nearest tree. Embers explode across his back as he lands on all fours.

He tries to find his feet, struggling upward, only to quickly retract his wings like I did, reducing his body surface.

His focus is on the orb.

Then on me.

Viviana is screaming at my side, her head held close to the ground, her body curled around me like she wants to protect me, but her shadow form can't provide any sort of barrier and her voice is cutting in and out.

I'm closer to the orb than Atrox is, and I'm determined to reach it before he reaches me.

My fingers claw the ground. I grit my teeth, reaching deep for the will to move, shouting at myself to do it, even if it feels like I'm being torn apart.

I scream as I rise to my feet, my head down, shoulders hunched, and I push through the force.

Step by painful step.

I wish I could breathe fire like I did with the Book of Light Magic, but I can't draw a deep enough breath, can only snatch boiling-hot air that scorches the inside of my throat and chest.

Hell... it's so hot that I *might* be breathing fire, for all I know... but if I am, it isn't helping me. Not against this dark energy.

I push myself forward until my legs are screaming, my muscles cramping, and my mind is breaking, little puzzle pieces of my life scattering.

When the force becomes too great to bear, I drop to my knees.

I'm only three steps away from the pedestal.

So close, but I can't get any closer.

Tears flow down my cheeks, their paths trails of lava. My lips are cracked and dry and my armor feels like it's melted onto my skin.

The Celestial Ascendant promised that the orb would destroy me. I was so certain I was meant to find it, so single-minded about my path, but now...

When I tip my head back, my torso buffeted in the storm, I can finally make out the orb's outline, not quite spherical and too large to fit within my fist.

I try to connect with the gold it's made from, try to make a connection with my mind, but the screaming wind around me is flooding my senses and I can't cut through all the noise.

Movement on my right makes my heart sink.

Atrox has caught up with me.

I have no idea what he's going to do, but I'm prepared for his attack, his rage, his fire. I've brought him to the orb—but he must know that he'll have to go through me if he wants it. Assuming it doesn't destroy him just as it's destroying me.

I swing to him just as his wing slips around my back. My defensive move has the effect that I turn into his chest, which allows his other wing to slide around my other side, trapping me in his arms. I struggle against his hold, freezing when he lowers his head to mine and presses his lips to my ear.

"Not-Lana."

My eyes flash to his.

His scales are burning, his golden eyes bright, his lips set in a determined line. I can't inhale his scent. Can't be sure who he is right now, but he presses his cheek to mine within the cocoon of his wings and a trickle of calm breaks through the storm.

His lips move, a kiss brushing my burning cheek. "You can do this."

Tears flood my eyes. I want to believe him, but I can't do it alone. "Callan," I say, allowing myself to speak his name. "I need your help."

"You have it," he says. "For as long as you want it."

He opens his wings just a little, the slice of vision between their edges showing me the orb. The sudden rush of screaming wind emphasizes how much quieter it is inside the canopy of his wings, but I'm aware that with every passing second that he shields me, the orb's energy rages at his back, tearing at him while he protects me.

I should be able to connect with the gold. Should be able to sense it, break through the rage around it, and—

My eyes widen because I suddenly realize that I *am* sensing it. I *am* hearing it.

This wind shrieking within my ears. It's the orb.

It's fucking *screaming*.

The orb is in agony.

I close my eyes and turn within Callan's arms so that my back rests against his chest. I don't know how long he'll keep Atrox at bay, but I trust him to help me for as long as he can.

Slowly, I extend my wings within his, forming another layer within the cocoon he's created, a buffer in which I can start to piece together my thoughts again.

I'm facing outward now, my head tipped back while Callan lowers his cheek to mine. A dragon's touch. A bond that will never break between us.

Outside, the storm rages, but he is my shelter against it.

Viviana's shadow flickers between the gaps in our wings, her luminous gaze seeking mine, both worry and fury on her face. Her lips part as if she's going to try to shout over the raging storm, but she stops when her focus falls on Callan where his cheek rests against mine.

She wouldn't have known that it was him until this moment.

Her features smooth out, her agitation appearing to fade as she settles down onto the ground and I picture her shadow body curved around us as she rests her head down, one big eye visible through the gap in our cocoon.

Taking a shaky breath, I extend my senses to the orb's gold, sensing its smooth surface, the way it curves unevenly in places, and then—surprisingly—the way it's layered in on itself.

Layer upon layer of dragon's gold is wrapped over and over to form the orb.

But that's not all.

As I push myself to delve deeper, I sense that there's another object at its core, and whatever that object is, I'm certain it *isn't* dragon's gold.

My eyes flash open.

The dragon's gold is merely a shield, a covering that's full of rage and sadness and pain while the real power lies in the core.

As if she senses my sudden mental turmoil, Viviana lifts her head, her one visible eye bright as she stares back at me.

She guarded the orb in her lifetime, and I need to ask her if she knows what lies at its core; most importantly, what will happen if I strip away the damaged gold that's surrounding it?

Will I destroy the core, or will I save it?

I don't have a hope of communicating with her in this storm. Even though she's spoken directly into my mind, I've never done the same with her. And I know I'm running out of time.

We all are.

Callan has slumped against me, bearing the brunt of the destructive power around us, defending me from it, but it's killing him.

His thready heartbeat tells me so.

It's fucking killing him, and it's time to put a stop to it.

I tuck my wings and spin in his arms, my heart wrenching at the pain in his face.

I press a kiss to his lips. "I love you."

"Wait—" he rasps.

I'm already pushing out of his arms, propelling myself through the gap in his wings, through Viviana's shadow and out into the storm.

Pain and heat and agony scream through me, tearing at my senses, but I don't fight it this time.

I spread my wings and let the wind lift me off the ground, let it tear at my burning feathers as it casts me upward.

While it rips at my body, I close my eyes and reach out to the golden shield, focusing only on connecting with it, focusing only on understanding it.

You and me, I say. *We're the same. Layers of rage and pain and having nowhere to turn. Nowhere to find love or warmth or safety.*

I open my eyes and seek Callan below. He's struggling to stand, his wings ripping at the edges. His golden scales crack across his chest. He may be a fire dragon, but there's no surviving this inferno.

You gave a part of yourself to me, I continue. *Maybe you didn't mean to, but it happened. You gave me light, but you also gave me fury.*

Well, now I'm here. Brimming with rage.

I could give you a choice, but I'm not going to.

I grit my teeth, ignore the burning hell around me, and gather my strength for one last push.

One last flight.

With everything I have left, I beat my wings against the current and dive straight for the orb, reaching through the energy around it, screaming as it tears my hands and arms bloody as fast as Viviana's power can heal me.

My palms close around the golden orb, my fingers claw against its surface, and I drag up every dark thread within my body and mind, the memory of every death I've ever caused, the *snap* of bones and the silence after, the cold of my cell, and the pain of a lash against my back, and I send a single, merciless command at the dragon's gold:

Break.

CHAPTER FORTY

*T*he orb cracks in my bleeding hands, fissures forming across its surface.

I tear at them, pulling on the gold, ripping at each layer as the storm continues to rage around me.

It's a mindless act as I fall to the burning ground and take the orb with me.

All I know is that I have to break away every darkness that surrounds its core, strip away all the anger, and free what lies within it.

Like breaking open a cage.

I can see it—the core. It's silvery and as bright as a diamond. It glints up at me, a power like nothing I've felt before. Beautiful like nothing I've ever seen.

But only a sliver of it is exposed and, while lumps of gold already rest in my lap, my hands won't work to free it further. My mind is shattered and all I can do is kneel where I've landed to the left of the pedestal, my tattered wings drooped at my sides and my breathing ragged.

But maybe... it was enough.

I manage to raise my eyes as silence falls while the light

within the core continues to shine, growing stronger with every passing moment.

Like mist clearing, the crimson energy raging through our surroundings begins to disappear. Burning leaves fall to the ground, cooling as they drop and turning into little piles of ash.

Viviana rises to her feet. Beside her, Atrox—and I know it's him now because of his scent—has also risen, the edges of his wings slowly healing.

His focus is on Viviana and not on the orb, his voice low when he speaks. "We finally have a chance to live."

She shakes her head gently. "We had our chance."

He responds with vehemence. "I won't accept that. The light will give you back to me."

"It won't," she whispers, stepping toward him. She heard everything the Vanem Dragon said. She knows that as soon as the orb is taken out of the veil, their old souls will be extinguished. "I know how much your heart hurt when I died, but there is no second chance for us."

His features harden before he leaves her side and strides over to me. He towers over me, his golden wings catching the growing silver light and reflecting it around me.

My throat hurts, but I need to speak. "We want the same thing," I whisper. "We both want dragons to live—"

"No!" he snarls down at me. "I want the life I lost. I want the years I never had with Viviana. I want the children that were never mine. I want what was taken from me."

I exhale a quiet sigh. "Then claim the life you want. Kill me and take the orb. You believe that its power will bring Viviana back to you. Well, I can't stop you from trying."

His golden eyes widen, then narrow, but I can't fathom what he's thinking. Maybe he doesn't trust that I don't have a final move up my sleeve. My glaive has survived the ordeal—I can feel its life at my back and I'm not weaponless—but my body is too damaged.

I'm catastrophically wounded.

Just like Solomon.

Just like Dominus.

Besides, I have no reason to stop him.

The moment he steps beyond the veil, he'll do what I no longer can. He'll return the dragons' light to the world, and it will do its work.

Atrox's soul will be extinguished.

The dragons I care about will be strong and free again.

Callan will be able to hug his family.

As for the angels, the Celestial Ascendant isn't alive anymore to spread her poison against dragons, and I'm sure that Isaac will advocate on their behalf. I can only hope that the heavenly realm will finally seek peace with the dragons.

Maybe I'm hoping for too much, but hope is all I have left.

Atrox crouches in front of me, his shoulders tense, watching me warily while his big hand hovers over the orb.

When I do nothing to stop him, he shoves aside the broken pieces of gold from around the diamond and scoops the core into his fist.

As soon as he lifts it from the gold, its light washes across me, and it's like standing in the sun again. A final moment of peace that I can take in and accept.

At the same time, the chunks of gold he left resting in my lap are hurting. I feel their pain in my heart. Taking my focus away from Atrox, I try to pull them toward me, using my forearm to awkwardly gather them close to my armor.

Atrox pulls to his feet, but, to my surprise, he continues to tower over me. His forehead creases and I suppose it's because, for the first time, I've stopped fighting him.

I told him I never would, and now... I have.

His voice is a dangerous growl as he stares down at me. "Viviana only lives through you. I'm taking you from the veil and then the light will do its work. You will no longer exist, and Viviana will live again."

I gasp when he scoops me into his arms, wrapping me up,

broken wings and all. The orb remains in his left fist, which now rests across my shoulder. The fragmented chunks of gold scatter from my lap but rise up into the air and follow us as he strides back to Viviana.

"I will bring you back, and we will live the life we were meant to live," Atrox says to her, vehemently.

Tears glisten down her cheeks as she returns his gaze and simply replies, "Thank you for your fierce love."

She meets my eyes for the seconds it takes Atrox to move on. She gives me the briefest of nods and I hear her voice inside my mind: *Thank you, Asper, for the peace you will bring us. Atrox and I will finally be at rest together.*

I don't have time to speak, but I hope she senses my gratitude toward her. She could have ended me, but she chose not to.

I'm not sure how the exit from the veil will open, but it seems that getting out of here is far easier than getting in. The wall disappears as Atrox approaches it, and within seconds, he will carry me, and the orb, through it.

No matter what happens, I won't make it. I will die and my rage will die with me, but I'll do it knowing that I set things right.

He pauses one step from the exit, staring down at me, his golden eyes inscrutable. "Goodbye, Asper Ashen-Varr."

I raise my eyes to his in a final acknowledgment of this fierce beast, who had the power to dominate his world but lost the one thing he loved.

Without another glance down at me, Atrox steps outside the veil.

The diamond resting on my chest glimmers as if sunlight had suddenly reflected off it. Or maybe starlight. Maybe both.

There's a flash, a *thud*, and then the world turns white.

CHAPTER FORTY-ONE

A golden light glows at the corners of my vision as I slowly open my eyes.

My first response is surprise at the simple fact that I'm still alive. Second, that I'm free of pain, although... something's digging into my back and it takes me a moment to realize it's my weapon pressing uncomfortably against the back of my armor.

I'm nestled against a chest that houses a heart whose calm beat I was afraid I'd never hear again.

"Callan?"

He strokes my hair away from my face, a light, slow touch that makes my breath catch.

I'm bundled up in his arms and my wings are still closed around me, forming a blanket of feathers. I manage to slip my arm free. I have to touch him. I need to know it's really him.

I trace his strong jaw, the slight cleft in his chin, the curve along the bottom of his lower lips... his smile... up to his cheekbones and his warm, cinnamon-brown eyes, which now have...

My forehead creases at the changes in his appearance.

His eyes now have golden flecks in them, and not a hint of juniper green. His hair is a distinct chocolate-brown color, no more charcoal. Along with the subtle changes in his appearance, his presence feels different, and I wish I could pinpoint why.

"Breathe, beautiful dragon-angel," he says softly.

Huh?

Oh, damn. It seems I've forgotten the simplest function.

I take a deep breath, inhaling his warm sunshine scent that feels like basking in the light of a new day. I moan with relief as his familiar scent fills my chest and I exhale all of my tension.

Breathing also seems to expand my awareness of my surroundings. We're still in my cell with the same dingy walls, although the bars are destroyed. The orb rests on my chest, neatly nestled within my feathers so it isn't in danger of rolling off. The diamond glows gently and I sense the immense power within it, but also its restraint. It seems smaller than before, but I didn't really get a good look at it after I broke the thick layers of gold from around it.

Quickly extending my senses beyond my cell, I discover that the Cathedral is peaceful.

No more clash of weapons. No more cracking walls or bones.

I don't know what might have happened up there, but it's serene, and that's all I need to know to return my focus to Callan.

My fingertips pause on his jaw. "You're here," I whisper, struggling to convey how much he means to me.

I missed you doesn't even come close.

"I am." His voice is a low rumble, the same as he used to sound, but now there's something else in it, a deeper growl like a new beast. The corner of his mouth hitches into a broader smile as his pupils constrict to reptilian slits and golden scales form across his forehead and cheeks. "And it seems that I can shift however I like."

I gasp when he extends his wings—a careful move since he's sitting on the floor between my shower and my bed. His wings are still golden, but now they're even more breathtaking with

348

threads of silver winding through the membrane between his golden wing bones.

I can hardly breathe. "You have a new dragon?"

He shakes his head, but his smile doesn't fade. "It's just me. I am the beast."

My eyes widen, but then uncertainty rises inside me. "Are you sure? What if there's a dragon waiting to emerge?"

"Even when I couldn't communicate with Atrox—before he took over—there was a weight in my mind," he says. "A constant sense of threat and dread. It's gone now. I feel whole and complete and in control of every part of my body."

"Then... what kind of dragon are you?" I pause, rethinking my question before I ask more quietly, "*Who* are you?"

His eyes crinkle. Slowly and carefully, he rises to a standing position, still holding on to me. He pulls me up and around so I can easily slip my legs around his waist. Being in this position also frees my wings and I stretch them behind me, conscious of how dark they are. They gleam like perfectly cut black diamonds as I spread them wide, and then, to my surprise, they ripple and shift to a matte black, a color that could allow me to blend into shadows.

I'm so surprised by the changes in my wings that it takes me a second to realize that the orb didn't drop to the floor when Callan changed our position.

I glance down at my chest, only to discover that the third— and previously puzzling—item that my gold formed in the Celestial Ascendant's quarters suddenly has a clear purpose.

Each petal of the lotus flower shape that sits across my heart is gently closing over the top of the diamond and encasing it. Attaching it to my armor. Within moments, it's completely covered.

I can't stop my surprised exhalation. "Oh."

Callan's heated smile draws my attention as he asks, low and soft, "Who are *you*?"

Trusting him to hold on to me, I lift my arms to study them.

They're completely healed, and I sense a new energy within them—within my whole body, in fact. It's a tingling sensation and I latch on to it, sensing it swell.

In the next instant—

"What the—?"

My eyes fly wide as black scales ripple across my arms, gleaming at first just like my wings did and then fading to matte black. I sense the same ripple up my neck and my cheeks before it recedes and the scales fade from my arms.

What kind of dragon-angel am I?

The Vanem Dragon said that my rage must die with me, and it has. My rage died with the old me.

And now...

"Are you Lana?" Callan asks, a soft twinkle in his eyes.

A piece of string to be woven to someone else's purpose? I shake my head. "No."

"Not-Lana?" he asks.

Again, I shake my head, although more slowly this time.

He asks quietly, "Asper?"

"No more," I whisper, leaning in and discovering that the new bump on my armor above my heart is in the way of what I want.

I need to be close to him, but I suddenly feel vulnerable, wondering what might have changed between us.

He's different.

I'm different.

I bite my lip, and he doesn't seem to miss a moment of the stream of emotions that I can't hide. Hope and worry. Want and anxiety.

His voice is soft and calming as he starts to speak. "I don't think I ever really knew who I was. A dragon. A soldier. A leader. A brother." He shakes his head before a vulnerable courage fills his eyes, the kind that only a truly strong person is willing to show. "But I know what I want."

The flecks in his eyes heat like melting gold as his voice becomes a low rumble that thrums through me.

"I want *you*, beautiful dragon-angel."

I cast aside my worries and send a quick request to my armor, waiting the brief moment for it to peel away from my body and rise up into the air, along with my harness, glaive, and armband, leaving me in my bra and black jeans.

Finally, I can slip my arms around Callan's chest and close the gap between us.

He pulls me close but pauses, nudging his nose to mine before he presses his cheek to my cheek.

A dragon's bond.

His voice is thick with emotion. "Whoever we are, and whatever we become, I'm offering you my hand to hold whenever you want to. Whenever you need to," he says. "I'm offering you my shoulders, to help you carry any weight you want help carrying. I'm offering you my heart. To break, if you wish. Or to keep safe. That's your choice, too."

My breathing is ragged, and my heart is warm. Glistening scales ripple across my skin as I give up trying to control everything that I'm feeling.

I press my lips to his cheek, inhaling his scent, so much like the sun. So much like the dawn of a new day.

I breathe in this moment and never want to let it go.

"Whoever we are," I whisper. "We'll find out together. We'll keep each other's heart safe."

I plant kisses across his jaw and to his lips, withdrawing just enough to see his eyes. Still cinnamon with molten-gold flecks, but now his eyes are growing warmer.

I feel it in his smile and the desire in his eyes, the tension in his body, the shift from calm to... *not* calm...

He is his own dragon.

And so am I.

My lips crash against his, and he responds with all the heat I need, matching the wild that swirls within me. The dragon, the angel, every part of me wants him. His lips, his hands, all of him.

Within moments, our clothing lies on the floor and his mouth explores my body from my neck to my breasts to my sensitive inner thighs to my center, every flick of his tongue making me moan with need.

"Callan." I growl, relishing the sound of the dragon within my throat, but damn, my body was ready from the moment I took my armor off.

He looks up at me with a lazy smile before he rises and spreads his wings, scooping me up as he sweeps us out of my cell and into the higher area in front of it.

A thrill passes through me. Other than his wings, he's completely human right now, but he's just as strong as he's always been, and I trust him not to drop me.

With a groan, he guides my legs around his hips before he tips back so that I'm now on top. I position myself over him and gravity brings his hard length deep inside me.

I moan with relief, my hands planting on his chest as pleasure spears through me. I take every burst of heat and I give back in kind. Every thrust and every moan, the air against my skin, our ragged breathing. All of it drives me closer to crashing.

I arch back as the crash takes me. The waves only continue to build until my world is heat and fire that tears me apart. But there's no fall, because Callan is right there in the crash with me.

His arms and wings close around me as we glide back to the ground and I remain with my legs around his waist, our bodies connected, his heart thumping as hard as mine.

I find his lips, kissing him deeply, acutely aware that my body will never have enough of him.

His fingers trace the contours of my face from my forehead to my chin before I press my lips to his.

I want to slow time. Extend these moments for as long as

possible. But we have to leave this place, even though, for possibly the first time, I'd rather stay a little longer.

We take our time cleaning up and getting dressed, never once losing contact with each other's bodies. It's an old habit now but one I'm starting to love.

As I call my armor back to my body, Callan asks, "What do you think the orb is made of?"

I bite my lip as the gold clicks back into place. "I have a theory, but it's not very likely."

He finishes pulling on his shirt—what remains of it, since it's tattered and scorched. "Tell me."

"When the Vanem Dragon spoke to me—"

Callan's eyes widen. "The Vanem Dragon spoke to you?"

I smile. "I have to tell you all about that." I want to explain everything right now, but I force myself to stay on track. "When he spoke to me, he said that the power in the human heart is beyond measure. I think... I mean it's possible..."

"The power of a heart," Callan says.

"Yeah," I whisper. "Maybe not a human's heart. It might have been a dragon's. Maybe even a thunderbird's heart. It's just that he kept telling me that humans were our allies." I shake my head. "I guess we'll never know."

I pause, suddenly remembering. "What happened to the gold that was encasing it?"

"It was gone when I came to," Callan says.

"Destroyed," I whisper. I guess I hoped I could help it, but perhaps it's for the best.

Finally, we're ready to leave, and even though I'm not sure what awaits us outside this cell, I'm filled with a sense of peace.

Maybe it's the orb resting against my heart.

Or Callan's hand brushing my arm.

Either way, as we ascend the stairs, I'm certain that I'll never step foot inside this cage again.

It's quiet as we make our way along the ivory-paneled corridor.

Callan pauses beside Dominus's hammer before he takes hold of the handle. I wonder if he'll claim it. There's a part of me that believes it should be his, but he says, "This is a dangerous weapon of light magic. It should be kept somewhere safe, where it can't be misused."

I give it a moment's thought. "We can take it to the veil—the Avenging Angel's haven. It will be safe there."

He nods, and his serious expression softens. The Avenging Angel's home is a place where we can fly freely. I want nothing more than to return there with Callan and experience the true beauty of the veil's environment.

We continue out into the Cathedral, where I sense a larger number of heartbeats than I was expecting. Definitely more than there were during the battle.

Callan meets my eyes for a moment, a wary expression on his face. Not exactly worried, but cautious.

We hurry through the next room and I use my senses to discern what lies ahead: the shimmering forms of angels—both warrior angels and Roden-Darr—along with other figures that don't give off any kind of supernatural aura.

My heart leaps into my throat. "Dragons?"

We pick up our speed and burst into the central atrium, only to pull up abruptly.

In the center of the room, all of the Roden-Darr sit with their hands and feet bound in bands of gold. Thin bands cover their mouths, although their noses are clear so that they can breathe.

The Serene Commander stands tall as she guards them. Her pale skin and blonde hair are marred with blood, as is her dress, which is torn in places. Standing in an arc behind her are the remaining warrior angels, including Aria. A quick count tells me that they all survived, although they're slumped and weary.

Isaac stands beside the Serene Commander, tall enough to tower over her. He looks exhausted, his hair and clothing also bloodied, but his gray eyes are riveted on the woman standing beside him.

Beatrix. She appears the same as she did when I left Zahra's home, her short hair straight and dark, wearing all black, although her eye makeup is a little smudged. But, just like with Callan, there's something different...

I quickly take in every other dragon in this room and the way they're all guarding the Roden-Darr, although they're keeping their distance from the warrior angels. The other Dread dragons—Felix, Sophia, and Zahra—stand to the right of the Roden-Darr, while the five Grudge dragons, including Micah and Leon, stand to the left.

I can't help but notice the way that Micah and Sophia are sending silent communications to each other across the space between them.

Finally, my focus falls on two teenage dragons I wasn't expecting to see: Dane, the Scorn dragon I allowed to live when I fought him on the rooftop, and Gisela, the young woman with the blue-black hair who's Sienna Scorn's daughter.

Members of all three clans have gathered together, which might be a first, let alone the fact that they're standing in the center of angel territory.

And then, my heart leaps to see my mother step out from behind Leon, the Grudge dragon who once reminded me of the desert, but whose new nature I've yet to discover.

The moment that Callan and I step into the room, all eyes are on us. For a moment, nobody moves, and then Zahra breaks off from the Dread.

Callan doesn't wait for her to reach him, placing the hammer down and striding forward to meet her halfway.

I can't tell what she's thinking, but there are tears in her eyes. It's been years since Callan could safely touch any other supernatural without his dragon's fire igniting, but now she heads straight into his arms without hesitation.

He wraps her up in a hug, nearly pulling her off her feet, but she doesn't seem to care. Behind her, Sophia, Beatrix, and Felix also pull away from the rest of the guard, each of them hurrying toward Callan.

Felix bear-hugs him and I'm sure there are tears in his dark eyes. Sophia openly cries, wiping her eyes between hugs. Beatrix appears the most stoic, although her mascara is soon running.

In the background, Micah says something to Leon, who nods, and the Grudge dragons spread out a little to make up for the gaps in the guard caused by the Dread dragons' absence.

Then Micah and my mother make their way over to me.

Mom gives me a hug that makes my heart squeeze, the worry in her eyes fading as she takes me in.

Micah is holding the Book of Light Magic, and I'm surprised to see that it's glowing softly at the edges. Unlike the Dread dragons, who are dressed in black, he's in his usual scuffed, brown pants and camo-green field jacket.

"Mom. Micah," I say, trying to comprehend what I'm seeing. "What are you doing here?"

Micah holds the book out to me. "It came alive," he says. "The moment that you stepped into the Cathedral, the book lit up and opened itself. It was recording every step you took. We didn't know what we were looking at until we realized we were watching you in real time. Then we saw Dominus and the Roden-Darr attack and we couldn't stay away. Beatrix and Felix had already gone out to find Dane and Gisela. I went to get my clan. We met on the way here."

"But the angels—"

The Serene Commander's terse voice sounds behind Micah. "We were losing," she says, holding her head high as she approaches, the admission appearing to sting. "The Roden-Darr were beating us. Oh, that trick you did with their spears gave us a few seconds' reprieve, but it was only a matter of time before they would have slaughtered us."

Her crisp, winter's scent is clouded with fog. She's angry and uncomfortable. She fucking hates dragons and she'll hate even more that they came to her aid.

"Just to be clear, we didn't do it for you." Micah growls. "We came for Asper. We'll leave as soon as the Roden-Darr are safely imprisoned. We aren't here to start another war."

I set my features into a neutral expression before I give Micah a nod. If the Roden-Darr had defeated the other angels, they would have found my cell soon enough, and I might have had to fight them when I emerged from the veil.

While we've been speaking, I catch snippets of the rapid conversation Callan is having with Zahra.

"Your human friends, Jada and Brock, are watching Emika," Zahra says. "Sophia apparently set up a way for them to contact her." Zahra's lips thin a little at the risk that Sophia took. "But I'm glad to tell you that they're safe."

Closer to me, the Serene Commander is already backing away, but I call out to her. "Wait."

She turns, poised on the back foot, a rolling fog of anger filling the air around her.

My command for her to wait wasn't lost on anyone around me—certainly not the angels—and nor was the fact that she obeyed. To my right, the Dread dragons turn toward me while across the way, Isaac gives me a tired but reassuring nod.

"The Celestial Ascendant is dead," I say clearly. "As the Avenging Angel, I judged her guilty. You will convey that message to the heavenly realm and if they take issue with it, they will come for me and only me. I acted alone in this."

I pin the Serene Commander with my gaze. "The war with the dragons is over. Any angel who breaks this command will answer to me."

She sniffs. "The old regime is dead. It was high time the Celestial Ascendant passed on the mantle."

I arch an eyebrow at her. It seems she's already thinking about making a play for the position. *Well, I guess we'll see.*

She spins way from me and rejoins the other angels, and that's when Isaac finally approaches me.

"I'll take the Roden-Darr to the veil," he says. "But I'll need help."

"I..." I stop speaking as I consider all of the dragons gathered around me.

Micah is a powerful figure standing next to my beautiful mother. His brown eyes flicker to Sophia, who casts him a soft smile. In the background, the other Grudge dragons, each of them fierce and strong, continue to guard the Roden-Darr.

To my right, the Dread dragons remain gathered around Callan, although they've turned toward me now.

Beatrix mouths, *"Hey, Night Sky,"* and Felix tips his chin at me.

Zahra gives me a single, firm nod.

Sophia drags her attention away from Micah for the seconds it takes her to shoot me a grin that tells me there's a hug coming my way soon.

The two Scorn dragons hover in the background, both of them young and with a battle ahead of them, but from the way that Beatrix beckons them to join her, I know they'll have the help they need.

The air around all of the dragons is different. Each of them, in their own way, is more alive than I've ever seen them.

They are all their own dragons, and I can't wait to discover who they are now.

I return my attention to Isaac. He asked for help taking the Roden-Darr to the veil and now I say, *"We* will help you."

I continue with a conviction I feel in my heart and soul. "But, Isaac, you'll need to recruit new Sentinels."

He tips his head. "I will?"

I nod as my smile grows certain and sure. "I am what I am."

An Avenging Angel.

A dragon of night.

The hunt will always be mine.

A gentle light grows in Isaac's gray eyes. "You found your home."

"And I will protect it," I say. From anyone and anything that threatens it or the people I care about.

Except now, I'm not alone.

I catch Callan's eye and he returns to my side, his golden scales flickering in the late afternoon sunlight while my black scales wash across my skin and make the shadows around us seem darker.

He is calm and I am rage.

He is sunlight and I am the dark of the night sky.

My path won't be easy, but I'll walk it with him and together, we'll make it through.

As he leans in and nudges his cheek to mine, I whisper to him the question he once asked me that changed my life. "Will you come with me?"

The smile in his eyes promises me everything. "Always."

To complete the series, and for an exclusive life after scene with Lana and Callan, find out what happens next in
Claim the Light.

CLAIM THE LIGHT

(SUPERNATURAL LEGACY #4)

Shadows spread across the city.
Whispers of a new darkness.

All my life, I've been at war. Fighting for my survival. Never knowing my worth. Never believing that love could be mine— until my enemy stood by my side and fought for me.

The alpha of the ruthless Grudge Clan asks for my heart. He offers me the heat of his body, the warmth of his home, and the liberty to explore my new strength.

Peace is at my fingertips.

And yet...

Across the city, shadows grow. With the darkness comes whispers of a rising power—a dragon who could destroy the light that forged our freedom.

He is a nightmare from my past. With scales as black as coal, he steals the air from my chest and the hope from my soul. He is a destroyer who threatens to crush my heart and the future of all dragon shifters.

But I will not wait for him to tear me down.

I will not stand by and watch my found family perish.

I will not be hunted again.

No.

I will hunt him.

The light may flicker and fade, but shadows won't claim my heart.

Content information: Claim the Light is a dark paranormal romance, a fourth chapter in the Supernatural Legacy series. Recommended reading age is 17+ for sex scenes, mature themes, violence, and language. NO cliffhanger.

*Includes an exclusive life after scene for Lana and Callan.

BRIGHT WICKED

If you'd like to know more about the Vanem Dragon, start the epic fantasy romance today. A complete series!

One forbidden touch.

I am the Bright Queen's Champion. The only fae to control the power of starlight, I am sworn to protect my people from the dark Fell who live in the wilderness beyond our border.

But when a Fell more powerful than any other challenges me, I'm not prepared for his fierce strength and skill.

Or the dangerous desire in his eyes when he looks at me.

Two champions bound to destroy each other.

One misstep is all it takes for me to invoke an ancient law that binds my fate to his. Suddenly, my life is no longer my own.

I am tied to him in a promise of pain and destruction.

Three days to live.

Now, I have only three days before I must fight him in a battle to the death that will determine the future of our two lands.

Every heartbeat counts.

But how can I kill the only man who sees me for who I truly am?

Content information: Bright Wicked is a fantasy romance, slow burn, the first in the Bright Wicked series, a trilogy told over three consecutive days. Recommended reading age is 16+ for heat level.

WOLF OF ASHES (DARK MAGIC SHIFTERS #1)

His dark crown will be mine.

My mother was imprisoned for a crime she didn't commit. She was locked away in darkness, never to see light again.

I was born into that darkness, that perpetual night. I learned to survive without sunlight and to thrive on the scraps that were thrown to me.

All because someone didn't want me to claim my birthright.

Now I'm free. And I'm coming for what's mine.

I'll go deep into the nightmares of an empire built on blood and bones to find the wolf whose name my mother couldn't utter.

A beast who stole my place among shifters.

I'll do whatever it takes to slice his empire apart, piece by little piece.

Even if it means making a deal with a man whose thirst for vengeance exceeds my own. A broken king. The darkest of them all.

In return for his power, he wants more from me than I can give.

He wants my heart.

Content information: Dark Magic Shifters: Book One is a dark paranormal romance, the first in the Dark Magic Shifters series. Recommended reading age is 17+ for sex scenes, mature themes, violence, and language. Ends on a cliffhanger.

ALSO BY EVERLY FROST

SUPERNATURAL LEGACY - COMPLETE

(Angels and Dragon Shifters)

1. Hunt the Night

2. Chase the Shadows

3. Slay the Dawn

4. Claim the Light

DARK MAGIC SHIFTERS

(Dark Urban Fantasy Romance)

1. Wolf of Ashes

2. Bond of Flames

3. Crown of Fate

KINGDOM OF BETRAYAL

(Fantasy Romance)

1. A Sky Like Blood

2. A Sin Like Fire

3. A Storm Like Iron

4. A Soul Like Glass

BRIGHT WICKED - COMPLETE

(Fantasy Romance)

1. Bright Wicked

2. Radiant Fierce

3. Infernal Dark

STORM PRINCESS - COMPLETE

(Fantasy Romance)

1. Book 1
2. Book 2
3. Book 3

ASSASSIN'S MAGIC - COMPLETE

(Dark Urban Fantasy Romance)

1. Assassin's Magic
2. Assassin's Mask
3. Assassin's Menace
4. Assassin's Maze
5. Rebels
6. Revenge
7. Rogue
8. Assassin's Match

SOUL BITTEN SHIFTER - COMPLETE

(Dark Urban Fantasy Romance)

1. This Dark Wolf
2. This Broken Wolf
3. This Caged Wolf
4. This Cruel Blood

DEMON PACK - COMPLETE

(Dark Paranormal Romance)

1. Demon Pack
2. Demon Pack: Elimination
3. Demon Pack: Eternal

MORTALITY - COMPLETE

(Science-Fantasy Romance)

Mortality Complete Set: Books 1 to 4

1. Beyond the Ever Reach
2. Beneath the Guarding Stars
3. By the Icy Wild
4. Before the Raging Lion

<u>Stand-alone fiction - dark romance</u>

Corrupt Me: Immortal Vices and Virtues

ABOUT THE AUTHOR

Everly Frost is the USA Today Bestselling author of fantasy romance, urban fantasy and paranormal romance novels. She spent her childhood dreaming of other worlds and scribbling stories on the leftover blank pages at the back of school notebooks. She lives in Brisbane, Australia with her husband and two children.

amazon.com/author/everlyfrost

facebook.com/everlyfrost

instagram.com/everlyfrost

bookbub.com/authors/everly-frost

goodreads.com/everlyfrost